A HARD BARGAIN?

"I have been contemplating the terms of your bargain," July announced. "As for you, losing your innocence is probably a long-forgotten memory. No doubt it happened so long ago that you don't even remember where, when, or with whom, but I—"

"Skip the lengthy dissertation and get to the point," Nacona said, puffing on his cigar.

"I have come to negotiate your terms," July said. "I have decided to accept your partnership in exchange for my maidenhood. For one night. But I have one stipulation to add. You will marry me. If I am to lose my innocence, I should at least be allowed to maintain my respectability."

"If I agree to a wedding, then I deserve more than one night in your bed!"

"Those are my terms."

With unconscious masculine grace, Nacoma moved toward her. July made one fluttering gesture of retreat, then moved fluidly into his arms. And when he captured her lips in a deep and sensuous kiss, when he molded her against the hard-angled and -muscled contours of his body, her traitorous flesh responded, and a knot of longing unfurled inside her. . . .

GINA ROBINS

WYOMING ECSTASY

PINNACLE BOOKS
WINDSOR PUBLISHING CORP.

PINNACLE BOOKS are published by

Windsor Publishing Corp.
475 Park Avenue South
New York, NY 10016

First Printing: August, 1993

Printed in the United States of America

This book is dedicated to my husband Ed and our children—
Christie, Jill, and Kurt—with much love.

Lovely but determined July MacKenzie did not know the meaning of the word "no," and when swarthy gunslinger Nacona Bleu rejected her bid for partnership as a private investigator, she saw to it that the ornery pistolero was backed into a corner—and into a jail cell to which she held the key. But July hadn't counted on falling beneath the handsome half-breed's potent spell when Nacona captured her in his brawny arms and introduced her to an entirely different kind of investigation—one that was wild and sensual.

The last thing Nacona Bleu needed while he searched for the mysterious outlaw who had murdered his brother was complications. But that was exactly what he got when the feisty, strong-willed July came barging into his hotel room to interrupt his bath. The sassy blonde didn't seem to know her place, though he was sure she would refuse to stay in it even if she did. A loner by nature and by habit, Nacona had been lured into partnership with this green-eyed leprechaun, and the instant he'd touched her luscious curves and felt her cherry red lips melting beneath his, he knew this was one showdown he was going to lose. The passion he experienced with *July* was as hot and steamy as a summer night. . . .

Chapter 1

Dodge City, Kansas
1878

The patrons of Dodge City's finest hotel parted like the Red Sea as a looming giant made his way through the lobby, his progress punctuated by the foreboding clink of spurs. All conversation died; all eyes focused on the swarthy, shaggy-haired man who moved with pantherlike grace.

One of the most celebrated gunmen this side of the Mississippi had returned from a foray to enjoy the luxury of his headquarters in Dodge City. Trail-weary, dusty, and sporting several days' growth of beard, the notorious gunslinger presented an ominous appearance. Yet, even when this muscular pistolero looked his very best, he commanded attention and demanded wary respect. His very presence was intimidating. It drew all eyes and caused speculation.

Silence hung over the lobby, save for spurs striking the planked floor as Nacona Bleu strode toward the stairs, his

9

worn saddlebags draped over powerful shoulders, an unlit cigar clamped between his teeth. He spoke not a word as he strode to his room, but his dark gaze scanned the crowd, taking in everything at a single glance.

Some folks said the legendary gunslinger had eyes in the back of his head because he seemed to be aware of all that transpired around him. Others claimed the half-breed pistolero possessed a sixth sense that alerted him to danger and kept him attuned to his surroundings, giving him the cutting edge. And there were those who swore Nacona Bleu was the devil himself, that he knew all, saw all, and broke the law as often as he upheld it.

"I thought Bleu had been killed in a showdown in Ellsworth," someone commented as Nacona ascended the steps in long strides accompanied by the click of row-eled spurs.

"I heard he'd been bushwhacked outside Fort Worth," somebody else reported.

It was difficult to keep track of gunfighters. Phantom sightings and false reports always spread like wildfire, growing more preposterous and fantastic with each telling.

"Hell, I heard he'd killed three desperadoes in a shoot-out near—"

The sporadic conversation that had resumed in the lobby died instantly when Nacona pivoted at the head of the staircase to survey the congregation staring up at him.

"As you can plainly see, the reports of my death were patently false," he drawled mockingly.

Not only did Nacona seem to have eyes in the back of his head and a nose like a bloodhound's, he had ears like

10

a fox. The pistolero also could nail an entire group to the wall with one penetrating glance.

His gaze caught and lingered on the shapely beauty who had tucked herself into a far corner of the lobby. Nacona assessed her unfamiliar face and arresting figure from beneath the brim of his hat and found himself staring into a pair of startling eyes—eyes as innocent and curious as they were green. But to Nacona's surprise the shapely blonde didn't avert her gaze the way most folks did when he pinpointed them with his unnerving stare. Instead, the chit gave him the once-over, twice, just as he had given it to her—thoroughly, deliberately, and unhurriedly.

Nacona's thick black brows furrowed over his ebony eyes when the bewitching minx continued to match him stare for stare. Damn, he must be losing his touch. This penetrating stare of his had become as legendary as his expertise with a six-shooter. He had backed men down from gunfights with such bone-chilling glares. Although others in the room were nervously glancing in one direction or another, this intriguing young woman met the challenge in his eyes, showing remarkable spirit and fortitude.

Although Nacona had willfully trained his voice and face to express very little emotion, he now had difficulty maintaining his cool facade. Not allowing others to know what he was feeling and thinking had become a habit, and was a necessity in his dangerous profession. But as he faced this dazzling blonde he suddenly didn't feel in control of his emotions. She was so pretty, she took his breath away. It was like staring into the sun and being blinded to

11

all else. He could feel the tug of his male body toward hers.

From beneath a fan of long curly lashes those sparkling green eyes keyed in on him, assessing him. Along the brim of her prim bonnet, wispy blond curls caressed the sides of her oval face—a face God had created with the utmost care. Two delicately curved brows arched over almond-shaped eyes, and she had a dainty upturned nose. Her skin, the color of peaches and cream, looked like satin. And her lips reminded Nacona of pink velvet. They curved naturally upward at the corners, even when she wasn't smiling.

Nacona's astute gaze made a deliberate sweep of her alluring assets. He found himself staring at one hundred ten pounds and five foot two inches of the most well-developed beauty he'd seen in all his thirty-two years. All too easy on a man's eye, this woman was tremendously hard on his blood pressure. Speculation as to how this enchantress would look nestled beside him in bed left a warm throb of forbidden desire pounding in Nacona's loins, and he was assaulted by an urge to charge down the steps, scoop her up, and cart her off caveman-style. But squelching that urge was the sensible realization that he would never know the pleasures this sophisticated beauty could offer a man. They hailed from two different walks of life. He had perceived that at first glance. This newcomer was the epitome of breeding and refinement, yet she had it all—eye-catching poise, a delicate bone structure, a tantalizing figure, and the finest clothes money could buy. She represented everything Nacona wasn't—and had never tried to be.

Like a victim of a trance, July MacKenzie stood in the

corner, meeting Nacona's bold stare. She had been awed by his mere presence the instant he'd swaggered into the lobby, captivated by the sensual rhythm of his movements. Now she was stunned by the strange sensations that had assaulted her when he'd visually assessed her. Her breath had lodged in her chest, and it had been several seconds before she'd thought to draw in much-needed air. July had often found herself in the presence of men who brazenly appraised her, and she had trained herself to stare back, refusing to be intimidated or subdued in any manner whatsoever. But this looming giant tested her composure more than any man alive. Something lured her to him, like metal to a magnet.

Nacona was clad in buckskin shirt and breeches that fit his powerful physique like a second skin. A black sombrero adorned with a rattlesnake band was set low on his forehead, and a pair of scuffed black boots encased his feet. He stood like a stunning portrait to rugged masculinity, his sleek body rippling with muscle and hinting at the raw driving force within him.

July gazed, spellbound, at his broad shoulders, narrow hips, powerful legs, and sinewy arms. His snapping black eyes set off a wave of electricity that she could not ignore. It added to the aura of primitive maleness he exuded. The casual menace in his stance, in his lopsided smile, intrigued her.

Strength emanated from him as with each breath he inhaled his deerhide garments strained across the whip-cord muscles of his chest. The silver-studded holsters slung low on his hips supported two pearl-handled Peacemakers, and a sheath containing a bowie knife was strapped to his right thigh. Nacona Bleu looked to all the world like a swarthy renegade who could handle any sort of trouble that came his way. Indeed, he seemed to challenge anyone to cross him.

His high cheekbones and bronzed complexion suggested Indian ancestry, and a decade of hard living was stamped on his craggy but undeniably handsome face. The cynical slant to his sensuous lips left July speculating as to what ironic twist of fate had led this dynamic man into such a dangerous profession, transforming him into the forceful hardened creature he was.

There was a certain arrogance in the way he held himself, the way he moved, yet each step was calculated and precise, expending not one iota of energy in wasted motion. July had no doubt that wariness and constant danger were always with this pistolero. She could almost feel their presence in the lobby, and he looked as unapproachable as a coiled rattlesnake. This was the kind of man who thrived on danger. No doubt, Nacona Bleu had been to hell and back a dozen times, yet he still had not found a worthy challenger.

He piqued July's curiosity, and left her wondering at her own peculiar need to prove to him that she was his equal. She had challenged his penetrating stare for the mere sport of it, just to determine how a man like Nacona Bleu would react. Now pure orneriness prompted her to meet the dare he silently offered and assure him that she had every bit as much gumption as he did.

The faintest hint of a smile quirked Nacona's lips as he assessed July's challenging glance. His gaze narrowed on her creamy complexion and on emerald eyes that dominated her exquisite face. Then his attention deliberately—and rudely—slid downward to reappraise the

14

voluptuous swells of her breasts and the tiny indentation of her waist. But even this bold visual affront didn't seem to faze the sophisticated bundle of aristocratic grace wrapped in mint green silk, for the lady countered by measuring the broad expanse of his chest before focusing directly on the powerful columns of his thighs and hips.

One dark brow elevated as Nacona clamped his teeth into the unlit cigar. Then he broke into a grin. Although there had been damned little amusement in his life these past two years, this saucy elf intrigued him. Of course, he had no intention of losing this staring contest to a beguiling bit of fluff. He had a reputation to uphold—a reputation which gave him the necessary edge that often meant the difference between life and death.

Vividly conscious of the fact that every pair of eyes in the lobby was bouncing back and forth between him and this daring woman, Nacona would not walk away without assuring everyone that he was in firm command of this—and every other—situation. No female, no matter how alluring and distracting she happened to be, was going to ruin *his* bad reputation, so before somebody started thinking he'd turned soft, he set about putting the gorgeous woman in her place.

Nacona tipped back his hat so that the shadowed brim no longer concealed his blatant appraisal of the curvaceous blonde. Eyes like polished obsidian boldly raked over the woman's distracting curves and swells, drawing gasps from several pious females who read his look with startling clarity.

Still, the daring beauty didn't bat an eyelash. Nacona had visually undressed her in front of a rapt audience, and yet this strong-willed nymph didn't turn away in shame or embarrassment. What did it take to get her goat? He'd employed the technique that customarily caused females to cower and blush profusely.

Pushed to the point of desperation, Nacona was determined not to be outdone by this minx. His ebony eyes drilled into her with challenging directness. "The price of my gunhand comes high, honey," Nacona drawled in a ridiculing tone. "But for *that* . . ."—his voice trailed off, and his probing gaze left no doubt as to the *that* to which he referred—"I don't charge at all."

Another wave of astonished gasps arose from the crowd. With a rakish smirk, Nacona touched the brim of his sombrero in a mocking parody of courtesy and then sauntered down the hall, his hat set at a jaunty angle. That should do it, he thought. That gorgeous nymph wouldn't challenge him again. He had ensured that she keep her distance from him. Lovely though the woman was, she wasn't his type. To her, he was a curiosity—like a freak in a circus.

He had actually done the woman a favor, Nacona told himself. He had felt an instant attraction to the shapely blonde, but they were as different as dawn and midnight. Her reputation would be ruined if she was seen in his company. Though bewitching, this beauty was the kind of woman with whom a man like Nacona was not allowed to associate. But she was good to look at, even if he couldn't permit himself to touch.

July was vaguely aware of all the attention she was receiving, thanks to that ornery and incredibly cocky gunslinger. Nacona Bleu had certainly lived up to his reputation. The raven-haired giant was everything July's inquiries in Dodge had led her to expect. The six-foot-three-inch, two-hundred-ten-pound mass of masculinity was a legend, a force to be reckoned with. Cynicism and wariness were *his* best friends, as well they should be!

And the look in those eyes! July inhaled a steadying breath and listened to the retreating clink of spurs echo in the hall above her. In her twenty-one years she had never before felt captured or paralyzed by a man's intense stare. But Nacona Bleu had perfected staring down challengers. He made Medusa seem a novice at stony stares. July had spent months before a mirror, practicing her own stare. But hers was dimmed by comparison to that of the skilled gunslinger.

Irma Billingsly materialized out of nowhere to comfortingly pat July's hand. "Now don't you fret, sugar. Nacona Bleu delights in intimidating men and women alike," the plump matron informed her. "Don't pay him any mind a-tall. We all know a respectable lady like you wouldn't give that scoundrel the time of day."

July inwardly smiled while she kindly thanked the overprotective woman for her words of consolation. But the rotund matron had July figured all wrong. Nacona Bleu was July's sole purpose for traveling to the "Queen of the Cow Towns." In fact, July had just spent five days anxiously awaiting Nacona's return.

Despite the arrogant gunslinger's attempt to humiliate her in front of a captive audience, July surged across the lobby and ascended the steps. For almost two weeks, she had mentally rehearsed what she had intended to say to the legendary gunman. Their first accidental meeting had changed nothing. July was dedicated and determined. She had not made the long trip from Kansas City just to be demoralized by a cocky rapscallion, and she wasn't the

17

slightest bit interested in what he was giving away to female companions. It was his expertise as a detective that lured July to him. She also wanted his skills with a pistol and his commanding presence, nothing more—despite his insinuating that every female on the planet served only one purpose for a man. That infuriating attitude commonly found in males could get July's hackles up in nothing flat.

She came to a halt in front of Nacona's room and glared at the door that separated them. She had rapped on this particular door a dozen times since her arrival, but until this moment, her raps had met with silence. Now was her chance to speak her piece. Inhaling deeply, July mentally prepared herself for her second encounter. Thankfully, she came armed with the knowledge that this midnight-haired, coal black-eyed gunslinger was as ornery and intimidating as they came. He was a hard man, and July doubted sentiment clouded his mind. He seemed to be ruled by instinct rather than emotion. But a rock-hearted man was about to meet an unstoppable force.

July MacKenzie called no man master. Not even the dangerous hulk who had tried to embarrass and intimidate her!

Nacona heaved a weary sigh and tossed his saddlebags onto the foot of his bed. An appreciative smile brimmed his lips as he surveyed his room. As always, the hotel clerk had seen to his comfort the moment Nacona had returned to Dodge. For a few extra dollars, he had set a full bottle of whiskey and a glass on the dresser. Fresh towels were draped over the rack on the commode, and the brass tub had been filled with steaming water. Nacona liked hot baths—the hotter the better.

With reckless ease, he shucked his dusty clothes and sank into the tub. Expelling a relieved sigh, he leaned over to retrieve the whiskey and fill his glass to capacity. Nacona forgot the nagging knife wound in his forearm, the aches in his joints caused by hand-to-hand combat with a ruthless renegade in Abilene, and the endless hours he'd spent in the saddle.

Ah, it was good to be back in Dodge to rest and recuperate. His last case had been exhausting. The criminal he'd tracked had proved to be a worthy competitor—and damned vicious with a dagger. But Nacona's client had paid him extremely well to track the murdering butcher down. Nacona now had more money than time to spend it because of all his grueling expeditions. And since bank robberies were a common occurrence, he had spread his savings hither and yon to keep losses at a minimum.

Nacona chuckled to himself, remembering the bank in Kansas City where he'd invested part of his money. The banker had posted a sign stating that Nacona Bleu was a patron of the establishment and any thief who thought to rob the bank would be asking for more trouble than he could handle. Nacona doubted the sign would deter many criminals, but the notice had gained Nacona several potential clients.

The firm insistent rap at the door jerked Nacona from his pensive contemplation. Instinctively, he grabbed his Colt .45 which he always kept within easy reach.

"It's open," he drawled as he trained the silver barrel of the pistol on the door.

He bit down on the end of his cigar and his eyebrows

jackknifed when the very same female who had caught his attention in the lobby sailed into his room. He had assumed his parting remark would send this gorgeous nymph out of his life. Obviously he'd been wrong. Demoralizing stares and degrading remarks didn't seem to faze this courageous chit.

Again noting her delicate features and elegant poise, Nacona was reminded that he and this wealthy sophisticate had absolutely nothing in common. He simply couldn't imagine what a woman like her would want with a man like him. Most decent women took a wide berth around him. Only the saloon girls and prostitutes in dusty cow towns offered him the time of day. Usually, his reputation and profession worked as effectively as insect repellent. Yet, here stood this vision of loveliness, blundering into what could become a most compromising situation. And much as Nacona enjoyed fantasizing about how delectable she would look in the altogether, lying in his arms, she simply had to go. The only problem was that he was in no position to stand up and escort her out the door. If he did, she would see far more than she had bargained for when she breezed in.

Chapter 2

July very nearly swallowed her tongue when her gaze fell on the hair-matted chest and long muscular legs that protruded from the rim of the brass tub. Mother Nature certainly hadn't skimped when she'd done her handiwork on this awesome man. Nacona Bleu had shoulders like a buffalo, and his bronzed flesh rippled with muscles. The shock of seeing the sinewy giant in such a state of undress caused July's heart to slam against her ribs. Atlas had nothing on Nacona Bleu, that was apparent.

Forcefully, July got herself in hand, fighting the embarrassed blush working its way up from the base of her throat to the roots of her blond hair. When Nacona's muscles flexed and rippled while he straightened himself in the tub, July tried very hard not to notice how appealing he was to the feminine eye. But that was virtually impossible when there was so much of him to ignore.

Get hold of yourself, July! she told herself. She had three older brothers, after all. Over the years, she had seen each and every one of them in various states of undress. This situation was only slightly different. It changed nothing. She could cope. She had taught herself to deal with every situation she encountered. She was well disciplined and determined. Wasn't she . . . ?

A smile quirked Nacona's lips while he peered up at his unexpected guest. This was the second time in fifteen minutes that he had misjudged the shapely nymph. Most women of her station would have wailed in humiliation and torn out of the lobby, never to be seen or heard from again. But this five-foot-two-inch package of well-sculpted femininity stood her ground. Nacona was sorry to say he couldn't figure her out. She did not react as he anticipated.

"What the hell do you want?" he questioned impolitely.

July dearly wanted to tell him, and she intended to, just as soon as her vocal apparatus began to function properly. But it took a few moments. In the meantime, she closed the door behind her and drew herself up proudly, making the most of her standing position. When she felt prepared to speak without her voice shattering, she proceeded.

"First of all, I feel compelled to point out that it doesn't cost extra for you to be nice to people," she admonished him. "I did not appreciate your previous remarks or your insulting tone. In fact—"

"Do you want something, lady, or did you just pop in here to annoy me?" Nacona could be polite and tactful when he felt like it. He just didn't happen to at the moment. He wanted this bundle of temptation out of his room before he started entertaining thoughts that had no business skipping through his head.

Without pointing out the fact that he was being unnecessarily rude again, July cut right to the heart of the matter. "I have come to request your services, Mr. Bleu," she declared, her voice one octave higher than normal.

One black brow arched as Nacona looked July up and down for the umpteenth time, wishing he didn't like what he saw quite so much. "Oh, you have, have you?" he chortled sarcastically. "In what capacity? The one I mentioned downstairs?"

"Blast it, must you make a mockery of everything?" she burst out, unable to control her temper another second.

He was lounging in his bath, but that didn't mean they couldn't carry on an intelligent conversation. She had come to bargain with him—person to person, *not* man to woman. He was in no position to shove her out the door until she had stated her proposition. July was determined—by nature and by habit—and she was not about to be intimidated by this ornery rascal.

"Despite the fact that you seem immensely proud of what is submerged in your bath water, I have come to request your assistance because of your expertise with weapons and in criminal investigation. You call yourself a detective of sorts, do you not, Mr. Bleu?" Considering the awkwardness of the situation, July thought she was handling herself rather well, even if she did say so herself.

Nacona expelled a volcanic snort and set his pistol aside. "Cut the fancy talk and get to the point," he demanded impatiently. "What do you want me to do? Follow your husband or fiancé to determine if he is cheating on you?" He raked her with a scornful look. "No doubt, a woman like you is all talk and no action. Your man probably searched elsewhere for affection."

July's fingers clenched in the folds of her gown, itching to put a stranglehold on his thick neck. This scoundrel's crude remarks were stoking the fires of her Scotch-Irish temper. Silently July counted to ten and cursed Nacona up one side and down the other before regaining a small degree of composure.

"For your information, Mr. Bleu, I have neither a fiancé nor a husband, nor do I want one. I have found that most men are plagued with your narrow-minded philosophies. Or, to be more specific, your warped theories on sex. As far as I can tell, love and passion do not make the world go 'round. In my estimation, they cause it to stall out." July drew in a deep breath and courageously plunged on, "I happen to be a detective myself, and I have come to—"

"*You?*" Flabbergasted, Nacona gaped at the enchanting sprite. "You're kidding." She certainly didn't look like a detective.

"There are such things as women detectives and lady lawyers, which I also happen to be!" July assured him tartly. "And—"

"Not where I come from, there aren't!" Nacona declared with a disrespectful snort.

"Well, welcome to the planet Earth, Mr. Bleu," she sassed.

Damn the rascal. He was acting intolerably superior, as only a man could.

Nacona took one look at the saucy intruder and decided he was headed straight to hell if this spitfire was part of his future. Even though she was positively gorgeous, they clashed. And if she was the prime example of the new breed of investigators, the world was headed toward ruin. *She* was a detective? And a lady lawyer? Good Lord!

July abhorred Nacona's reaction. It was the one she

faced when male clients learned that J. B. MacKenzie was actually a woman. Men were so entrenched in their offensive opinions of women that they assumed a female could have no other occupation besides that of housewife or whore.

While Nacona threw another drink down his gullet, causing his Adam's apple to bob up and down, July squared her shoulders and continued. "I am sad to report that, when I have stated my profession, I have received similar responses before," she begrudgingly admitted. "And that is exactly why I have sought you out. I would like to merge your reputation with my knowledge of the law and detective investigation in order to launch my career. I have already contacted my latest clients who are willing to pay a very generous fee for our combined efforts."

For a full minute, Nacona sat in the steaming tub, mulling over this intriguing female and her unexpected proposition. It wasn't that he wasn't tempted, for he most certainly was . . . if only for the prospective fringe benefits. But he had been working alone for over two years, driven by a need for vengeance that had yet to be appeased. His first and last partnership had ended in disaster, leaving emotional scars that had haunted all his days and too many of his nights. What this saucy minx offered would only invite trouble and distraction. She and Nacona were worlds apart. And unless he missed his guess, she only fancied herself to be a detective. What the hell could she possibly know about investigation, about the grueling hours required to track desperadoes? In his estimation, nothing.

"You've been reading too many of those dime novels

that depict women as adventuresses in the Wild West," Nacona scoffed disdainfully. "I imagine your library is stocked full of such fantastic titles as *Hurricane Nell, Queen of Saddle and Lasso, Bess the Trapper,* and *Mountain Kate.*" He guzzled another glass of brandy in one swallow. "Take my advice, honey. Find another profession. You don't look the part, and you'll only get yourself into the kind of trouble no woman can handle."

"And *that,* Mr. Bleu, is the very reason why I chose to pursue investigation, to prove you—and every other narrow-minded man on this continent—wrong! As a woman, I do not arouse the suspicion of the fugitives I intend to track. You, on the other hand, attract trouble and invite unnecessary confrontations."

"Then why the hell do you want to team up with the likes of me?" he couldn't help but ask.

"It is not by choice, I assure you," she muttered before pacing about like an attorney in a courtroom. "My brothers and I own and operate a detective agency in Kansas City."

Nacona plucked up the sponge and soap, and lathered himself while July circumnavigated his room. He had a pretty good idea how Little Miss Detective had tracked him down—the banker in Kansas City who'd bandied his name about for the protection of his establishment.

"I met with the superintendent of the detective force for the Union Pacific Railroad. George Hershberger is his name."

That was nothing new to Nacona. He had worked for George when he was a detective doing work for the Pinkerton Agency. He had taken a case for George in Missouri and had recovered several thousand dollars which had been stolen from the railroad.

"George and C. L. Chambers—a banker in Cheyenne, Wyoming—have banded together to investigate the rash of bank robberies, cattle rustling, and train holdups that have plagued the area with alarming regularity," July elaborated. "Our home agency was contacted, and I met with George and C. L. while my brothers were involved with other pressing cases."

July slanted Nacona a brief glance, valiantly trying to concentrate on the conversation rather than the appealing picture this swarthy giant presented to the feminine eye. The man could have been listed as the Eighth Wonder of the World. He was that impressive in the flesh, even if he was as ornery as the devil.

"I wanted to take this assignment myself because my infuriatingly overprotective brothers—"

"How many?" he interrupted.

July grumbled at Nacona's annoying knack of distracting her with his inquiries. It always took a second to recover her powers of thought. "I have three older brothers," she replied. "They are thirty-four, twenty-nine, and twenty-seven years old, if that makes any difference to you—though I cannot imagine why it should. My brothers are defensive and overprotective when it comes to my welfare and I resent it. They offer me the safe assignments, such as trailing cheating husbands for broken-hearted wives and doing legwork for court cases. My oldest brother is also an attorney. He helped me pass the board examination so I could assist him with legal matters."

"And now you want to carve your own niche, burst loose from confinement, appease your sibling rivalry, and make a name for yourself, woman or no," Nacona speculated as he assessed the shapely sprite.

Oddly enough, he wasn't surprised. He had only met this vivacious female, and he could detect her undaunted spirit. It oozed from her pores and danced in those intelligent green eyes that dominated her pixielike face. She reminded Nacona of a leprechaun who possessed too much independent spirit and enthusiasm for her own good. She was headed for trouble. That was as obvious as a wart on the tip of one's nose. This saucy elf was straining against the rigid limitations of womanhood, itching to test her wings and her skills—underdeveloped though they undoubtedly were.

July paused in her pacing to stare Nacona squarely in the eye. "You are very astute, Mr. Bleu. I do indeed wish to be my own person, woman or no. I thought Wyoming would be the perfect place to begin my operations since the Territory seems more progressive in granting equality to women. After all, it gave women the right to vote nine years ago.

"I am tired of living in my brothers' shadows, doing their busywork for them," July confessed. "I know the law forward and backward and all the tricks of the detective trade. But because I am a woman, I was politely but firmly told I was not the *man* for this job."

A puzzled frown plowed Nacona's brow as he absently reached for the razor to clear the stubble from his cheeks. "Then why did you come looking for me if you were rejected?"

July stared at the air over his shiny black head and

swallowed nervously. "I was not rejected . . . exactly," she hedged. "I told the bank and railroad representatives that you and I had teamed up together and that, if they gave me the assignment, you would be assisting me."

Nacona very nearly cut a chunk out of his chin. Wide black eyes drilled into her as their truce ended. If there was one thing Nacona detested, it was having people take him for granted. "You little witch! You don't go around dropping names and making promises you can't keep. The answer is *no!*" he roared at her. "Nobody decides what I take on but me, especially not a woman." His muscled arm shot toward the door. "Now get out of here before I lose my good disposition."

As if he has one, thought July. The man was like a dragon—full of fire and venom—even though he could mask his emotions when it was his wont. All the same, he had met his match in July MacKenzie. She was determination personified and she had not come all this way for nothing.

Even though Nacona had showed her the door, as if she were too stupid to know where it was, she tilted her chin to a defiant angle and refused to budge. "The purpose is noble," she declared, her voice rising testily. "If you've kept up with events in the West, as all professional detectives and law officials should, you know that Wyoming is becoming a hotbed of trouble. Unfortunately, every marshal, ranger, and detective west of the Mississippi is overloaded with pressing cases. The Lincoln County War in New Mexico erupted in February, pitting Pat Garrett and his posse against Billy the Kid."

Like a conscientious attorney, July formulated her thoughts and spouted her case. "In Deadwood, South

Dakota a band of desperadoes has been preying on stages and ranchers. Every available lawman in the area is on constant surveillance. And Big Nose George is still at large, terrorizing the Black Hills. The Pinkertons and U.S. marshals are trying to track down the James gang which is wreaking havoc all over the country. The Texas Rangers are busy trying to track down Sam Bass, who robbed a Union Pacific train in Nebraska and flitted off with sixty thousand dollars in gold before robbing two stages and four more trains near Dallas."

To Nacona, she did sound like a lawyer arguing in court. He hated to admit it, but this woman impressed and fascinated him in ways he hadn't expected. Of course, he was still mad as hell at her for volunteering him without his permission. But he was intrigued by her intellect, her gumption, and her delectable body that seemed to beg for a man's touch.

"And let's not forget the Army of the West has its hands full trying to chase down Geronimo and Victorio, not to mention Dull Knife and Little Wolf who took a band of Cheyenne and Arapaho and sneaked off from the reservation just last week. Nor can we forget that Black Bart's clever stage holdups are giving the detectives of Wells Fargo fits in California."

Good Lord, thought Nacona. He hadn't realized there had been such a rash of criminal activity this year. The country was crawling with ne'er-do-wells, renegades, and thieves. No wonder he always found a stack of telegrams requesting his services when he returned from a manhunt.

"Besides that, every cowtown in Kansas is being overrun by unruly trail hands from Texas cattle drives, professional gamblers, and scalawags." July stared pointedly at the lounging giant who had shaved the left side of his face. "And even closer to home, Sheriff Bat Masterson's older brother, Marshal Ed Masterson, was shot in the chest just last winter when he tried to break up a fight between Bob Shaw and Texas Dick in the Lone Star Saloon. Dodge City has its hands full, and it's only one of the many towns plagued by riffraff and thieves."

"You've made your point," Nacona grunted before laying the razor to the right side of his face. The nymph would make one whale of an attorney. She sure could rattle off facts. "Unfortunately, when it comes to upholding the law and trailing desperadoes, your only chance at success would be to talk them to death. The most dangerous weapon in your possession—and all you probably need, in fact—is your tongue," he added insultingly. "But you're no detective, at least not the kind it takes to hunt down robbers and rustlers." His piercing stare cut to the bone. "Even if I agreed to take the assignment in Wyoming, which I won't, you'd be more trouble than assistance to me. And the next time you blurt out somebody's name and imply he's in the detective business with you, make sure it isn't *my* name." He made a stabbing gesture with his left arm and winced from the nagging knife wound. "Now get the hell out of here. I'd like to finish my bath in peace and privacy."

July puffed up like an inflated bagpipe. "You are just like every other man," she spewed out in frustration. "You assume, since I committed the unpardonable sin of being born a woman, I am useless and incompetent. I want this assignment more than anything in this world!" Her fist slammed down on the edge of the commode, rattling the pitcher and basin. "I want to be something besides my brothers' shadow! You don't even have to help me crack this case if you don't want to. You only have to make a brief appearance in Denver for the bank and railroad representatives. I'll do the rest, and you will receive a fair fee for it."

"And lose my reputation when you bungle the job and maybe even get yourself killed—or worse?" Nacona exploded. "No thanks, honey. I don't want your death on my conscience." I have one death there already and it's hounding me, he silently added. "No dice, lady. You aren't using me for a front and you aren't standing on my reputation, either!"

"Isn't it just like a man to be unreasonable," July muttered acrimoniously.

Nacona glanced at her sharply and frowned. "You're the one who bluffed your way through your interview. I don't even know who the hell you are, and I don't care. I have my own purpose to serve. For two years I've been searching for a murdering bastard who seems to have dropped off the face of the earth. I have no definite description of this scoundrel and clues to his whereabouts. Every assignment I take is ultimately designed to find that son of a—"

He stopped short and willfully clamped down on his temper. There was damned little in this world that could crack his iron-willed control. That vicious killer had done it, so had the woman standing in the middle of the room and spouting a foolhardy proposition, tempting a man with that delicious body and exquisite face of hers.

July leaped at the opportunity to toss in her two cents' worth when Nacona's deep baritone voice cut off and his eyes wandered over her in silent inspection. "The murderer you're tracking might very well be in Wyoming," she baited him. "Why, he might even be involved in robberies or rustling. And if he isn't, I promise you the MacKenzie Detective Agency will do all in its power to help you track the man down—*if* you assist me in this case. You need only give me what little description and background you have on the elusive killer and I will assume the investigation myself."

"The answer is no," Nacona declared in a tone that invited no further argument. He wasted his breath.

"This is important to me, to my career!" she flared in frustration. "I want to make a name for myself."

"A lot of good a career will do a corpse."

Nacona scowled at her; she scowled back.

He had learned to keep his emotions under lock and key, to analyze and examine before proceeding. But this spitfire exasperated him beyond words. He looked at her and he wanted things from her that had nothing whatsoever to do with corporate or private investigation, but rather with the personal investigation of her tantalizing body and those luscious lips that were now puckered in a pout. Her cultured accent and her impressive command of the English language told him she had an education that surpassed his. He studied the expensive cut of her clothes, her poise, and he knew damned well that he and this tempting beauty were all wrong for each other. He'd come up the ladder the hard way, having learned by firsthand experience. She had textbook knowledge, idealistic standards. Good Lord, wouldn't they make a fine pair—worn rawhide and dainty lace. It was laughable!

Muttering as a riptide of emotion drew him in, Nacona directed her attention toward the door again. "Get out of here before you ruin your unblemished reputation, honey. If the respectable citizens downstairs discover you've been up here, flinging propositions at me while I'm in the tub, your name will be bandied all over town. This discussion is officially over!"

July stamped her foot in frustration. She would have preferred to throw something at this stubborn, mule-headed man. She had tried to reason with him. She had pleaded. She had plied him with a half-dozen examples, hoping he would feel an obligation to lend assistance, if not to her then to the good citizens of Wyoming. But nothing had worked. She had no option left except black-mail, even if it went against her grain.

"Very well then, I will be forced to scream my head off," she insisted with childish vindictiveness. "And when those decent citizens downstairs hear the commotion and come to investigate, I will insist that you tried to take unfair advantage of me. They will side with me, of course, especially after the crude remarks you made to me in the lobby. And you, Mr. Bleu, just might wind up behind bars in Bat Masterson's jail, which is probably where you belong anyway. *Your* kind of detective gives respectable investigation agencies a bad name because you prefer to shoot first and ask questions later."

"You can scream at the top of your lungs, honey," Nacona generously offered. "But it will change nothing. My reputation will keep those so-called decent citizens from crossing me. On that you can depend—"

His challenge died beneath a piercing female shriek that rattled the rafters and shattered his eardrums. To his utter disbelief, July took in an enormous breath that caused her ample bosom to strain against the confines of her bodice. Then she let loose with another bloodcurdling shriek that could have raised the dead in Boot Hill Cemetery.

Nacona was on his feet in nothing flat. Cursing a blue streak, he bounded from his bath to clamp a hand over the blonde's mouth.

The sight of naked masculine flesh glistening with water caused July to screech in earnest. Her startled voice hit a shrill pitch that made even the hair on the back of *her* neck stand straight up. She hadn't expected this swarthy brute to rise like a genie from a bottle and pounce on her. Obviously she had misjudged him.

As Nacona Bleu dashed toward her—buck naked—July very nearly crashed through the door in her haste to escape him. Instinct bade her to make a hasty departure, but nothing could erase the image frozen in her mind. July had never fainted, but she had come as close as she ever wanted to when he had bounded toward her in all his glory.

A low rumble rattled in Nacona's chest when the swish of petticoats was followed by the slamming of the door. That sassy female detective had just learned a valuable lesson, in more ways than one. It was important to expect the unexpected if she was ever going to become a good detective. And, judging by the expression on her face, she'd just gotten a lesson in male anatomy she'd not soon forget.

It was just as he'd thought, that minx didn't know beans about men. She was as pure as driven snow. When nothing else had worked effectively, the sight of a naked man had shocked her into flight. He had made his contribution to that high-spirited misfit's education. And that

35

was the *only* contribution to it she was going to get from him—drastic though that most certainly had been. The last thing Nacona needed was to take a greenhorn detective under his wing, especially a female. And especially *that* female. She was too damned distracting. A man couldn't concentrate on his work with that shapely nymph underfoot. Throughout their conversation, Nacona had found his mind wandering down the most arousing avenues, wondering how it would feel to take her velvet-soft lips under his, to map the curvaceous terrain of her body with bold caresses.

Another skirl of laughter erupted from his lips when his mind lingered on that tantalizing thought. If he'd dared to lay a hand on that sophisticated bit of fluff, she really would scream for all she was worth. Imagine him and her together . . . doing anything . . . *anything* at all. Making wild sweet love? Mmm . . . To be sure, the scintillating prospect caused his male juices to percolate, but she was nowhere near his type. Imagine the two of them investigating robberies and rustling. He and that lovely firebrand as partners? Inconceivable! Even with his brawn and her brains it would never work. They were hopelessly and completely mismatched—and she had a phenomenal ability to ignite his temper. That wasn't a good thing. She rattled him, and he wasn't accustomed to those kinds of feelings.

Nacona plunked himself into his tub and scowled at the tormentingly lovely image that floated above his head. He didn't want to spare that gorgeous nymph another thought. But she was there, like an intriguing picture drifting across his mind's eye.

"Forget it," he growled at himself before taking a huge

swig of brandy as a substitute for the steamy kiss he was never going to get from that curvaceous beauty. He had seen the last of her, and that was best for both of them. Nacona sealed that sensible thought with another drink and scrubbed himself clean.

Chapter 3

Humiliated beyond words, July streaked down the back stairs of the hotel. The instant she stepped into the darkened alley she half-collapsed against the clapboard wall to recover her composure. At that moment thunder rumbled overhead, and that didn't help matters. July had an irrational fear of storms, the result of a tragic incident in her childhood. When lightning flashed, what little control she had over her chaotic emotions evaporated. Blast it, she had to get a grip on herself! Wouldn't you know she would have to confront her worst fear immediately after the jolting encounter with that cocky pistolero. Obviously this wasn't her day.

July blinked once and then twice, trying to get herself in hand. But nothing could erase the shocking image at the front of her mind, spotlighted by irregular flashes of lightning. The picture of a virile Nacona Bleu stuck with her like a porcupine quill, causing her heart to *ker-thump* in her chest with every erratic beat of her pulse.

The infuriating man! He had refused her request and then had sent her running by exposing himself to her. He had no scruples whatsoever. She had heard it said that this deadly gunman played by his own rules, that he made them up as he went along. She had also heard it said that Nacona Bleu was one of the best in the business because he was unpredictable, utterly fearless, and incredibly daring. Well, he had lived up to his reputation.

July sucked in a shuddering breath and pushed herself upright. Two could play his cunning game, she decided. Nacona Bleu wanted to play rough, did he? If he could dish it out, time would soon determine just how well he could take it. David hadn't bowed down to Goliath, and she wasn't admitting defeat to that ornery giant.

With angry jerks, July pulled the pins from the right side of her hair, allowing sandy blond tendrils to dangle down her neck and then be caught up by the brisk breeze that swirled past. Clenching the bodice of her gown, she tore enough cloth to look slightly indecent without exposing too much bosom. Cursing Nacona, she reached down to rip the fabric at her waist, exposing the white petticoats beneath it. Still fuming over the embarrassing encounter, July pinched her cheeks and lips until color blazed on her face.

She then made her way to the sheriff's office, cautiously remaining on the covered boardwalk to protect herself from the inclement weather. Meticulously planning her strategy, she mustered a few crocodile tears along the way. Once or twice in the past she had called upon her theatrical abilities during investigations made with her brothers. But none of her performances had been as gratifying as the one she was about to play for Bat and Ed Masterson's benefit. As sheriff of Ford County, Bat would be obliged to apprehend the scoundrel who had molested a young, respectable woman in town. And as marshal of

Dodge, Ed Masterson would also feel it his duty to ensure a woman's safety. With July's knowledge of the law, she was about to play the situation for all it was worth. Propelled by a gust of wind, she blew into the sheriff's office to repay Nacona Bleu for infuriating her.

Bat Masterson bounded out of his chair when July burst through the door in tears, clutching at the gaping fabric which barely concealed her bosom. His slate blue eyes drifted over July's comely figure and her enchanting face. He didn't have to ask what had happened. He could see well enough that the young lady had narrowly escaped with her virtue . . . if she was that lucky.

July peered watery-eyed at the sheriff. Bat Masterson was a striking figure of a man with a thick mustache and a mop of jet black hair. When the twenty-four-year-old Bat had arrived in Dodge the previous year, it was said that a flashy scarlet neckerchief had encircled his throat, and a Mexican sash had been draped around his waist. Gleaming silver-plated Peacemakers had hung on his hips and gold-mounted spurs were strapped to his polished boots. July had heard it said that Masterson's finery gave him the edge when he faced outlaws on Front Street. He could blind his foe in a gunfight.

Since Bat had been elected sheriff, he had changed his personal image and style of clothing to lend himself an air of respectability. Now he was garbed in a black tailor-made suit and a fashionable pearl gray bowler with a high-curled brim. Two silver-mounted, ivory-handled pistols rested on his hips and a diamond stickpin glistened on his jacket. To complement his striking appearance, Bat carried a cane which served as a walking stick and at times as a weapon.

According to reports, Bat had gotten into a gunfight two years earlier at Fort Griffin, Texas, over a woman. Gossip had it that Molly Brennan had thrown herself in front of Bat when her former sweetheart, a U. S. Army sergeant named Melvin King with a bad reputation had tried to shoot him down. The bullet had passed through Molly's body, killing her instantly, before lodging in Bat's pelvis. But before Bat fell, he had pumped lead at the enraged sergeant, who was in the process of cocking his pistol to fire a second time. Bat was the only one to survive the showdown, but his limp was a constant reminder of the deadly ordeal.

Despite this ex–buffalo hunter, Army scout, and gun-slinger's checkered past, he and his older brother were riding herd over Dodge City while Marshal Wyatt Earp took a leave of absence to try his luck in the goldfields near Deadwood, South Dakota. Although July knew Bat and his brother had their hands full, she intended to retaliate against Nacona and the Mastersons were going to help her even the score.

"I want that horrible man arrested," July wailed. She then muffled several sniffs with her hankie. "I will not have my reputation ruined by that lecherous scoundrel. I wish to file charges this instant. I want that rascal shot, poisoned, and hanged!"

Bat surged forward to assist the damsel in distress into the nearest chair. "You needn't worry, ma'am," he consoled her. "I'll have your assailant behind bars as soon as possible. Just tell me who he is and where he was the last time you saw him."

July spilled a few more tears into her hankie and expelled several sobs. "That vermin tried to"—she clutched at her gaping gown, pulling it back into a more decent position—"he—"

"Who was it?" Bat asked her, his expression testifying to the extent of his concern.

July muffled her sniffles and dabbed at her eyes. "Nacona Bleu is his name. The man's a threat to womankind!" This she punctuated with a howling wail and a shoulder-shaking sob.

Bat jerked upright and blinked in surprise. "Nacona? Are you sure about that?"

Bat had met the half-breed gunslinger the previous year when he'd worked as a deputy for Wyatt Earp. He counted Nacona as one of his friends, and he had a habit of remaining fiercely loyal to friends. As far as Bat knew, Nacona had never stepped out of line in Dodge. The gunslinger lived a peaceful existence while he was in town, relaxing between assignments that took him far and wide. Bat and Nacona had a good working relationship. When trouble erupted in Dodge, Nacona offered his gun hand to quell disturbances.

Nacona frequented brothels and saloons, it was true. Who didn't? But the famed shootist knew his limitations. And yet, it only took one glance at this lovely female to imagine what had come over Nacona. He had probably been without a woman for weeks during pursuit of a fugitive. Whiskey and lust made a man do crazy things sometimes. Nacona was as vulnerable to a pretty woman as the next man.

"Well, don't just stand there," July howled. "Arrest him before he abuses some other poor defenseless female. I want to file charges."

The door to the cells creaked open, and Ed Masterson

appeared on the scene. A curious frown clouded his brow. "What's going on?"

"The young lady claims Nacona Bleu assaulted her," Bat reported.

"Nacona?" Ed's square face registered surprise. Bewildered, he stared at his younger brother and then at the weeping blonde. Bat pensively stroked his well-manicured mustache and shook his head. "I never would have thought Nacona—"

"I want to see justice served," July blubbered. "Do something and be quick about it!"

Spurred into action, Bat and Ed whizzed toward the door. Although it went against their grain to arrest a man they considered a friend, the hysterical young lady demanded action.

When the door slammed shut, July smiled triumphantly. Very soon, she would see just how cocky that dark-eyed scoundrel was while he was sitting behind bars alongside the drunks and ruffians who had given Dodge City a bad name. She hoped the cells were crammed full of criminals awaiting trial—enough to crowd Nacona in like a sardine.

And there would probably be more unruly ruffians shepherded into jail within the next few days, she reminded herself with a spiteful smile. A cattle herd was reported to be approaching from the south, and that meant more trouble for the town. Cowboys had a nasty habit of shooting the place up and causing one ruckus after another in the streets. While Bat and Ed were trying to keep the peace, Nacona Bleu would be mildewing in the calaboose until he finally agreed to join forces with July for the Wyoming assignment. By hook or crook, she was going to acquire Nacona's assistance, and then she would soon be well on her way to a successful career in investigation, flaunting the kind of credentials no man would ever scoff at.

The rap at the door caused Nacona to curse under his breath. He'd been drinking hard and fast since his encounter with the saucy blonde, and the more whiskey he imbibed, the more his mind wandered to forbidden fantasies. He could see that gorgeous imp standing in the middle of his room, tempting the man in him, leaving him wanting what he'd done without for more weeks than he cared to count. The craving now had Nacona tugging on a clean set of clothes in his eagerness to seek out a warm, willing female to make him forget the one he couldn't have.

And if that pretty nymph was standing on the other side of his door, she might get more than a frontal view of a naked man to further her education in the birds and bees department. After all, it was her fault his male desires were running rampant. Considering all the whiskey he'd consumed, he might not be able to stop himself.

Sluggishly, Nacona staggered toward the door, a pistol in one hand and a half-empty bottle in the other. He could still smell the fragrant perfume that permeated his room, could still visualize the voluptuous figure and the enchanting face that preoccupied his thoughts even when he'd vowed to put her out of his mind.

"Did you come back for more, honey?" Nacona drawled as he swung open the door and leaned negligently upon it.

But it wasn't the alluring blonde who greeted him, and Nacona had no way of knowing that his remark sounded very incriminating to Bat and Ed Masterson.

"You were expecting someone else, I presume." Bat ambled inside to survey the room. Although there was no sign of a struggle, one look at this giant of a man assured Bat that a struggle would have been futile for the wailing young woman who waited in the sheriff's office. The petite blonde hadn't stood a chance against this rugged gunslinger. Nacona Bleu had the strength of three good men.

Nacona tossed his pearl-handled pistol on the bed and chugged a drink straight from the bottle. "Actually, I'm glad you aren't her. She really wasn't my type. If she had been . . ." He waggled his thick black brows suggestively, leaving Bat and Ed to form their own conclusions. That wasn't a good thing, not in lieu of what July had told the law officers.

"Care for a drink?" Nacona generously asked.

"No thanks." Ed propped himself against the door-jamb. "I'm afraid we're here on business."

"Oh? Is somebody in town disturbing the peace? You need an extra hand?" Nacona questioned before sipping his whiskey to drown the tempting vision that floated above him. It didn't help.

"Yes, as a matter of fact, someone did disturb the peace." Bat reached over to grab Nacona's hat and then plunked it on his ruffled raven hair. "That *somebody* turned out to be you. You dallied with the wrong woman while you were drinking and carousing."

Nacona stared blankly at the two pairs of slate-blue

eyes keyed on him. "What the hell are you talking about?"

"We're referring to the young lady you molested while you were celebrating your return to town. She's in the office, crying her eyes out and demanding your arrest," Ed explained as he steered Nacona into the hall.

"Just for *that?*" Nacona blinked like an owl, assuming the ornery imp had filed a complaint after he'd exposed himself to shut her up and get her out of his room. "Well, she asked for it," he asserted. "I should have *her* arrested for disturbing *my* peace."

"I'm afraid the law will rule in her favor," Bat countered as he shepherded Nacona down the steps. "But maybe if you apologize real nicely to her, she'll drop the charges and you can be on your way."

"I'd rather not see her again, thanks just the same," Nacona muttered sourly.

"I'm sure you wouldn't, not just now anyway." Ed chuckled. "The young lady is fit to be roped and tied."

Nacona scowled at the thought of another confrontation, especially in his present condition. He could barely think straight after drinking on an empty stomach. And that minx was too quick witted and intelligent to encounter when a man was not functioning at full capacity.

The instant Nacona staggered into the sheriff's office he came to a halt. With jaw sagging, he stared at July. His droopy gaze fell to the luscious swells of her breasts which were exposed by the gaping gown. July shrank back in her chair, giving her most convincing performance for Bat and Ed's benefit.

"I hope that vile beast rots in a cell," she sobbed.

When Bat and Ed tried to usher Nacona toward the back room, he refused to stir another step. "What the hell is this?" He didn't call July a maniac, but the look he flung at her clearly implied that he thought she was one.

"Pretend you don't know, you odious man," July blubbered, hiding her mischievous smile behind her hankie. "Respectable women aren't safe on the streets while lecherous scoundrels like you are running loose, victimizing every female in your path."

Nacona gaped at her, realizing that ingenious improvisation was this crafty witch's forte. She seemed to have a most unnerving knack of getting what she wanted, one way or another.

"Come on, Nacona," Bat insisted with another nudge. "We don't want to add resisting arrest to your first offense."

Nacona glanced over his shoulder, watching with fuming irritation while July flung him a goading grin. But the instant Ed Masterson spared her a glance, July sobbed noisily and dabbed her reddened eyes.

"I never touched that little witch," Nacona growled. "But I'd like to."

"Keep your mouth shut. You're only making it worse," Bat warned as he opened the cell and guided Nacona into it. "As soon as you get yourself in hand, I'll send the lady in to see you. The two of you can have a powwow and work this out. And if you behave yourself, maybe she'll forgive you and reconsider pressing charges."

Nacona didn't know how long he'd sat there stewing and brooding before the hinges on the door creaked and his dream-turned-nightmare appeared in the shadowed room. A muffled curse passed his lips as he unfolded himself from his cot and clamped his fingers around the iron bars, wishing with all his heart that they were clenched around the mischievous imp's swanlike neck!

"I can see why you studied the law, lady," he muttered. "You delight in bending the rules to suit your purposes, don't you?"

"And let that be a lesson to you, Mr. Bleu," she chastised. "Force doesn't always have to be applied in investigation work. There are more subtle but effective ways of getting things done."

Nacona scrutinized July, annoyed that she had trapped him like an unsuspecting rat. "You're a shrewd, manipulative woman, I'll give you that," he said in a begrudging tone. "What did you tell Ed and Bat? That I raped you?"

"I didn't have to explain myself," she informed him smugly. "The picture was worth a thousand words. And as soon as you agree to assist me in this investigation, I will tell the Mastersons that all is forgiven and that you have promised to be the perfect gentleman in a lady's presence henceforth and forevermore."

Nacona loosed his stranglehold on the bars and plopped back onto his cot to regard the dazzling beauty for a long pensive moment. He needed to turn the tables on this cunning sprite. If he hadn't pickled his brain with liquor perhaps a solution would readily spring to mind.

"Well?" July crossed her arms over her torn gown and impatiently tapped her foot. "Are you going to agree to my bargain, or shall I shriek my way back to the sheriff and marshal and claim you have attempted to molest me again?"

What he really longed to do was give her something to

shriek about. Curse her ornery hide! He would feel a damned sight better if he *had* done the things implied by her torn gown and tangled blond hair.

A scampish smile quirked his lips when that arousing thought converged with an idea. Nacona rose to his full height and approached her. "Very well, Miss . . ." He waited for her to fill in the blank.

"MacKenzie. July Beth MacKenzie," she supplied.

"July?" Nacona frowned curiously. "Where the hell did you get a name like that?"

"Probably from the same place you got yours. From my parents, of course. I was born on the fourth of July. Being hopelessly patriotic, Abigail and Bernard MacKenzie named their only daughter in honor of Independence Day. That is no more peculiar than the name Nacona, so don't poke fun."

"I suppose your brothers are August, September, and October," he scoffed sarcastically.

July sent him her best glare—the one she had practiced in the mirror. It didn't faze Nacona one whit. "Gresham, Calvin, and Ethan wouldn't care for your snide remark, Mr. Bleu."

"I wish they were here. I have a few choice comments to make to them about their brat of a sister," he snapped back at her. "The name suits you, I'll admit. July—hot and testy."

"Insults will get you nowhere, Mr.—"

"Nacona," he corrected with a scowl. "If you call me Mr. Bleu again *I*'ll scream *my* head off and declare that you tried to rape me through these cussed bars!"

She sniffed haughtily. "And who in his right mind would believe you?"

"Anybody who isn't bedeviled by that deceptively angelic face and delicious body of yours," he muttered. Damn it to hell, this minx was giving him such grief, he *did* want to scream in frustration.

July struck a sophisticated pose, covered herself as best she could, and flung her dainty nose in the air. "I can see that this discussion is going nowhere. You are too surly to be reasonable. Sleep well, Nacona."

When she lurched around to make a theatrical exit, Nacona's hand shot through the bars to snare her. He dragged her back, intending to breathe down her neck and curse her fluently, but the scent of her perfume clogged his nostrils and clouded his brain. He could feel her delectable body pressed against his. Even the bars didn't detract from the shocking contact. Lightning struck, he was paralyzed by riveting sensations.

She was such a temptation! She appealed to everything masculine in him. How she'd escaped being molested before now was beyond him. To see her was to want her. She inspired dreams and aroused his desire, preying on the hungers that simmered beneath the surface, causing mental and physical distress. In fact, the ache she aroused inside him was so pronounced it burned like fire.

This wasn't the time or the place to be entertaining such arousing thoughts, but Nacona couldn't seem to keep his hands off her. Suddenly, unappeased desire was eating him alive, and the bars that separated them were all that prevented him from committing the crime that had landed him in jail. Hell, since he was locked in the calaboose for molesting this gorgeous nymph, he might as well get some sort of satisfaction.

Chapter 4

July froze when her body came into contact with Nacona's powerful frame. Unspoken awareness flowed between them, setting off riveting sensations that both paralyzed and sensitized her. A lump the size of a cantaloupe ballooned in her throat, and her circulation suddenly seemed restricted from the neck up. She couldn't think when trapped by his male magnetism. The masculine scent of him saturated her senses. Solid, unyielding muscle forged against her as iron bars pressed against her back. She couldn't breathe without "inhaling" him, couldn't move without feeling the warm, powerful threat of his body communicating with hers.

This ruggedly handsome rogue was dangerous, not only to fugitives of justice, but to every female on the planet!

Before July could take control of her wayward thoughts the vision that had shocked her senseless earlier in the evening flashed through her mind. She went hot all over, seeing Nacona standing naked before her, behind her, beside her. . . . He was everywhere, suffocating her, monopolizing her thoughts, stirring feelings that had no business assaulting her then or now!

Frantic, July strained against him with all her might. "Let me go!" she gasped, appalled at herself for being so affected by this rapscallion's nearness.

One touch and Nacona was throbbing with unappeased hunger. A shudder racked his body as his lips grazed her bare shoulder, marveling at the silky texture of her skin. Mmm . . . she tasted as good as she looked. She was soft and exquisite as satin. Basic instinct gnawed at him like a termite on wood, crumbling the logical side of his brain, leaving him highly susceptible to lusty desire.

A shiver skittered down July's spine when warm sensuous lips drifted over her throat, causing her pulse to leap. She told herself that she could become immune to his amorous assault if she set her mind to it. Determination was her most admirable virtue, after all. But it failed her when she needed it most. When Nacona molded her against the hard angles and muscled contours of his body, her traitorous flesh responded. Involuntarily, she swayed backward, unable to battle the needs his skillful touch had awakened.

What was happening to her? She wasn't even sure she liked this rascal, but her body betrayed her by surrendering to the wicked pleasure of his kisses and caresses. Men had never affected her this way before. She had not permitted such weaknesses of the flesh. It was only that this midnight-haired devil had caught her off guard with his sensual assault, July tried to reassure herself. Although his first touch had been demanding and forceful, within a heartbeat, this formidable lion had become as gentle as a lamb—almost worshipful with his caresses that glided around her waist to tantalize and entrap her. While his reverent kisses distracted her by skiing over the slope of her shoulder, leaving a knot of fire uncoiling deep inside her, his skillful hands set off on a journey of discovery. His brazen caresses swirled over her hips and trailed over her thigh before ascending to encircle the taut peaks of her breasts. Her traitorous body quivered in instantaneous reaction to his wildly sensual assault.

This couldn't be happening! It was totally illogical. But it *was* happening, and her legs trembled beneath her as if they meant to fold at the knees. July clutched at the sinewy arms that encircled her waist, more for support than an attempt to escape, she was sorry to say. Her breath came in ragged spurts as his moist lips traced a burning path to the sensitive point she didn't even know she had just beneath her ear. When his arm shifted so that his hand could cup the mound of her breast, July gasped for air, but none was forthcoming. Her lungs might well be filled with mortar. His searching hands glided over her ribs, counting them one by one before they measured the trim indentation of her waist and settled familiarly on her hips. July gulped hard when another knot of longing unfurled inside her.

Sweet merciful heavens! She had never been prone to fainting spells, but this was the second time in the same evening that the world shrank and she felt lightheaded. His tenderly erotic assault on her body and her senses was worse than seeing this Adonis of a man in the altogether. She was alarmingly close to collapse.

Nacona had partaken of far too much whiskey to question his impulsive need to steal what little pleasure this jail cell offered him. One touch, one kiss and caress, and he was addicted. The feel of July's curvaceous body resting against his made him ache. White-hot fires prickled beneath his skin, and a pulsating ache burgeoned in his loins. It angered Nacona that he was so easily and explosively aroused by this imp who had purposely landed him behind bars. But it wasn't spite that prompted his amorous efforts. His body had become far more demanding than his brain, though his male desire was never going to be satisfied with those damned iron bars standing between them. Damn it, if he didn't get a firm grip on himself and quickly . . .

Nacona steadied himself against the bars and eased his grasp on the trembling beauty. The agony of wanting her beyond bearing was killing him. But if he pursued this hopeless fantasy he would drive himself mad. His meager consolation came in knowing that his brazen touch had devastated July as thoroughly as it had devastated him. Her breathing was definitely disturbed, and her body had quivered in response to his daring kisses and adventurous caresses. He had felt the sensual vibrations undulating through her to him. When they touched, sparks flew. It was as simple and as complicated as that.

Swallowing hard, July wheeled away, willing her weak knees to support her. Were it not for the far wall she leaned against, she would collapse, embarrassing herself even more. This unexplainable biological attraction was impossible to control, but why was it this black-eyed demon affected her that way? She had artfully dodged wily adventurers and cunning rogues for years without being stirred by wanton desire. In the past, she'd had three brothers as chaperones, July reminded herself. Now braving the world alone, she found herself tempted by a man so daring and skillful he could seduce her while he was locked in a cell. Lord, what was she letting herself in for? Considering the phenomenal effect this rough and rowdy rapscallion had on her, she would be flirting with danger if he *did* agree to her bargain.

As her lashes swept up she saw Nacona peering at her with the penetrating gaze that probed deep enough to pluck the carefully guarded secrets from her soul. Each time those glistening ebony eyes focused on her at point-blank range her knees wobbled. Exerting, will power, July got her erratic pulse under control, then drew herself up to what she considered a remarkably dignified stature and marched toward the door.

"I'll agree to join forces with you on one condition," Nacona stipulated, his voice rustling with disturbed desire. "I want you, July, without a fight, for one uninterrupted night in my arms. . . ."

His words echoed through the shadowed chamber and reverberated in July's mind, causing her to stop dead in her tracks. Nonplused, she wheeled to gape at the towering giant who demanded what no man had ever taken from her. The swine! How dare he put such a high price on this bargain that *she* had engineered!

A scampish smile pursed Nacona's lips when July's face flushed crimson red. He wanted her, it was true. But he knew she would reject his terms. And when she did, it would be *she* who denied *his* assistance. Nacona had turned the tables on this sassy firebrand and now he would see how she liked being backed into a corner. Turnabout was fair play, wasn't it?

The warm, unexplainable sensations that had flooded through her a few moments earlier suddenly were transformed into fiery outrage. July jerked herself to attention and glared at him. "Not only are you a gunslinger, you are an opportunist. I should have anticipated such an underhanded tactic from a good-for-nothing rascal like you!"

Nacona shrugged off her insult. He could handle this spirited imp far better when they were at odds. He didn't feel quite so out of control, so unhinged by the desire she aroused in him. Mocking disdain was *his* forte. He had developed it into an art, and it had worked to his benefit in many a showdown when he'd needed the edge. In this instance, he employed the technique to build walls between him and this alluring nymph. His sarcasm would prevent what happened a few moments earlier from occurring again.

"It's your decision, honey," he drawled as his onyx eyes raked over her with penetrating effectiveness. "I doubt you would bring me much pleasure anyway, being the innocent you are. I prefer my women experienced in pleasing a man. I'd wager you wouldn't even know how to start."

Rage boiled inside her, and July would have slapped the insolent smirk off his face if she could have done so without breaking her hand on iron bars. "You are beneath contempt," she spluttered, shooting him a venomous look.

Nacona delighted in watching her hiss and sputter. A deep rumble of laughter echoed in his massive chest as he swaggered over to stretch out on his cot. Cushioning his head on his linked fingers, Nacona glanced sideways to survey the fuming female who was glaring at him.

"I'm not changing my mind, honey. Those are my terms. Take 'em or leave 'em." A crafty grin quirked his lips. "I don't know why you're in such a snit. You said yourself that you wanted neither a fiancé nor a husband. So what does losing your innocence matter if you aren't saving yourself for your knight in shining armor? And you did proclaim that this assignment meant more to you than anything else in this world." Nacona flashed her a mocking smile that provoked her to swear in a most unladylike manner. "Now's your chance to prove it, sweetheart. I want your virginity in exchange for my expert marksmanship and renowned reputation. It's up to you."

July was thankful that she didn't have a loaded pistol in her possession. She was certain she would have blown this ornery scoundrel to smithereens without a second thought. She had tried to bargain with the devil and just look where it had gotten her. She had been too naive to consider the consequences of such foolishness.

"You can sit here and rot for all I care," she spat out, her green eyes snapping.

"And your career as a detective will never get off the ground," he replied with as much boredom in his voice as he could command. "But it's your loss, honey. I could have taught you far more than how to be a successful detective."

In a burst of fury, July lurched around and stormed away. She had definitely met her match when she'd challenged this unscrupulous gunslinger. He had lived up to his reputation, displaying the most uncanny knack for turning every situation to his advantage. He was accustomed to success, to maneuvering for position. Dealing with him was like playing a mental game of chess. July was in jeopardy and the stakes were as high as they came. Check to her king . . .

"Did you and Nacona come to some sort of agreement?" Bat questioned when July sailed through the office, accompanied by a rumble of thunder and a flash of lightning.

"No." July spewed out. "You can hang him high tomorrow and that wouldn't be soon enough to suit me!"

With that, she zoomed outside and the entire office shuddered and groaned when she slammed the door behind her.

"That certainly went well," Ed snickered as he watched the fuming firebrand whiz past the window as if propelled by a cannon.

Heaving a sigh, Bat ambled back to the cells to find Nacona leisurely sprawled on his cot, trying to make the best of his meager accommodations. "You've put Ed and me in an awful spot," Bat grumbled. "I can't let you out without inviting that feisty female's wrath. She wants your neck in a hangman's noose."

"By now, she should be mad enough to leave town," Nacona calmly predicted. "Tomorrow you can release me and she'll be none the wiser."

"I hope you're right," Ed said as he strode up beside his brother. "But mad as she was when she left, I'm wondering if she's entertaining thoughts of organizing local support and returning with a lynch mob to ensure that you're the honored guest at a necktie party."

Bat unlocked the cell and swung open the door. "How about a game of poker to while away the hours."

"And supper," Nacona requested. "I'm starved."

"Just how did you get mixed up with a woman like that in the first place?" Ed questioned as the threesome ambled back to the main office.

Nacona settled himself comfortably in the chair beside the desk. "I was just damned unlucky."

"Amen to that," Bat said. "Pretty though she is, that terror in green silk is out for your blood."

Nacona didn't bother to mention what he'd been out for when he'd tried to bargain with that high-spirited beauty. Some things were better left untold.

When Ed strode off to order their meal at the restaurant, Nacona plucked up the deck of cards and shuffled with experienced ease. He was sure he'd seen the last of July Beth MacKenzie. And that was for best, he reassured himself. That rambunctious blonde was too great a temptation. She should never have left her protective brothers in Kansas City. Nacona wished he could forget he had ever laid eyes on her!

Gresham MacKenzie ambled up the steps to a spacious home that set on the outskirts of Kansas City. He stared absently at the telegram he had received from July—one that assured him she was having a grand visit with their elderly aunt in Wichita.

Of course, July was nowhere near Wichita, and she had taken great pains to keep the truth from her brothers who usually kept her tucked so closely under their wings she was nearly smothered.

A fond smile pursed Gresham's lips when visions of his lively sister sprang to mind. Quite honestly, it had come as a relief that July had decided to visit their mother's sister. She needed to get away from the detective agency and distract herself from her obsession.

For the past three years July had been straining at the bit, constantly demanding to become an equal partner with her three brothers, no matter how difficult or dangerous the assignments. She had very nearly driven Gresham crazy while she prepared to read for the law. He had assisted her with her studies to ensure she passed the bar examination with flying colors. But that hadn't been enough to satisfy July's adventurous, independent nature. She had thrown herself into criminal investigation with her usual vim and vigor, leaving her brothers to stew about her safety. The little hoyden was difficult to handle, and she always had been. The older she got, the worse the problem became. Gresham was glad to have July out from underfoot for a few weeks, while Aunt Betty coped with her irrepressible spirit.

Calvin and Ethan were just descending the steps when Gresham strolled into the foyer. Their eyes narrowed on the telegram in their oldest brother's hand.

"Not another assignment," Calvin groaned. "Good Lord, we've got enough to handle already. You haven't even finished the paperwork on the last court case we turned over to you."

Gresham gave his sandy blond head a shake and extended the message to his disgruntled brothers. "This is from July. According to her, she and Aunt Betty are having a marvelous time in Wichita and she's thinking of extending her vacation another few weeks."

"Good," Ethan said with a relieved sigh. "I hope that means our little sister has recovered from her compulsive need to outdo us in the detective business. The last case she took it upon herself to resolve very nearly gave me a heart seizure. She was getting too damned daring for her own good."

"I've been giving our sister some serious thought." Gresham strode into the office to pour himself a brandy. "It's time we selected a suitable husband who can take July's mind off her hunger for adventure. She needs to pursue a more sedate life-style. She is a woman, after all, even though she insists being born a female was the curse of her life."

"And who do you know in Kansas City who possesses all the necessary qualifications?" Calvin questioned as he filled his glass. "Her intended will have to be every bit as determined as July, and he'll have to be able to stand his ground when she tries to walk all over him. You know perfectly well that July refuses to take *no* for an answer when she sets her mind to something."

"Our little sister is extremely particular as well as determined," Ethan noted. "To hear her talk, there isn't a man on the planet who is worthy of her affection. She goes through suitors like an elephant goes through peanuts."

Gresham shrugged off the negative remarks and settled into his favorite chair. "I have four eligible bachelors in mind. Each might prove to be good husband material."

"Oh really?" Calvin smirked. "Name one."

"John Witherspoon," Gresham supplied.

"That upstart lawyer you've faced in court?" Ethan scoffed at his oldest brother. "July has twice as many brains as he does. He couldn't even handle her on his good days. The bad days would breed disaster."

"Then how about Dr. Fitch," Gresham suggested. "He has a prospering practice."

"Justin Fitch?" Calvin gave his blond head a vetoing shake. "He's too kind and tender hearted. July would walk all over him. He'd have to perform surgery on himself to remove her footprints."

"Well then, how about Robert Crayton? He is assertive and plainspoken and he has made a huge success of his mercantile stores. He could put July to work as his accountant, to keep track of the money he's making hand over fist."

Calvin and Ethan thought it over and nodded agreeably.

"Robert has possibilities," Ethan agreed. "He can deal with tough customers, and he can provide for July in the manner to which she has grown accustomed."

"There's only one problem that I can see," Calvin mentioned. "Robert melts at the very sight of July when she passes him on the street. He runs his business with a firm hand, but July may be another matter entirely. I think he's been sweet on her for some time now, and that will put him at a disadvantage." His fair features furrowed curiously. "Who is your last prospect, big brother?"

"James Harrison, the rancher who lives six miles south of town," Gresham informed them. "I admit I don't know much about him, but he does seem to be prospering."

Calvin scoffed at the suggestion. "James is too rough around the edges. He was a cattle drover for almost two years before he stocked his ranch and settled down. He lacks sophistication, and he has a bit of a reputation as a gunslinger." This last Calvin followed with a distasteful snort.

"I agree with Cal," Ethan piped up. "James wouldn't suit July. I have no use for gunslingers who try to pass themselves off as lawmen or detectives, and I'm not so sure James hasn't ridden on both sides of the law. In fact, the details of how he acquired the cash to set up his ranch are sketchy at best. I wouldn't want July mixed up with a man with a questionable past. No one seems to know much about James, and he isn't one to reveal it or to confide what he did before he turned to ranching. He could have been an honest-to-goodness outlaw for all we know."

"Robert Crayton would come as close as any man in town to being able to handle July," Calvin decided.

A ponderous frown puckered Ethan's brow. "But how do we go about coaxing July into marriage when she insists she wants to pursue a career? If we depended on her to manage this house and cook, we would have starved to death by now. She has never been very domestic."

"July doesn't have to be domesticated, only properly wed," Gresham insisted. "We are responsible for July. It is up to us to ensure that she settles down as a well-bred lady should. This business about July opening her own law and detective agency is utterly ridiculous. I hope we've got that notion out of her head for good." He glanced at his brothers. "Despite the difficulties we might face, are we all agreed that Robert Crayton is our man?"

Calvin and Ethan nodded.

"Good. I'll have a chat with Rob. When July returns from Wichita, we'll invite him to the house so he and July can socialize with proper supervision."

Having agreed that it was time for July to join the ranks

of married women and to relinquish her profession before she got herself hurt, the brothers three raised their glasses in a toast to their well-laid scheme.

"Even if we do convince July to marry Robert, we'll still have to keep a watch on her," Calvin said.

"Haven't we always?" Gresham snickered. "Having another man to keep that rambunctious female under control can't possibly hurt. In fact, it will make our duties easier, the way I see it."

"Robert will make a fine addition to the family," Calvin said with perfect assurance. "He will need some guidance in handling July, but he has promising possibilities."

"I'll run a check on his past, just to be on the safe side," Ethan volunteered. "We can't be too careful where our sister is concerned. I hope Rob doesn't have any skeletons in his closet."

"Well, at least he isn't a vagabond bounty hunter or something equally disgusting," Gresham snorted distastefully. "I have no respect whatsoever for men who go about depopulating the country under the pretense of seeing justice served. Gunslingers always seem to hover on the edge, just between law and corruption. John Henry Brown is a perfect example of a lawman gone bad. He was the marshal in Caldwell before he robbed a bank in Medicine Lodge and was shot down trying to escape. If you ask me, he got exactly what he deserved."

"My pet peeve is pistoleros and shootists who become detectives and marshals. Their personal conduct makes a mockery of law and order," Calvin chimed in. "Investigation should be handled in a respectable, dignified manner. If July ever wound up with some no-account scoundrel, I'd be ready to shoot the both of them—her for not having more sense and him for being the kind of man who plays the law to his advantage rather than upholding it!"

"I doubt we'll have to fret over July ending up in the company of such a despicable character." Gresham chuckled at the ridiculous thought. "We've never let men like that near her. And for certain, Aunt Betty will ensure July meets only the *crème de la crème* of Wichita."

It was a pity the MacKenzie males didn't know where July was or what she was doing. If they had they would have beaten a path to the depot to catch the first express train to Dodge City, but they thought they had resolved their problems with their independent, high-spirited sister. As her brothers spoke, however, July was taking her life into her own hands, rather than permitting her brothers to plan her future. In her estimation, what her brothers didn't know wouldn't hurt them. She was trying to launch her career in criminal investigation, and that ornery Nacona Bleu wasn't cooperating. She had decided there were times when a woman had to do what a woman had to do. And she was on her way to do it. . . .

Chapter 5

Pensively, July stared down Front Street, which represented the more civilized side of this town of a thousand inhabitants. The Atchison, Topeka and Santa Fe railroad tracks cut Dodge City in two from north to south. Front Street paralleled them fifty yards to the north. At the edge of town Roth and Company hide yard sat beside the tracks. Mounds of buffalo hides were being unloaded, stretched, dried, and bundled for shipment to tanneries in the East.

The buffalo hunters and skinners had done more to starve out Indian tribes than the entire Army had done in the past thirty years. July had little use for the rough and rowdy hunters, but she thought even less of them after she saw the thousands of hides and pondered the plight of the Indians and buffaloes that would soon be wiped out if some type of regulation wasn't established—and quickly.

Mulling over that disheartening thought and many others, she had spent the past few days pacing in front of business establishments, saloons, gambling houses, and, more particularly, the jail to ensure that Nacona was still locked behind bars. Occasionally she saw Bat, Ed, or Nathan Haywood, the deputy marshal, patrolling Front Street on which the carrying of guns was prohibited. Unfortunately, that was not the case on the rough side of town.

July glanced past the railroad tracks to the South Side where citizens were very much on their own if trouble broke out. The South Side was located fifty yards south of the rails, separated from the respectable district by one hundred yards of sand and sagebrush. The "Plaza" as it was called—though July could not imagine why since there was nothing there except sand, weeds, and steel rails—saw much traffic after dark. Buffalo hunters, renegades, rowdy cowboys, gamblers, and restless soldiers visiting from Fort Dodge were known to frequent the wild side of town. July hadn't bothered to investigate South Side which was lined with dozens of bawdy theaters, dance halls, and brothels. She wondered how many times Nacona Bleu had swaggered down those boardwalks in search of painted women and . . .

Tamping down the thought, July glanced back at the sheriff's office. She knew perfectly well that Nacona Bleu had mingled with the wilder elements of Dodge City society, being a little wild himself. In fact, according to Irma Billingsly, who paid July daily calls and who nurtured and pruned the grapevine of gossip, Nacona was still entertaining his lady friends—if one could call calico queens and doxies that. Irma had claimed some of Nacona's paramours had stormed the jail, demanding his release. And since Bat and Ed were unable to free Nacona until July decided whether or not to drop the charges, the floozies saw to it that the prisoner enjoyed as many luxuries as possible. Vases of flowers were said to adorn Nacona's cell to counteract the customary stench of the jail, and according to reports, the calico queens had decorated the barred window with curtains. They had also supplied fresh linen for the cot.

July had never heard of anything so outrageous, but it appeared Nacona Bleu carried a lot of weight in Dodge. He was a friend of both Bat and Ed Masterson, men known to be fiercely loyal to their cohorts. They would have released Nacona in a minute if July hadn't kept a close surveillance on the jail.

Time was becoming a factor for July. She had promised to meet with the railroad and bank representatives in Denver the following week. If she decided to abandon the investigation, she had to notify George Hershberger and C. L. Chambers. And if she agreed to Nacona's offensive bargain . . .

July let her breath out in a rush. Although she realized that desperate conditions demanded desperate measures, she had never expected to make such a monumental sacrifice. Curse it! How could she reverse the advantage that Nacona held over her? Nacona's words echoed through her mind until she was plagued with a nagging headache—a six-foot-three-inch, raven-haired, black-eyed headache, to be more specific! Nacona had pointed out that her loss of purity was inconsequential if she had no intention of saving herself for the man of her dreams. And since July had never fantasized about the existence of such a man, he had wanted to know why she was making such a to-do about nothing?

July hated to admit that Nacona had made a reasonable point, though she had never thought about it from that particular perspective. And if the truth be known, it was that ornery rapscallion who had awakened her slumbering desires with bold caresses and kisses—and in a jail! July supposed Nacona was as good a candidate as anybody to introduce her to passion. Though he had infuriated her by ridiculing her lack of experience and expressing his preference for women who were seasoned at passionate pursuits.

The man had her over a barrel. He had challenged her to prove her intent to take this investigative assignment no matter what the price. And of course Nacona planned to reap every benefit he could. She was nothing more than an amusing challenge to that scoundrel. He wanted her only to say he'd had her, so he could carve another notch on his bedpost. The lout! He was a shining example of the kind of man her brothers detested—a scalawag who posed as the long arm of the law and then turned every situation to his personal advantage. Well, he wasn't dealing with the local idiot. July wasn't going to bow down without . . . A fleeting thought whizzed through her mind, causing her to miss a step as she paraded past the sheriff's office.

Check to Nacona's king, she mused, plotting her move in this mental game of chess. Now it was her turn to back Nacona into a corner. An impish smile pursed her lips as she made a beeline for the jail. She couldn't wait to see the look on Nacona's ruggedly handsome face when she offered her stipulation to his stipulation. Let the worm squirm and see how he liked it!

* * *

Bat and Ed Masterson glanced up when July breezed into their office. Ed rose to his feet to greet the comely blonde. The city marshal was well known for his ability to talk rowdy cowboys into submission. He had a quiet, sincere way about him, and he was using diplomacy to resolve July's problem with Nacona.

"Miss MacKenzie, this conflict between you and Nacona should be settled without further delay," he urged. "I've known him for several years, and I assure you he has never made an attack on any other respectable lady in town. I'm sure it was only bad whiskey and an eagerness to unwind after his last foray to bring in offenders of the law that prompted his uncharacteristic behavior. I would like to work out some sort of compromise."

"So would I," July surprised him by saying. "If you don't mind, I would like a few words with Nacona. If he is willing to agree to my terms, I will drop the charges against him."

Ed made a sweeping gesture with his arm. "Be my guest."

Determined, July sailed across the office and into the back room to find Nacona puffing on his cigar and lounging on a red velvet bedspread supplied by one of his lady-of-the-evening friends. The rumors July had heard were indeed true. King Bleu was holding court in his cell. His improvised accommodations no longer resembled the crudely furnished chamber she remembered. Bouquets of flowers graced the nightstand that had been placed in the corner. A small drop-leaf table set in the center of the eight-by-ten-foot cell, and an oak commode, complete with pitcher, basin, and towels, had been stashed on the far side of the chamber.

July had spitefully hoped Nacona's sojourn in jail would be nothing short of hell. It was anything but. And what annoyed her beyond belief was the buxom brunette who had come to keep Nacona company. She sat in the padded rocking chair beside his cot, running her fingers through Nacona's hair and whispering sweet nothings in his ear. Disgusting!

The instant Nacona noticed July, he was on his feet. Although he had made the best of an intolerable situation, he was frustrated by his inactivity. Another day of confinement and he swore he would drop dead from sheer boredom. He had grown accustomed to a Gypsy life-style, and these four walls had begun to close in on him. Now here stood the prim and proper sophisticate in pink satin, the source of his exasperation and the cause of his severe case of cabin fever. July had left him cooped up for days on end. Enough was enough!

She ignored Nacona's scowl and drew herself up proudly. "If you can tear yourself away from your visitor for a few moments, I would like a private word with you."

On cue, the painted doxie called to Bat to release her from the cell, leaving July and Nacona in privacy.

"Now what do you want, woman?" Nacona glared at her through the confining bars. "Hell, considering all my unpleasant dealings with you, I'm almost afraid to ask!"

He is frustrated and annoyed, July thought. Good. That made two of them. It was small solace to see this cunning rascal frying in his own grease. Her three brothers would thoroughly enjoy this. They were of the opinion that every gunslinger should be refused a position as sheriff, marshal, or detective and that the entire lot of social deviants should be locked away until the end of their days. July tended to agree with her brothers' assessment. No matter what her dealings with Nacona might be, he was what he was, and nothing would change that. If she knew what was good for her, she would never let herself forget she was dealing with one of the most dangerous and unscrupulous men who inhabited the West.

"I have been contemplating the terms of the bargain," she announced as she flicked an imaginary piece of lint from her lacy sleeve.

Nacona scoffed sardonically. "Does it always take you this long to make a decision?"

"The stakes were high, if you recall," she countered with a disdainful sniff. "At least on my part. As for you, losing your innocence is probably a long-forgotten memory. No doubt, it happened so long ago that you don't even remember where, when, or with whom, but—"

"Skip the lengthy dissertation and get to the point, little miss prosecuting attorney. I don't need a lecture on my wayward youth or my love life."

"Very well, I will get right to the point."

"That will be a first," Nacona grumbled.

July glared him down. She may have been long winded, but he was forever interrupting her, then leaving her to recall where she had left off. "I have come to negotiate your terms."

Nacona puffed on his cigar and purposely blew smoke in her face, staring irritably at her through the gray cloud that separated them. "Well? What's your counteroffer?"

He could not imagine. He thought he had sufficiently backed this firebrand into a corner. It was either yes or no and nothing in between, the way he had it figured.

"I have decided to accept your proposition—my innocence for your reputation and expertise as a shootist."

When he bit down on the end of his cigar and gaped at her in astonishment, July frowned. So he hadn't really expected her to accept. He had been trying to force her to reject her own request. He was even more clever than she'd allowed. An oversight on her part. She would make a mental note never to take this man lightly again. But just wait until she presented her proposition and shoved the shoe on the other foot. He would feel the pinch. Nacona Bleu hadn't outfoxed her yet.

"I have one stipulation to add," July declared. "I will drop the charges against you and meet your terms if you will agree to marry me."

Nacona bit through his cigar and nearly swallowed part of it. He gaped at July as if she'd sprouted antlers. Although he opened his mouth to speak, no words formed on his lips. His breath slammed against the portion of cigar stuck in his throat.

"It seems, if I am to lose my innocence, I should be allowed to maintain my respectability—or at least as much as can be salvaged by wedding a man like you. Surely you realize you are not what the upstanding citizens of Dodge refer to as a fine catch," she added with a ridiculing smile. "Of course, it will be a marriage in name only after your initial terms are met. There will be no ties to bind. You don't want a wife, and I don't really need a husband. But marriage is my price. I will give you one uninterrupted night in exchange for the temporary use of your name and your legendary reputation. When our assignment is over, I will have the marriage dissolved quicker than you can say good-bye."

There, let him stuff that in his smelly cigar and smoke it.

"One night?" Nacona hooted like a disturbed owl. "If I agree to a wedding, I deserve more than one lousy night in your bed!"

She flashed him a pretentious smile that made her emerald eyes sparkle devilishly and, with immense satisfaction, tossed his words back in his face. "Those are my terms. Take 'em or leave 'em."

Check to his king. July now enjoyed the advantage in this chess game of wits.

Nacona's fuming glance sought to fry July to a crisp, but she deflected his glare with a mocking smile. With a curse and a scowl, he paced from wall to wall. Defeat was something he had always refused to accept, as July Beth MacKenzie obviously had. And when it came at the hands of this clever nymph it rankled. July was the most difficult and cunning female he had ever run across. For each of his strategic moves, she posed a countertactic. And just when he thought he'd outsmarted her, she tipped the scales in her favor.

Pulling up short, Nacona focused on the elegant beauty, trying to picture her as his wife. Wife? Imagine that! Nacona Bleu, the confirmed bachelor, married? To this sassy hellion? Inconceivable! Agreeing to such a preposterous union seemed to be the act of a madman—which he would become if he spent too many more days in this damned cell.

Married? Married . . . ? His mind very nearly exploded

at the outlandish thought. He and July would probably kill each other before they completed the Wyoming investigation. And why should he agree to a marriage in name only? One night in her arms when he could have legal rights to her luscious body every night? How would she contest his demands? he wondered. Knowing this crafty witch—and he had come to know her quite well in a short span of time—she would probably force him to sign some sort of premarital contract that limited his husbandly rights and entitled her to every savings account with his name on it. She would do all of the taking and none of the giving.

Well, he ought to marry this ornery hellion, no matter what the terms. He'd delight in taming her and leaving her heartbroken when they completed their assignment. He would enjoy ultimate victory over this sassy female. It was what she deserved.

Nacona stared at the curvaceous beauty again, mulling over his options, of which there were damned few. He could serve time for the assault or give her his name to preserve her dignity. Did July expect him to reject her offer, as he had expected her to reject his terms? Probably. In that case they would both retreat to dream up another form of negotiation. This could go on for weeks. And in the meantime, Nacona would be climbing the walls.

Hell, teaming up with July Beth MacKenzie and tramping off to Wyoming had to be better than rotting in the calaboose. Having her in his arms for one night had to be better than spending time in jail and fantasizing about this witch-angel who occupied his thoughts far more than she should have. After all, nothing this pure and innocent had ever been within ten feet of Nacona until now. He should take advantage of this once-in-a-lifetime opportunity.

After he had taken her for his pleasure, this infuriating spell she had weaved around him would be broken. Then he could get on with his life. Inexperienced as July was, one time would undoubtedly be enough to satisfy him. No woman had ever captured his interest for extended periods of time. This spitfire was no different. No different at all, Nacona assured himself confidently. And besides, he might happen onto the murderer who had eluded him for two years during his trek to Wyoming. . . .

"Well, Nacona?" July demanded, jostling him from his reverie. "Do we have an agreement, or don't we? Or would you like another day to contemplate your decision?"

"And just how are your three overprotective brothers going to take the news that you have wed a gunslinger? That is, if I decide to accept your offer?" he questioned, puffing vigorously on his cigar.

"They will never know. In fact, they think I'm in Wichita visiting Aunt Betty. They don't know I met with the Wyoming representatives or that I'm in Dodge negotiating with the likes of you. When this assignment is over, I will simply return to my life and you will return to yours. My brothers will be none the wiser."

"Sneaky little thing, aren't you?"

"Detectives often have to be. It is a necessary evil of the profession," she said with a haughty toss of her blond head. "You are the epitome of sneakiness yourself. I am only sharpening my skills."

With unconscious masculine grace, Nacona moved toward her, and July involuntarily backed out of his reach.

She wasn't risking a repetition of those mind-boggling kisses and heart-stopping caresses. She couldn't think straight when this sensual man touched her.

A wry smile quirked Nacona's lips at noting her cautious retreat. July was leery of him now, she would be squirming in her lovely skin when she was forced to come to his bed, ready and willing to satisfy him. It would very nearly kill her. That thought alone was enough to prompt Nacona to agree to her bargain.

"I've thought it over, and I have decided to accept your offer," he announced. "But I have one more stipulation."

July wasn't surprised, but she was wary of what was to come. A man like Nacona Bleu was an expert in playing circumstances to his advantage. Only God knew what the raven-haired devil had on his mind now.

"What sacrifices do you expect me to make, as if I'm not forfeiting more than enough already?" she asked with wary trepidation.

Nacona propped himself against the iron bars and grinned like a barracuda. "I want a honeymoon rather than just one night of your love and devotion."

July staggered back to brace herself against the dingy wall and cursed under her breath. Blast it! Next he would be asking for unrestricted privileges throughout the entire investigation. Well, she wasn't compromising more than she already had.

"No. It's one night or nothing," she snapped with finality.

"It will be a three-day honeymoon or you can trot back to Kansas City and shrivel up in the shadows while your detective brothers steal your limelight," Nacona negotiated. "You're the one who wants to launch your career.

I can teach you what your brother won't allow you to learn. Your brothers have a personal interest in you while our relationship will be strictly business."

"I hardly consider a three-day honeymoon strictly business," she sniffed in contradiction.

"It is in this case," Nacona contended. "For three days you will be at my beck and call. In return, you will receive the benefit of my experience in investigative methods. When I'm through with you, your big brothers will be asking for advice from you."

That was a tempting possibility. For years, July had longed to be accepted as her brothers' equal. And what could three days with this rough-edged rascal possibly hurt since the damage would already be done? The first night was the crucial one, wasn't it? If she could endure one night with Nacona, the next two should be a snap. If only he wouldn't be domineering and forceful with her, determined to prove his superiority as men had a natural tendency to do . . .

"What's it going to be, darlin'?" Nacona cooed tauntingly. "Do we have a deal or don't we?"

Since Nacona had mocked her for taking forever to accept the terms of his first offer, she made a quick decision, just to prove that she could. "We have a deal," she confirmed.

That said, July spun about and marched off. "It's settled," she informed Bat and Ed Masterson.

Bat raised a hopeful brow. "Does that mean you plan to drop the charges?"

When July nodded affirmatively, the Masterson brothers trooped off to release the prisoner.

A curious smile brimmed Ed's lips as he stabbed the

key into the lock and swung the door open. "If you don't mind my asking, what did you do to persuade that lady to set you free?"

Nacona chewed on his cigar and grabbed his hat. "Nothing much. I just agreed to marry her."

"What?" Bat's eyes very nearly popped out of his head. "You? Married? You're kidding."

"I couldn't be more serious," Nacona declared. "And if I could impose on the two of you, I would like for you to stand as witnesses to the wedding."

Bat snickered in amusement and clapped Nacona on the back. "My friend, I wouldn't miss this monumental occasion. In fact, I'll have to see it for myself to believe it."

The instant Nacona moseyed into the front office, July nervously toyed with the folds of her gown. She couldn't believe she had actually agreed to this. She must have suffered a temporary lapse of sanity. She peered at the swarthy gunslinger and tried to imagine them as husband and wife. Her brain quickly rejected the vision. True, she found herself physically attracted to Nacona for some unaccountable reason, but this was definitely *not* a match made in heaven. In fact, Nacona would probably be hell to live with and impossible to work with. Yet, July needed this alliance, and she would make the best of the situation—somehow.

With exaggerated politeness, Nacona offered his fiancée his arm. "Shall we go, my beloved?" he murmured in a syrupy tone. "I do believe I hear wedding bells chiming in the distance."

"Must you make a mockery of everything?" July grumbled as he hustled her out the door, forcing her to jog to keep up with his long, swift strides.

"Must you trudge through the ceremony like a condemned prisoner on her way to the gallows?" he countered with a taunting grin. "This was your idea after all, my sweet."

"So it was." July grimaced at the thought of what she had done and what she was going to have to do to elicit Nacona's assistance to further her career. "So it was . . ."

Chapter 6

Disbelief registered on Irma Billingsly's plump face when July was escorted into the office of the justice of the peace on none other than Nacona Bleu's arm. Behind the unlikely twosome stood Bat and Ed Masterson and Deputy Nathan Haywood who were anxious to view the ceremony firsthand. Irma's husband clambered to his feet when Nacona demanded to be married there and then. While Daniel Billingsly was bustling about, searching his files for a marriage certificate, Irma drew July aside.

"My dear girl, do you have the faintest idea what you're doing? Did that barbarian force you into this? Although you confided nothing to me, rumors have been flying all over town that this renegade assaulted you and that was the reason he landed in jail. I have not been so bold as to ask for a confirmation of the report until now, but considering your predicament . . . Well, if that dangerous creature has threatened your life just to have you in his—" Irma clamped down on her tongue and tried another approach. "I will be happy to confer with the Women's Society in town and form a protest in your behalf. We decent women must stick together to ensure our rights. Why, this is prepos—"

July cut in before Irma worked herself into an emotional tizzy. "I agreed to the marriage."

Although July and Irma were casual acquaintances, the older women's maternal instincts were hard at work. For some reason, Irma had taken a liking to July the moment the younger woman arrived in town. July appreciated her concern, she truly did, having lost her mother and father at a tender age, but she had decided to further her career despite the sacrifices demanded. There was naught else to do but to play this farce out until the investigation in Wyoming was over and done.

While Irma stared at her in amazement, July rejoined Nacona in front of Daniel's desk. She tried to project the image of a willing bride as the ceremony began. With Irma as her matron of honor and the Mastersons and Nat Haywood as witnesses, the justice of the peace rattled off the vows that would join this mismatched pair in wedlock.

July felt she was experiencing a dream that hovered on the fringe of reality. It wasn't the idea of the ceremony that rattled her, but rather the upcoming wedding night. Thoughts of it kept her nervously distracted, wondering if Nacona would be rough and abusive just to spite her. . . .

Daniel Billingsly's voice trailed off when two men rushed through the door, right smack dab in the middle of the ceremony.

"Sheriff, I thought you should know that several small cattle herds from the Panhandle just arrived," one of the men reported. "They're being held on the Arkansas River until morning. But we saw a rowdy group of cowboys ride across the south toll bridge to celebrate the trail's end. There may be trouble."

"I'll go keep a lid on the South Side," Ed Masterson volunteered. "Bat, you can join me after the ceremony."

After Ed and Nat Haywood strode off, the justice of the peace continued. It wasn't five minutes before the same two informants had returned to interrupt the ceremony again.

Nacona scowled sourly at the second intrusion. "Just get to the "I do's" and be done with it," he demanded impatiently.

Daniel complied, then Nacona wheeled to face the uninvited guests.

"Now what's the problem?" he questioned.

"Marshal Masterson and Nat were walking down Front Street when a flurry of gunfire erupted across the Plaza at the Lady Gay Saloon," one of the informants reported. "Ed and Nat rushed over to disarm the drunken cowboys and their trail boss. I think Ed needs more assistance. It's a surly crowd."

To July's astonishment, Nacona snaked his arm around her and sealed their wedding vows with a possessive kiss. Still stunned, she watched Bat Masterson slide one of his ivory-handled Peacemakers from its holster and toss it to Nacona. The nod of Bat's dark head silently deputized Nacona. And suddenly both legendary pistoleros were sailing out the door to lend Ed Masterson and Nat Haywood assistance.

July had only taken two steps toward the door when Irma gasped in dismay. "You can't go out there!" she croaked. "You don't know what it's like around here when a group of rowdy cowhands roars into town. They drink themselves insane and start shooting the place up. You're liable to catch a stray bullet."

July didn't bother to inform the rotund matron that investigation was her business and she could handle a pistol if the situation demanded. As far as July was concerned, she was in training, learning from the masters. She wasn't about to miss Nacona or the Mastersons in action. If she could profit from the experience, she would broaden her horizons in the detective business.

"July! Come back!" Irma howled. "Don't go out there!"

But she was gone, leaving Irma to wonder at her sanity for the second time in less than an hour. Irma was certain that marrying Nacona Bleu was July's first drastic mistake, and dashing out into a gunbattle was going to be her last.

"Damn it to hell, get back inside," Nacona growled when he heard the swish of petticoats behind him. "Dodge City after dark is no place for a lady."

"I just got finished promising to stand by you for better or worse," July argued as she scurried to catch up with him and Bat.

"Too bad I asked Daniel Billingsly to skip over the part about honoring and obeying," Nacona muttered. "Not that it would have mattered. You delight in clinging to the rules you favor and bending or simply ignoring the ones you don't."

The loud voices and scuffling noises coming from the Lady Gay Saloon brought a quick end to the conversation and prompted the threesome to hasten their pace. They dashed across the tracks of the Plaza and scampered toward the saloon.

A muffled shot resounded in the street like the peal of impending doom.

"Damn it to hell!" Nacona darted forward, matching Bat step for step.

July gasped in horror when she realized Ed Masterson had been shot at such close range that his shirt and waistcoat were afire. When he staggered back, clutching his right side, Nat Haywood led him across the tracks toward Hoover's Wine and Liquor Store.

When Bat and Nacona opened fire on the two men who had shot Ed Masterson, July plastered herself against the outer wall of the saloon and fought down palpitations. She had groomed herself to expect the worst when it came to showdowns, but a real-life gunbattle shook the very foundations of her soul. The smells of smoke and blood permeated her senses and caused her stomach to flip-flop.

Ivory-handled pistols spit flames as Nacona and Bat resumed the battle Ed Masterson had been unable to finish. When the smoke cleared, the two men who had assaulted Ed were riddled with bullets. The drunken cowhand who had shot Ed stumbled into the Peacock Dance Hall and collapsed, three bullets in him. The other wrangler had apparently survived two gunshot wounds, but he offered no more resistance.

The instant Nacona and Bat wheeled around to rush across the tracks, July scuttled after them, willing her wobbly legs to support her. When the threesome reached Front Street, they were told that Nat had taken Ed to Bat's room and had put him to bed after he'd collapsed.

As they dashed off to check on Ed's condition, Nat Haywood appeared on the boardwalk in front of them. His face had lost all color, and his expression was grim.

"Ed's dead," he reported in a broken voice. "He never had a chance."

The words dropped like stones in the deafening silence.

Muffled curses gushed from Bat's lips. "What happened?"

"Ed and I walked into the Lady Gay to stop the gunplay," Nat said bleakly. "Ed convinced Wagner to hand his gun over to A. M. Walker, his trail boss. Ed told Walker to keep the pistol until Wagner sobered up."

Nat raked shaky fingers through his hair and heaved a shuddering sigh. "We thought the incident was settled, and we stepped back onto the street. But Walker and Wagner followed us outside. Ed glanced over his shoulder to see Wagner trying to regain possession of his pistol. When Ed tried to disarm Wagner a second time, Walker whipped out his pistol and threatened to kill *me* if I interfered in the struggle. When Ed and Wagner were scuffling for control of the weapon, it went off."

Nacona clamped his hand around Bat's arm for support. "Come on, Bat. We have arrangements to make." His somber stare shifted to July whose face had turned as white as flour. "I'll take care of Bat tonight. You go back to the hotel." His gaze shifted again. "Nat, get some men to . . ." He didn't finish the dismal request. Nat knew what his last duty as assistant marshal to Ed Masterson was going to be.

Numbly, July did as she was told, fighting down the wave of nausea that threatened to crest on her. Although she had only known Ed for two weeks, she had admired him. He hadn't possessed the sharp instincts and skills of gunfighters like Bat and Nacona. His method was to talk his adversaries into submission, but he was respected and admired by the citizens of Dodge City. His death would be a disheartening blow.

Muffling a sniff, July washed her face and paced her room restlessly. The incident erupted in her mind, again and again. It only took one rough night in Dodge to realize there were two vastly different types of police work. Nacona and the Mastersons specialized in the kind that involved showdowns and constant life-and-death situations. The MacKenzie brothers pursued a far more civilized and largely nonviolent type. July realized she had been living in a dream world. She hadn't been prepared for the nightmare she'd endured.

Maybe she wasn't cut out to be a detective after all, at least not the kind required in cowtowns. Maybe she had been suffering from delusions in thinking that law and order could prevail without six-shooters to speak for it. And why had she chased after Bat and Nacona as if she could have lent them assistance? When the shooting started, there had been no time for words. But curse it, she had been concerned about Nacona's safety. Now that he was her husband it seemed natural for her to rush to his defense, incapable though she had turned out to be in her first gun battle. Why, the ink hadn't even dried on their marriage certificate before she was dashing after Nacona like a loving, devoted wife! It was inconceivable that she could have reacted in such an irrational manner.

Thoroughly shaken, July wobbled down the hall to

Nacona's vacant room. Although she had been a teetotaler who advocated the prohibition of liquor, she picked up the bottle of whiskey on the night stand and helped herself to a drink . . . and another. The confrontation at the Lady Gay Saloon had sickened her. And she was shaken by her fierce need to protect a man who was obviously capable of fending for himself.

Her *husband?* Nacona Bleu was really her *husband?* July gulped down a drink and wheezed when fire seared her throat. She could have been a wife and widow, all in the same night. The image of dark eyes embedded in a ruggedly handsome face appeared above her. Lord, Nacona could have been plugged with lead when those pistols flared. He had laid his life on the line to repay the men who had killed Ed Masterson. What would she have done if he had wound up in the same condition as Ed?

July shuddered at the gloomy thought and at the horrible incident that had taken Ed's life. Why did the prospect of watching Nacona fall beneath an assassin's bullet turn her inside out? There was no love between them. They had only formed a working partnership at her insistence. The night's ordeal had rattled her and caused an upheaval of emotions, July thought realistically. She certainly hadn't fallen in love with that midnight-haired gunslinger. She just regretted the senseless loss of human life. Watching Ed Masterson die, and seeing his assassins cut down in a blaze of bullets, had torn her apart.

To counteract the horrible flashbacks of the disaster, July took another drink, though she had never touched anything stronger than dinner wine before this night. She felt personally responsible for Ed's death. If it hadn't been for this farce of a marriage she had arranged, Bat, Ed,

Nacona, and Nat would all have descended upon the South Side to quell the disturbance at the Lady Gay. But no, she had dreamed up this bargain to salvage her pride and dignity. Now she had Ed Masterson's death on her conscience, and nothing she could do would turn back the hands of time and bring him to life. He had needed his brother and Nacona as reinforcements.

July heaved a tremulous sigh and stared blankly at the walls. It had been a cold, dark night in Dodge. Now she fully understood why the bustling cowtown and trade center had been labeled the "Gomorrah of the Plains." The community was still trying to live down the fact that its moral code was no more than honor among thieves. Its tainted virtue was prostitution, and its favorite beverage was whiskey. Dodge City was only six years old; it had a lot of growing up to do before civilization and respectability took over.

That depressing thought spurred July into having another drink. She didn't care that she had turned to liquor for surcease. She wanted to forget the deadly gunfight that had cheated Ed Masterson out of the prime years of his life.

And she even found herself wishing for Nacona's sinewy arms, to comfort her, to reassure her that what she had just witnessed was the exception and not the rule in the West. Lord, had she called herself a detective? Nacona was right. She had a lot to learn if she was going to cope, woman or no. And a lot of growing up to do if she was going to endure the cruelties of this world without falling apart at the seams when trouble broke out. She had been too idealistic. One eye-opening experience had shocked her so she was guzzling whiskey like a lush.

Wearily, Nacona trudged up the steps to his hotel room. He had planned to stay the night with Bat, but after a few hours of hard drinking, Bat had sent Nacona on his way before drifting off to sleep. Nacona had roused the telegraph agent and requested a message be sent to Wyatt Earp in Deadwood, South Dakota. After Ed's untimely death, Nacona imagined Wyatt would want to resume his duties as marshal since he had worked closely with the Mastersons the past few years. Nacona was also assigned the grim task of sending a message to Masterson's parents who owned a farm near Wichita, informing them that the eldest of their five sons had lost his life in a gunfight.

Scowling, Nacona mulled over the odd sensations that had plagued him the instant he'd realized July had followed him down the street and into calamity. The whole time his pistol was blazing to bring down Ed's assassins, he had been tormentingly aware of the green-eyed beauty behind him. Nacona had wanted to remain emotionally detached in the heat of battle, but the prospect of July being riddled by a stray bullet had unnerved him. He knew he had begun to feel a certain affection for this female. A greater one than he had realized before that particular moment. That, compounded with the incident from two years past, had plagued Nacona when he should have been concentrating solely on the ruffians who fired back at him.

For two years he had been looking out for himself, feeling no responsibility except to his own hide in a showdown. Having July one step behind him had left him with an uncomfortable feeling of vulnerability. He had needed

to be good enough with a gun to protect *himself* and *her.*
Suddenly, he had unconsciously positioned himself between her and the drunken cowboys, like a protective shield, and he hadn't even realized it until the battle was over.

It had almost felt as if the other half of himself was standing in the shadows—the half that exemplified sophistication, elegance, refinement, and all the good things he'd been deprived of. Nacona swore at that peculiar thought, then wondered what it was about the feisty daredevil that preyed so heavily on the emotions deep inside him. Within four days July had burrowed into his thoughts, leaving him to fantasize, distracting him beyond belief. And through it all, she had been his antagonist— the proverbial thorn in his side. She was like a lovely, delicate—and prickly—rose.

He and she had been playing a chess game of wits, jockeying for position until the night he had dared to tug her into his arms. Then, suddenly, fires of forbidden desire had burned in him. Against his better judgment, he had decided to marry the sassy firebrand. Now he had a wife, for God's sake! *Him!* The man who had dedicated his life to hunting down that murdering bastard who had . . .

Nacona's thoughts trailed off when he sailed into his room to see July doing hand-to-glass combat with his private stock of whiskey. His jaw nearly fell off its hinges as he assessed the inebriated imp sprawled half on, half off his bed. Her discarded shoes lay beside the nightstand, and the hiked hem of her gown was draped at a tempting angle across her silky thighs. Her fashionable coiffure was in disarray, shiny tendrils of sandy blond hair cascading over her shoulder. She presented a most appetizing picture.

A tormented groan tripped from Nacona's lips as his hungry gaze toured her delectable body. The night had been frustrating enough as it was, but it looked as if it was going to get worse before it got better. Nacona had plenty of difficulty dealing with this saucy sprite when she was sober. He shuddered to think what July was going to be like when she was really sauced—which she most certainly was.

The tragic incident had already taken its toll on Nacona. His heart had gone out to Bat, and he grieved the loss of a good friend. Now he was faced with the bleak realization that he had left July alone to cope with her shock and grief. She had needed him, in her own way, to soften the blow of watching men die violent deaths. And although Nacona was hesitant to admit it, he'd felt the need to be with her, had wanted the comfort of understanding arms.

Poor July, thought Nacona as he assessed the inebriated beauty. So bold and brave, and yet so very naive and inexperienced. She was like a little girl wearing blinders, sipping drinks she couldn't handle. She was both comical and pathetic . . . and she made him feel things he hadn't allowed himself to feel in years. Damn it to hell, how could one mere wisp of a woman entangle a man so completely? It wasn't fair. It wasn't logical. . . . And what the blazes was he going to do with this gorgeous female who was lying on his bed, polluted with whiskey?

Chapter 7

July's thick lashes fluttered up at the creaking of the door. Her glassy green eyes leisurely scanned the broad expanse of Nacona's chest. Solitude, grief, and whiskey had a fierce hold on her. If she had been sober, she would never have confessed that she was relieved to see him. The admission would have gone against her feminine pride. But she *was* happy to see Nacona and, with the whiskey working like a truth serum, didn't hesitate to tell him so.

"I'm ever so glad you're back," she croaked, and then frowned at the odd sound of her own voice. Her vocal cords had rusted, she was certain of it. Tipsily, she propped herself against the headboard and clanked the bottle against the glass she was refilling.

"You're drunk," Nacona observed.

"Am I?" July sent a cursory glance down her own torso, as if some visible sign of inebriation had been printed there. An audible sigh escaped her before she downed another drink. "So this is what being drunk feels like," she slurred out.

Despite the grim events of the evening, Nacona felt a

smile tugging at his lips. July was half reclined on her throne of pillows, clinging to the bottle as if it were her salvation. In their brief but enlightening acquaintance, Nacona had viewed various facets of her complex personality. This, however, was a new twist. The lady definitely wasn't herself tonight. The street fight had rattled her, so she had made a crusade of drinking to forget what she didn't want to remember.

Before July could down another swig of whiskey and drink herself into a coma, Nacona surged across the room to snatch away the bottle. Without ado, he gulped some whiskey to settle his own nerves. His wedding night had been plagued with calamity, and his new bride was soused. He wondered what it would be like to lead a normal life. Not damned likely that he would ever find out, not when married to this daring beauty and involved in a dangerous profession. Hell, he wasn't sure he would recognize "normal" if it walked up and sat down on top of him!

"I killed him," July burst out. Then she wiped away the shiny tears that streamed down her cheeks. "I'm the one who killed Ed."

A muddled frown plowed Nacona's brow as he stared down into her tormented features. "How do you figure that?"

July muffled a sniff and sighed dispiritedly. "If I hadn't dragged you off to that marriage ceremony, you and Nat and the Mastersons would have been on the South Side to prevent the killing." Her tormented gaze lifted to Nacona, wondering which of the blurred images was really him—and which of the bottles he was holding was the one with the whiskey in it. "I killed Ed just as surely as if I had been holding a pistol," she added on a choked sob.

"You can't blame yourself," Nacona murmured as he sank down on the edge of the bed. "Ed laid his life on the line hundreds of times. We all have. We know the risks going in. When a man makes his choices, he lives and dies by them. That's the way it is, July."

His consoling words didn't lift her sinking spirits. She was too sick at heart, too upset by the tormenting scene that kept flashing in front of her bloodshot eyes to find solace in them.

"Gimme that bottle," July demanded sluggishly. "I need another drink."

"What you *need* is a good night's sleep to combat the hangover you're going to have in the morning," he diagnosed before pouring another drink down his own gullet. It was killing him to watch July punishing herself for something over which she had no control.

"I can't possibly feel worse than I do tonight," July mumbled, the whiskey taking full effect.

"Wanna bet? You'll be ready to swear your head is trying to break away from your body. Your stomach will feel as if it's undergoing a volcanic eruption. Take my word for it, honey. I've been there myself, lots of times."

July heard the rich baritone voice resounding around her as if it were echoing in a long dark tunnel, but her pickled brain had difficulty deciphering the rapidly delivered remarks. Her toes were numb and so was the tip of her nose. Her eyes felt as if they were about to slam shut and a gray haze was gliding lazily around her like criss-crossing shadows moving in slow motion.

"Can you stand up?" Nacona spoke slowly and distinctly, as if English were July's second language. At the moment, "mumble" seemed to be her native tongue.

She wilted on the pillow and drew in a ragged breath. "Do I have to?" she chirped when his question finally soaked into her saturated brain.

Nacona shook his head in disbelief and rolled his eyes ceilingward. My, what a wedding night this had turned out to be. And although he had always thought drunks deserved to sleep in their clothes, he relented in July's case, this being July's first offense. It wasn't as if she didn't have excellent reasons for drinking herself half blind. What she had witnessed firsthand had come as a shock, and she was grieving the loss of one of Dodge's favorite sons, just as Nacona was.

Bracing his hands on either side of her shoulders, Nacona bent down to peer into her bloodshot eyes. "July, I'm going to undress you and put you to bed," he forewarned. "So don't go crazy on me."

"Mmm . . . that's nice," she muttered over her thick tongue.

Nacona had often visualized peeling away expensive garments and satisfying his obsession for this lovely nymph. He still ached to do that, but his fantasy wasn't unfolding exactly as he'd imagined when he and July had negotiated the terms of their marriage. Instead of an amorous lover, Nacona suddenly found himself a lady's maid and compassionate friend.

Gently, he eased July onto her side to unfasten the stays on the back of her pink gown. As he pulled the garment from her shoulders, his attention focused on her lacy chemise and on the silky flesh beneath it. When July stretched like a kitten, Nacona swore the temperature of the room shot up ten degrees. Her knees accidentally brushed against his lap and he groaned uncomfortably. The throb of desire hammered at him as he worked the crumpled gown down to her waist, exposing the full swells of her breasts covered only by sheer satin and transparent lace.

She was even more exquisite than he had imagined. Nacona had seen more than his fair share of feminine bodies in one state of undress and another. He knew there were damned few perfect figures in this world, and this nymph possessed one of them. Most women had to resort to makeup and garments to emphasize their assets and downplay their defects. July MacKenzie Bleu had no defects whatsoever. She possessed the kind of body and face that inspired male fantasies and confounded men's dreams.

Good Lord a-mighty, this vision of loveliness was actually *his* wife! Nacona still couldn't believe that he had laid claim to this delicate bundle of sophisticated beauty and untamed spirit. She was too good for a man like him.

Nacona drew the dress away and tugged off July's petticoats. An audible sigh escaped his lips as his dark eyes roamed unhindered over her full breasts and the trim indentation of her waist. Intrigued, he reached out to trail a forefinger over the satiny flesh of her thigh, and his pulse leaped into triple time.

July giggled drowsily when his tickling touch migrated over her flesh in the whisper of a touch. When she turned onto her side to cuddle the pillow in her arms, Nacona could hear his thundering heart beats. His eyes fell to her long, well-formed legs and the tempting flair of her hips before he focused on the dusky crests of breasts that peeked at him through lace and satin. This goddess struck the most tantalizing poses imaginable, even while she was oblivious to the world. If she were only aware of how tempting she was, she could become the most devastating seductress.

Nacona groaned when his heart hammered against his ribs like a tom-tom. July was too damned good for the likes of him. He must have had rocks in his head to agree to this arrangement, tempting though the proposal had sounded at the time.

Almost hesitantly, fearing another tormenting assault on his senses, Nacona drew the straps of her chemise off her shoulders and tugged it away. He swallowed a roomful of air and his overinflated lungs nearly burst at the luscious sight of rose-tipped breasts. One would have thought he had never seen a naked woman in all his born days. For sure, he'd never seen one as well sculptured and elegantly formed as this one.

Nacona poured another drink down his gullet to steady himself. It didn't help.

Cursing the maddening need to drag July beneath him and appease the monstrous craving she unknowingly aroused in him, Nacona peeled off the last of her clothing. Valiantly, he clung to the frayed threads of his noble restraint as he turned back the bedspread to maneuver July beneath the sheet. He covered her up—except for her head. But that didn't matter. The damage had already been done. When he stared at that bewitching vixen he could see every delicious inch of her, as if she were still lying naked before him.

Scowling, Nacona helped himself to another drink.

102

Lord, what a night he was having! He had been dragged from one end of the emotional spectrum to the other in the course of five hours. First he had encountered July in jail; then he had sailed through a whirlwind wedding ceremony before the fatal showdown. And now *this* on top of all else!

Well, after all this visual torture, he deserved to pleasure himself with his new bride's half conscious body, didn't he? He was entitled, wasn't he? There should be some consolation for all the frustration and torment he'd been through. He owed it to himself to take what he wanted from her. Well, didn't he?

Nacona tipped up the bottle and took another drink, but his conscience kept giving him hell for wanting July while his body was giving him hell for refusing to satisfy the gnawing hunger that was eating him alive. July would probably prefer that her first encounter with passion came while she was in a whiskey-induced stupor. She was innocent and inexperienced, unsure of what Nacona expected of her. He would probably be doing them both a favor if he stole her virginity while she was oblivious. She would experience no pain, no fear of what was to come.

Miserable cad, how could you even consider such a thing? his offended conscience roared at him. This is your wife, not some strumpet who pleasures men for a price. She's a bona fide lady. Taking her now would be nothing short of rape!

"Oh shut up," Nacona growled irritably. This mental tug-of-war he was having with himself was draining him.

Take what you want, his desire tempted. She probably won't even remember the night she spent in your arms, but you will. . . .

Nacona scowled before downing another drink.

After thrashing around the room, while his conscience and his instincts warred with each other, he snuffed out the lantern and shucked his clothes, determined to do the honorable thing, even if it killed him. All he had to do was ease beneath the sheet on his side of the bed and pretend he was sleeping alone. The liquor he had consumed would work like a sleeping potion, and he would be out like a light in a matter of seconds.

But the instant Nacona plunked down his large body the mattress sagged and July rolled toward him. She snuggled up against him as if he were a warm, cuddly blanket and sighed against the sensitive flesh of his neck. Her silky arm slid across his chest, and her head burrowed into the crook of his arm. And there she lay, sleeping like a contented child, safe from harm . . . or so she thought.

What man would turn down such a golden opportunity? Nacona could feel the delectable imprint of her satiny flesh, the beating of her heart. And when her knee insinuated itself between his thighs, he swore his own heart was about to beat him to death. What unpardonable sin had he committed to deserve this?

How was he supposed to sleep when he could barely breathe? His male desires were running rampant, making outrageous demands. He, a man who had become the personification of frontier justice, was getting no personal justice whatsoever. Here he lay, wanting July beyond bearing, refusing himself because of some noble thought in his brain.

If anyone dared to make a teasing crack about his wedding night, Nacona was going to plant his fist squarely in the middle of his face! He had endured physical torture that was nowhere near as painful as this. He did not expect to survive the night. Having and not having was going to be the death of him.

The shifting of a warm, muscular form on the bed brought July up from the groggy depths of slumber. A muddled frown knitted her brow as she fought her way through the cobwebs that clogged her mind. Bright sunlight tapped at her eyelids and thumped on her spongy brain. She became aware of hair-matted flesh molded intimately to hers. . . .

July's eyes popped wide open at the expense of her throbbing headache when she realized she wasn't wearing a stitch and neither was the masculine body beside her. She darted a startled glance at a ruffled raven head and at the rakish grin plastered on Nacona's face. Crimson red splashed across her cheeks when the implication soaked in. July vaguely remembered Nacona returning in the middle of the night, but then she drew a complete blank. He could have informed her the world had disintegrated and she wouldn't have remembered it.

Had Nacona taken his husbandly privileges while she was wallowing in a puddle of whiskey? Had she disappointed him? Why did she even care a whit if she had?

"Mornin', darlin'," Nacona drawled.

The previous night had been pure and simple hell. After counting all the tortures of the newly damned, he had finally drifted off to sleep, wanting this tempting minx in the worst possible way. He had awakened a half dozen times, still wanting her, but she had been oblivious to the world. Now his only solace was knowing that July was enduring a meager part of the frustration he had tolerated all through the night. She didn't know what had happened, and Nacona was in just the right frame of mind to let her squirm a bit. She deserved that for depriving him of the satisfaction of his obsession while she lay in a liquor-induced coma.

July stared goggle-eyed at the bare muscular shoulders and arms that protruded above the sheet. She was so awkward and embarrassed that she couldn't meet his dancing brown eyes. "Did we . . . ?" Her mouth was so dry she could have spit cotton. She swallowed to lubricate her vocal cords and tried again. "Did we . . . ?" Her face turned all colors of the rainbow.

Like a rousing lion, Nacona levered himself up on an elbow. He peered down at the strands of blond hair that rippled out from July's flawless face in a shimmering pool of gold. Willfully, he stifled the makings of a smile. It was amusing to watch July's enchanting face blossom with color and to hear this articulate intellectual fumble with words like a tongue-tied idiot. He knew she was as embarrassed as any woman could get, but it was oddly pleasing to know that he was the only man who had ever seen her in the altogether, the only man who had slept with her, even if he had ached for so much more. A strange feeling of possessiveness overcame him as he stared into her bewitching eyes. First, protectiveness had overwhelmed him in the face of danger, now it was possessiveness. What next? Damn it, this female had gotten under his skin worse than he'd thought.

"I'm sorry," July chirped, wondering why she felt the need to apologize to her new husband. "I had no experience and you were probably disappointed that I—"

106

His index finger dropped to her lush lips to shush her. He'd had every intention of razzing her unmercifully, letting her think he had taken her while she'd been drifting in whiskey-induced sleep. But something strangled the mocking retort he had planned to voice. Suddenly, he didn't want to play to his advantage or incite another argument. He only wanted to feel those heart-shaped lips beneath his, to discover the pleasures that this marriage arrangement promised and had yet to deliver.

His mouth slanted over hers as the weight of his body pressed her into the mattress. Nacona sensed July's shock at the intimacy of his kiss, her unfamiliarity with a masculine form moving possessively over her. He was probably frightening her senseless. He had never touched a real lady, let alone one who knew nothing of the fiery sensations of passion. Her untutored responses surprised him, as did his realization of how wildly sensual each touch was to her. Since everything he did was new to her, she reacted on pure instinct, her responses setting him on fire.

As his kiss deepened, savoring the soft recesses of her mouth, his hands drifted off to rediscover every silky inch of her. July shivered and gasped as his adventurous caresses sought out the sensitive points of her flesh, memorizing each curve and swell. Her pulse leapfrogged through her bloodstream, leaving her dizzy and too dazed to resist the wanton magic of his touch.

The soft texture of her skin aroused Nacona. The timid response of her petal-soft lips excited him. Each exploring caress and breath-stealing kiss demanded more, making him a prisoner of his own unfulfilled longings, and yet he was aware of her innocence and the need for gentle patience.

July tensed and then immediately melted as his masterful hands flooded over her like surf tumbling toward the shore. She had expected this powerful giant to swallow her alive, to urgently take possession, but to her surprise he made no hurried attempt to appease his male needs. He took her inexperience into consideration and allowed her to adjust to the startling sensations caused by the newness of a man's kisses and caresses whispering over her body. The overpowering tenderness he bestowed on her was far more devastating than brute force. July surrendered to his titillating caresses without putting up a fight. Responding to his erotic touch had become as natural and reflexive as breathing.

As if her hands possessed a mind of their own, they lifted to cruise over the whipcord muscles of his chest and the lean wall of his belly. This giant of a man was like a sleek, muscular tiger, and July marveled at the potential strength that flexed and relaxed beneath her inquiring fingertips. She felt she was drawing energy from him, as if she had been absorbed into the aura that enshrouded his awesome strength.

A muffled moan tripped from July's lips when his fingertips skied over the swells of her breasts to tease taut peaks. Fire blazed in the core of her being and channeled through every nerve and muscle in her body. She swore she had melted down into the consistency of hot lava when his roving hands mapped the indentation of her waist and swirled over the ultrasensitive flesh of her inner thigh. She heard and felt the groan that rattled in Nacona's chest as his knee glided between her legs and his body half covered hers, bending her into his aroused contours.

Nacona had never touched flesh so soft and exquisite in his life. This green-eyed elf was a treasure, a dream come true. But wanting her was playing havoc with his self-control. He tried to proceed at a slower pace, to melt July's resistance and generously return every ounce of pleasure she gave him. Addicted to the luscious body lying so temptingly close to his, desire raging within him, Nacona vowed not to startle this innocent nymph when she had just begun to trust him, to enjoy the prelude to lovemaking.

Slowly but deliberately, he lowered his head to erase the breathless inches that separated them. His lips feathered over hers in a whispering kiss, and his hands retraced their leisurely path over the creamy swells of her breasts, drawing a moan of helpless surrender from her throat. Over and over again, he caressed her, taught her the silent language of passion until her innocent body arched instinctively toward his.

A shudder shot through Nacona when he felt hungry desire gnawing at his self-restraint. He wanted to devour her, to feel her ripe body molded intimately to his as they moved in the ageless rhythm of unleashed passion. His slow, seductive advances had taken July past the point of no return; he could sense it. Now he longed to take complete possession of this bewitching siren, to end this maddening agony of wanting her, to glide into her silken fire and burn in ineffable pleasure. . . .

The abrupt rap at the door made Nacona curse. He and his innocent bride had stood on the threshold of a new awareness of each other when the erotic spell had been shattered.

"Who the devil is it?" Nacona growled in frustration.

"Nat Haywood," came the subdued reply from behind the door. "I'm sorry to bother you, Nacona. But Bat asked me to fetch you. He's not coping very well. He wants you to help with the final arrangements. Can you come?"

Only a request from a friend in desperate need could have torn Nacona away from the exquisite nymph in his arms. He glanced from the door to the wide green eyes below him, seeing the spark of passion he had ignited in those shimmering pools. July's lips were swollen from his demanding kisses and her expression tugged at Nacona's heart. She looked so vulnerable, so stunned, hungry and yet totally confused by the sensations that had assaulted her. She was simply too naive to understand the potent effect of passion, and Nacona didn't have time to show her where this mystical spell could lead, to satisfy the cravings that left them both trembling with profound needs.

"I'll be down in a minute, Nat," he called out in a strangled voice.

Reluctantly, Nacona rolled away to grab his clothes. He didn't look back for fear that July would misread his mood. She had erroneously assumed that her lack of experience had disappointed him the previous night. Anything but! He couldn't remember wanting a woman the way he'd craved his lovely, innocent wife. He didn't want July thinking she couldn't satisfy him because he had the instinctive feeling that with patient instruction, she could make a man's wildest fantasies come true. Nacona just wanted to take up where they had left off. But he couldn't, not now. . . .

Mustering his composure, Nacona grasped the door

knob and glanced back at the wide-eyed beauty who peered unblinkingly at him. "I have to go. Bat needs me. You understand, don't you?"

July nodded mutely, her admiration for this complex man increased by knowing he would forsake his personal pleasures to console a grieving friend. Nacona Bleu might have been rough around the edges, but beneath that tough exterior beat the heart of a tender, understanding man. He was sympathetic and aware of the needs of others. The gentleness in his caresses and kisses had stirred July. He had given rather than taken selfishly. He'd made her feel she was a woman with feelings and desires of her own, not a possession to be used and discarded on a whim.

When the door clanked shut behind him, July sighed. Had she experienced these incredible sensations the previous night when they'd made love? Why couldn't she remember? And how could she keep her emotions on an even keel when this intriguing rake was tugging on her heartstrings?

Curse it, she had to keep her wits about her, no matter how difficult it became. She wasn't a romanticist. She was a realist. Sex was second nature to a man like Nacona Bleu. There had obviously been dozens of others in his arms. She was nothing but his latest conquest. Only a fool would allow herself to think they shared something unique and special. Nacona was her first experience with passion. That was why the aftereffects of his seduction played havoc with her body. He, on the other hand, was a master of seduction, a man could bend an inexperienced woman to his will by creating sensual illusions.

July cautioned herself not to make more of the moment

than was actually there. Indeed, she would have resisted his advances if her mind hadn't been saturated with too much whiskey. Besides, she had bargained for that raven-haired devil's legendary skills as a shootist, not his heart—if he had one. She had better watch her step, or she would learn far more than how to become a skilled detective. She would also learn how it felt to nurse a broken heart.

Nacona Bleu would go on his way when their assignment was concluded. July knew that as well as she knew her own name. She couldn't, *wouldn't* allow herself to forget that this was only a temporary arrangement. That would prove as dangerous as being caught in the crossfire of blazing six-shooters. As soon as her body stopped tingling from the remembered feel of practiced hands skimming across her flesh, she was going to forget all about this romantic interlude and become her old sensible self.

However, forgetting Nacona's bone-melting caresses and heart-stopping kisses took a good while longer than she'd anticipated. Hours, in fact. She simply could not stop marveling at the tender, attentive lover who had emerged from beneath a hard, callous shell to bring her innocent body to a level of exquisite consciousness that she never realized existed.

Chapter 8

After the tragedy on the South Side the previous night, Dodge City was incredibly quiet. Every business in town had shut down, and all doors were draped with black crepe. The fire company, to which Ed Masterson had belonged, requested the honor of conducting the last rites. Later that afternoon, July joined the procession of mourners, which consisted of every buggy, wagon, and citizen in town. The cortege moved solemnly toward the military cemetery at Fort Dodge, rather than to Boot Hill where renegades who had no family to mourn them were buried. The members of the city council led the somber procession five miles east to Fort Dodge. They were followed by Bat Masterson and sixty uniformed volunteers from the Fire Company.

July caught an occasional glimpse of Nacona in the distance. He and the deputy marshal were always nearby when Bat needed moral support or consolation. Nacona had proved himself a loyal friend in times of crisis, and July found herself admiring this facet of his character. Even Irma Billingsly, who had cringed at the very idea of

113

July wedding a man with Nacona's reputation, commented on his attentiveness to Bat.

Once the bleak ceremony ended and the crowd dispersed, the Billingslys escorted July back to the hotel, where she wrestled with her feelings of guilt and remorse. She had made no attempt to contact Nacona, only to extend her deepest sympathy to Bat. When she ventured out onto Front Street to go for her evening meal, she saw Nacona and Nat making their rounds to ensure that all remained quiet out of respect for the marshal's passing. When Nacona spied July, he paused, as if he meant to speak. But before he could approach her, one of the townsfolk scurried up to him to inquire about Bat.

July went on her way to take her supper alone, struggling with the maelstrom of emotions that hounded her. She found herself unusually depressed and oddly restless that evening as she curled up on her bed, a book in hand, to take her mind off the series of events that had plagued the past few days. She actually missed sparring with that black-eyed gunslinger. Nacona had challenged her, annoyed her, unnerved her. And that morning he had introduced her to unfamiliar sensations that . . .

When a warm flood of pleasure washed over her traitorous body, July squirmed uneasily. She simply couldn't allow her thoughts to be derailed by wanton feelings. She was suffering from emotional turmoil and from a ridiculous infatuation based purely on a physical attraction.

It was only natural to respond as she had to a wildly sensual man who knew his way around a woman's anatomy better than a practicing physician. It didn't mean a thing. Any naive maiden would have reacted similarly had she found herself in that rake's swarthy arms. Nacona

114

Bleu was as good at seduction as he was with a pistol, while she was hopelessly inexperienced with men.

After giving herself that silent pep talk, July set her book aside and snuggled beneath the quilt. She had to put her relationship with Nacona into proper perspective, and she couldn't dwell on the tragedy that had upset her. Because of circumstances beyond their control, she and Nacona had been detained in Dodge. Now they would be forced to make hurried arrangements, if they were to meet the bank and railroad representatives in Denver at the beginning of the week.

Since she and Nacona had missed the train from Dodge to Pueblo, Colorado, and its northern connection, July knew they would have to trek cross-country to reach the southern branch of the Union Pacific at Oakley. If they were lucky, they could catch a passenger train bound for Denver and arrive with a few minutes to spare.

Mentally listing the supplies they would need for a fast flight across the Kansas plains, July fell asleep, but her dreams were tangled and confused. She awoke several times during the night in a cold sweat, reliving the nightmare of the gunfight, and then trembling from sensations like those Nacona had aroused in her.

"This is ridiculous," July muttered to herself when she awakened with thoughts of that raven-haired rake tormenting her. "One would think I was a harlot in a previous life the way I'm behaving!"

Pummeling her pillow to relieve her frustrations, she ordered herself to sleep. But things didn't get better; they got progressively worse. The more she tried not to think about the tragedy, the more she found herself dwelling on the morning she'd spent in Nacona's brawny arms. Lord-a-mercy, trying not to think about anything at all was downright exhausting!

Bat extended a hand to Nacona. "Thank you for helping me through a rough time," he murmured appreciatively.

Nacona noted the lack of sparkle in Bat's slate blue eyes. "That's what friends are for."

He wished he'd had someone to help him through the torment two years ago. He knew what Bat was going through.

"You have another investigation awaiting you," Bat speculated.

Bat knew the legendary shootist was in constant demand. While Nacona was away from his headquarters, Masterson collected the telegrams that arrived for him. This competent pistolero had always been too restless to take over a town that needed taming. Nacona preferred to come and go as he pleased. Wyatt Earp was a lot like that, Bat mused. When the cattle season was over in the spring and fall, Wyatt took a leave of absence to cure his restlessness. He had wintered in Deadwood, South Dakota, while Nacona had been in Texas tracking down cattle thieves for a group of ranchers before heading for Abilene, Kansas, to pursue a rapist and murderer for a distinguished citizen who wanted justice served.

"I'm headed for Cheyenne," Nacona informed Bat. "But if you need me, all you have to do is send me a wire and I'll be here."

"Thanks, Nacona, but it's time I picked up the pieces and got on with my life. You have to get on with yours, too. I've already taken you away from your new bride longer than I should have. I had planned to celebrate with you, but . . ." His voice trailed off and a mist clouded his eyes. "Ed was dedicated to keeping the peace in Dodge. He'd want me to carry on, just as he would have."

After Nacona bid Bat farewell, the sheriff resumed patrolling the streets. Thankfully, Bat's younger brother, Jim, had sent a message that he was on his way to lend a helping hand. At least Bat had family to console him. When tragedy had struck Nacona, he'd had to go it alone.

Shaking himself loose from his gloomy thoughts, he made his way back to the hotel. Heaving an exhausted sigh, he flounced onto his bed. The past two days had been long and draining. Nacona had not only assumed Bat's duties, he had also provided companionship for him during his torment.

Since July had mentioned the conference in Denver earlier in the week, Nacona knew they would have to make tracks if they were to reach their destination on time. But he intended to make good use of the overland trek to Oakley to board the Union Pacific Railroad. Before he plunged into this assignment he needed to know what skills his new wife possessed. Having her in the street during the showdown in Dodge had unnerved him. She had proved herself to be a daredevil, but how competent she was in the face of adversity Nacona didn't know, though he certainly planned to find out. He only hoped July wasn't in for unexpected on-the-job training during their fast-paced race northward.

Nacona stared pensively at the door, lost to the alluring vision that constantly burrowed into his thoughts. He hadn't seen much of the captivating blonde during the day. He had actually missed her. Imagine that! He had never given women much thought before. They had served their purpose now and again, but this emerald-eyed nymph was another matter entirely. Already, she had touched off emotions Nacona wasn't accustomed to experiencing in his customary liaisons with the female of the species. In the past he had flitted from one shallow affair to another without regret. But with July . . .

A warm tingle trickled down Nacona's spine. He would like nothing better than to join his new bride in her room, to relieve his depression by cradling her in his arms and forgetting reality. But after his amorous advances that morning, he imagined he had rattled July enough for one day.

Would she be receptive to him now that the sluggish side effects of her bout with whiskey had worn off, or was she dreading their next intimate encounter? July had had the entire day to grapple with their morning interlude. Knowing how feisty she was, Nacona imagined she had cursed him for touching her so intimately and had chastised herself for responding to him. Considering July's highly analytic mind, she had probably reduced their spontaneous reactions to each other to some mathematical equation.

Nacona recalled having haughtily declared during their earlier confrontations that he was no stranger to a woman's bed, just to infuriate her. July wasn't the kind of woman who forgot or forgave such brash remarks. He could well imagine what she thought of him and his previous indiscretions. Out of pride she would undoubtedly hold his promiscuity against him for the duration of

118

their marriage. But then, Nacona had an oversupply of pride and stubbornness himself, so who was he to criticize her?

"And what difference does that make?" Nacona asked aloud.

He was not going to analyze everything they did. He would take this bargain at face value. July only wanted his assistance—and instruction in the art of criminal investigation—Nacona reminded himself irritably. She had negotiated this marriage to preserve her pride and had arranged to have it dissolved the instant they completed their mission in Wyoming. So why the devil was he forgoing sleep, wondering what she thought and how she would react when he demanded his conjugal benefits on their three-day honeymoon? If he had a lick of sense, he would regard his new wife as a conquest and quit getting tangled up in the concept of marriage—a marriage neither of them really wanted. This was only a temporary arrangement, after all. Hell, he was starting to think and act like a possessive, protective husband. He hadn't wanted ties or obligations. He'd been on a personal crusade for two years. And until he located the murdering thief who had . . .

Nacona forced this frustrating thought aside, deciding Bat Masterson was the lucky one. Bat had gotten immediate revenge for his brother's murder, but Nacona couldn't rest until the assassination that had disrupted his life was avenged. And in the meantime, that green-eyed firebrand would become a temporary distraction, which was all she would ever be. That was the way she wanted it, too, the way he wanted it—the way it was. On that sensible thought Nacona fell asleep. But there was nothing sensible about the dreams that awakened him during the night and left him in a sweat.

July was befuddled by the change that had come over Nacona when he appeared at her door the following morning. The tenderness and concern she had noticed in him the past two days was gone. He was all business when he ordered her to pack her belongings and meet him downstairs within the hour. July had expected as much from him after he had taken what he wanted from her while she was submerged in whiskey on their wedding night. Nonetheless she was disappointed by his remote, standoffish manner. Quite honestly, she didn't know what approach to take with the man. She decided to ignore him and see how that worked.

As she struggled out the door, her arms and hands laden with satchels, Nacona gaped incredulously at her, refusing to rush to her assistance like a doting admirer. "Woman, there isn't a horse big enough and sturdy enough to tote you and all that paraphernalia. Did you bring everything you owned with you from Kansas City?"

So much for ignoring him, thought July. His wisecracks burned the wick off her temper. She jerked up her head and glared at the swarthy giant in buckskins. "I and my necessities cannot possibly weigh more than you do," she argued defensively.

"Lord, wouldn't you know I'd get stuck with a fashion-conscious wife who needs an entourage of attendants," Nacona countered in a sarcastic tone.

His mocking disdain had returned, and July sorely resented it. "And wouldn't you know I'd get stuck with a complaining husband who refuses me even the most basic necessities."

"Necessities?" Nacona hooted as July tossed her satchels behind her saddle. "If you ask me, these are extravagances."

"I did not ask you," she snapped. "Just get on your horse and ride. We have a train to catch in Oakley, and we're wasting daylight."

"Surely you don't plan to ride in that frilly gown?" Nacona smirked, as he looked her up and down with a critical eye.

"Surely I do. Lady Godiva may have ridden about stark naked, but I assure you, I'm not as good a sport as she was."

Despite his annoyance, Nacona couldn't suppress the grin that tugged at his lips. He could easily picture this gorgeous goddess naked on horseback. For sure, Lady Godiva had nothing on this shapely undaunted woman who had brought so much along.

"Suit yourself," Nacona said with a shrug.

"Never fear. I plan to," she assured him grandly.

"But I still think breeches and a shirt would be more appropriate," he mumbled.

"I don't happen to own any." Her brothers had confiscated the two pairs she'd worn several years ago, declaring it was time for July to dress and behave like a lady.

Nacona tugged a package from his saddlebag and tossed it at her. "You do now. Your wedding present, my dear wife."

"And I didn't get you anything," July cooed pretentiously.

He scowled at her. "Just put the damned things on. You probably can't even ride well enough to stay in the saddle for a full day as it is. You may as well dress the part."

July tucked the package under her arm and sailed back into the hotel. Although she was the recipient of several astonished stares and whistles when she emerged from the building in tight-fitting buckskins, her attention was fixed on Nacona. Couldn't ride? Ha! She would show Nacona Bleu a thing or two about horsemanship. Her parents had put her on a horse before she could walk.

Nacona's jaw dropped when July leaped onto her steed in a single bound and thundered off like a house afire. Well, at least he wouldn't have to teach her to manage a horse, in the event this harebrained assignment led them into a breakneck pursuit of desperadoes. If only she could handle a pistol at a full gallop, thought Nacona. No doubt, he would have to teach this saucy nymph how to survive in the wilderness and acquaint her with the finer points of criminal investigation. What could a woman possibly know about such things?

Nacona growled sourly as he gouged his bay gelding into a canter, but he knew he was involved up to his neck with this spitfire, all because of his obsessive need to have her in his bed. As of yet, he had enjoyed only a foretaste of heaven, even though July thought otherwise, but it had been enough to keep his male glands in a state of distress and to play havoc with his disposition.

Nacona watched July ride her steed with the versatility of the Comanches, those warriors well known for their equestrian skills. How had he gotten himself into such a mess? And why did he find this hellion so damned distracting? She had him on an emotional teeter-totter, and he couldn't dismount.

"Where'd you learn to ride like that?" Nacona questioned when he finally caught up with July a mile later.

She smiled triumphantly. She couldn't say exactly why it pleased her to know she had impressed this dark-eyed rogue, but it did. "My father fancied himself a horseman," she explained. "He loved to train and race thoroughbreds. My mother shared his enthusiasm, so she insisted I have the chance to ride as expertly as my brothers."

"Another suffragist in the family." Nacona smirked. "I imagine your parents battled every morning to determine who would get to wear the breeches for the day." He slid her a mocking glance. "Did your father ever win the battle?"

"I'll have you know that my parents had respect for each other, and they shared responsibility," July parried, highly offended. "I see nothing wrong in that. My father knew my mother was headstrong and independent when he married her. He gave her the space to be an individual rather than dominating her as most males try to do to women."

"Well, you can hardly complain that I haven't given you space," Nacona pointed out. "In fact, it was *you* who proposed to *me*. If that isn't liberal minded, I don't know what is."

"I hardly see why you should complain when I set no restrictions on you," July shot back. "And I know perfectly well that the relationship my parents shared was the exception, not the rule. I certainly don't expect more of you than you are capable of giving."

"All the same, I don't like being manipulated by a strong-minded female."

He had missed their repartee more than he'd realized. Verbal fencing with July made time fly. Of course, he'd kill himself before admitting he actually enjoyed arguing with her. Why allow her to gloat?

"You wrote the book on manipulation," July flung back. "I may have accomplished my purpose by gaining your assistance, but you took—" July slammed her mouth shut and looked everywhere except at Nacona. She had not intended to refer to their wedding night, but she couldn't keep from wondering. . . .

"You're living on assumptions," Nacona declared. "A good detective assumes nothing. He formulates logical conclusions, but he does not *assume* in the absence of substantial evidence. You'd be wise to remember that when we reach Wyoming. I don't want you leaping from one erroneous conjecture to the other like a mountain goat." As his taunting gaze slid over her arresting figure, he wished he weren't so aware of how tantalizing she was in the close-fitting breeches and the shirt. Too late he realized he should have bought those garments two sizes too large. That was his mistake . . . and his misery. "For your information, my dear wife, we had no wedding night. You passed out. I undressed you and that, I'm sorry to say, was that."

Wide, disbelieving eyes swung back to him. "You mean you didn't take what you wanted when you could have had it? Whyever not?"

That was a good question. Nacona only wished he had a reasonable answer. If July had been any other woman he would have taken her—and without a second thought—because his dalliances had always meant nothing more than the appeasement of his physical cravings. But he had been damned noble where July was concerned, at his own expense.

"Why not, Nacona?" she prodded when he didn't immediately respond. Curiosity was one of her most noticeable faults—the kind that had brought about the ruin of the proverbial cat.

"End of discussion." His deep voice had the finality of a judge's gavel. In one swift fluid motion, Nacona slid his Peacemaker from its holster and leaned over to slap it into her hand. "In case trouble arises—and I have been involved in damned few assignments in which it hasn't—I need to know how good you are at guarding my back. You've flaunted your ability at riding, but—"

"I was not flaunting!" she interrupted in protest.

"There is no need to split hairs, honey." Nacona rudely snorted. "You were showing off for my benefit. Don't bother denying it. So you can ride as well as a man. Big deal. I need to know if you can ride and shoot at the same time."

July sent him a glare that would have drawn blood—or ice water—from most mens' veins. She had demonstrated her equestrian skills to impress him, but it galled her that he realized it. Curse him. He probably thought his opinion of her mattered. Well . . . it did, she admitted, much to her dismay. Of course, she would cut out her tongue before she'd let him know. His male pride was already swollen to such monumental proportions that it was on the verge of bursting.

"If you'll kindly ride ahead of me," she spitefully suggested, "I'll shoot you out of the saddle to display my skills. Will that be proof enough that I am an excellent markswoman?"

"If you're going to take offense every time I open my mouth, this partnership will never work," Nacona grumbled.

"Then I suggest you keep your mouth shut."

"What the hell's eating you, woman?" he demanded. Suddenly everything he said set her off. Just why was that?

"Nothing is bothering me." She tilted her chin so she could look down her nose at him. "If you want proof, here's your proof!"

She took two rapid-fire shots at the grass beneath Nacona's steed. Dirt danced beneath the horse's hooves and the startled animal kicked up his heels and bucked like a rodeo bronc. Cursing a blue streak, Nacona drove his knees into the steed to keep his seat. When he finally got the gelding under control, he wheeled about, only to have another shot bark in the afternoon air. His sombrero flipped off his head and landed crown down in the grass. With jaw gaping, he watched July make a theatrical production of blowing the cloud of smoke away from the barrel of the pistol, then grin smugly.

"I haven't practiced for two weeks. I'm sorry I'm a mite rusty." Her tone was certainly not apologetic.

"My Lord!" Nacona croaked, goggle-eyed.

"You needn't call me that," she replied airily as she trotted her steed past him. "July suits me just fine."

With a mixture of amazement and irritation, he watched the shapely blonde canter off. Damn! She could have blown his head off if she'd missed her mark. Lucky for him that she hadn't. He hadn't given her credit for being a horsewoman or crackshot because she was so incredibly dainty and feminine. That was the last time he'd judge her by the standards he had set for normal women. July was nowhere near normal. She had undoubtedly grown up like a tomboy, following on her brothers' heels, determined to prove that she was their equal. Now, though she was every bit the lady in appearance, she was still a hoyden at heart.

Reluctant admiration dawned in Nacona's eyes as he followed in July's wake. With her skills with pistols and horses, and with her legal training, maybe she could become a top-notch detective. It seemed she was full of surprises. However, Nacona quickly reminded himself that practicing one's marksmanship on bottles, cans, hats, and such was vastly different from squaring off against a desperate man in a life-and-death situation. That took nerves of steel, ice-cold emotions, and absolute concentration.

Oh sure, he scoffed to himself. How many men would draw down on a lady? Why, even if a man won, he'd lose.

Society frowned on men who gunned down females. In some ways, being born a woman had given July the advantage in the profession to which she aspired. This might just turn out to be a successful partnership after all, if he could manage some degree of control over this gorgeous misfit. . . .

Nacona's thoughts trailed off when he noticed the telltale signs that another party had trekked through the area ahead of them. He and July had been tracking northwest toward White Woman Creek, where the plains dropped off into a craggy, spring-fed valley that had long been the site of Indian camps during hunting expeditions. Unless Nacona missed his guess, they were trailing a band of

Cheyenne who had escaped the reservation in Indian Territory.

Before they reached the ledge where the land sloped into a rock-filled canyon, Nacona snaked out an arm to halt July. Without a word, he dismounted to inspect the tracks.

"What the matter?" she questioned impatiently. "Must I remind you that we are on a tight schedule. We have to be in—"

Nacona jerked her out of the saddle in midsentence. "Keep your voice down," he hissed. "It can carry like echoing cannon fire along this ridge." He indicated the hoof prints that encircled them.

July blinked owlishly when Nacona pressed his palm into the tracks and then circled around, pausing every now and then to inspect one particular spot. "Was it a buffalo herd?"

Nacona glanced up at her and scoffed before continuing his investigation. "Hardly. Do you remember your reference to the Indians who sneaked away from their reservation a couple of weeks ago?"

July nodded bleakly.

"Well, I think we just found them. If we leave them alone, they probably won't bother us, but all the same—"

The crunch of rocks somewhere in the near distance brought a quick end to their conversation. July and Nacona were in their saddles in less than a heartbeat. The cry of a bird that sounded a little too human to be genuine drifted toward them. Without thundering off and alerting uninvited guests to their presence, Nacona quietly circled the rim of the canyon. He preferred not to test July's sharpshooting skills on real-life targets who shot back.

And he wanted no trouble with the Cheyenne. His Indian ancestry made him sympathetic toward all the tribes that had been forced into confinement, as his mother's people had been when they'd been herded down the Trail of Tears from their native lands in Mississippi. Nacona wasn't about to go looking for trouble and he'd just as soon trouble didn't find him, especially with this comely blonde underfoot.

While they detoured off their path to avoid calamity, July studied Nacona's broad back. With each passing day she found herself more infatuated with and impressed by this magnificent man. Despite her firm resolve to resist his sensual allure, she could not negate the knowledge at his disposal.

Although Nacona had never divulged his past to her, she knew Indian blood flowed through his veins, and had noticed that he seemed attuned to all that transpired around him. She had never before met a man who possessed knowledge of the terrain and the skills of tracking man or beast. Nacona had noticed the tracks that indicated trouble while she had been oblivious to them. In a matter of minutes he had determined whether they belonged to buffalo, wild horses, or humans. He had deduced the nature and size of the party from studying the tracks, overturned stones, and patches of crushed grass. July felt if she knew half of what Nacona knew she would be the best female detective on the planet. But what did that matter? she asked herself bitterly. No one would hire her because she could never overcome the handicap of being a woman. . . .

A resounding war whoop banished such thoughts from her mind. Suddenly she was on full alert. When Nacona gouged his steed and plunged down the steep slope, July followed suit, afraid to look back for fear of what she'd see. In a matter of seconds, she was forced to push her riding skills to their very limits. While her frantic steed bounded right and left to avoid the sharp, jutting boulders, July clamped her legs against its flanks. The thunder of hooves echoed around them, and July very nearly leaped out of her skin when the bark of a rifle sent fragments of rock into the air around her. Quick as a wink, she collapsed onto her steed as if she were an extra saddle blanket. Her heart was hammering as they zigzagged down the rocky terrain to the floor of the canyon.

She didn't know if it was to their advantage that the sun had disappeared on the horizon. Did Indians truly call it quits for the evening, forgoing battle until the light of day? She hadn't anticipated any mishaps during their journey north to catch the train, but she reminded herself of what Nacona had told her during one of his lectures on honing her skills for investigation and survival. Always expect the unexpected, he'd said.

When they reached level ground, Nacona motioned toward the clump of cedars in the distance and silently ordered July to take the lead. He refused to alert other warriors to their location by firing at the braves who had pursued them. He had no beef with the Cheyenne, unless they decided to relieve him and July of their scalps while they still had need of them. In that instance, his truce with his blood brothers was off.

To July's relief, they reached the cedar break without further incident. The braves who had chased them had apparently ceased their pursuit. When Nacona paused only long enough to quench his steed's thirst, and his own, at the creek and then trotted off, July stared at him in astonishment.

"Surely you don't think you can navigate your way through this labyrinth of canyons in the dark!"

"I'm part Indian," he told her as he peered into the moonlit distance. "I'll *feel* my way." His obsidian eyes swung back to her, and a taunting smile quirked his lips. "Going without sleep is really to your advantage, my dear wife." His gaze drifted down her curvaceous physique, its effect as powerful as touch. "It will spare you from our thrice-belated wedding night, but sooner or later you're going to be mine. I would have preferred sooner, but later will suffice. Now we won't dare pause for more than a couple of hours, for rest. You're safe from me—and the Indians—for the moment. We'll catch a few hours of sleep in the wee hours before dawn."

When he rode off, July glared at his departing back. He wasn't going to allow her to forget that she had yet to uphold her end of the bargain. And if the truth be known, she had mixed emotions about the prospective loss of her innocence. She had heard that women were forced to endure the amorous attentions of their husbands, out of obligation and duty. And yet, the morning Nacona had attempted to seduce her, she had experienced erotic pleasures she hadn't expected.

At first she had presumed her body only remembered the experience of the previous night and that was why she had made no attempt to resist him. But as it turned out, he hadn't taken complete possession. July still didn't have the foggiest notion of what to expect from Nacona. If she resisted him, would he become abusive and forceful? Would she suffer at his hands when the critical moment came? Would he try to prove his dominance over her, gloat over his conquest? And why should he care if she found pleasure? She was only a challenge to him, a temporary and convenient means for release of his physical desire. Damn, in some ways, July wished he had taken her while she'd been too inebriated to remember. Now she had to nervously dread her belated wedding night.

Nacona glanced sideways to see her chewing thoughtfully on her bottom lip. He could have kicked himself for spouting that last sarcastic remark at her. But taking this lovely blonde was constantly in his thoughts. The longer he was forced to wait to make her his, the more frustrated he became. It seemed Fate had conspired to torment him.

The way things were going, this elusive nymph might escape the farce of a marriage with her innocence still intact. If Nacona didn't know better, he would swear July had somehow schemed to avoid the marriage bed. She, after all, could maneuver with the best of them.

Chapter 9

Just as Nacona had promised, they did pause from their journey to catch up on missed sleep—and not a moment too soon. When Nacona finally called a halt to the night's trek, July was on the verge of dropping off her steed, she fell sound asleep the instant her head hit her makeshift pillow, her saddle.

When the first rays of dawn spilled over the countryside, July moaned groggily and squirmed in her bedroll. Something tapped her on the shoulder, nudging her from the depths of slumber. Reluctantly, she stirred. A quiet moan tripped from her lips when another tap brought her to a higher level of consciousness. July sensed sunlight beaming beyond her closed eyes, fleeting shadows swaying in front of her. . . .

Her lashes fluttered up to greet the day, and a startled gasp burst from her lips when she found herself surrounded by a congregation of Indians whose rifles were trained on her chest. Grim faces stared down at her, and July instinctively sidled toward Nacona, as if he could resolve their problems. Unfortunately, he couldn't. Another dozen rifles were aimed at *his* chest. The only difference was that his emotional reaction was masked behind a carefully controlled stare.

"Smile sweetly for our guests," he instructed.

Struggling for composure, July propped herself up on a wobbly elbow and tried to control the frantic beat of her heart. With effort, she displayed a friendly smile, doubting it would do her any good.

"Some scout you turned out to be," she muttered through her tense smile. "We might as well have fallen asleep several hours ago and saved the Cheyenne the trouble of tracking us down."

Leave it to this sassy minx to point out his error in judgment, Nacona thought. He shouldn't have halted their trek north, not even for a second. But she had looked exhausted, so he had offered her the rest she needed. And this was the thanks he got—her ridicule and a party of Cheyenne warriors armed to the teeth. *Damn!*

Although Nacona couldn't speak the Cheyenne tongue fluently, he did know a few words, and he improvised with the sign language employed by most tribes for communication. In fact, the system had proved more versatile and expressive in his dealings with Indians than any other means of communication developed on the plains.

Nacona's level gaze circled the stony faces, searching for the leader of the band. He quickly made the sign indicating that he wished to parley with their chief. Though none of the braves lowered their rifles, they stepped back a pace to let their leader emerge from their ranks. Nacona found himself facing Dull Knife himself. He displayed the sign for peace and friendship and spoke a few words in the chief's native tongue.

July sat up, cross-legged, to watch Nacona converse with the old man whose opaque eyes looked weary from his exodus north. The chief was wrapped in a buffalo robe, and gray braids dangled beside his long, thin face with the weathered features. Silently, she chided herself for razzing Nacona for being unable to second-guess the Cheyenne. He seemed very competent and confident in handling every situation he encountered. Of course, they still ran the risk of being tortured and killed. But so far so good, July mused. At least Dull Knife was willing to talk before he disposed of them and left their remains for the buzzards.

When Nacona explained that he was of Chickasaw and French blood, the rifle barrels dropped, and July breathed a sigh of relief. Dull Knife eased down to offer Nacona his hand in a gesture of friendship, then began to explain his purpose while Nacona translated for his curious wife.

"My people and I have no wish to live on the reservation near Darlington on the land Father Washington calls Indian Territory," Nacona translated.

Dull Knife grunted disgustedly and went on speaking, implementing with sign language. "We want nothing more to do with the soldiers, and we can fight no more wars. Thirteen summers ago the cavalry massacred our people at Sand Creek. Ten summers ago Custer attacked our people on the so-called reservation. Black Kettle survived the attack at Sand Creek, but he was slain on the Washita. Now our leaders are few and our people are battle weary."

The old chief's gaze stretched across the rolling plain. "We huddled on the reservation like cattle, with poor food rations. We tried to adapt to the white man's ways

135

when we were left with no other choice. But the southern climate does not suit our people. Already, hundreds have died of malaria. When we begged to go north to live out our lives on our own land, we were refused."

Dull Knife peered somberly at Nacona. "We want no more death, and we want no more war. We want only to live near the Tongue River in Montana, to be buried on the sacred ground from which we came. We will not go back to the reservation and those intolerable conditions!"

"I do not blame you, Dull Knife. If a man has no freedom to choose then he has nothing at all," Nacona murmured sympathetically. "I will send a message to Fort Reno to tell the commander that you want no trouble, only the freedom of your fathers and your father's fathers to live on the land given to you by the Great Spirit."

"You understand how it is for us," Dull Knife said with a weary sigh. "We cannot live like the white man, and we have no wish to try." With Nacona's assistance he rose to his feet and gave a command in his native tongue. Instantly, the warriors dispersed.

"I pity the Indians," July confessed as she struggled to toss the saddle on her mount. "I wouldn't take kindly to a bunch of men in blue uniforms telling me where to live, what to eat, and what to do. And I'd hate those prison camps they call reservations."

"Free spirits usually do," Nacona replied with a teasing grin. "And here you thought being a woman was oppressive. Things could be worse. You could be a member of one of the many tribes who have been herded onto a reservation, or you could be a half-breed. Women aren't the only people who are treated badly."

July peered at the column of warriors who wound their

way northward. She hoped Dull Knife and his people could proceed without incident. She shuddered to think how harsh and cruel life had been to them. Nacona was right, she decided. She was better off than some folks. But as far as she could tell, equality—the right to live one's own life—was still a vision. Those with power and influence were always trying to maneuver less fortunate people into doing their bidding.

Mulling over that depressing thought, July followed Nacona northward, wondering how many centuries would pass before all those beneath the yoke of oppression would finally enjoy freedom. Too many, she supposed. Progress was always slow in coming.

She had certainly encountered many eye-opening experiences in the past few weeks. They served to remind her of just how naive and idealistic she had been while her brothers protected her. She felt that she had aged years in the short time she'd been on her own and with Nacona Bleu.

To July's relief, they met with no further mishaps during that day. But the following morning was another matter entirely. A spring storm rumbled across the Great Plains, leaving vaporous mountains piling high on the western horizon. July was already exhausted from the rigorous trip with only occasional rest stops to graze the horses and to appease their own gnawing hunger. She was sure Nacona was testing her stamina and endurance. It seemed he was intent on knowing just how far she could go before she collapsed, wailed, or implored him to stop.

Fortunately, determination was one of July's greatest

assets. She had spent years trying to keep up with her older brothers, proving she was made of the same sturdy stuff they were. She made a mental note to send a wire from Oakley, assuring her brothers that she was still enjoying her vacation in Wichita with Aunt Betty.

Thunder crackled above them and July instinctively ducked. Her concerned gaze swept across the rolling hills. Where in the world would they find protection from the inclement weather? The plains of Kansas were unforthcoming when it came to providing humankind with shelter against the elements.

A muddled frown knitted her brow when she noticed the peculiar rock formations that jutted up from the river bank in the distance. The three monolithic boulders, as tall as two-story houses, were shaped like flat-topped pyramids. When huge raindrops splattered around her and the wind howled like a coyote, July gouged her steed and aimed herself toward the rock towers and what little cover they could provide.

A wry smile quirked Nacona's lips as he watched July ford the narrow channel of the river and lunge up the slope to seek protection amid the huge rock mounds. He had thought her to be near collapse, but she seemed to have phenomenal resilience. It allowed her to generate energy when the situation demanded it. He knew she couldn't have been as seasoned on the trail as he was, but she was determined to keep up with him . . . or die trying.

When a raindrop slapped him in the face and pellet-sized hailstones thumped him on the head, Nacona urged his steed across the river. By the time he reached the pyramids, hail hammered and zinged against the stone slabs, startling the horses. Before they bolted away, Nacona grabbed both sets of reins and dallied them around a jutting edge of rock.

The instant lightning flashed directly above them and thunder boomed, July plastered herself against Nacona. Her damp body quivered against his as she burrowed her head into his shoulder and squeezed the stuffing out of him.

"You risked death to dash into the middle of a show-down in Dodge and you're afraid of storms?" He chuckled incredulously. "I never would have thought it!"

July was sorry to admit her weakness. Though she had tried to control her apprehension, the spears of lightning and the earth-shaking thunder had really rattled her.

"My parents were killed by lightning while they were trying to herd my father's prize race horses into the stables," she mumbled against his soaked shirt. "I was only ten years old at the time, and I'm afraid their deaths left emotional scars. I'm sorry to be such a coward, but . . ."

He cupped her chin, lifting it so she could see his comforting smile. Odd, how this mere wisp of a woman could draw upon the emotional well he'd kept hidden from the rest of the world. One look into those lustrous green eyes rimmed with thick curly lashes and he softened like butter in a skillet.

Another spear of blinding light stabbed through the gray clouds, accompanied by a drumroll of thunder. Like an octopus, July clamped onto Nacona. "Talk to me," she requested shakily.

The jagged edge of panic in her voice made him frown.

"And talk loud. Tell me everything about yourself and your past. Don't stop talking until the storm blows over," she insisted.

Nacona had always been a very private man, but July's desperate plea put words on his tongue that hadn't been there for years, not even when he was sloshed from whiskey. And suddenly he was shouting the chronicles of his past to high heaven, to be heard above the pounding hailstones.

"My father was French," he blurted out. "My mother was Chickasaw. My brother Shandin and I were raised in a village near Tishamingo City in Indian Territory. Since our father came and went with the wind, Shandin and I were put in our uncle's care. He taught us the ways of our people until we were old enough to be placed in the Chickasaw Manual Labor School for Boys. We . . ."

Nacona paused in his tale when thunder exploded and the horses tried to rear up and lunge away. He secured the wild-eyed steeds, then July, like a boa constrictor, latched onto his neck.

"You're strangling me!" Nacona croaked as he pried her arms loose and resettled them around his waist. "Aw hell, July, you don't want to hear all this. It's—"

"Yes, I do!" she croaked, cursing her irrational fear.

She hated this weakness. But the incident that had taken her parents' lives kept flashing before her, torturing her beyond words. This had happened each time she'd found herself out in the elements during a storm. She preferred to huddle inside, allowing no one to know of her vulnerability. It was illogical, but she never could stop shaking, nor could she forget that fateful day eleven years ago.

Heaving a frustrated sigh, Nacona propped himself and July against the wall of stone, shielding her trembling body from the driving rain. "When the Civil War broke out, Shandin and I went to Kansas with two hundred and fifty other tribesmen to fight for the Union. We were young, but we got our first taste of battle against Confederate guerrilla bands that ravaged the war-torn state. When the fighting ended and we returned home, our mother had passed on and no one knew what had become of our father. He hadn't been around in years.

"Shandin and I joined the Chickasaw police force to support ourselves. Then we rode for Judge Parker out of Fort Smith for four years, tracking down Indian and white outlaws who preyed on the territory. We had been given a tip about some whiskey peddlers who were operating in the Choctaw nation, and we went to investigate. It was an ambush. The two white outlaws in cahoots with the peddlers had set us up and . . ."

When Nacona's voice wavered, July lifted her head to peer at his stormy expression. Intuition told her tragedy had struck when she saw Nacona's control crack. She forgot about her own anxiety.

"What happened?" she queried.

"Those sons-a-bitches riddled Shandin with bullets." He erupted, scowling. "He never saw them coming. When I got to him, he just stared blankly at me and asked me to give those bastards hell for him. . . ."

July quickly realized why Nacona had been so compassionate and understanding when Bat Masterson lost his oldest brother to tragedy. He had lived through his own nightmare, but there had been no one to offer him sympa-

141

thy, no family to help him endure the tormenting ordeal. He had had to make his way alone.

As difficult as it had been for July without her parents, her brothers had provided security, moral support, and comfort. Nacona had had no one. No wonder he had become such a callous, self-contained man. He had come through life the hard way, enjoying few pleasures and shouldering more than his share of burdens and responsibilities.

"I tracked two of those murdering butchers down after they split up," Nacona continued, as if he were trapped in a hellish trance. "Judge Parker didn't have to bother bringing them to trial and sentencing them to hang. I launched them into hell. But the third one . . ."

He stared at the looming clouds as the cold wind whipped through his damp clothes, bitter rage just beneath the surface. "His partners were loyal to the very end," Nacona growled.

"I never caught up with the ringleader. I had no accurate description of the man who carefully plotted to have Shandin and me killed for investigating his whiskey and theft ring. He's still a mystery. I have no accurate description. All I know is that he—supposedly—has dark eyes, brown hair, beard, and mustache, and is of average build and weight. After the ambush, that bastard disappeared off the face of the earth. I've taken on every job with the aim of finding him and avenging Shandin's death. But wherever that murderer is, he's as elusive as he was while operating his ring in the territory. Do you know what it's like to hunt for a man who could be any one? It's pure hell!"

A wave of sympathy washed over July as she studied Nacona's tortured expression. Now she understood the various influences that had shaped this legendary shootist. He had refused to allow the rest of the world to know he was haunted by the past, that his restlessness was spurred by an obsession to hunt down his brother's killer. Bat Masterson had found instant satisfaction in Dodge, but not Nacona. He traveled far and wide, ever searching for a man who might not even still be alive, a man he couldn't even recognize on sight.

July was finding out a great many things about Nacona. But these discoveries only confused her. She kept receiving contradictory vibrations from him, and she wasn't sure what to make of him. He could be cruel and insulting at times, downright dangerous at others. And yet, beneath that rock-hard shell was a vulnerability that made July realize just how human he really was.

Tenderly, she reached up to tilt his face toward hers. He had offered her comfort from her nightmares, and in return she felt the need to console him, to heal his wounds with the milk of human kindness. But when her lips met his, Nacona froze as he drew away he was scowling.

"Don't," he muttered as he set her away from him.

"I only wanted to—" July was cut off by an explosive snort.

"I know what you were doing," he snapped, cursing himself for letting this nymph inside his tough shell.

She had already burrowed in too deeply. He didn't want her pity, and he refused to accept it. He was unaccustomed to compassion. Her tempting kiss enflamed the smoldering coals of banked desire. Nacona didn't like the riptide of emotions that hounded him. He had already waited two weeks to appease his need for this captivating woman. July was sure tempting.

But this wasn't the time, nor were these the circumstances under which to satisfy his craving. The Good Samaritan in July was offering comfort to his troubled soul, but she knew nothing of the savage passions in him. Each touch, each careless glance had kept him on a slow burn, waiting and wondering how it would feel to lose himself in the soft, feminine warmth of her delicious flesh—in that body too temptingly close and yet too tormentingly far away.

Hell and damnation, the time never did seem to be right for them. And why was he always fretting about that and postponing taking his husbandly rights? Since when had he become so particular about appeasing his male appetite? Since when had he turned out to be so blessed considerate and noble? And why the blazes did this sassy, exasperating vixen have to bring out the best in him? She would ruin his reputation. He found himself wanting her first experience of passion to be a positive one. But sex was sex, or at least it had been until July MacKenzie barged into his room to turn his bath into a cloud of steam and his mind to mush. Still, he was showing her all sorts of consideration, even when she had his emotions tied in knots.

"Get on your horse," Nacona ordered in a voice that cracked like a whip.

July blinked, puzzled, when he thrashed around to retrieve their mounts. Blast it, if she lived to be a hundred she wasn't sure she would ever figure this perplexing man out! The first time she had made the slightest advance toward him, just for comfort's sake, he'd chewed her up and spit her out. She was far better at repelling advances than instigating them, it was true, but for a man who had mockingly declared he wanted her innocence in exchange for his assistance, he was acting damned peculiar. Had he decided she wasn't worth the trouble? Most likely, July decided. After all, what would a worldly, experienced man like Nacona Bleu want with a naive maid who hadn't the slightest idea how to go about making love, even if she wanted to.

Thanks to Nacona's harsh reaction, July's pride was smarting and her confidence was low. Attempting to salvage what was left of her dignity, she piled onto her horse. The storm had passed, but a cloud of despair hovered over her as she trotted north, deciding she should never have let visions of a career in investigation lure her away from Kansas City. She had lied to her trusting brothers, and she had tangled with a man she could never understand. She had even gone so far as to propose marriage to salvage her pride and dignity. Heavens, why would Nacona want anything to do with her? She had seen to it that he'd spent time in jail, and she had forced him to help her. If that wasn't bad enough, she had inadvertently caused the death of his friend. He probably considered her a curse—and justifiably.

These dismal thoughts cut July to the quick. She was the one who had insisted on a marriage with no real ties, no promises to keep. Deep down inside, Nacona knew as well as she did that it was her fault Ed Masterson had lost his life. He didn't really want her with him. He had only been toying with her from the beginning, for the sport of it. She wasn't the least bit special to him. He could probably have any woman he wanted. So why did the vision of this dark-eyed rake nestled in someone else's arms stab at her heart? She and Nacona weren't bound by love, were they? Surely she would know if she had accidentally fallen in love with this complex man . . . wouldn't she?

Nacona scowled when he noted her gloomy expression. "Don't sit there thinking. Just forget everything I said and did. Knowing how logical and sensible you pride yourself on being, you'll be analyzing the entire morning to death. Just forget it."

"Forget what?" July drew herself up proudly in the saddle and raised her chin a notch. "I don't have the faintest idea what you're talking about."

"Hell yes, you do," Nacona persisted, goaded by his unaccountable bad humor. "I didn't want your kiss of compassion, and now you're sulking."

"I am not!" July vehemently protested. "I didn't even want to kiss you. I was only trying to be supportive and compassionate. But considering how *un*sentimental you are, Mr. Hard-as-a-Rock Bleu, you don't need anybody's pity. I simply forgot that in my momentary lapse of sanity. In fact, I'd prefer to kiss a stone. I could have drawn the same amount of emotion from it as I could from you. So there!"

That was just what he'd thought. July had tolerated him when she'd needed moral support; then she had attempted to extend the same courtesy to him. Her heart hadn't been in it. She had acted out of moral obligation. And what the hell was the matter with him anyway? He was behaving like a female at risk of becoming a man's object of pleasure.

Damn him, July fumed, shooting him a lethal glare. He

could infuriate her faster than any man alive. "I should have known I'd wind up in hell when I bargained with a devil like you!"

"Well, welcome to hell, honey," Nacona flung back, along with a flaming glower. "I hope you like it hot!"

"I can tolerate being in hell with you because I know I won't have to put up with you all my life," she retaliated, her tone insulting. "Hell will only last as long as this farce of a marriage. Thank God!"

And that, was the last fragment of conversation to pass between them for the duration of the afternoon.

Nacona flashed her mutinous glares as he fished in his saddlebags now and then to retrieve a cigar and puff fiercely upon it.

July sat atop her horse, mentally alphabetizing each and every flaw in his personality, so she could dislike him more. Curse the man! He was making her crazy, what with his quick changes of mood and his ridicule.

She couldn't wait to reach Oakley, to enjoy the luxury of other humans milling around her. Spending the past few hours with Nacona Bleu had been comparable to squaring off against a fire-breathing dragon. She had drawn strength from the feel of his protective arms around her during the storm, and then, suddenly, he was jumping down her throat, flinging glares hot enough to melt rock. Let him appease his voracious male appetite in someone else's arms. What did she care? Not one blessed whit!

From this moment forward, she was dedicating herself to her assignment, and that was that. Yes, sirree, Wyoming was the place for her. Suffragists like Susan B. Anthony had complimented Wyoming's enlightenment and had urged women everywhere to migrate to the model state. Women had acquired the right to vote, and they had even elected Esther Morris of South Pass City as their first female justice of the peace. Since the citizens had forbidden discrimination because of sex in the paying of qualified schoolteachers, maybe they would even see their way to clear to accepting a female investigating attorney who hung out her shingle and decided to stay. Yes, indeed, Wyoming was the place for her. When Nacona went on his way to only God knew where, she would bid him good riddance. He wasn't an *ass*et, she thought bitterly.

Chapter 10

July was never so relieved to hear the jingle of harnesses and the creak of wagons. The bustling railroad community at Oakley was her salvation. Without informing Nacona, who was going through his supply of cigars at a record rate, she made a beeline for the railroad roundhouse to inquire about the train's departure to Denver. To her dismay, the train from Hays City wasn't due until the ungodly hour of three o'clock the following morning.

"But the good news, ma'am," the ticket agent cheerfully assured her when her shoulders sagged in disappointment, "is that you will arrive the following afternoon in Denver, barring any unforeseen delays."

Such delays were what worried July. The way her luck had been running, the cursed locomotive would derail while rounding a bend and she would never arrive at the conference in Denver.

"There's a hotel just down the street, and it offers comfortable accommodations," Jefferson Bell continued with his customary enthusiasm. "And I recommend Ma Bell's restaurant right next door for your dining pleasure." His wrinkled face beamed with pride. "She's my wife, and she makes the best apple pies in Kansas."

July plunked down the money for two tickets, only to find Nacona shouldering her out of the way. He stuffed the coins back in her hand and offered his cash to the agent.

"I hope your wife isn't as independent as mine," he remarked.

His voice was pleasant enough, but July detected in it the faint purr of irritation. Everything she did seemed to rub him the wrong way.

"My new bride keeps forgetting that she no longer has to pay her own way, that she is my responsibility."

When July opened her mouth to contest being anybody's responsibility, especially his, Nacona placed his boot on her foot in warning.

"Newlyweds, huh?" Jefferson Bell brightened. "There's a fancy hotel suite that would suit the occasion. I'll tell Ma to rustle you up something special for supper. Ma loves weddings. She must. I'm her third husband."

"What happened to the first two?" Nacona inquired with a faint hint of mockery in his tone. "Died of food poisoning, did— Ugh!"

July had jabbed him in the ribs with her elbow, and she now produced a smile for Jefferson Bell. "My husband has an odd sense of humor."

"Indeed I do," Nacona concurred as he pinched July's cheek a mite too hard. "I married you, didn't I, darlin'?"

Jefferson didn't know exactly how to take Nacona, but he had dealt with various types in his line of work. With a shrug, he handed over the tickets and smiled. "You two enjoy your stay, and don't be late for the train. It only stops here for ten minutes before it roars off again. More than one sleepy-eyed passenger has missed his connection."

As July and Nacona ambled out of the depot, she shot him a disdainful glare. "That was uncalled for. As I've told you before. It doesn't cost extra to be nice to people. Try it once in a while."

"There's a difference between being nice and being sticky sweet," he snorted as he gathered his saddlebags. "You were batting your eyes at the man. If Ma Bell bumped off her first two husbands for flirting, the ticket agent might wind up with a buffalo steak laced with arsenic."

"I wasn't flirting," July hissed.

"Tell that to Ma, honey," Nacona insisted before he stalked off.

July stared after him in disbelief. What was eating him now? Obviously the rain had warped that chunk of wood he called a brain. Flirting indeed!

July stamped off in a huff, to send a telegram to her brothers, and assure them she was having a marvelous time in Wichita—where she wished she was. She certainly wasn't having a marvelous time in Oakley. That impossible man she had married was making sure of that.

It wasn't until July breezed through the foyer of the hotel and opened the door to their suite that she realized she was about to share a bed with this irascible husband of hers. She told herself there was no reason to fret. Nacona would probably prefer to appease his lusts with someone else since he had been snapping and growling at her for the better part of two days. Brothels were never hard to find, and he had undoubtedly noted their locations on his way through town.

"I ordered a bath for your pleasure," he informed her as he rummaged through his saddlebags. "I'll be at the bathhouse and barber shop down the street. After I send a telegram to Fort Reno to clear the way for Dull Knife and the Cheyenne, I'll meet you at Ma's at six o'clock."

"You needn't rush back on my account," July purred pretentiously. "I'm sure I can find someone to occupy my time during your absence, other than Jefferson Bell, of course."

One thick brow lifted at a mocking angle as he studied July from beneath the drooping brim of his rain-damaged hat. "No strings, is that it? What about our bargain? Or is that something you have conveniently chosen to forget?"

July whirled around to meet his taunting expression, wishing she could annoy him as effectively as he annoyed her. "Damn the bargain," she spewed out, falling victim to her Scotch-Irish temper. It happened all too often when Nacona was underfoot. "You'll find no satisfaction with me, I promise you that. I don't know the first thing about pleasing a man. And even if I did, I wouldn't waste my energy on you. For two cents I'd bed a total stranger, just to deny you the conquest!"

Nacona came uncoiled like a rattlesnake and jerked her to him with a back-wrenching jolt. Dark fires flickered in his eyes as he stuck his face in hers and bared his teeth. "Don't challenge me, July. Dangerous men have tried and failed. You belong to me, but I'll be damned if I'll fight another man for my rights to you!"

"Belong?" July shoved the heels of her hands against his inflated chest, but his encircling arms refused to release her. "I *belong* to no man!"

"Don't you? You're the one with the law degree, honey. You tell me what right I have now that we're husband and wife. Unless I've been misinformed, I have all sorts of privileges which I've overlooked because extenuating circumstances demanded it. But I've run clean out of patience. Tonight will find you in my bed, and we'll be doing a lot more than sleeping together. And you"—he made a stabbing gesture at her heaving chest to emphasize his point—"won't make one move to resist me because that was the bargain. You don't have to like it, but you'll do it because I'll be here to make certain you do!"

"I *won't* like it. You can depend on that!" July spluttered, infuriated by his harsh demands, his predatory stance, and his thunderous scowl. How dare he treat her like his dutiful slave!

A scampish smile curved the corners of his mouth upward as he released his hold on her and stepped away. "We'll just see how well you like your too-long-postponed wedding night, Missus Bleu. Time will tell which one of us walks away from this tête-à-tête unaffected. And being a betting man, I'd put my money on the one with the most experience, not the one *without* it."

He scooped up a saddlebag without breaking stride and sailed out the door. July childishly stuck out her tongue, then flinched when he wheeled around to catch her red-handed.

"Grow up, July. You're about to become a woman instead of a starry-eyed little girl who lives on dreams."

153

"And who married a nightmare," she qualified with a scathing glance.

His sensuous lips lifted in a devilish grin, and he chewed on the cigar he had clamped between his teeth. "I told you it was hot in hell, honey. And tonight, you're going to find out just how hot the fires can burn. . . ."

The clank of spurs echoed in the hall as July stamped over to slam the door, wishing she could lock Nacona out of their room as easily as she could shut out the rest of the world. Muttering, she paced about until the maid and her attendants arrived with a small tub and buckets of heated water. She was determined to devise a way to avoid that horrible man and his humiliating intentions. He was hellbent on making her regret ever crossing him. She wished he had taken what he wanted while she had lain in an intoxicated stupor. Then this ridiculous bargain would have been over and done. But the three-day honeymoon she had promised him stood like a barrier between them, and the torment of not knowing what to expect from Nacona was tearing her to pieces.

When July was alone, she tugged off her soiled breeches and shirt and plopped into the tub. Frustration hounded her. She very nearly scrubbed off her hide while she plotted and schemed to get even with the ornery Nacona. She could resort to whiskey again and ensure that she was oblivious to his attentions. Or perhaps she could gorge at supper and make herself nauseous. Surely even Nacona wouldn't force himself on her when she was green around the gills.

An impish grin pursed her lips as she settled back in the tub. If she became indisposed, he would search elsewhere for female companionship and . . .

July cursed the unappealing vision of Nacona in another woman's arms. Blast it, she'd be damned if she carried out this plot and damned if she didn't. Maybe she wouldn't be so spiteful if she thought Nacona had one smidgen of affection for her. But he didn't. He was the kind of man who trained himself to be emotionally detached, the kind of man her brothers thoroughly detested for a hundred good reasons. And why should he care about her anyway? July asked herself realistically. He felt trapped, and he simply wanted to fulfill the terms of their bargain out of spite. She should make him feel guilty for compromising her, that's what she should do. If she preyed on his sense of decency—provided he had some—maybe he would relent and let this marriage continue to be in name only.

While drying herself off, July made her decision. She was going to kill that oversize brute with kindness. She would be gracious and dignified. She could if she wanted to. And Nacona's conscience would hound him if he thought to be rough and forceful with her. She would give him the long-winded spiel about the sanctity of wedlock and the genuine concern that should bind husband and wife. Yes, siree, she would make him feel all of two inches tall when she got through with him.

Having decided how to turn the tables on Nacona, July shook out her most elegant gown. She would do everything within her power to remind him of just how much of a lady she really was. Hopefully, he would respond accordingly. And if he didn't, she'd whack him over the head and take the train to the conference in Denver without him. Surely he wouldn't wring her neck with a railroad dignitary and a prestigious banker as witnesses.

155

July smiled wryly and wriggled into her emerald gown. It seemed she and Nacona were back to their mental game of chess. If she calculated her moves, maybe she could checkmate his king. Wouldn't that get his goat! The mischievous thought provoked her to grin.

Ma Bell was not the husband-poisoning female Nacona had made her out to be, July soon found out. Anything but. The instant July breezed into the clean, well-organized restaurant, a spry older woman who was pushing fifty scurried toward her.

"You must be the new bride Jefferson told me about," Ma gushed. Bursting with vim and vigor, she herded July toward the corner table that had been decorated with a bouquet of wildflowers and a white lace tablecloth. "Now you just sit yourself down and await your husband. Dinner is on the house, my dear. Ah, how I love to see the budding of new romance." She clapped her hands together in sheer delight.

"You are very generous, but this isn't necessary—"

"Ah, but it is!" Ma proclaimed with absolute certainty. "I remember the way it was with me—so wonderful and new. I found love three times, you know. I wish my husbands could have lived longer, to enjoy it. But it was marvelous each time, while it lasted." She bent down to stare July squarely in the eye. "Make the most of love, my dear girl. It never seems to last long enough."

When Ma buzzed off like a busy bumblebee, flashing smiles to every customer she passed, July frowned curiously. She would have liked to know what quirks of fate had cut Ma's two other marriages short. But it was obvious the wiry little woman was an optimist who believed in living life to the fullest. It also was evident that Ma's zest for living spilled over into her work. The cafe was filled with appetizing aromas, and July was anxious to sink her teeth into a decent meal. The rations she had choked down the past few days had left a lot to be desired.

Nacona halted in his tracks when he spied the fetching blonde in green velvet. July's gown reeked of wealth and elegance, and the string of pearls that encircled her swan-like neck bespoke of her close association with all the luxuries the gentry could afford. The MacKenzie brothers had seen to it that their little sister was adorned with finery. And not only was this bewitching imp dressed fit to kill, but she had swept her waist-length hair into a mass of shining curls, leaving wispy ringlets dangling around her oval face. Nacona wasn't the only man in the place who had been blinded by such radiant beauty. Some men cast speculative glances at July, while those who were less refined openly gawked at her.

Now what was that cunning sprite up to? Nacona asked himself warily. After the ultimatum he had delivered in a burst of bad temper, he knew she would retaliate in her ingenious way. It hadn't taken him long to determine that this hellion gave as good as she got. July was a natural-born competitor who met every challenge. She simply couldn't tolerate defeat. Nacona knew the feeling.

A frown plowed his brow when he noticed the bottle of champagne—July had drunk half of it—that graced the table. Ma Bell had certainly rolled out the red carpet for them. Nacona had made it a point to glean information from the townsfolk while he'd bathed, shaved, and had his shaggy mane clipped. He had expected to learn that Ma Bell was a shady character who disposed of her unwanted husbands when she tired of them. But his cynicism had turned out to be unjustified. According to all reports, Ma Bell was one of the most endearing, best-respected citizens in the small community. It seemed she just had a penchant for launching new romances and treating newlyweds like royalty. Nacona had also heard that Ma served meals that could leave mouths watering before and after the dinner hour. She was *that* good a cook! But her husbands hadn't died of overeating—or food poisoning. One had perished in a railroad accident, and the other had been stricken with a disease that called him to the pearly gates before his time.

Casting his wandering thoughts aside, Nacona tugged at the cuffs of his waistcoat and proceeded down the aisle. He was halfway to July's table when a vivacious, grayhaired woman intercepted him.

"You must be the new groom," Ma speculated as she bustled Nacona along beside her. "You certainly did well for yourself, didn't you? Not a man in the room has been able to take his eyes off your bride since she appeared like an angel from heaven." Her hazel eyes slid up and down Nacona's muscular torso. "And your bride didn't do too bad for herself, either. You make a handsome couple. Now, you just set yourself right down and I'll bring out your plates. I always did say good food was the foundation to a fruitful marriage and true love was the mortar that held the institution together."

Amusement glistened in Nacona's eyes as he sank down in the chair to watch Ma flit off with her customary

158

amount of energy. He rather liked being just a face in the crowd for a change. In fact, he'd signed the hotel register under an assumed name to ensure he drew no unnecessary attention. Nacona was known more by reputation than by sight, and he had decided to keep a low profile— or as low as he could with Ma treating him like a king and July like his reigning queen. Folks didn't take such a wide berth around him since they were unaware there was a shootist in their midst, and he had left his holsters in his saddlebags, opting to carry a concealed weapon. He looked rather respectable in his black waistcoat and breeches, even if he did say so himself.

July had intended to dazzle him with dignified charm, but she wound up staring at him in open appreciation. The garments he had donned fit his well-sculpted physique like a glove, accentuating his masculine assets. His face was devoid of whiskers, and his raven hair had been clipped in the style of a gentleman. There was still an air of wild nobility about him, but it was toned down by the veneer of sophistication. In fact, Nacona looked so dashingly handsome and elegant he was receiving plenty of admiring stares from the females present. He certainly could be a lady-killer if he had a mind to. July only hoped she wasn't within firing range if he declared open season on blondes.

To steady her nerves, she took another sip of champagne. She was contemplating the inevitable encounter with Nacona. She intended to keep her wits about her, but she saw no harm in taking the edge off the experience with liquor. She had done a smashing good job of that already.

"You look breathtaking," Nacona complimented as he

raised his glass to toast his bride. His dark eyes never wavered as he sipped champagne and stared at her over the rim of his glass. "I'm honored that you took such pains to impress me, my lovely wife."

He had expected her to show up in breeches, making herself as unappealing as humanly possible. He had misjudged her tactics—again. This female was totally unpredictable.

"And you, my dear husband, look positively devastating," July countered.

Why had he strapped himself into the fancy trappings of a gentleman? she wondered suspiciously. What ploy was this? The last time she had seen Nacona he had been quite vindictive. Now masculine charm oozed from his pores. *Confusion* must be his strategy, July decided. He didn't want her to know what to think until he pounced on her. She cautiously reminded herself that beneath that fashionable coat and those trim-fitting trousers beat the heart of a lion. Nacona was up to something. She just hadn't figured out what.

When Ma reappeared with two heaping plates and rattled on about the magic of love, July glanced discreetly at Nacona from beneath a fan of thick lashes. He had settled into the role of the smitten husband for Ma's benefit. July played the adoring wife, just to prove she possessed some theatrical ability, and she conversed on a myriad of subjects when Ma left them, pretending she was with any other man who had escorted her to dinner.

And to her surprise, she found the evening immensely enjoyable. She was at ease without trying to be. She simply behaved like her old self, like a person who wasn't constantly countering the disdainful shootist she had met in Dodge City. And Nacona proved to be well informed and amusing when he wasn't trying to irritate her.

If July was having trouble figuring Nacona out, he was even more baffled. Here were no sassy retorts, no suffragist flags waving in the breeze. July was the epitome of good companionship and gracious charm. Nacona felt like Cinderella's prince wandering through some childhood tale. What was this crafty leprechaun trying to prove anyway? Surely she wasn't being nice to him for the sake of being nice. She had to have an ultimate purpose.

"If you're finished with your meal, let's return to our suite," July suggested.

Nacona did a double take. Just what the hell was going on? Was this an open invitation to resolve their bargain? If he weren't so suspicious of her, he would have grabbed her hand that very second and taken the steps two at a time in his haste to appease his long-harbored craving for her.

July's lashes fluttered down as she gracefully rose from her chair. Nervous though she was about the events that would take place when they were alone in their room, she projected an air of nonchalance. She would get through this night, somehow or other. And if she handled the situation cunningly, nothing might happen.

With Ma's best wishes resounding around her, July exited from the restaurant and peered up the flight of stairs. Nacona's hand gliding around her waist caused her to flinch. She swallowed down her heart when it polevaulted to her throat, and she mentally rehearsed what she planned to say to him. One way or another she would tame this tiger of a man, she promised herself. He was not going to gobble her alive.

Nacona spoke not a word as he escorted her to their suite. Anticipation was gnawing at him, but wariness called forth restraint. This gorgeous sprite was too keen minded to meekly succumb to him. She was up to something, and he was about to find out what.

When Nacona brushed against July in his attempt to open the door, he felt her tense. This was a carefully plotted charade, he decided. She was nervous as hell, though she was trying to disguise her true feelings. And within an hour, she would know exactly what she had to be nervous about because the tormenting wait would be over. At long last, Nacona was going to see his obsession merge with reality. The time of bargains paid in full had come. . . .

Chapter 11

The instant the door creaked open, July swept inside and pirouetted to face Nacona. Squaring her shoulders, she looked him straight in the eye, even though she was shaking on the inside.

"Nacona, I have a confession to make." She would appeal to his sense of decency with sincerity. Surely that would work. If it didn't, she would try an alternate tactic.

"I have always prided myself on possessing self-confidence. But when it comes to . . ." Here she faltered, striving for just the right effect. She cleared her throat and continued, "When it comes to intimacy with men." July inhaled deeply and slowly expelled a breath. "The truth is I feel terribly ignorant and inadequate in such a situation. However, I did agree to this bargain, and my sense of integrity demands that I keep it."

If only his sense of integrity will prompt him to disregard this damned bargain. July waited, but Nacona didn't speak when she gave him the chance. She hadn't really thought he would. Still, he did seem to be pondering her words like a reasonable, intelligent human being. That was a start.

"I have always thought the bond between husband and wife should be a sacred trust, a mutual admiration. Perhaps it is my own conscience which is rebelling against making a sacrilege of this marriage." July glanced down to hands tangled in the folds of her gown. "You and I have taken something which should be precious and special, and have bent it to suit our own purposes. I am ashamed of my part in these dealings with you, I truly am."

So far so good, July complimented herself. She was handling this uncomfortable situation superbly.

"Perhaps if we truly cared for each other the way a man and wife should, I wouldn't be battling such feelings of guilt and apprehension. Tonight at dinner I tried to be the kind of wife I expect a man would want."

Well, that should explain her behavior to his satisfaction. Her gaze swept up to meet his unblinking stare, and her fingers fumbled with the dainty buttons on the front of her gown, as if to dutifully undress.

"If and when I married, I pictured myself disrobing before my husband, offering myself to him, offering my affection to him above all others." July drew the gown away from her shoulders, leaving only her chemise to conceal her from his hawkish gaze. "I thought modesty and awkwardness would be forgotten in that moment, that I would welcome my husband's eyes on me for I would be his precious treasure, not a conquest."

That was really good! July congratulated herself. That should prey on Nacona's conscience, his sense of decency. "I would want my husband to realize that I was sacrificing all to him . . . willingly. I regret that, given the terms of our bargain, this cannot be what it should have been."

July pushed the gown past her hips until she was standing in a pool of green velvet. "But I won't resist you," she promised. Her lips trembled in apprehension, and she bit down on them in an effort to control her uneasiness. "And please don't hurt me, Nacona, even if I do deserve it for the hell I've put you through. Despite our conflict, I don't want tonight to become a nightmare. . . ."

Well, if that didn't beat all! Here stood this bewitching sprite, playing the martyr to the hilt. And here he stood, feeling as tall as a table leg for backing her into a corner and spouting ultimatums at her. July was an innocent maiden, a full-fledged lady; and they were hopelessly mismatched. He had known that from the very beginning, but damn it . . .

Nacona struggled to draw in a breath while his ravenous gaze flowed over her barely clad figure. He remembered that morning when he had come within a hairbreadth of paradise, and unappeased desire sizzled through him.

Maybe a gentleman would have folded his tent and honorably retreated, but Nacona did not aspire to be a gentleman. And a deal was a deal, no matter how this lovely nymph tried to sugar-coat the bargain with fancy words and meek glances. She was attempting to make him feel guilty, he realized. That was what she had been up to all along. But this time she was going to get exactly what she deserved, and he would derive excessive pleasure from seeing that she did.

And yet, when July peered apprehensively up at him, requesting gentleness and understanding, he felt himself waver. That soulful look of hers cut right to the bone. Nacona had been unscrupulous in his dealings with her, he knew. He had made unreasonable demands. The noble thing to do would be to turn around and walk out. Unfortunately, he wasn't noble!

When he continued to stare pensively at her, measuring every square inch of her with those probing ebony eyes, July shifted nervously from one foot to the other. Lord, the tension in the room was so thick it was suffocating her. Her legs wobbled like a newborn foal's. Since Nacona hadn't turned around and walked out, she was forced to meet his terms. Marshaling her courage, she moved toward the bed to fold back the quilts. Gracefully, she eased herself down and waited, while butterflies fluttered about riotously in her stomach.

Nacona's expression gave none of his thoughts away. Only when he leisurely shrugged off his jacket and draped it over the back of the chair did July realize that her colloquy truly had been for naught. He had every intention of staying to take what she had promised him. She hadn't talked him out of a blasted thing.

When his shirt joined his jacket, July found herself staring helplessly at the wide expanse of his hair-matted chest. Her pulse leapfrogged through her veins when he tugged his breeches from his hips. She well remembered that unsettling moment when he had bounded up from his tub to shock her out of screaming her head off. It was no less shocking now to see him looming over her, wearing nothing but the faintest hint of a smile. Her face flushed beet red, but her eyes clung to him, marveling at his rippling muscles and the bold evidence of his . . .

July swallowed hard when Nacona sauntered toward her with masculine grace. Nacona Bleu was many things, some of which July didn't approve, but he was a most

166

impressive specimen of a man. Not a woman on the planet who would argue with that, especially not while she was staring at every magnificent inch of him. Nacona's dynamic masculinity seemed to enfold her as if with invisible tentacles. July was all too aware of this breathtaking mountain of a man. "You can't talk your way out of my arms this time," he told her as he towered over her. An amused smile quirked his lips as his eyes slid over her in bold, visual possession. "But it was a nice try, July. . . ."

When Nacona eased down beside her and wrapped her in those swarthy arms, July melted. Suddenly she was caught in the same spell that had overcome her in Dodge. She wanted to know this remarkably complicated man as she knew no other. She wanted him to unveil the mysteries of passion to her, to pleasure her as he once had, if only briefly, before he subjected her to complete masculine possession. Instinctively, she reached out to limn the hard-rock wall of his chest, remembering with vivid clarity the morning he had allowed her to touch him before they were interrupted.

Nacona swore he deserved a medal for lying there and allowing this inquisitive nymph to touch him familiarly. It sure was hard on his self-control. Desire pounded through him, leaving him throbbing in every fiber of his being. When her slim fingers cruised over his shoulder and rose to trace the curve of his lips, Nacona became ravenous for the taste of her. He could hold himself in check no longer. He wanted to feel those petal-soft lips beneath his, to lie with her, flesh to flesh.

A tiny moan bubbled from July's throat when his full lips descended on hers. His mouth was warm and faintly demanding as it slanted over hers—probing, exploring, evoking erotic sensations that she had only just begun to discover a week earlier. A hot sweet ache blazed in the core of her and her body began to throb in places she didn't remember having. When his hands slid beneath the straps of her chemise, languidly removing the garment from the path of his exploring caresses, wild tingles flew up and down her spine. His lips left hers to greet every inch of flesh he had exposed, his warm breath sensitizing her body by tantalizing degrees. Fingertips encircled the thrusting peaks of her breasts before his tongue flicked at their dusky crests. When he drew the buds into his mouth, July gasped at the scintillating sensations that splintered through her.

When his hands drifted down her ribs to stroke the ultrasensative flesh of her inner thighs, July honestly wondered if she would survive the devastatingly tender assault. His gentle patience amazed her, baffled her. There was nothing rough or forceful about Nacona. His lazy seduction hypnotized her. He was deliberately and effectively crumbling her defenses, banishing all thought from her mind. He teased and tantalized her until her innocent body became a shell that housed a maelstrom of soul-shattering yearnings. His slow exploration and practiced touch tormented and satisfied. But for each hungry ache he appeased, a multitude of unexplainable needs burgeoned from out of nowhere.

Aware of the sensual threat of his powerful body, of the intimacy he promised with each heart-stopping kiss and mind-boggling caress, July no longer feared him. Her nerves hummed, and her body glowed with indefinable pleasure as he tasted and touched her with skillful expertise. Helplessly, she arched toward his seeking hands and lips, giving whatever he asked, in return asking only that he make her maddening hunger go away.

When his hands glided over her thighs and guided her legs apart, spasms of pleasure ribboned through July, intensifying until her entire body quaked in response. His knowing fingers delved into her womanly softness to excite and arouse, and she forgot how to breathe and why she even needed to. His hands and lips seemed to be everywhere at once, stimulating every sensitive point on her body. He knew how to send her senses reeling. She felt the warm draft of his breath, heard the quiet compliments that testified to his desire for her. The world shrank to the space she and this seductive wizard occupied, and she surrendered in hopeless abandon.

An uncontrollable tremor riveted her as he plied her with tormenting kisses and caresses. She clutched him desperately, consumed by needs she couldn't even begin to understand. "Nacona, please . . ." she whispered raggedly.

It thrilled Nacona to know he had brought her pleasure, that he had made her want him as wildly as he wanted her. The women in his past had never really mattered all that much, but this jewel-eyed goddess mattered more than she should. It aroused him to watch her, to know that she experienced erotic pleasure. To her, every touch was unique and new. And in return for her innocence, he brought to her the gift of unparalleled gentleness, a sensitivity to her needs, and an attentiveness to her newly awakened desires. Nacona had never given so much of himself. He realized that to him July was a priceless treasure, not a conquered prize. The very thought of how precious this moment was caused him to tremble beneath the weight of his responsibility to the innocent in his arms. This was her first encounter with passion. It was within his power to influence her impression of lovemaking.

Bearing that in mind, Nacona worshipped her with his hands and lips, drawing responses from her untutored body, while his own need burned within him. He tested the moistness of her, and he ached to bury himself in the silken heat of her desire.

"Nacona?" Wide, astonished eyes focused on him as a convulsive shudder undulated through her, making her gasp in wonder.

"Do you want me, love?" he rasped as his lips feathered over the tips of her breasts like fluttering butterfly wings. "Not because of the bargain, July, but because of the rapturous pleasures we can bestow on each other." Nacona lifted his raven head to stare into her passion-drugged eyes. "This isn't about bargains anymore. It's about you and me and the hungry needs we arouse in each other."

July watched unblinkingly as his sinewy body glided over hers. His hands migrated over her quivering flesh, setting off more sparks that ignited raging fires. When his knee was insinuated between her legs and she felt the velvet sheath of his manhood gliding across her thigh, a breathless moan tumbled from her lips.

"Must I say the words?" she whispered brokenly. "Surely you know when your other lovers—"

"I remember no one but you," he assured her huskily.

Oddly enough, he didn't. He had undergone a drastic transformation. With this innocent nymph it was as if he had just discovered the meaning of unbridled desire, though he'd once thought he knew all there was to know. This enchanting angel played havoc with his body. The sensations that gripped him exceeded all physical boundaries. They touched emotions he never knew existed. This was like a glimpse of paradise—a spendorous new dimension that defied time, space, and explanation. Nacona was first experiencing the difference between physical appeasement and sensual lovemaking.

With a tormented groan, he settled upon her pliant body, aching to appease his need. He felt July flinch at his penetration and clutch his forearms. Sensing her pain, he longed to banish it, to recapture the pleasure she had just begun to experience before he'd possessed her. Ever so slowly, he moved within her, until she relaxed and instinctively arched up to meet him.

Suddenly the sharp stab of pain was no more than a dim memory compared to the kaleidoscope of everchanging sensations channeling through her. July knew she was about to die. No one could withstand such intense pleasure and live to tell about it. Sweet mercy! Was this what she had dreaded and schemed to avoid? This miraculous pleasure that left her spiraling in wild, fiery ecstasy?

The hazy world split asunder as one incredible sensation after another riveted July. Her body was ablaze and her soul suddenly cast off the hindering garment of the flesh to soar. Like an eagle testing its wings for the very first time, she let go of every last inhibition and glided in motionless flight.

Nacona's swarthy arms crushed her to him as he shuddered above her and gasped for breath. July could feel the thundering beat of his pulse, the ragged draft of breath against her cheek. It was as if they were not only flesh to flesh but soul to soul, sailing somewhere beyond the horizon of reality, their hearts beating in perfect harmony. And then the wind beneath her wings stilled and she was spiraling downward to bob on the hazy sea of contentment.

Even later, when the fog of rapture lifted, July still felt she was drifting, and she marveled at the pleasure that lingered in the dreamy aftereffects of passion. She lay limp and drowsy in Nacona's encircling arms, her cheeks flushed with the blush of satisfaction, her breath whispering softly against his sturdy shoulder.

"My goodness," she said with a shaky sigh, "is it always like this?"

That was a loaded question. If Nacona said yes, July would assume he was calling upon past experiences. That would offend her. If he answered no, he would imply that what they had shared was rare and special to him. He wasn't sure he wanted to admit anything of the kind to a woman like July. To do so would be like aiding and abetting one's enemy. The fact that nothing he had ever known had been this sweet or lasted this long rattled Nacona. In the past, he had gone through the paces of passion at play for the sole purpose of appeasing his sexual appetite. He had always been eager to be on his own way after the sensations ebbed. Now he couldn't even move. His strength, his will to leave this angel's arms, were nonexistent! What in the name of heaven had come over him?

"I was under the impression that when—" July was cut off by a silencing kiss.

Nacona didn't want to analyze the sensations that assaulted him. The way he had responded, one would have thought this was his first encounter with passion. But that was laughable, Nacona chalked up his excessive craving for this delectable beauty to his long abstinence. He knew that when he made wild sweet love to her again he would finally be satisfied, the mystical spell would shatter, and he could put his affair with July back into proper perspective.

Astounded by this midnight-haired rake's second siege on her body, July swore every ounce of energy had been spent, that it would take hours to recover her strength. But in no time at all, the now-familiar fires were again smoldering. And this time July employed seductive tactics on him, discovering each place he liked to be touched. She familiarized herself with every square inch of his muscular body, inventing tantalizing ways for a woman to please and satisfy a man.

She delighted in her newfound power over this Goliath, and his responses encouraged her to explore the dimensions of passion, her fingertips drifting to his flat belly and beyond. . . .

When her hand brushed against his bold manhood, Nacona gasped for air, but his lungs had collapsed. He had given this curious imp license to do what she would, but at the price of self-control. Her touch had set off a chain reaction that left desire rumbling within him.

Sensations hammered at him like hailstones, leaving him to wonder at his unexpected vulnerability. He had foolishly assumed a woman needed scads of experience to satisfy a man, but July instinctively knew how to turn him into a human torch, and when her whispering kisses drifted over his chest and belly, Nacona swore he had suffered heart seizure. July was doing impossible things with her hands and lips. Her touch was tender yet tormenting, and he wanted her so badly he was shaking!

When Nacona rolled sideways to draw her body under his, July peered up into the glowing coals of his eyes. She could see her own emotions mirrored in them—the obsessive wanting, the undeniable hunger. Her arms lifted and she raked her fingers through the thick mass of raven hair that capped his head, drawing his lips to hers as she arched to meet his lean, muscled body as he came to her.

It was a wild coming together, an explosion of the senses, an overflow of indefinable sensations. July reveled in the pleasure. She was a meteor blazing across the heavens, consumed by white-hot fires that signaled her own destruction. Shudder after convulsive shudder wracked her when Nacona clutched her to him and trembled in helpless release. For this one glorious moment, there were no conflicts between them, only sweet satisfaction.

In the aftermath of love, Nacona cradled her against him, marveling at the tide of possessiveness that washed over him. Making love to July had soothed his troubled soul and brought a sense of inner peace. It was a shame there were only a few short hours left to hold her, to relive the magic they had discovered. Very soon, reality would intrude and they would board the train bound for Denver. He wished they had more time to build upon this fragile bond their lovemaking had created between them.

As he listened to July's rhythmic breathing, he stared pensively into the darkness. He felt changed somehow. He couldn't quite puzzle out why. Something about this vixen made it impossible to remain emotionally unattached. He never felt in complete control when he was with July. She was too keen-witted, too vital, too much like him in some ways and yet diametrically different in others. He couldn't quite explain what he was experiencing, even to himself. A warm, unfamiliar feeling flickered in his soul and tugged at his heart. He felt vulnerable when he really wasn't. He had been bedeviled, and he knew it. He was . . .

Nacona shook his head and relinquished his deep thoughts. Whatever the cause of these unaccountable sensations, he was going to have to get himself in hand—and soon. If he went lollygagging about like a starry-eyed schoolboy he might well have to retire from his dangerous profession. Every would-be gunslinger was out to test his skill. He couldn't afford to be so damned distracted by this bewitching siren that he wound up riddled with lead.

Yes, he and this curvaceous elf had certainly come together, but he couldn't allow their encounter to distract him. Until he found his brother's killer, he had to hold firm to his objective, his convictions. If he traveled far enough, long enough, he would eventually locate Shandin's murderer. The mysterious assassin would know Nacona on sight, but Nacona couldn't recognize him. It was maddening, not knowing his enemy except by name. Charley Brazil . . . And that name could be an alias, Nacona reminded himself. Where was that bastard? Had he changed his appearance—his name? Was Charley Brazil even alive?

When July sighed in her sleep and cushioned her head against his chest as if he were her pillow, his gaze dipped to the tangled blond hair that cascaded over his arm. A tender smile hovered on his lips as his eyes wandered freely over her shadowed form. God, how could this vivacious bundle of femininity keep setting off such a myriad of emotions inside him? *She* was the one who had lost her innocence, but *he* felt like a different man!

"In answer to your question, my curious little imp," he murmured ever so softly, so as not to wake her, "lovemaking was never like this before. And if only . . ."

His voice trailed off. He and July had found their place in the sun, but sometimes sunlight casts shadows. Some lives simply aren't destined to be united. It was bad enough that this rambunctious beauty had touched his carefully guarded heart. Things would have been much simpler if that had not happened. But life had never been simple for Nacona. He just didn't seem to have that sort of luck. . . .

Chapter 12

July was chagrined to find that the accommodations on the train bound for Denver offered little in the way of comfort and no luxury whatsoever. On the second-class day coach she and Nacona were forced to sleep in their seats. They managed to settle into semicomfortable positions and dozed off once or twice, but each time they nodded off, the train invariably paused at one of the tank towns or whistle stops that dotted the western route, jostling them awake.

To contribute to her discomfort, July had noticed Nacona's quiet, remote attitude toward her. Oh, he hadn't ridiculed her or taunted her the way he usually did. He wasn't that obvious. But it seemed that once their lovemaking was over, it was business as usual for him. According to her perception, Nacona hadn't experienced the same degree of pleasure she had found in his arms. That had to be it, she reasoned, casting him a discreet glance. He was accustomed to skilled paramours, and she was still a novice. It was depressing to realize she had begun to feel a tenderness for him, yet he was unaffected by their intimacy. Suddenly everything had changed between them—at least on her part—and she felt awkward and on edge.

July was jolted from her musings when the train abruptly screeched to a halt, flinging her forward and mashing her face against the seat in front of her. She and every other passenger peered out the window to determine what had caused the delay.

"Buffaloes!" someone bugled from the rear of the car.

To July's amazement, men from all walks of life grabbed their pistols and rifles and pushed open the windows. And to her further astonishment they began to blast away at the herd that grazed on either side of the tracks.

July was on her feet in a single bound, raging at the top of her lungs while Nacona sat there and stared at her as if she were insane. "Stop this madness at once!" she trumpeted.

Her loud, high-pitched voice served its purpose. The bushwhackers paused to gape at her.

"Don't you realize that buffalo hunters are wiping out these herds, that this entire species is on the verge of extinction?" she shouted in outrage. "Yet here you are, supposedly sensible, civilized men, taking potshots at those animals for pure sport. And what is to become of those creatures you have killed, crippled, and wounded?"

"July, sit down and shut up. You're making a scene," Nacona muttered, pulling his hat over his face as he sank a little deeper into his seat.

July had no intention of quieting down. She was just getting up steam. "I have heard it said that Indian tribes find a use for every square inch of those animals and that they hunt only enough of them to provide food, clothing, and shelter. But not you. You engage in senseless slaughter and leave the carcasses to rot—for no other reason than to boast that you felled a buffalo. If you were the men you think you are, you'd march out there and take your chances with those creatures, give them a sporting chance instead of sitting here and shooting at them. I have never seen anything so disgusting."

"July . . ." Nacona's voice held a hint of warning that she flagrantly ignored. He never knew what was going to come out of this woman's mouth, and once she got on one of her rampages she wouldn't stop.

"In my opinion, there should be a law against such useless slaughter," July spouted. "And I intend to see that there—"

A shriek burst from her lips when the locomotive surged off, flinging her off balance. To her shock and humiliation, she flipped backward over the seat and landed on the lap of one of the men who had been ambushing buffaloes.

Stifling an amused grin, Nacona swerved around to pluck July up in his arms and deposit her in her original seat. "How are you related to Susan B. Anthony and the other suffragists who spout reform and hold forth on one issue after the other?" Nacona mocked as he rearranged the squished bonnet that sat askew on her head.

July settled herself in her seat with as much dignity as the situation permitted, straightening her gown. "I do not think I should have to sit by and watch senseless killing and mutilation," she proclaimed self-righteously.

"Well, you made your point, honey," he said snidely

179

before settling back to catch forty winks. "You got the attention of every passenger in the car. Of course, they all think you're a lunatic."

"I suppose you think I'm deranged as well," she muttered.

Nacona tipped his hat up just far enough to meet her gaze. His dark eyes twinkled with teasing humor. "I knew you were demented the moment you barged into my bath and had me herded off to jail for sins I hadn't even committed."

July squared her shoulders and stared straight ahead. Her chin tilted to that proud angle Nacona had come to recognize at a glance. "I'm sorry if I embarrassed you. And I will understand perfectly if you prefer that no one knows I'm your wife."

The fact that he *did* like everyone knowing she was his wife had been bothering him since the night they were wed. He shouldn't have cared, considering this was only a temporary arrangement. But damn it to hell, he did. This sassy little firebrand was really beginning to get to him. He wasn't accustomed to the multitude of emotions she stirred in him, and he was trying very hard not to let sentiment cloud his thinking. This was a business arrangement, he reminded himself for the umpteenth time. No ties to bind. That was the bargain.

When he didn't bother to respond to her comment, depression closed in on July. She knew this self-reliant man had no need of a wife. But she had hoped . . .

Don't expect more from this kind of man than he is capable of giving, she cautioned herself. She wasn't a silly romantic with stars in her eyes. She knew Nacona was hell-bent on his own purpose of finding his brother's murderer. He had confided that much to her. So why did she keep thinking of him as her husband, her soul mate? It was absurd, and she'd only get hurt if she started seeing things in this raven-haired rogue that weren't really there.

July was allowed to wallow in her disturbing thoughts for only a quarter of an hour. The piercing whistle of the locomotive indicated they were approaching a round-house. The instant the train screeched to a halt, passengers practically trampled over each other to purchase their late breakfast or early lunch. It really didn't matter which. The meals were all the same along the line—beefsteak, fried eggs, and fried potatoes—morning, noon and night.

The express train on which they traveled did not compare to the accommodations July had enjoyed when she'd left Kansas City almost a month earlier. She had traveled first-class, partaking of meals prepared by Pullman chefs and served by waiters in the dining car. In that luxurious car July had savored a twelve-course meal that was comparable to the fine cuisine served in big city restaurants. Of course, the Hotel Express had sleeping cars equipped with hinged berths to allow passengers to sleep in a prone position, and morning parlors accorded the luxury of sitting on a tufted couch rather than hard wooden seats that numbed the backside and left kinks in the spine.

Sighing heavily, July rose to her feet to follow Nacona down the aisle. What was left of her good disposition evaporated. When the whistle tooted and the conductor's trumpetlike voice urged all passengers to climb aboard, she had consumed only half her meal at the roundhouse, yet she was expected to forgo the food to return to her seat.

When July opened her mouth to protest, Nacona jerked her to her feet. "If you didn't find it necessary to chew every morsel twenty times you'd be finished already," he told her as he marched her toward the steps.

"Had I known I would have to swallow my food like a python, I would have," July grumbled sourly.

He turned her to face him, forcing the other passengers to swerve around them to board the train. "What's really bothering you, July?" he demanded. "You've been on one crusade or another all morning."

"Nothing is bothering me," she snapped, more harshly than she'd intended. "I'm perfectly fine, but thank you so much for your concern."

Dark, probing eyes sought out the secrets of her soul. "What is it? Does it have something to do with last night?"

It had everything to do with the lingering sensations and tender feelings that July knew were one-sided. Blast it, she was trying to cope, and she did not need Nacona's prodding.

Refusing to respond to his question, July wormed free. With snickers to the right of her and chuckles to the left of her she stalked off, ignoring the clump of men who were whispering behind her back.

"Your wife, I presume."

Nacona half-turned to see the rotund gentleman who was leisurely puffing on a corncob pipe. Pale blue eyes glistened up at him as Nacona nodded affirmatively to the comment.

"Feisty little thing, isn't she?" the well-dressed gentleman observed as he ambled along beside Nacona.

"As feisty as they come," Nacona agreed.

"Well, if a man's going to have a wife at all, better that she has some spunk. But you, my good man, have your work cut out for you."

Didn't he just! Nacona shook his head and expelled a sigh. He couldn't imagine how he was going to keep that spitfire under his thumb during the investigation, short of nailing her lovely hide to a tree. July MacKenzie Bleu had the kind of fiery spirit that wouldn't quit. Her dainty, sophisticated exterior was damned deceiving. She was a rabble-rouser through and through. What had he let himself in for? It was bad enough that he was having difficulty in dealing with their personal relationship. That, compounded with a criminal investigation, would be trouble enough. For certain, Nacona was going to have to lay down a few laws for that headstrong female—if July wasn't going to get killed by going off half-cocked as she had a habit of doing. He could see her sniffing out rustlers and thieves with daring panache. It was a scary thought. He must have lost the good sense he'd been born with when he'd agreed to team up with that blond-haired terror in blue silk.

Gresham MacKenzie raced his buggy through the entrance of the family estate situated on the outskirts of Kansas City. A look of irritation was stamped on his handsome features as he stormed up the steps and into the foyer. The eldest MacKenzie skidded to a halt in front of his two younger brothers, who were conversing over an after-dinner brandy.

183

"What's up, Gresh?" Calvin questioned, frowning at the unpleasant expression that puckered his brother's brow.

"That's what I'd like to know," Gresham muttered grouchily. He jerked open the letter and slammed it down on the end table. "Have a look for yourselves."

Ethan and Calvin put their heads together to read the missive. Their green eyes widened in disbelief, and they simultaneously glanced up at Gresham who was looming in front of them like a thundercloud.

"Aunt Betty sends her love to the *four* of us?" Ethan croaked.

Gresham nodded grimly. "Sounds a mite suspicious, doesn't it?"

Calvin bounded to his feet and strode across the walnut-paneled study to paw through the stack of letters on the desk as if he were a dog unearthing a bone. Having found what he was looking for, he whizzed back to his brothers. "According to July's last telegram, she was having a wonderful time in Wichita."

"She's probably having a *time* all right," Gresham scowled. "But it isn't in Wichita, visiting Aunt Betty." He dug into his pocket again to reveal another telegram. "Now take a look at this. I received it just before I left the office this evening."

Again, Calvin's and Ethan's narrowed eyes swept over the message. "July plans to extend her vacation a few more weeks?" Calvin snorted.

"Her vacation? Where?" Ethan grumbled.

"That mischievous little imp!" Gresham exploded. "You don't suppose she's gone off to take an assignment without our permission?"

184

"As if you even have to ask," Calvin growled. "You know damned well she has. Why else would she be using Aunt Betty as a cover?" He glared at the eldest MacKenzie. "And it's your fault that she's hoodwinked us."

"*My* fault?" Gresham hooted.

"Yes, yours," Ethan chimed in. "She's been straining against confinement for months and you refused to let her do anything except dig through law books for your court cases and interview witnesses."

"Well, I didn't see you and Calvin offering her any substantial assignment," Gresham protested hotly. "I thought we all agreed to keep July away from dangerous cases. You know perfectly well how she enjoys throwing herself into her work. Even though we did train her to use weapons and teach her other techniques of self-defense, I had no intention of allowing her in situations that could call for her to utilize that training."

"From the look of things, she's thrown herself into harm's way *somewhere*, and only God knows where." Ethan scowled.

"It is my opinion that we should all track her down," Gresham announced. "The verdict on the Fredricks case just came in this afternoon, so I'm free to leave town."

"We wound up our last assignment this morning," Ethan informed his oldest brother. Then he gestured toward the half-empty glasses of brandy. "We were celebrating."

"Good," Gresham paced the room, thinking aloud as he went. "We'll have those telegrams traced first thing in the morning and find out what July is up to—and where. That will give us time to pack this evening. Tomorrow we'll be on the first train to wherever she was when she

185

sent the telegrams. And when I get my hands on our cunning little sister—"

"You have to wait in line," Calvin assured him as he leaped to his feet to collect his belongings.

"Having a grand time at Aunt Betty's, indeed." Ethan snorted. "She'll think *grand time* when we get our hands on her!"

All three men barreled up the spiral staircase, then whizzed into their respective rooms to pack for their journey. And that evening, not one of the MacKenzie clan was thinking nice thoughts about their younger sister. July had deceived them and they didn't take kindly to that.

"Your husband?" C. L. Chambers croaked when July made the introductions in the elite executive car at the Denver depot. "You said Bleu would be working with you on this assignment, but I had no idea that a lady like you would be married to—"

"Don't you think a man in my profession can have a wife?" Nacona growled defensively, causing the haughty Cheyenne banker to retreat a pace.

"Well, of course, you can," C.L. bleated as he tugged at his cravat to relieve the discomfort of having a man like Nacona Bleu stare him down. "But with your reputation with a pistol and your—" He bit down on his runaway tongue and averted his gaze from those stony black eyes. "That is to say . . ."

George Hershberger stepped forward to save C.L. from stuffing his other foot in his mouth. "Nacona, I don't know if you remember me or not, but I hired you to take an assignment for the railroad almost two years ago while you were a detective who accepted assignments from the Pinkerton Agency. Do you recall the train robberies in Missouri?"

Nacona glanced at the tall, thin gentleman who had passed the half-century mark. "I remember. It's good to see you again, George."

So that was why George's eyes had lit up during that first conference when July dropped Nacona's name, July thought. George had changed his tune in a hurry when she'd promised that Nacona would be working with her, if they were given the assignment.

"Why don't we all sit down?" George gestured toward the red velvet wing-backed chairs that lined the luxurious private car utilized by the railroad executives. "We were quite pleased that you and your wife agreed to come to our assistance. The sad state of affairs in Wyoming demands immediate attention."

"My bank has been robbed twice in the last three months, and I want those scoundrels behind bars as quickly as possible," C.L. blurted out. Tact, it seemed, was not one of his virtues.

After casting C.L. a silencing glance, George continued, "Because of this rash of train and bank robberies between Cheyenne and Laramie, my company and several of the bankers in the area decided to form an alliance and hire investigators. The dangerous nature of this assignment requires a man of your capabilities and expertise, Nacona. We're not even certain what kind of men we're dealing with or how they operate."

George offered Nacona a drink from their stock of whiskey. "There also seems to be a ring of cattle rustlers operating in the area. These thefts and robberies are playing havoc with the economy in Wyoming and cutting wide gashes in Union Pacific's profit."

"I had to shut down my bank when alarmed citizens demanded their money after the last holdup," C.L. interrupted. The man simply couldn't keep his mouth shut for more than a minute.

"Do you have some particular method of investigation in mind?" Nacona addressed George, ignoring C.L. as much as possible.

George nodded his gray head and settled back to nurse his brandy. "One of the local ranchers in the area lost his life during a rustling incident two weeks ago. Since Bob Foster was heavily indebted to Chambers Bank for cattle loans, the property falls back to C.L. With his permission, you can utilize the ranch just outside Cheyenne as your headquarters. I think it best if you infiltrate the area as a would-be cattleman. Although your name and reputation are well known, I hope you can convince the local citizens that you have decided to settle down on your new property and assume another profession. And since you have married, the setup should provide a perfect cover."

Nacona nodded agreeably. George was very methodic in his arrangements, just as he had been when they had discussed the situation in Missouri. George Hershberger was in charge of the railroad's detective forces. He had previously served with the Chicago police. Nacona liked the man, and he respected George's opinions and suggestions. As for C. L. Chambers, Nacona could find little use for the pompous dandy who flaunted his extravagant wealth by wearing jeweled rings and flamboyant clothes that had undoubtedly been imported from the East.

George dug into his vest pocket and extracted a certificate which he handed to Nacona. "I also thought it might be a good idea if we presented you with a few credentials. The U.S. Census Bureau is hiring men to gather livestock statistics in the West. I took the liberty of volunteering you for the assignment. I hope you don't mind. I thought you would be able to inspect other ranches and holding pens along the railroad without drawing suspicion."

"You're very thorough," Nacona complimented with a wry- smile.

George broke into a grin that affected every feature on his wrinkled face. "I'm highly paid to be. And I wanted to provide a reasonable excuse as to why you are riding the rails up and down the Union Pacific lines that have been under siege the past few months. The more logical your reasons for appearing in Cheyenne, the less suspicion you'll arouse. With your lovely wife to verify your reason for seeking a new occupation, I cannot imagine who would dispute you. You should be able to come and go as you please, posing all sorts of pertinent questions."

July slumped in her chair. She'd had visions of being equally involved in this conference. But it seemed George viewed her as nothing more than a convincing prop. Blast it, what did she have to do to be recognized as a working member of this partnership—round up a ring of rustlers single-handed?

George reached into his left vest pocket to retrieve a stack of bank notes. "Considering your efficiency on your last assignment for Union Pacific, the president of the company has offered you a generous fee. The railroad's share of your payment is five thousand dollars in advance. Of course, the bounty on any outlaws you take into custody will be yours as well, just as before. C.L. and the other area bankers have collected three thousand dollars for expenses and fees."

July's eyes popped. My goodness, Nacona's name and reputation afforded him tremendous wages. Even her own brothers weren't accustomed to receiving such astronomical fees.

"Well, July, do you think the salary and the arrangements are satisfactory?" Nacona questioned.

The wonderful man! July could have squeezed the stuffing out of him for asking. Until this moment she had virtually been ignored. Nacona had been aware that her pride had been smarting because he was in the limelight and she was in his shadow. He was sensitive to her needs and her moods. That pleased her. Even if he felt no true affection for her, at least he didn't treat her like an inferior just because she had been born a woman.

"I think the fee is reasonable. But I suggest we draw up a contract, to protect all parties concerned."

Nacona grinned to himself. The lawyer in July was bursting at the seams. No doubt, she would volunteer to write up the legal document, if only to show these men that she was more than just a pretty face. Nacona couldn't begrudge her that. He had taken women for granted himself until this high-strung, keen-witted sprite showed up to confound his theories about the fairer sex.

"Then we have a deal?" George asked hopefully.

"A deal," Nacona confirmed with a handshake. "July will prepare the document and we will return it to you before your train leaves Denver."

George drew his timepiece from his pocket and stared thoughtfully at it. "We were scheduled to leave for Cheyenne in two hours. Do you suppose we could have the contract in hand by then?"

"I'll see to it immediately," July promised.

"I hope you understand that we cannot offer you the luxuries of our private train," George apologized. "If you were traveling with us, it might draw unnecessary suspicion."

Nacona shrugged nonchalantly. "We'll arrive in Cheyenne in a few days. We will need ample time to gather a few supplies to lend credence to our intention of taking over the operation of the ranch."

After another round of handshakes, July and Nacona stepped from the private car to locate a room for the night. She was thinking nothing but nice thoughts about Nacona as they ambled down the street. Even though George and C.L. had focused their attention on the famed detective, Nacona had made them aware of July's presence and of the importance of her opinion. And just why had he done that? He had been remote and distant for the better part of two days. Had the gesture been just an act for the dignitaries' benefit? July's shoulders slumped when logic told her it had.

"Nacona Bleu, is that really you?"

July glanced up to see a buxom redhead moving toward them, her painted face aglow with delight. Suddenly she wasn't thinking kind thoughts about Nacona. Unreasonable jealousy knifed through her.

"Hello, Lilian." Nacona got the greeting out the instant before he became the recipient of an overzealous hug.

"What brings you back to Denver? Another dangerous assignment?" Lilian smiled conspiratorially.

July was certain the redhead never even noticed her. Lilian was all over Nacona, like ivy on a trellis.

"Excuse me." July wedged past the chummy couple who were blocking traffic on the boardwalk. "I have to rent a room at a reputable hotel and see to the contract."

Before Nacona could call her back, she had threaded her way through the crowd. It was just as well, Nacona assured himself. He and July needed a few hours apart. He had been having trouble keeping his emotions on an even keel when it came to that bewitching blonde, and she had been spoiling for a fight since her protest of the buffalo hunt.

"Come have a drink with me, Nacona." Lilian steered him down the street. "I have a few free hours on my hands this evening." Her brown eyes twinkled with unspoken suggestions as to what they could do with their time after they finished their drinks.

Nacona entertained thoughts of accommodating the shapely dance-hall queen who ran her own establishment in Denver. He had met Lilian shortly after Shandin's death. She had been in her late twenties the first time he'd arrived in town. Lilian had been the mistress of more than one gold magnate who operated in the Denver area, and she and Nacona had enjoyed a brief but satisfying affair while he'd been on assignment in Colorado.

Now Lilian had appeared at a time when Nacona was trying to evaluate his relationship with that green-eyed nymph. He needed to spend some intimate moments with Lilian to remind himself that his arrangement with July was purely business and would be concluded with their investigation.

As far as Nacona knew, the only sure-fire method for a man to recover from a fascination with one woman was to distract himself with another. And that was exactly what he should do. July had wanted a marriage in name only and had only agreed to his terms because of her fierce desire to make a name for herself with the Wyoming case. He needed to assure her that *no woman* would ever lead him around by the nose. He had no intention whatsoever of becoming emotionally involved.

It was for the best, Nacona lectured himself. Hell, if he didn't watch himself he might wind up falling in love with that wild-hearted harridan. Now that would be the last straw! Him in love? Nacona scoffed at the absurdity of it. He could no more imagine himself in love than he had been able to imagine himself married to that gorgeous sprite. But now that he was—albeit temporarily—he had been a little too comfortable with the outlandish idea. It was high time he remembered his primary objective in life—avenging Shandin's death. And until he found that shrewd bastard who had dropped out of sight, he wasn't going to lose track of that purpose. Who knew? That murderer might be swaggering down the street of Denver at this very moment.

After his tête-à-tête with Lilian, Nacona would check the wanted posters at the sheriff's office, just as he always did when he arrived in a different town. If he was lucky, he might come upon an outlaw in the area who matched Charlie Brazil's sketchy description, even if the name on the wanted poster didn't match. Nacona was always on the lookout for that sly fugitive, and it was easier to keep his mind on business when July wasn't underfoot. She always caused momentary lapses in his sanity.

Out of sight and out of mind, Nacona told himself sensibly. Lilian was going to help him forget that curvaceous blonde.

Chapter 13

With a furious curse, July crumpled her attempt at writing out the terms of the contract and then hurled the unsatisfactory effort into the wastebasket. Unjustified jealousy was clouding her thinking and coloring her thoughts. She damned Nacona and his incurable case of wandering eye. His response to Lilian testified to the fact that what she and he had shared was nothing special. He'd just reacted to her the same way he did to everything in skirts. Nacona Bleu was, and always would be, a womanizer, the unscrupulous kind of man her brothers had always warned her away from.

When Nacona saw a familiar face in Denver, off he went to renew an old acquaintance, latching onto his former paramour without the slightest consideration for July's feelings. It had been obvious that Nacona had known the redhead before, and in the most familiar sense. He had mentioned that he had been on assignment in Denver earlier in his career, but July hadn't considered how she would react to meeting one of his lovers face-to-face.

Damn it, how could that dark-eyed devil be so cognizant of her needs one minute and so infuriatingly inconsiderate the next? Curse him. If he felt anything—anything at all—for her he would have followed after her, wouldn't he? Well, of course he would, even if July *had* granted him license to do whatever he pleased with whomever he pleased, whenever he pleased.

Heaving an exasperated sigh, July glanced at the blank paper. She had only thirty minutes to draw up the legal agreement and return the contract to George Hershberger's private car. Concentrate on the business at hand, she ordered herself. Forget that rat Nacona Bleu and his redheaded courtesan.

Determinedly, July formulated her thoughts and committed them to paper. With no time to spare, she folded the document and zoomed down the hall. Like a shot, she whizzed down the darkened street, deftly dodging passersby in her haste to keep her appointment at the depot.

"Why didn't your husband accompany you?" C. L. Chambers questioned with his customary lack of tact. "I have a few pieces of information to convey to him about the bank robberies."

"Nacona is seeing to other important matters," July managed to get this out without biting off the banker's shiny bald head. He always said the wrong thing. "I will be happy to relay the information. After all, Nacona and I are handling this case *together.*"

Taking command of the situation, she unfolded the contract and read it to C.L. and George. In the terms, the railroad and bank representatives agreed to forgo the expense monies and half the fee, in the event that the case remained unsolved. If she and Nacona did bring the renegades to trial, they would be entitled to the full amount negotiated and they would be presented with any bounty for wanted criminals. She, of course, would handle the prosecution in court to obtain convictions. All costs would be incurred by the railroad and banks who pressed charges.

"I think we should be allowed to collect the full fee if you fail to meet with success," C.L. grumbled.

July stuck to her guns. "Those are our terms," she said firmly. "We are the ones who will be forced to risk our lives in your behalf. Although we cannot put a monetary price on life itself, we do expect compensation for the time and the risks involved. We will be dealing with murderers and thieves, Mr. Chambers. One of the ranchers has already lost his life in his effort to protect his herd from rustlers."

C.L. tried to object. "But I still—"

George waved his hand for silence. "The terms are reasonable. Nacona and I had the same understanding when he took the Missouri assignment." His eyes twinkled as he regarded the quick-witted female who obviously had no intention of adding any stipulations to her legal document. "Just sign your name, C.L., and let's be done with this. Nacona has a reputation for employing every technique possible to ensure success. He'll find the men responsible for this rash of rustling and robberies. I'll stake *my* reputation on that."

C.L. begrudgingly scrawled his signature on the document. Then he handed it to George to validate. After the legal matter was settled, C.L. related the information about the holdups in the area. July took notes, only to ensure her wary associate that she wouldn't misplace the facts in her miniature-size female brain before she regurgitated the information to Nacona who had yet to return from his rendezvous with his lover.

Still fuming over C.L.'s attitude toward women handling business and Nacona's heartless betrayal, July stamped off down the street. She hadn't gotten very far when a drunken prospector made an attempt to flirt with her.

Flinging her nose toward the north star, July elbowed past the offensive-smelling hooligan, only to be shackled by the arm and dragged toward an alley. Fury more than fear whipped through her as she writhed for freedom. Her indignant shriek echoed in the darkness when she felt groping hands and heard the rending of cloth. Revulsion seized her when slobbery lips fastened on her mouth. July lifted her knee, catching the besotted lecher in the groin. A howl of pain erupted from his throat as he doubled over, taking July with him to the dirt. Her breath came out in a whoosh when the big brute landed on top of her.

A terrified yelp burst from her lips when impatient hands tugged at the hem of her gown and growled words vulgarly promised what was to come. Suddenly, fear had a stronger hold on July than fury. Wildly, she fought to unseat her assailant before he was able to do as he had threatened.

A snarl that sounded almost inhuman wafted through the shadows. And suddenly, there was no threatening weight bearing down upon her. It was as if her brutish assailant had been launched through the air like a rocket to crash into the crates that lined the alley. Although July's brothers had taught her a few techniques in the art of self-defense, she realized she was a novice compared to the pouncing lion of a man who had mercilessly attacked the drunken prospector. Nacona had appeared from nowhere to defend her. She watched in fanatical fascination as he jerked the scoundrel to his feet and treated him to a meal of beefy fists. The crack of flesh was followed by a pained groan and the stumbling retreat of her assailant. But the drunken galoot had only staggered back five paces before Nacona hurled himself forward to hammer him again.

Pulling her gown into decency—or at least as close a proximity as possible—July wobbled onto her feet, shoving tangled tresses away from her face. She had never seen a man pulverized with such deadly efficiency. It was glaringly apparent that Nacona was as good with his fists and feet as he was with a rifle and pistol. He fought like a wild Indian, an enraged white man, and a destructive grizzly all rolled into one, and although Nacona needed no assistance, July's offended dignity demanded restitution. She dashed forward to grab the milk can that sat beside the smashed crates. When her assailant's head snapped back in response to another bone-jarring blow, July crowned him.

As her attacker folded like an accordion and dropped in a heap, she inhaled a steadying breath. She glanced up to thank Nacona for coming to her rescue, but she wasn't allowed to utter one word of gratitude. He stuck his snarling face into hers and set about chewing her up one side and down the other.

"You little fool!" His black eyes flashed like fire and brimstone. "What did you do? Flirt with that drunken oaf to retaliate after I abandoned you?"

July gasped, indignant at the ridiculous assumption. And here Nacona had told her a good detective never assumed anything until he had gathered all the facts. It sounded as if he should heed his own advice.

"I did nothing of the kind, you arrogant lout!" she all but yelled at him. "I couldn't care less that you swaggered off with your latest conquest draped on your arm. I certainly didn't invite that scraggly cretin's attention. I did everything to avoid it, but that mule of a man was plagued with the same amount of lust that spurts through *your* veins. He refused to take no for an answer!"

Nacona tried to get hold of himself, but he was too damned upset to be reasonable. The instant he'd heard July's shriek he had raced into the alley to see two shadowed forms squirming in the dirt. The thought of July enduring such abuse sickened him, but knowing how ornery she could be, he suspected she had purposely attracted the big ape, just to punish him for leaving with Lilian. After all, July had landed him in the Dodge City jail to spite him for exposing himself and flatly refusing her business offer.

While Nacona was standing there fuming, July swished past him and headed for the boardwalk. "I am going to file a complaint at the sheriff's office. And forgive me for inconveniencing you." Her hissed words conveyed not the slightest tinge of apology. "I'm sure you and your hussy have plans for the remainder of the evening. I have no intention of detaining you."

With that, she zoomed off, cursing that midnight-haired rake every step of the way. To her disgust, she heard the clink of spurs behind her and glanced back to see Nacona striding after her, her assailant's limp body jackknifed over his shoulder and a lit cigarillo clamped between his teeth.

After Nacona deposited the unconscious galoot in a cell, he busied himself with the stack of wanted posters on the marshal's desk.

Mustering her composure, July presented a precise account of the incident, and the officer filed the charges. Without waiting for Nacona to accompany her to her room, July stomped toward the door and flashed him a glare as hot as the hinges on hell's door.

Invite a mauling, indeed! July silently seethed as she stalked toward the hotel. That black-eyed imbecile had leaped to the most ridiculous conclusion imaginable. How dare Nacona even think that she cared what he and that doxie had been doing. Well, she didn't—because she detested Nacona. The night they had spent together meant nothing, nothing at all. She had kept *her* part of the bargain. . . . Almost, she amended huffily. But if that cocky rascal thought for one minute he would ever again join her in bed, he had damned well better reconsider.

Grumbling to himself, Nacona stamped back to the street. He had located a wanted poster that fit Charley Brazil's vague description, and the marshal had offered promising information about the fugitive whose thieving operation sounded suspiciously familiar to Nacona. This could be his opportunity to avenge Shandin's death and yet . . . Nacona puffed on his cheroot, surrounding himself with a cloud of smoke. And yet, if he went in search of the fugitive, he would have to leave July to her own devices immediately after she had been attacked in the street and while she was so furious with him that she was ready to spit tacks. Damn! He had invited all-out war with her by blurting out his biting accusations, but how was he to have known that July was only returning from her business meeting when she was attacked without provocation? Should he shrug her off and follow the promising lead he had waited two years to find?

His keen gaze scanned the boardwalks, trying to determine where she had gone. He caught sight of her as she passed under a street light and then veered into a fashionable hotel. Nacona raked his fingers through his tousled raven hair and heaved an exasperated sigh. He had to make a decision. Should he attempt to make amends with July or pose questions around town about the fugitive?

Before he realized it, he was following in July's wake, forsaking the possibility of locating his brother's murderer. He had made a decision that forced him to break his solemn vow to Shandin, had placed July above his long-standing need for justice and revenge. He could feel walls going up around him, imprisoning him, confining him. The harder he fought, the more tightly he was trapped. He hated this feeling of vulnerability, detested these contradicting thoughts that played tug-of-war with his emotions. He wanted to locate Charley Brazil more than anything, but he couldn't bring himself to allow July to travel to Cheyenne alone. She had already proved she could get herself into all sorts of trouble.

Puffing vigorously on his cigar and cursing under his breath, Nacona strode forth to confront July, disgruntled by the commitment he had just made in doing so.

* * *

July stood at the commode, holding one cool compress against the bump on her forehead, another against the nail marks on her bosom. A surge of revulsion shot through her at the thought of having had that offensive beast's hands on her. The drunken swine! Because of his attack her gown had suffered irreparable damage and she had endured a most disgusting ordeal. Even though the ruffian hadn't been able to have his way with her before Nacona beat the tar out of him, the man had scraped off a few inches of her hide.

Men! They were all alike—insufferable, disgusting creatures. They could never see a woman in any capacity other than as the object of their lust. July couldn't help it if men found her visually appealing. One look in the mirror assured her that she was reasonably attractive; at least she had been until she had been mauled. Now she looked as if a herd of wild mustangs had trampled her. Just once, she wished a man could appreciate her for her intellect and personality instead of fantasizing about some sordid affair. Blast it, she hadn't asked to be pretty. It had been an accident of birth and the curse of her life. Honestly, sometimes she wished she had been born male; then perhaps she could get somewhere in this world. For the female of the species it always seemed to be an uphill battle. . . .

The creak of the door caused July to lurch around. When Nacona strode inside, she wheeled back to tend her injuries, making a spectacular display of ignoring him. He, however, refused to take the hint and leave.

"Your room is next door," she informed him waspishly. "I thought you and your paramour would want privacy so I rented my own chamber. Now kindly take yourself off. I prefer to nurse my wounds and retire for the night while you do whatever it is you and Lilian feel compelled to do."

Nacona scowled when he saw the reddened scratches that dipped beneath the torn bodice of her gown, and he had an insane urge to stalk back to the jail and pound some manners into the disgusting bastard incarcerated there.

Instead he walked over to retrieve his saddlebags, which July had had sent over from the train depot. He dug down to find his first-aid kit and aimed himself toward July. When she retreated and put out her chin, he indicated the chair and silently ordered her to seat herself on it. When she defied the unspoken command, Nacona snaked out a hand and jerked her down. She bounded up like a jackrabbit.

"I can tend my own injuries, thank you just the same," she stated testily. "In fact, the sooner you leave the better I'll feel." This she added with a glower that testified to her disgust at having to share the same space with him.

"You'll let me apply this healing salve—and you'll like it!" he growled ominously.

If he expected silent obedience he was sorely disappointed. July reflected his glare with one of her own. "I've been mauled once tonight. I don't want another man's hands on me now—or ever!"

Nacona was quickly losing patience. She could be as rebellious and belligerent as she liked, but he was her husband and he fully intended to see to her wounds—

which she wouldn't have sustained if he had been with her as he should have been. The incident was all his fault. He'd gone off to prove a point to her, and to himself; she had suffered the fright of her life because of it. He owed her compensation and compassion.

Setting the ointment aside, Nacona gently but firmly planted July in the chair and held her there with one hand while he retrieved the salve. "I had no right to jump down your throat. I'm sorry I did," he apologized. "The truth is I was afraid for you. I'm not used to fretting over anybody else. I lashed out at you because I knew I should have been there with you to prevent the attack."

"You owe me nothing. Your time is your own, unless we are working on the investigation. And furthermore, I expect nothing from you. Not protection, not compassion, nothing!"

Talk about defiance personified, Nacona thought. July was dead set on giving him the cold shoulder. Be that as it may, he smoothed the ointment on the scratches and felt her flinch at his familiar touch. His probing gaze held hers, searching for a sign that, despite her anger, she didn't despise him as much as she claimed . . . because the frustrating truth was he liked her a lot more than he wanted to, even though he fought those feelings in his saner moments. He was with her rather than searching out leads on a wanted poster, and he was fighting the maddening urge to take this green-eyed sprite in his arms and console her, to replace groping touches with tender caresses.

The need to erase the haunting incident from July's mind prompted Nacona to brush his lips over hers. She stiffened like a ramrod, refusing to succumb to the betrayal of her body. She wanted no man who could jump from one bed to another like a grasshopper. Nacona was only being nice to her because he felt guilty, because he pitied her. Well, she could do without that. He hadn't wanted *her* pity and she didn't want *his*.

"I'm sure I must be keeping you from Lilian." She cursed her vocal cords for failing her when she needed them most.

Nacona expelled an enormous sigh and drew the stubborn beauty to her feet. "Look, July. I'm here because I want to be." He did not mention that he had bypassed a golden opportunity to track down a promising lead to his brother's unsolved murderer. "I took time out earlier this afternoon to visit a former acquaintance—"

"Visit?" July pounced on his choice of words. "The woman draped herself all over you like Spanish moss. That suggested she had something more stimulating in mind than conversation. And you looked every bit as anxious to accommodate her. I'm sure you were doing much more than paying *lip* service to a former acquaintance."

"Stop interrupting, lady counselor," Nacona growled. "I didn't touch her."

"Oh? Did she suddenly contract leprosy?" July sniffed sarcastically. "I can think of no other reason why a man like you would deprive yourself."

Nacona wheeled around and stalked toward the door. "I didn't touch her, and that's the truth," he muttered, struggling with the confession that hovered on the tip of his tongue. "I didn't touch her because she wasn't *you*." To salvage his male pride, he added, "A deal is still a deal, July."

There. He'd said it, and it had nearly choked him to do so, just as he expected it would. But he had saved face by tacking on that last comment. And damn it, he was annoyed to admit that the instant Lilian had sidled up against him, she had felt all wrong in his arms. Her hair and eyes were the wrong color. Her curves and swells were in the wrong places and didn't fit perfectly against him as those of this frustrating bundle of trouble did. And the overly sweet fragrance of Lilian's perfume offended him. He didn't *want* to want this sassy blonde the way he did, but . . . He'd even gone so far as to tell Lilian that he was married. Not that it mattered one whit to Lilian. Her lovers were all married men. And worse, he had turned his back on the chance to track down a man who might have been responsible for his brother's murder.

What the devil was the matter with him these days? One would have thought the instant he'd scribbled his name on that marriage license his whole perspective had changed. He and July had spoken the vows for convenience. And all of a sudden he was behaving like a loyal, true-blue husband! Even while this saucy sprite spouted that there were no ties to bind them, he felt as if he were bound to her by silken chains that were as sturdy as iron. July didn't really want or need him. She had said as much, and quite often. So why was he feeling so devoted to a woman who had given in to his passions only because he had bargained for the privilege of being the first man to make love to her? If their lovemaking hadn't been so wild and fulfilling and sweet maybe he wouldn't keep sailing back to her . . .

"Next time you venture out on the street after dark, tuck a pistol in your purse," Nacona ordered grouchily.

207

"You scared the living daylights out of me. I don't like that feeling. Having you at the borderline of disaster unnerves me. Don't let it happen again."

July blinked in disbelief when Nacona, having muttered these remarks, stalked off. When the door banged shut behind him, she just stared at it. Temptation had been tossed in his lap and he had done nothing about it. Why? Her delicately arched brow furrowed. Nacona had been afraid for *her* sake? He was upset that he hadn't been able to prevent the attack? Why?

Bemused, July aimlessly ambled around the confines of her room. Could it possibly be that he, like she, was experiencing this affinity, that they were trapped in a web of their own making? Did Nacona actually *feel* something for her besides obligation and responsibility? Probably not, she decided. Not too long ago he had made the statement that he was responsible for her. Her brothers felt that same protective obligation, which ended up smothering her and provoked her to strike out on her own. In Nacona's case, however, feeling responsible was an awkward, unfamiliar experience and more than likely he resented it.

Yet, he expected her to meet the stipulations of their bargain. She still owed him two nights, she reminded herself with a blush. Wasn't that what Nacona had meant when he'd insisted that Lilian wasn't her? Hadn't he been suggesting that he was waiting for her to uphold her end of the bargain? Apparently he was prepared to overlook July's inexperience, if only to enjoy ultimate victory over her. Well, she'd learn what that skilled philanderer had to teach her and then turn his provocative techniques back upon him. That would show him! To become Nacona's match in eliciting passion she would have to arouse him to the same mindless degree that he excited her. Then *she* would enjoy ultimate victory over him. . . .

Sweet mercy! What sordid and spiteful thoughts! Was this the same woman who'd left Kansas City as a dedicated spinster vowing to make a name and a place for herself in this man's world, insisting that she needed no husband or lover to make her life complete? July glanced at her reflection in the mirror. No, it definitely wasn't. Her association with that rough-edged rake had made a woman of her—a woman who had discovered wants and needs she had been unaware she possessed until Nacona awakened her slumbering passions and provoked feelings of . . .

Although July had battled those feelings tooth and nail, she wanted Nacona to want her. But how could she make that come about after she had twisted his arm a half-dozen different ways to ensure his cooperation and had sidetracked him from his personal crusade for justice? How did a woman make a man feel more than obligation, resentment, and simple lust when she longed for that particular man's . . . affection?

There it was then, July realized—the elemental truth that had been hounding her all night. She had wanted to draw and keep the interest of a man who had attracted her, even when she had never expected any such thing to happen.

July glanced over at the satchels stacked in the corner. Well, the first thing a woman had to do if she wanted to gain a man's true interest was get his attention. July fished into her bag to locate the delicate negligee and matching robe. Although she knew it wasn't love or lasting affection that had brought Nacona back to her, it was still a small commitment of sorts. And if Nacona was man enough to admit that he'd wanted her instead of Lilian Whoever-she-was—even if the need was born of a challenge that had become entangled in unwanted obligations—then July intended to swallow her damnable pride and admit to herself that she found pleasure in joining him in bed. She hadn't wanted to face those shameless feelings, but in truth she had discovered something wondrous in Nacona's masterful kisses and caresses.

An impish grin pursed July's lips. She was entitled to her wifely rights, wasn't she? And of course, there was that old cliché about practice making perfect. She had always been plagued with a competitive nature that prompted her to be the best at all her endeavors. . . .

She had tried to convince herself that Nacona did want her—physically at least. Perhaps because she wanted to become more than a bargain and a responsibility to him, perhaps because she longed to revisit that erotic paradise she had discovered in his arms. Whatever the case, July had made her decision, and she was sticking with it.

Once she had wormed into her gossamer gown and smoothed it over the slope of her hips, she picked up her brush and untangled her hair, allowing its long strands to fall over one shoulder like a shiny waterfall. Carefully, she drew a few wispy tendrils over the bruise on her forehead, then adjusted her gown to conceal the unsightly scratches. Inhaling a determined breath, she eased open the door to inspect the darkened hall. Since the coast was clear, she moved silently toward Nacona's room, wondering how he would react to having her waltz in wearing a seductive negligee.

July gulped apprehensively. Since she had never made such overt advances toward any other man, she couldn't help but wonder how good she was going to be at initiating a romantic interlude. If Nacona dared to ridicule her, she feared she would turn and run. This was definitely not her forte, but that dark-eyed devil had cast a fierce and mighty spell on her and she seemed helpless to resist the tantalizing memories they had made together. Her traitorous body and her wayward mind had conspired to put her pride at risk, forcing her to disregard the biting words and sizzling glares that continually kept them at odds.

For this one night, July wanted to forget the near brush with disaster she had endured in the street and to lose herself in Nacona's skillful embrace. If she could set that stubborn pride of hers aside, perhaps she and Nacona could make a fresh start and give this manufactured marriage a chance.

With that thought echoing in her mind, she stepped into Nacona's room without awaiting an invitation. . . .

Chapter 14

Nacona bit down on the end of his cigar and very nearly swallowed it whole when a vision materialized before him. July looked like an angel standing in the doorway. Golden lantern light formed a translucent halo around her head and speared through the fetching gown that lay diagonally across her breasts, accentuating the tempting peaks beneath it. The matching white robe did more to tantalize than to conceal her exquisite form from his hungry eyes, and Nacona savored the tempting sight of her.

To his disbelief, July shrugged off the robe and approached him. A faint blush of embarrassment heightened the color in her cheeks as she untied the ribbons on the shoulders of her gown, allowing the diaphanous fabric to drift down her curvaceous body in the most titillating manner imaginable. To Nacona's further astonishment, she eased down beside him on the bed. He almost strangled on a breath when she reached out to run her hands over the muscles of his chest before gliding her fingertips over the taut tendons of his arms.

July marveled at the unique pleasure she derived from

touching this magnificently built man. His sleek, rippling flesh indicated incredible power, and she found herself recalling how he had launched himself at her assailant. Nacona Bleu had certainly lived up to his legendary reputation as a fighter, yet she knew he could be remarkably tender when he was in one of his gentler moods.

"You were right," July confessed as she investigated the broad expanse of his chest with inquiring hands. Self-consciously, she watched her fingertips flow across hair-roughened planes and rippling contours instead of braving a glance into those dark eyes that could hypnotize and entrance. "I was . . . jealous. I didn't want you to leave with Lilian because I was afraid she would . . . take my place with you. I wanted you here with me. I have no right whatsoever to be possessive because that was not part of our bargain, but—"

His forefinger settled on her heart-shaped lips, shushing her. He placed his hand beneath her chin, lifting her enchanting face to his, urging her to meet his gentle smile. Learning that July was just a tad bit jealous pleased him, but he wasn't sure why. He had no place in his life for commitments, obligations, and selfish whims. He had promises to keep, and he had been distracted from them once already tonight. But despite his determination and his instinctive need to remain emotionally detached, this spell-casting siren had bedeviled him, distracted him from his long crusade. They both seemed to resent the attraction that pulled on them, straining against it like kites against a strong wind. Yet, the magnetism was there, bubbling just beneath the surface despite their fierce pride and their dedication to individual purposes. The very fact that July had come to him was a concession, and Nacona would not have destroyed her fragile femininity for the world, even if she occasionally made him so mad he erupted like Vesuvius.

When he peered into those luminous eyes that reminded him of polished emeralds, he made a startling discovery about himself. His disciplined control and firm convictions didn't amount to a hill of beans where July was concerned. He had wanted this enchanting nymph since the first time he had touched her. She had become an itch he could never sufficiently scratch. She was the geometrical equation he couldn't puzzle out, the fever he couldn't cure. Though she had become his challenge and his conquest, making passionate love to her hadn't quenched what had become an insatiable thirst. One night in her arms hadn't curbed his craving for her. He honestly wondered if ten times ten would even be enough to make this nagging need go away.

He decided there was naught he could do but satisfy his hunger for her until this irrational fascination ebbed. Once he learned all there was to know about this intriguing imp he would be ready to go his own way. It was just a matter of time. But until then . . . Nacona's thoughts scattered when his eyes dropped to the tempting curves of her luscious body. He was wasting precious time thinking. And he was being as analytical as this sharp-witted sprite when he really just wanted to fan the fire inside him, to lose himself in the rapture he had discovered in her satiny arms.

When his sensuous lips drifted over hers as if he were a bee courting nectar, July swore the skin had melted off her bones. As he caressed her intimately, her body instinctively arched toward his, aching to dissolve the agonizing

215

inches that separated them. She longed to feel his masculine body forged to hers, to experience that same breathless ecstasy that had engulfed her once before.

Suddenly they were clutching urgently at each other like two lost souls who had been separated for eternity. Her senses took flight when his searching hands and greedy lips rediscovered every ultrasensitive point on her flesh and brought it to life. It was as if Nacona had perfect recall, as if it had been only minutes since he had touched her. Her skin tingled as if tiny fires burned beneath it— growing hotter, wilder, raging out of control. Her breath came in ragged spurts as the aching pressure built and sensation upon indescribable sensation channeled through her. She quivered with the wanting of him, with her responses to each phenomenal sensation he aroused in her.

Over and over again, Nacona traced the voluptuous terrain of her body, reveling in her uninhibited responses, longing to taste her, touch her, and leave her gasping with the overwhelming need of him. Shock waves of pleasure sizzled through him at knowing that each technique he employed was new to her. He was teaching her about passion, and she was learning to respond only to his lovemaking.

His hands refused to remain still for even a second, and his lips fluttered over her breasts, his tongue flicking the throbbing crests. With a tremulous groan, he savored and worshipped her with his hands and lips, provoking fervent responses that further ignited his passion. He shifted beside her, yearning to teach her things—wildly intimate things that he hadn't dared reveal the first night he had taken this innocent siren in his arms.

216

July caught her breath as Nacona introduced her to new dimensions of lovemaking. He was doing incredible things to her, making her burn like wildfire, causing needs to burgeon inside her until she feared they would consume her. Shudder after tormenting shudder shattered what was left of her composure. But the wild pleasures he bestowed on her left an empty, gnawing ache that his hands and lips had only teased into a monstrous craving. She longed to feel his muscular body upon hers, to know the pulsating warmth of his total possession.

When she reached out in desperation to guide him to her, Nacona smiled in satisfaction. "Not yet, sweet witch," he whispered against her quaking flesh. "There's much more I want to teach you about the pleasure a man can offer a woman."

"I'll die of it, I swear," July gasped as his hands and lips began to work their wild sensual magic all over again.

"For you, life's little death will come again and again . . . until you fully understand the sensual explosion of new life in its purest form."

His words confused her, but it wasn't long before July began to understand what he meant. She had never believed it possible to experience such devastating sensations: wild, convulsive tremors converged in her and then ebbed before engulfing her again . . . and again. When his moist lips skimmed her thigh and his masterful hands splayed across her abdomen, July held her breath. He shifted above her to teach her even more of the intimate things that transpired between a man and a woman— things that sent her over the edge into erotic spasms of pleasure.

Desire clenched Nacona's body as he tasted and

touched this lovely siren in ways he had never before dared. He could feel the sweet core of her femininity contracting around his fingertips, searing him with silken fire, making him burn as wildly as she was burning for him. Her uncontrollable need for him was on his fingertips, his lips. He caressed her until he heard her cry out to him again, until the hot spasms of passions were calling him to satisfy each soul-shattering sensation he had instilled in her.

When he finally came to her, tears of ecstasy were streaming down July's cheeks. His sleek body uncoiled upon hers, and he took her lips as a prelude to merging his powerful body with hers. His slow, erotic penetration was another form of delicious torture that left her quaking in his arms. Her nails bit into the rigid tendons of his back, and she clung to him as if he were the only stable force in a whirling universe. For what seemed forever the wondrous sensations spilled from her trembling body into his as he drove into her, taking her higher and higher still.

A muffled groan flooded from Nacona's lips when the fiery surge of passion engulfed him, assuming absolute control of mind and body. Primal needs multiplied as he and July moved in perfect rhythm, giving and sharing the indescribable wonders of passion. He couldn't ease his tight grasp on her as they soared through time and space, circling the twinkling stars and gliding over rainbows, his intense pleasure mounting until he feared he would burst with it. And when the shudder of sweet, satisfying release rippled through him, Nacona let go with body, heart, and soul because that was the price he had to pay for passion so unique and devastating.

A wry smile quirked his lips as he pressed a kiss to the swanlike column of July's neck in the aftermath of their lovemaking. This spirited female, who occasionally burned the fuse clean off his temper, could satisfy him in ways he'd never dreamed possible. She was filled with explosive passion seeking release. Now Nacona fully understood why he had backed away from Lilian's offer of herself and why he had walked away from that wanted poster. When he was with this green-eyed siren all seemed right with the world. July filled his senses to overflowing and left him drowning in a sea of ecstasy. She made all the difference.

Languidly, July wormed free and propped herself up beside the magnificent giant who had aroused inexpressible needs in her and then had satisfied them one by one. Earlier, Nacona had not allowed her to distract him from his intimate assault. Now she longed to offer that immense pleasure to him, to become as skillful at seduction as this ruggedly handsome rake. Only when he begged for mercy, as she had done, would she be assured that she had driven him over the edge to mindless oblivion.

Nacona's dark brows shot up when soft, exploring hands strayed over his chest and traced intricate designs on his belly. At the moment he was like a jellyfish out of water, unable to move to save his very soul.

"Don't," he croaked, his voice rattling with the aftereffects of unparalleled passion.

"No?" July tossed her long mane of blond hair over her shoulder and flashed him an impish smile. Her fingertips trickled over his ribs and scaled the washboarded muscles of his abdomen to encircle each male nipple.

"No," Nacona protested hoarsely. "I'm not sure I'll ever be able to rouse again as it is. I'm numb from the neck down."

"Then you can't possibly mind if I satisfy my feminine curiosity." Green eyes twinkled with mischief. "Curiosity is one of my worst faults, I'm sad to report. But don't mind me. You can fade off to sleep if you wish."

Her adventurous caresses left his body tingling, even though he'd seemed paralyzed as a result of their previous pleasure. And when her moist lips fluttered over his flesh to seek out every sensitive point, Nacona groaned in astonishment. This beguiling witch could create energy where there was none. Why, she could bring a stone to life and make it breathe! Good heavens, he had been positively certain he'd had nothing left to give and no strength left with which to give it. Obviously, he'd been wrong. July really *was* a spell-casting witch who could transform frogs into princes and turn a contented man into a starving beast.

This imaginative imp had taken the erotic techniques he had taught her, revised them to suit her own purposes, and then turned them back upon him. Nacona groaned in torment when her fingertips closed around the pulsating length of him, stroking him until he panted for breath. Her hands and lips coasted over him, her tongue flicking out to taste him, leaving him shuddering in barely restrained need. Her caresses, like fairies' wings, flooded and ebbed, tormenting him by delirious degrees to inward heat. Ever so slowly, she had drawn him up from the depths of lethargy to leave him aching to satisfy the gigantic cravings she had instilled in him. This woman had too much hold over him.

A look of satisfaction appeared on July's lovely features when she glanced up to see the flare-up of desire in his ebony eyes. He wanted her again. She had made him want her. She could feel the throb of his need for her, could hear the ragged breaths that tumbled from his parted lips. It gave July a sense of power and gratification to know she could stir him at will. Inexperienced though she was, her ingenuity and imagination had brought his passions to a fervent pitch.

"Come here, damn you," Nacona gasped when another intolerable wave of torment rippled through him.

Her hands enfolded the velvet length of him again, teasing him until he gasped for breath a second time. "I thought you said—"

"Never mind what I said," Nacona growled as he shifted to draw her supple body beneath his. "You little witch. You're downright dangerous."

July smiled impishly as his lean, hard body glided intimately over hers. "I thought you liked living dangerously. In fact—"

His mouth descended upon hers while his lithe body took absolute possession, and her playfulness evaporated when his penetrating thrusts demanded responses. Then together they set off on a wondrous journey beyond the sun, and July didn't really care if they ever returned from those erotic galaxies.

Nacona awoke feeling like a new man, even though he hadn't had many complaints with the old one. Although he knew the danger of becoming too deeply involved with this enchanting minx, he couldn't stop himself from enjoying her company or from marveling at the companionable silence they now shared. He and July had passed a new milestone in their stormy relationship. When he playfully teased her, she no longer took offense. She simply broke into one of those radiant smiles that left Nacona feeling as if the sun itself had dawned in their room.

They managed to climb out of bed long enough to tour the city of Denver and purchase a few supplies to lend credence to their new occupation, ranching in Wyoming. But Nacona was ashamed to say he couldn't wait to get July all to himself once again, to revel in the newfound wonders of their limitless passion for each other.

He kept waiting for the fascination to ebb, but it never did. Each time he made love to July was like the very first time, only better. With this ever-changing sprite everything seemed possible. Not only did she fulfill his wildest fantasies, but she was a most entertaining companion with a delightful sense of humor. She had even related the events from her life on the sprawling estate near Kansas City and had spoken of her childhood dreams. She described her brothers and confessed that she had indeed felt smothered by their overprotectiveness, that she had balked at standing forever in their shadows; yet she admired them, loved them, and aspired to be like them.

Nacona wondered what the three citified detectives would think if they discovered their innocent little sister had married the likes of him, even in connection with their business venture. Though a detective, Nacona had a reputation as a gunslinger and a shootist who could be bought for a price. Gunslingers and bounty hunters weren't exactly regarded as respectable citizens. They were always looked down upon, though begrudgingly admired for their abilities. Nacona imagined the MacKenzie brothers would go through the roof if they learned the truth.

The townsfolk in Dodge, as well as other towns, viewed him as a man to be feared, but their favorite hobby was speculating as to where he'd been and how many men he had launched into eternity. In the past, Nacona had provided these people with the excitement they wanted and expected, to amuse himself. And because of his own devilishness, his reputation had become bigger than life.

Most folks gave him a wide berth unless they required his expertise with a pistol, but they whispered behind his back. That was, Nacona amended, until he'd married this sophisticated beauty—whose brothers would throw a conniption fit if they ever found out. Now, lo and behold, Nacona seemed to have acquired respectability when July was by his side. It was the most remarkable phenomenon he'd ever experienced. The citizens of Denver, who had once looked down their noses at him, now tipped their hats and greeted him when he strolled by with July on his arm.

And that wasn't the half of it, either. Nacona suddenly found his worn buckskin clothes unappealing and out of place while he was escorting July about town. He bought himself two outfits in the current style. And during their meals he caught himself emulating July's polished table manners, as if his old ways weren't good enough when he was in her company.

His wandering thoughts dispersed when July curled up on his lap while they lounged in their suite and pressed an impulsive kiss to his lips.

"What did I do to deserve that?" he questioned as his

hand glided familiarly over her shapely derriere. "Tell me what it was so I can do it again."

"I was only trying to get your attention," July murmured as her wandering fingertips tunneled beneath the buttons of his linen shirt to make stimulating contact with his hair-matted flesh. "Thinking deep thoughts, Nacona?"

He wasn't about to share his pensive musings. He was a private man, and taking others into his confidence did not come easily. The odd feelings that had come over him the past two days were too new, too unfamiliar to discuss. "I'm thinking that we need to fetch a wagon and haul all this paraphernalia to the freight car," he hedged. "Our train leaves in two hours."

July regretted departing from Denver. Their sojourn in Colorado had been like a dream come true. She and Nacona had shared a pleasant camaraderie. They had toured the federal mint, enjoyed the theater, and consumed delicious meals together. And then there were those wondrous hours of . . . A warm blush stained her cheeks when arousing thoughts riveted every fiber of her being.

"Thinking wicked thoughts, July?" Nacona teased as his hand lifted to brush the taut peaks of her breasts. His dark eyes glittered knowingly. "Too bad we have a train to catch."

July bounded to her feet, trying to appear indignant that her betraying body had conveyed her thoughts to him. But the instant Nacona gathered her in his arms, all pretentiousness fell by the wayside. Knowing they would enjoy very little privacy in the next two days, she surrendered to the sensations that spiraled through her. At times like these she feared she had fallen in love with this seductive rake.

What would it be like to love a man like Nacona? she wondered. To have him love her back? Although he didn't have room in his life for love, nor did he intend to make room for lasting commitments, July found herself whimsically wishing she could give this tumbleweed roots. After the time she had spent with him, learning his every mood, watching him display his legendary skills, enjoying his wondrous brand of lovemaking, she wondered if she would ever be content to be escorted about town by a normal man.

She would not, July decided as she returned Nacona's passionate kiss. She had always been difficult to impress, her three brothers having been standards for excellence. Now it would be even worse. She would compare this midnight-haired rogue to every other man, and each would fall short of the mark. If she didn't watch her step, she would emerge from this marriage, clinging to pieces of a broken heart.

Oh, if only she could observe caution when he enfolded her in those brawny arms and made her body glow with the pleasures he had unveiled. But caution, like good sense, kept drifting off in the wind when Nacona communicated with her in that magical body language that banished all thought from her mind. . . .

Nacona made certain he and July acquired first-class accommodations on the train bound for Cheyenne. They boarded a luxurious car, much like the one July had described when she had made the first leg of her journey to Dodge City. The plush seats offered the kind of comfort second and third-class tickets couldn't provide. And for four extra dollars they were permitted to dine in the special dining car rather than at the roundhouses in which a body had to swallow his food whole and dash back to his seat in ten minutes.

For the first time ever, Nacona stretched out in a lavish sleeping car. Oiled walnut panels lined the top of the car, and marble and walnut wash stands stood in every available space. The floors were covered with costly Brussels carpet and the roof was etched in mosaics of gold and emerald green. It was the damnedest thing Nacona had ever seen. He supposed July was accustomed to such extravagance, but he sure as hell wasn't. Suddenly he felt like a peasant who had wandered into a royal court—definitely out of place, even if he had just spent two days pretending to be someone he wasn't.

The only consolation Nacona enjoyed while lying alone in the bottom berth of the sleeper was staring at July's reflection in the oiled paneling that lined the top of her bunk. The ceiling had been polished until it shone like a mirror.

With a rakish grin, Nacona watched July peel off her dress and worm into her nightgown. When she glanced up, she saw his reflection staring back at her, and she very nearly toppled from her perch. Then, realizing that Nacona was not really above her but below, she craned her neck over the edge of her berth to fling him a saucy grin.

"You beast," she admonished playfully. "You were spying on me."

"Indeed I was." He tossed her an unrepentant smile

that displayed pearly white teeth. "And I enjoyed every minute of it. In fact—*ooofff!*

July had overextended herself. When the train had rounded a sharp bend, sending drowsy passengers rolling into the aisle, she had hurtled down onto Nacona, forcing his breath out. While the other passengers were muttering and recovering their poise, Nacona scooted sideways to make room for July between him and the wall.

A triumphant grin pursed his lips as his head moved slowly and deliberately toward hers. "Mmm . . . this is much better," his baritone voice rumbled seductively. "I've grown accustomed to having you in my bed."

July dodged his oncoming kiss and darted a wary glance toward the waving curtains that separated them from the rest of the passengers, some still in the process of clambering back into their bunks. "What if somebody sees us?"

"What if they don't?" he countered with a cavalier smile. "I thought you enjoyed living dangerously, as I do."

The feel of his masculine body brushing suggestively against hers dissolved her self-consciousness. "So I do, Mr. Bleu, so I do. . . ."

It was difficult to contain the exquisite pleasure they created when they were in each other's arms, but they managed. In fact, they took a certain wicked delight in putting something over on the other passengers. Most folks were still grumbling about the incident that had landed them on the floor. As for July, she had no complaint whatsoever about where she had landed. She could think of no other place she would rather be.

Chapter 15

C. L. Chambers glanced up from the stack of papers on his desk when an insistent rap echoed throughout his office. As one of the local ranchers ambled inside, C.L. frowned irritably. Hub Butler was not one of his favorite people, for good reason. Besides, C.L. was expecting Nacona Bleu and his bride to arrive at any moment. Obviously he was going to have to tolerate Hub's presence in the meantime.

"What can I do for you, Hub?" C.L. questioned, without bothering with the social amenities.

Hubert Butler strolled across the bank executive's office and parked himself in a chair, despite C.L.'s less than cordial attitude toward him. "I came by to talk to you about the Foster place. I thought I might consider assuming the mortgage on the ranch and adding it to my syndicated properties."

C.L. squirmed uneasily in his seat. Bob Foster was the rancher who had been murdered during a rustling incident. His ranch was the one C.L. had offered to Nacona and July as their headquarters. He would have liked to collect the debt Foster had left with the bank, even if he sold the ranch to a man he disliked, but he had signed that confounded contract July had drawn up and he couldn't back out. . . .

A suspicious frown plowed C.L.'s winged brows when another thought suddenly struck him. "How'd you find out about Foster's mortgage? As I recall, the loan wasn't public knowledge."

Hub lifted a shoulder in a noncommittal shrug. "Foster's land joins mine on the south. We were neighbors, after all," he explained. "Bob mentioned the mortgage while we were sharing a drink at the Cheyenne Club. It was common knowledge to most of the ranchers, anyway. Naturally, I assumed the Golden Spur Ranch and its improvements were still under a lien. Bob didn't have investors backing him as I do. He was trying to make a go of it on his own."

"Well, I'd like to make some sort of arrangement," C.L. declared, though he would have preferred it to be with someone besides Hub Butler. "But the fact is the mortgage to the Golden Spur has been purchased. Four days ago to be exact."

A frown creased Hub's weathered brow. "Who's taking it over?"

C.L. eased back in his chair. "You probably won't believe this, but Nacona Bleu and his wife purchased it," he announced and then awaited Hub's reaction.

"Bleu?" Hub crowed in astonishment. "I thought he was a gunslinger operating in Kansas or Indian Territory or some place like that. I thought he got killed a few months back."

Again reports of Nacona's death had been greatly exaggerated. C.L. wondered if the whole town would react to the news the same way Hub had. He decided he'd better initiate gossip to counteract that. "He *was* a gunslinger," C.L. replied. "But Nacona decided to retire from his profession when he married. According to the letter"— C.L. was trying to concoct a believable explanation as he went along—"Bleu wanted to locate in an area where he wasn't so well known on sight, so he could make a fresh start without cocky gunslingers trying to draw him out to make their own reputations. Of course, he knows we've had trouble with rustling and robberies. I suppose he figures he can take care of himself and his new wife as well as anybody around here."

Hub grumbled under his breath. "I was hoping to add the Golden Spur to the Cabestro Ranch."

"With all the cattle rustling cutting into everybody's profits, I'm surprised you have the available cash for a down payment," C.L. replied tactlessly, uncaring that he annoyed Hub. After all, the man annoyed him.

"I have investors backing me," Hub reminded him. "They still think there is money to be made in the Wyoming cattle industry."

"Well, if Bleu and his wife decide ranching doesn't suit them, you'll be the first to know," C.L. promised. "But a deal is a deal. I offered the Golden Spur to Nacona Bleu, and he's already made a payment."

Hub unfolded himself from the chair, still muttering at the news. "If you ask me, having a former gunslinger in the area will only invite more trouble. I don't think the other ranchers are going to like it either."

"Plenty of ranchers in the area have hired gunslingers to defend their property. Cheyenne hasn't exactly progressed from lawlessness to respectability. Like Dodge and Hays and Caldwell, it has a bad reputation which will have to be lived down. Having Nacona Bleu around might make those pesky bandits think twice before they tangle with an ex-gunslinger with a new wife to protect."

When the door eased shut behind Hub, C.L. impatiently drummed his stubby fingers on the desk. He wished Nacona would show up, and quickly. He wanted the detective and his saucy wife to get a foothold in town before damaging rumors and speculations started flying. But he knew Hub would high-tail it straight to the Cheyenne Club where the ranchers congregated and would spill the beans.

Well, any ruffled feathers would be smoothed when the ranchers got a look at Nacona and his sophisticated wife. C.L. wondered how his own wife would adjust to having some competition. Angela delighted in flaunting her good looks, but she was about to find herself challenged as the "prettiest female in town." July Bleu was a sassy little chit, but she was damned good looking, and she would not escape notice, much to Angela's dismay.

Another rap at the door jostled the banker from his pensive deliberations. Relief washed over his face when Nacona's broad, muscular frame filled the entrance to his office. To C.L.'s surprise the rough-edged pistolero had donned fashionable clothing and looked very much the gentleman. But the most elegant attire couldn't conceal the unmistakable toughness about Nacona Bleu.

At least his new image should quell some gossip, thought C.L. Nacona and the delicate blonde at his side would make a most impressive couple. C.L. was feeling better already.

"I had a chance to sell the ranch you'll be utilizing," C.L. said after a brief nod of greeting. "But the Golden Spur is only a mile from town and it couldn't suit you better."

If Nacona was supposed to be impressed because C.L. had declined the chance to collect on the loan, he wasn't. Frankly, Nacona had little use for the banker whose favorite person seemed to be himself. A pensive frown furrowed Nacona's brow as he casually took inventory of the elaborate furnishings in the office. "Just who is the man who wanted to buy the ranch?"

C.L. waved away any potential suspicion. "It was Hub Butler, but he's harmless enough, except when it comes to . . ." He cleared his throat and began again, leaving Nacona to wonder what the banker had intended to say. "Hub manages the syndicated ranch just north of the Golden Spur. He's lost as many cattle as the next rancher. The only difference is that he has foreign investors to keep his operation afloat. The Cabestro Ranch bought Texas stock cattle for breeding and began their cow-calf operation like most of the other ranches. Half the ranchers in the area have investors from the East or elsewhere backing their operations. The rest are individuals like Bob Foster, who moved north to take advantage of the Homestead Act that allows folks to claim land for little or nothing if they built homes and corrals and stayed for five years."

"But there has been squabbling between the small farmers and the ranchers over the rights to graze public lands," July put in, annoyed that C.L. had pretty much ignored her. "According to my research, the farmers resent the big cattle barons because of their attempts to control the rivers and streams, and the barons are angered by small operators cutting their fences, as if they owned the whole territory. I have read reports in the papers that the ranchers suspect the farmers of stealing and branding cattle. If Wyoming's citizens aren't careful, they might find themselves embroiled in the kind of violence that erupted in New Mexico last February."

"Perhaps the cattle rustling is somehow connected to the squabble between large and small ranchers," C.L. contended. "But our major concern is the increase in bank and train holdups. It could be that some of the hired guns working for the big ranchers have stooped to robbery to acquire extra money. George Hershberger and I speculated on that theory. But that is why you two are here, to ascertain just who is at fault. And the sooner you get to work, the better I'll like it."

Before July and Nacona could pose more questions, C.L. hoisted himself out of his chair and directed their attention to the window. "That's the Cheyenne Club," he informed them, stabbing a stubby finger toward the large structure. "That's where the cattlemen gather to discuss their problems and politics, and to entertain themselves. I'm sure Hub Butler has already tromped off to the Club to inform his neighbors that the new owners of the Golden Spur are on their way to town."

He glanced at Nacona, overlooking July as usual. "Hub Butler recognized your name and I had to do some fast talking to explain that you had retired your guns to try your hand at cattle. I suggest you and your wife introduce yourselves to the ranchers and make a good first impression before they have time to speculate about your arrival over one too many bottles of whiskey."

"We'll do just that after we rent a wagon to transport our household furnishings to the ranch." Nacona lit his cigar and peered thoughtfully at the Cheyenne Club. "It won't hurt to have our new neighbors see that we have come prepared to stay indefinitely. That should alleviate some of their suspicions."

"Good idea," C.L. agreed before returning to his chair to take the excessive load off his feet. "A very good idea indeed. Of course, as experienced as you are at these matters, I doubt you need suggestions from me."

July rolled her eyes in annoyance. Although she was the first to admit she wasn't trying very hard, she didn't like C.L. He was an arrogant windbag, a pseudo intellectual. She was being cynical, of course, because she disliked the man. But she wouldn't have been surprised to learn he had instigated the robberies against the railroad to compensate for the bank's losses. He could very well be the kind of man who loudly protested injustice and then went about cheating others at every chance he got.

When Nacona had escorted July back onto the street, he glanced down at her. "What is your impression of C.L. Chambers?" he questioned as he guided her toward the livery stable.

"I don't like him. He has a narrow mind and a broad tongue. He's self-centered, shrewd, and obnoxious."

Nacona flashed her a wry smile. "Is that a professional or a personal evaluation?"

"Both," she replied as she hurried to keep up with Nacona's long, lithe strides. "C.L. could have joined forces with George just to keep abreast of the situation, especially if we are to report our progress to him."

"Which we won't," Nacona added emphatically. "I make it a habit of telling no more than I want known."

July paused to peer up at the ruggedly handsome pistolero who monopolized her thoughts more than she would have wished. "Does that policy apply to me as well, Nacona?" she wanted to know.

Nacona pivoted to stare into her lively green eyes. He was aware that C.L. had once again gotten her hackles up by regarding her as no more than a prop in the investigation. At times, as if she were a part of him, he could read her thoughts. But when he wanted to know how she regarded their personal relationship, he couldn't figure her out at all.

Shaking off this thought, Nacona glanced discreetly around him, noting that he and this dainty sophisticate had already attracted more than their fair share of attention. Apparently word had already spread about his reputation and his arrival. He intended to take full advantage of the situation, and to quell any unnecessary gossip that wasn't in his best interest.

A roguish smile pursed his lips as he framed July's face, tipping it up to his oncoming kiss. "You, my dear wife, are the exception to every rule," he murmured before his lips slanted over hers in front of God and anybody who cared to watch his public display of affection. "After all, we are in this together, through thick and thin."

When Nacona slipped his brawny arm around her waist to guide her toward the stables, July glanced sideways, aware of all the attention they were receiving. An impish smile pursed her lips. "And you, my dear husband, are as cunning as they come. Suddenly you've become the picture of manly devotion. Leaving lasting impressions and nurturing the grapevine for our own benefit, are we?"

Nacona chuckled scampishly. "If you think I was merely conducting a display for the good citizens of Cheyenne and their shady counterparts, you have misjudged me."

"Have I?" She reached up to pat his grinning face for theatrical effect. "Or is it just—?"

His quick kiss silenced her. "You're very good at this, love," he murmured. "But let's not wind up in a debate. It will spoil the effect we've just created."

After they had rented a wagon, Nacona drove back to the depot to collect their belongings. He swore that gossip traveled faster than a swift horse. Along the way, folks paused to stare at them. Some even nodded greetings and tipped their hats to July. So far so good, Nacona mused.

Part of him was anxious to dive headlong into their investigation. Another part was reluctant, knowing that this marriage, which had begun to grow on him, would end with the completion of the assignment. But a job was a job. He had to set his personal desires aside and concentrate on his purpose.

"I want you to subtly wheedle out every tidbit of information possible when we mingle with the ranchers at the Cheyenne Club," Nacona instructed July. "We need as much background information as we can get on everyone in the area." He cast her a somber glance. "If that means leaving yourself open to invitation, then do it. That in itself will help us discover what kind of men we're dealing with. Those with the least integrity deserve the most suspicion."

"You want me to flirt?" July croaked in disbelief. "At Oakley you accused me of doing that with Jefferson Bell

237

when I was innocent. Now you are encouraging me to throw myself at men?" She flashed him a disapproving glare. "I don't like it, and I'm not going to do it. I happen to be married."

"You're a detective," Nacona reminded her sternly. "A good detective employs every device available and preys on every opportunity. I've gleaned information in various ways and—"

"Are you trying to tell me that you've slept with women to acquire information?" The thought stung, though she told herself that being jealous and possessive was a waste of emotion.

"I'm saying that with your stunning beauty, you will have opportunities with men I won't have in this particular case," Nacona paraphrased, hoping to avoid argument. He didn't.

"I would prefer to gain information because of my intellect, not my body," July said huffily.

Nacona grumbled under his breath. "I didn't say you had to sleep with every rancher in the county, for God's sake, only that you should take a liberal approach to the limitations of wedlock. And don't you dare lose that Scotch-Irish temper of yours and start reading some amorous suitor the riot act."

"If I am to have loose morals, then what was that demonstrative kiss on main street supposed to prove?" she muttered.

"I want our new neighbors to think I'm hopelessly devoted to you. It is my reason for being here that they question," he retorted. "I'm supposed to be so smitten with you that I gave up my profession to settle down as a rancher and census agent, remember? I'll be doing most of the snooping, and you'll be doing the prying—no matter what form it takes."

"I don't think I like this," July grumbled.

What hurt the most was that, for all Nacona's amorous attention, he didn't care if she cavorted with other men so long as it got him the information he wanted. She thought he had come to care about her, just a little. Obviously, lust was all that motivated him. And worse, he had obviously begun to tire of her. This was his way of severing the bond between them.

"You're the one who was all fired up to become a fabled female sleuth," Nacona reminded her crossly. "If it means using your feminine charms, then you'll do it. Do you understand me, July?"

"I understand perfectly." She said, staring straight ahead. Something twisted in her chest. She had the sneaking suspicion it might have been her heart.

From here on out, July promised to remember her place on Nacona's list of priorities. She was a source of physical pleasure and a tool to wrench facts from love-starved men. She should have found a way to acquire this assignment without him!

Once they had retrieved their supplies and halted in front of the Cheyenne Club, July gathered her composure. If Nacona wanted her to charm the breeches off every cowhand, businessman, and wrangler in the territory, then she would do it, just to prove she could. She hoped it made him insanely jealous to watch her flaunt herself. It wouldn't of course. Nacona's heart—if he had one—wasn't part of this bargain. She would be a fool if she let herself forget that.

When Nacona entered the elegant social club, he put

his best foot forward to introduce himself and his wife. It was obvious that the curvaceous blonde was the main attraction. Male heads turned when July sashayed by, flinging her admirers smiles that could melt them in their boots. And she was even more effective with her come-hither glances than July had anticipated. She had thrown herself into the role of temptress and was playing it to the hilt, though all poise, grace, and elegance. Eager to make her acquaintance, every male in the establishment flocked to her.

Leaving July to her eager admirers, Nacona ambled off to fetch a drink, only to find a shapely young brunette eyeing him with obvious interest. The fashionably dressed female was aplume in her fine feathers that must have cost an arm and a leg. A bejeweled necklace adorned her bare neck, and her ample bosoms were exposed to their best advantage. Employing a drum-roll walk, the brunette sauntered over to loop her arm over Nacona's shoulder as if they were intimate friends . . . or were about to be.

"You're the former gunslinger-turned-cattleman I've been hearing about." She slurred the words, testifying to an overindulgence in liquor. "Since your wife has bedeviled all the other men, you can entertain me." She extended a hand as if she expected Nacona to bow over it and kiss the diamond ring big enough to choke a horse.

He complied of course, flashing her a cavalier smile.

"I'm Angela Chambers." She tossed Nacona a provocative smile. "My friends call me Angel."

Nacona was willing to bet his reputation that this seductress was no angel. Angel Chambers had undoubtedly married C.L. for his money and cuckolded him every chance she got. She, it appeared, was an incorrigible flirt.

Nacona had met her kind before. Angel was the type of woman who craved—and thrived on—male attention. And yet, she could never get enough of it.

Excusing himself, Nacona ordered a drink from the bartender, whose duty, it seemed, was to keep a watchful eye on Angel Chambers. Either that or the young man was fantasizing about things he wished he were doing besides pouring drinks. Was he one of the studs in Angel's stable? Probably, Nacona decided.

Before Nacona could amble away, Angel clutched at his arm and towed him to a table in a deserted corner. The other patrons had flocked around July. Waves of laughter wafted across the barroom, assuring Nacona that she was dazzling her admirers with her keen wit. She was far better at gathering prospective suitors than he had anticipated. Nacona winced at the nip of jealousy. He wanted to march over and claim his husbandly rights, but he had ordered July to endear herself to the cattlemen who were enjoying their leisure. He had no right to be agitated with her, no right at all.

"So, tell me why such a legend maker like yourself opted to migrate north to try his hand at ranching," Angel requested as she studied him with open appreciation. "I should think you would grow restless in such an occupation, having had such unlimited freedom of movement." When another round of laughter erupted, Angel noticed where Nacona's attention had strayed. "Ah, so that's how it is, is it?"

Nacona jerked his gaze back to the sultry brunette who had leaned forward, offering him an unhindered view of her cleavage. This female was very good at striking poses that drew a man's eyes. Nacona wondered how many somebodies knew C.L.'s young wife in the most intimate sense. She had invitation stamped all over her.

Shaking off this thought, Nacona mustered a dreamy smile for his companion's sake. "When I met July, my wandering days were over. It appears the male citizens of Cheyenne are as enamored with her as I am." His dark eyes strayed toward July, and he smiled. "When I found her it was like finding that part of myself that had been missing all my life."

"A reformed rake. How delightful!" Angel said in her most provocative purr. "I've heard it said they make the most devoted husbands." She reached across the table to trail a carefully manicured hand over his bronzed cheek. "Your wife is very lucky, Nacona. I wonder if she appreciates your devotion. She seems to enjoy being the life of the party."

Nacona knew exactly what Angel was doing, casting shadows on her rival, planting seeds of suspicion. She was damned good at it, too. Nacona, however, refused to pick up the gauntlet.

"July simply attracts men," he said with a nonchalant shrug. "She can't help it. She dazzles like the sun, drawing admiring gazes. Men gravitate toward her, much as they are drawn toward you." He gave Angel the kind of look she seemed to thrive on. "You are a very desirable woman, Angel."

Angel blessed him with another evocative smile. "Thank you for noticing, love," she crooned. "And if your wife doesn't appreciate you . . ." Her smoky gray eyes slid over his muscular torso in blatant admiration, making it obvious that she liked what she saw and that she wasn't opposed to seeing far more. Her remark dangled in the air, giving Nacona plenty of time to draw his own conclusions on how far she was willing to go to console him.

"Does your husband mind that you offer comfort to the lovelorn, Angel?" he asked with raised eyebrows and a roguish smile.

She eased back in her chair to strike another provocative pose that called attention to her well-displayed feminine assets. "Clarence Lee is so busy counting his stacks of money that he rarely notices where I am or what I'm doing."

Nacona offered the compliment she seemed to crave. "Then I'm sorry to say your husband is neglecting the best part of his life."

Angel shrugged a half-bare shoulder. "I'm like one of his costly furnishings," she explained before sipping her drink. "Clarence Lee likes to surround himself with expensive trinkets and keepsakes. But I have no complaint about the way of things." She peered meaningfully at Nacona over the rim of her glass. "The arrangement suits us both."

I'll just bet it does, Nacona thought to himself. Angel delighted in preying on men's physical urges. No doubt, she relished the power she had over them, using her body to get what she wanted whenever she wanted it.

"I'm sure we'll see each other again," Nacona said, rising.

"I'm counting on it," Angel cooed and then batted her eyelashes.

"My wife and I have a great deal to do before we settle in at our ranch. If you'll excuse me, I'll collect her and see to our chores."

"You're dragging your wife away at such an early hour? And in the middle of a dozen conversations with all her admirers?" Angel taunted.

This sorceress delighted in causing dissension. Obviously she resented anyone who seemed happily married. Nacona had met several "Angels" during his extensive travels, but this temptress was extremely seasoned at amorous exploitation. Angel Chambers was in hog heaven when other females were miserable, especially if she was the cause of their misery.

Without responding to the comment, Nacona moseyed across the room to find July still holding court by the billiard tables. He paused to survey the gaggle of men basking in the warmth of her radiant beauty and sunny smile. As always, he found himself surveying the men, looking for the killer who had eluded him for two years. The ranchers made him curious. Each was of average height and weight, and all had the general physical characteristics of Charley Brazil. The first one was a small-time rancher, John Gilman by name. The second was Hub Butler, who had been standoffish when they had first met. Nacona supposed the man's pride was smarting because he had wanted the ranch which was to become headquarters for the investigation. The third man who caught Nacona's eye, not good looking but rather ordinary and plain, was Hoyt Simpson. Hoyt was so bedeviled by July's beauty that it was almost amusing, and he avoided Nacona's direct stare.

Nacona had also noticed two other probable suspects while he had been on the street. One looked like a gambler, and the other was a hired gun, probably working for one of the ranchers ogling July.

It would have been nice if Charley Brazil had stepped forward and identified himself sometime in the past two years so Nacona wouldn't be searching every face he passed. But Nacona knew Brazil might be dead—or in Denver. And if he had encountered Brazil face-to-face, would he have known it? If only he had seen Brazil . . . But the scoundrel was as elusive as the wind. Charley remained a step ahead of lawmen and detectives alike. Nonetheless, when this investigation was over, Nacona was going to retrace his steps to Denver and pursue that last lead. He would never forgive himself if he didn't.

Tucking away those bitter thoughts, Nacona shouldered his way through the crowd to take his place beside July "Excuse me, gentleman," he drawled politely. "My wife and I would like to take a look around the Golden Spur before dark. It's been a pleasure meeting you."

That said, he ushered July away from her fawning admirers and shepherded her toward the door.

"For a woman who protested playing the role she was assigned, you certainly seemed accommodating enough," Nacona observed as he stepped outside.

"That was the idea, wasn't it?" July half-turned to wave farewell to the clump of men in the club.

Was that a chord of jealousy she heard in Nacona's voice? Probably not, she thought realistically. It wasn't as if he had lacked for attention. She knew perfectly well that Angel Chambers was hovering around him while she'd been posing questions to the ranchers.

"Did you enjoy yourself at the club?" July couldn't help but ask.

"It was enlightening," Nacona replied. "C.L.'s little Angel seems to enjoy airing her wings."

"She married C.L. for his money, of course," July deduced. "I can't think of any other reason why she would have anything to do with that pompous banker. Maybe he's the ringleader of the robbers and he's been stockpiling money to ensure he can keep his claim on Angel. No wonder he put up a stink about paying back the entire fee if we failed in this endeavor. He really expects us to fail and prefers that we do since he is involved up to his neck in the shenanigans."

Nacona burst out laughing. "You're dashing to cliffs again. How can you leap to such an ill-founded conclusion?"

"Leave it to you to spew cold skepticism on the fires of my inspiration," she grumbled resentfully. "C.L. could be breaking the investors and cattlemen who have been dallying with his wife. Jealousy has been the motive for many a crime."

Nacona rolled his eyes in disbelief. "Woman, you can take a half-dozen wild conjectures, piece them together, and actually make them sound logical. It's downright scary."

"Won't you going to feel silly if C.L. turns out to be our culprit?"

"Aren't you going to feel silly when he *doesn't?*" Nacona countered.

"With a promiscuous wife like Angel, a man could be forced into behaving like the very devil."

"How well I know," Nacona grunted sourly.

"Thank you very much for insulting me," July sniffed, highly affronted.

"You're very welcome." Nacona scooped her up and

deposited her on the wagon seat. "And don't glower at me. People might see you."

At the moment, July didn't care if someone did. Sometimes Nacona's cutting remarks rankled her. To prevent herself from glaring in his direction, she twisted on the seat to send another coquettish wave and a blinding smile to the ranchers who had wandered onto the veranda of the club. Nacona wanted her to entice every man in the county, did he? Well, she would! And if those men beat a path to her doorstep to woo her, then he would get exactly what he deserved. Besides, nothing would make her happier than being the one who cracked this case wide open. That would show this dark-eyed devil a thing or two.

Chapter 16

July instinctively clutched at Nacona's arm when a huge black mongrel bounded off the front porch of their new ranchhouse to warn them off the property. The wild-eyed team of horses backed away when the monstrous beast bared his fangs and lunged at the intruders.

"Whoa, boy," Nacona croaked at the snarling beast. He didn't know what else to say but whoa to a dog that was as big as a half-grown foal.

Nacona recoiled when the growling creature reared up on powerful hind legs and slapped big paws on the edge of the wagon. The bark that erupted from his curled lips was enough to make the hair stand up on the back of one's neck.

"That's got to be the biggest damned dog I ever saw!" Nacona's voice was carefully controlled. He didn't want to further upset the already infuriated brute. He managed the semblance of a smile. "Nice dog . . . Have you eaten any men for supper lately?" His crooning voice didn't put a wag in the monster's tail. But then, the dog didn't bite off his arm, either. "You're just plain mean and ugly. I've met wolves with better dispositions." His soothing tone disguised the insult in his words. Still, the massive dog refused to remove himself or to allow Nacona to step down from his perch.

"Killer! Git down from there!" The bellow seemingly came from out of nowhere. "Git over here, Killer!"

"Killer?" July peered at the beast's frothing mouth and daggerlike teeth and gulped hard.

"Killer certainly seems hell-bent on living up to his name," Nacona murmured before flashing the mongrel his most charming smile. It didn't soothe the savage beast one whit. Killer snarled viciously.

"Down, Killer!" came the insistent voice.

The dog finally dropped onto all fours and trotted toward the wiry little man who hobbled around the corner of the house, favoring his left leg.

"Killer must have taken a bite out of his trainer," July speculated. "If I were Killer's owner, I'd never let him go hungry, that's for certain!"

The spry, bandy-legged cowboy, who stood only five foot six inches in his boot heels, hobbled forward with Killer one step behind him. "Sorry about that," he apologized. "Mr. Chambers sent a messenger out to tell me you was comin'. I plain forgot to chain Killer up. He ain't a bad dog exactly."

Exactly? July cast an apprehensive glance at the black mutt. The animal looked positively dangerous to her.

"Killer just ain't bin hisself since Bob Foster got shot down durin' that rustler attack." The ranch foreman reached down to stroke the panting mongrel's broad head. "Killer guards the door of the house, waitin' for

Bob to come back. If Killer likes you, yer his friend for life."

"And if he doesn't?" Careful not to make any sudden movements that invited attack, Nacona eased a hip off the seat and slid to the ground. To his relief, Killer didn't pounce, but the mongrel did trot over to sniff at Nacona's trousers.

"If he don't like ya, then he ain't one bit friendly," the ranch foreman explained. A faint smile hovered on his lips, exposing the wide gap between his two front teeth. After cleansing his soiled right hand on his soiled breeches, he extended it to Nacona. "Otto Knott is my name. I've bin keepin' the place runnin' until C.L. Chambers found a buyer. I guess you'd be the buyer."

Nacona clasped the callused hand and firmly shook it. "Nacona Bleu," he introduced himself. "And this is my wife July."

Otto politely tipped his dusty sombrero and ventured another smile. "Pleased ta meet ya, ma'am." A muddled frown puckered his brows as he glanced back at the tall, muscular giant in fashionable clothes. "Seems like I've heard that name afore." He rubbed his whiskered chin and frowned thoughtfully. "Bleu, ya say? I thought there was a gunslinger down Kansas way who went by that name. I heard he got shot down in New Mexico a few months back. Was he a relative of yers?"

"I *am* him," Nacona informed the foreman with a grin, amused that someone always had him dead and buried before his time. A hazard of his profession, he supposed. "But I am no longer a gun for hire." He turned to lift July down beside him. His hand grazed her creamy cheek in

251

a gesture of affection. "I've found a far more rewarding purpose in life."

Ot peered at the lovely blonde who was staring adoringly at the muscular hulk of a man who was her husband, and a lump formed in his throat. He had never found his mate. Obviously the ex-gunslinger had, and it had turned his life around. Touching, thought Ot, very touching indeed.

Clearing his throat, Ot Knott limped around to the back of the wagon to unload the oak rocking chair and the stacks of unidentifiable packages. "Well, Mr. Bleu, even if ya ain't in the gunfightin' bus'ness no more, it will be nice to have yer expertise 'round here. We've had all sorts of trouble with outlaws. I guess C.L. told you 'bout that."

"Please call me Nacona." He cast Killer a wary glance before walking back to assist Ot with the supplies. "And yes, the banker mentioned the difficulties. But the Golden Spur seemed the perfect place to begin our new life together."

While Nacona and Ot toted the supplies into the house, Killer sniffed July up one side and down the other. "Nice puppy," July purred sweetly.

Killer growled and she froze. Obviously purring voices reminded Killer of cats. She made a mental note never to offend him again. "Come, Killer," she demanded, employing another tactic.

Bravely, July strode toward the porch with Killer sniffing at her heels. When she opened the door, Killer very nearly knocked her knees out from under her in his haste to barge inside. A startled yelp erupted from July's lips as she stumbled back in attempt to catch her balance.

She tripped on the hem of her gown and landed with a thud and a groan in an unceremonious heap. A gasp broke from her throat when Killer, who had caused her fall lunged at her. July stared goggle-eyed at the broad face poised two inches above hers while she lay spread-eagled on the floor. The mongrel's front paws were wedged against her shoulders, and his hind legs straddled her waist. Great black eyes stared down into her alarmed face for several unnerving seconds, and then, to July's amazement, Killer licked her cheek with his tongue.

"Well, I'll be damned." Ot Knot chuckled as he limped through the parlor. "It looks as if Killer likes ya."

July wasn't at all certain that was to her advantage. Friend or foe, the oversize mutt was a nuisance. And for all she knew, Killer was just getting a taste of her so he'd know where to come for his next meal.

When Nacona reached down to assist July to her feet, Killer growled deep in his throat. Nacona automatically jerked back his hand before the brute decided to bite it off at the wrist.

"If he likes ya, he'll take commands," Ot assured July. "Tell him to sit down and he will."

July gulped down the lump in her throat and mustered a firm, commanding voice. "Killer, sit down."

With a wag of his tail, the huge creature lumbered over and plunked its great body down on a rug which lay in the corner of the parlor. While Killer was lounging on his braided throne, Nacona set July on her feet and dusted her off. An amused grin quirked his lips as he readjusted her lopsided bonnet.

"Why don't you take a look around, my love, and

decide where you want Ot and me to stash the supplies?" he suggested. "And then you can coax Killer out of the house before he infests it with ticks and fleas."

"Nope," Ot cut in, shaking his head. "Bob Foster always let Killer sleep inside the front door. I tried to move him outside after Bob was . . ." His voice failed at the thought of his previous boss's death. "Well, I just wouldn't mess with Killer's braided rug, not if I was you. He'll take it personally. He's a good guard dog. He might be a comfort to the missus when yer gone."

"Is that how you acquired your limp?" July couldn't help but ask. "By trying to evict Killer from the premises?"

"No, ma'am. I got shot tryin' to stop the rustlers. Doc said I'll likely be stiff-legged for a few months. But if it weren't for Killer, I'd be pushin' up daisies myself. He couldn't get to Bob in time to divert the rustlers, but he did manage to rescue me. Killer startled the rustlers' horses while they was tryin' to shoot. Otherwise . . ." Ot shook off the bleak memories. "Well, we better git yer belongin's inside afore dark. I'll have Cookie send up yer supper afore me and the other men take our meal."

"Cookie?" July questioned curiously.

"That's what we call him." Ot grinned. "He don't mind it neither. His real name is Audey Ball. But when some of the cowboys shortened it and started calling him Aud Ball, he objected."

Ot Knott and Aud Ball? July smothered a grin. Strange names. Obviously the cowboys had weird senses of humor.

"He's my cousin," Ot informed them. "He can't ride, rope, or shoot straight, but he can cook dam-fi-no pie with calf-slobber meringue, molasses custard, and fricadilles like you've never tasted. Just ya wait an' see."

July could wait. Calf-slobber meringue? She shivered, repulsed by the image that leaped to mind. Suddenly she wasn't as hungry as she'd thought while they rode toward the ranch.

When Ot and Nacona ambled off to fetch the rest of their belongings, July inspected the compact house. It only took a moment to realize Bob Foster had been a bachelor. The decor was plain and without a woman's touch. He had obviously been a man of simple tastes, demanding only the barest necessities of life. The furniture was sparse and poorly arranged, at least in July's opinion. She set about remedying that situation immediately. Then, with the aid of soap, a mop, and several dust rags, she put the ranchhouse in livable condition, except for the mutt's Olympian throne in the corner. No amount of coaxing, no firm commands, prompted Killer to budge from his spot. He was there to stay, just as Ot Knott had said.

While Nacona ambled off with Ot to meet the wranglers in charge of the herd, July plopped into their recently purchased rocker to jot down the information she had acquired at the Cheyenne Club. She alphabetically listed each rancher she had met, noting all the background information she had managed to wring out of him. She had also inquired as to what the ranchers thought of the bankers in the area and the railroad and its contribution to the cattle business.

C.L. Chambers was not the most popular man in town, not by a long shot. But mention of his wife had raised several eyebrows. July was certain the fallen Angel had spread her charms around Cheyenne. No doubt, Nacona had been offered the chance to take a few liberties. July wondered if he would. All in the line of duty for the investigation, of course, she mused resentfully.

The jealous thought caused her to grumble in annoyance. Her emotions were in a tailspin. Nacona was paying her attention in order to convince the ranch hands and townsfolk of his devotion to her, but he had her half-believing he was sincere. She had to remind herself it was all an act. She couldn't let herself be caught up in this cunning charade. The investigation was their primary objective, and Nacona was just playing a role.

Killer's low growl announced Nacona's approach. Cautiously, Nacona craned his neck around the partially opened door to determine how well his entrance would be received. Killer didn't bound to his feet, but neither did he wag his tail in greeting.

"That flea bag has to go," Nacona declared as he trod lightly across the room.

"I already asked him to leave," July informed him. "He said no, as only Killer can."

Nacona forgot his preoccupation with the mongrel when he noticed the notes July had on her lap. After scooping up the papers, he folded himself into a chair and studied the information. "Your afternoon at the club seems to have been highly productive. Good work, July. I'm impressed."

July tamped down the pleasure his praise evoked and concentrated on the business at hand. "These are the two ranchers who have foreign and Eastern backers." She directed his attention to the names on her list. "Hoyt Simpson came up from Denver about eighteen months

MORE PASSION AND ADVENTURE AWAIT... YOUR TRIP TO A BIG ADVENTUROUS WORLD BEGINS WHEN YOU ACCEPT YOUR FIRST 4 NOVELS ABSOLUTELY *FREE* (AN $18.00 VALUE)

Accept your Free gift and start to experience more of the passion and adventure you like in a historical romance novel. Each Zebra novel is filled with proud men, spirited women and tempestuous love that you'll remember long after you turn the last page.

Zebra Historical Romances are the finest novels of their kind. They are written by authors who really know how to weave tales of romance and adventure in the historical settings you love. You'll feel like you've actually gone back in time with the thrilling stories that each Zebra novel offers.

GET YOUR FREE GIFT WITH THE START OF YOUR HOME SUBSCRIPTION

Our readers tell us that these books sell out very fast in book stores and often they miss the newest titles. So Zebra has made arrangements for you to receive the four newest novels published each month.

You'll be guaranteed that you'll never miss a title, and home delivery is so convenient. And to show you just how easy it is to get Zebra Historical Romances, we'll send you your first 4 books absolutely FREE! Our gift to you just for trying our home subscription service.

BIG SAVINGS AND FREE HOME DELIVERY

Each month, you'll receive the four newest titles as soon as they are published. You'll probably receive them even before the bookstores do. What's more, you may preview these exciting novels free for 10 days. If you like them as much as we think you will, just pay the low preferred subscriber's price of just $3.75 each. *You'll save $3.00 each month off the publisher's price.* AND, your savings are even greater because there are never any shipping, handling or other hidden charges—FREE Home Delivery. Of course you can return any shipment within 10 days for full credit, no questions asked. There is no minimum number of books you must buy.

4 FREE BOOKS

TO GET YOUR 4 FREE BOOKS WORTH $18.00 — MAIL IN THE FREE BOOK CERTIFICATE T O D A Y

Fill in the Free Book Certificate below, and we'll send your FREE BOOKS to you as soon as we receive it.

If the certificate is missing below, write to: Zebra Home Subscription Service, Inc., P.O. Box 5214, 120 Brighton Road, Clifton, New Jersey 07015-5214.

FREE BOOK CERTIFICATE

4 FREE BOOKS

ZEBRA HOME SUBSCRIPTION SERVICE, INC.

YES! Please start my subscription to Zebra Historical Romances and send me my first 4 books absolutely FREE. I understand that each month I may preview four new Zebra Historical Romances free for 10 days. If I'm not satisfied with them, I may return the four books within 10 days and owe nothing. Otherwise, I will pay the low preferred subscriber's price of just $3.75 each; a total of $15.00, *a savings off the publisher's price of $3.00.* I may return any shipment and I may cancel this subscription at any time. There is no obligation to buy any shipment and there are no shipping, handling or other hidden charges. Regardless of what I decide, the four free books are mine to keep.

NAME _____

ADDRESS _____ APT _____

CITY _____ STATE _____ ZIP _____

( )
TELEPHONE _____

SIGNATURE _____ (if under 18, parent or guardian must sign)

ZB0893

Terms, offer and prices subject to change without notice. Subscription subject to acceptance by Zebra Books. Zebra Books reserves the right to reject any order or cancel any subscription.

ago, trailing stock he bought in Texas. According to Hoyt, he met several prospective investors in Pueblo, all Easterners who were looking to expand their profits by buying into the cattle industry. He's thirtyish, or thereabout."

She pointed to the second name. "Hub Butler also operates a syndicated ranch—with foreign investments. He showed up about two years ago, but he came from Missouri to purchase Texas cattle with outside financial backing. He's the one who tried to buy the Golden Spur," she reminded Nacona. "His ranch sits just north of here. I suspect both he and Hoyt have other interests besides cattle. And they both appear to be close friends of Angel Chambers."

Nacona snorted caustically. "I'm almost afraid to ask what brought you to that conclusion. After a few minutes with the banker's wife, I'd swear she is partial to anything in breeches."

"I could certainly believe that." She flung Nacona a glance which suggested he ought to know just how promiscuous Angel was. Then, casting her unwarranted jealousy aside, July indicated the other three names on her list. "John Gilman, Derrek Paine, and Jordon Milner are successful ranchers, though they don't operate on such a large scale as Hoyt and Hub. I think all three men also have eyes for Angel Chambers."

"I don't know how they could have been eyeing Angel this afternoon. It looked to me as if they were all giving *you* the eye."

"That was what you wanted," she reminded him tartly. "But when I mentioned Angel's name in passing, I deciphered several smug smiles which could mean only one thing, and that is—"

Nacona flung up a hand in a deterring gesture. "I think we're getting sidetracked here. This is not an investigation to determine how many men are sleeping with the banker's wife to compensate for the interest on their loans. We need facts about which ranchers might have hired gunslingers who resort to rustling and robbery. You've been involved with too many cases concerning roaming husbands and unfaithful wives."

"Well, fine," July said huffily. "I'll approach this case from my angle, and you can come at it from your direction. I happen to think that C. L. Chambers is involved somehow because of his promiscuous wife. Jealous revenge could be the motive. I think it sounds logical."

"I think it sounds ridiculous," Nacona contradicted.

"Then you can saddle up first thing in the morning and trot off to locate the outlaws' hideout," July suggested flippantly. "I personally doubt you'll find one. Intuition tells me that—"

Nacona groaned loudly. "I knew this partnership wasn't going to work. We don't operate on the same plane."

"Your idea of investigation is to snoop around until you find somebody to shoot down. Then you start asking questions in hopes you'll stumble onto something. That is the primitive approach, as my brothers refer to it. If these rustlings and robberies aren't all connected, I'll eat my bonnet, feather and all."

"I'll see that it's boiled down, just the way you like it," Nacona mocked dryly. "You are simply implicating C.L. and Angel Chambers because you don't happen to like them. But even if C.L. is involved—and I'm only agreeing with you for the sake of argument—he is obviously not one of the eleven men who were reported to have been on hand when Bob Foster was murdered and Ot Knott was shot in the leg. I questioned the cowhands about the incident. They claimed the rustlers were garbed in linen dusters that made it difficult to describe their heights and weights. And they had concealed their faces with bandannas. I cannot imagine C.L. riding with them. He doesn't seem the type to straddle a horse for any purpose, not when his plump body fits better into a buggy."

"George Hershberger and C.L. informed me that the bank and train robbers were garbed in similar attire," July added. "The thieves are undoubtedly one and the same, and C.L. is probably the mastermind, even if he isn't riding with the bandits. He's only trying to throw us off the track."

"And how, Miss Know-it-all, do you suppose the thieves acquired information about which ranches to strike and when railroads carried payrolls for their workers?" Nacona snorted, trying to shoot holes in her unfounded theories.

"C.L. Chambers, of course," July declared with great conviction. "The man has his hands on the pulse of every coin that moves in the county. He knows when payrolls are to arrive and when cattlemen have sold their stock or when they are on roundup."

Nacona threw up his hands in exasperation. "Shall I go shoot him to see if the robberies in the area come to a screeching halt?"

July sent him her best glower. Damn his ridicule. He was just like every other man. He didn't give her credit for possessing a deductive mind. "You are so pigheaded that you refuse—"

The argument died quickly when Killer sprang to his feet, charged across the parlor, and skidded around the corner into the dining room. The rocking chair in which July had been sitting teetered sideways and crashed to the floor when Killer's swishing tail collided with it. From force of habit, Nacona clutched his pistol and wheeled toward the rattling sounds in the dining room.

"Hullo! It's me."

July and Nacona didn't have the slightest idea who *me* was, but Killer seemed to. The scratching and growling at the back door ceased immediately. Nacona and July surged into the room to find Killer sniffing at the edges of the door. His tail thumped against the the wall.

"Kin I come in?" Cookie called from outside. "I brought yer dinner. It's son-of-a-gun stew and cabbage pie. I would've fixed somethin' special for yer arrival, but I ran clean outa time."

July stood aside while Cookie waddled inside with steaming pots of food. The cook was as plump as his cousin was thin. Aud Ball reminded July of rising dough with his pudgy jowls and round shiny cheeks. There was a natural smile on his lips and a twinkle in his hazel eyes.

"Ev'nin', ma'am," Aud murmured before he set the meal on the stove. "I'm pleased to make yer acquaintance. Ot said ya was a real beauty." His assessing gaze flooded over her in blatant approval. "I thought Ot had just bin away from town too long, away from those of the feminine persuasion in particular. But his description didn't near do ya justice."

"Why thank you, Aud." July graced him with a blinding smile.

"Call me Cookie, if ya please. I've bin called Aud all my life. I've taken enough teasin' 'bout it a'ready."

"Very well, Cookie it is." July pivoted to sniff the aromatic pots on the stove. "Dinner smells delicious."

"The men think cabbage pie makes laripin' good lickin'. I hope you'll like it, too, ma'am."

July flashed him another smile. Somehow the sound of cabbage pie did nothing to tempt her taste buds. But who knew? She might learn to like Cookie's country cooking. One could only hope.

As it turned out, the meal was delicious. As Ot had said, his cousin's cooking was out of this world. Killer loved it, too. The mutt sat beside July, ogling her plate with eager eyes. July tossed him an occasional morsel, careful not to let her fingers become one of Killer's delicacies.

"I'm going to take a look around," Nacona announced after he'd wolfed down his meal.

"In the dark?"

"According to Ot, the rustlers usually work at night. That indicates the thieves are familiar with the terrain and with every ranch they strike. I want to determine just how familiar these bandits need to be to keep from breaking their necks while cutting out part of a herd at high speed."

"That's it!" July popped out of her chair, startling Killer who let out a bark.

"What is it?" Nacona half-turned to stare at this female sleuth who could leap from one wild conjecture to another like a confounded jackrabbit.

July stopped short and peered at his dubious expression. Evidently he was prepared to reject her speculations before she even voiced them. "Nothing. It was a silly thought," she said with a dismissive shrug. "After giving it consideration, I realize the hypothesis has too many loopholes." She turned back to scoop up the plates. "While you're gone, I'll make up your bed with the fresh linens we purchased."

"*My* bed?" Nacona's thick brows collided over narrowed black eyes.

July pivoted and tilted her chin. "If memory serves me correctly, and I'm certain it does, our bargain was a three-day honeymoon. Those were *your* terms."

"But I thought—"

"That I would be at your convenience indefinitely?" July cut in, having acquired Nacona's bad habit of interrupting in midsentence.

It may have been Nacona's intention to let her down gently, but she was cutting him off completely. He had bruised her heart, but he had not intended to crush her pride.

"As you told me, master detective," she continued with a saucy toss of her blond curls. "One must never presume assumptions to be fact."

Dark, penetrating eyes sliced through her. Nacona gave her a look that was worth a thousand words, none of which July dared to ask him to translate. But no matter how he disliked the arrangements, she was no longer going to lower herself to being available merely for his physical release. Ordering her to throw herself at men for the sake of information pretty much had said it all, in her estimation. It was obvious that she cared more than Nacona did and she had decided that this seductive rake was not joining her in bed unless she mattered to him, *truly* mattered to him. That was the way it was going to be, since Nacona had given no indication that he felt more than lust. A deal was a deal. The stipulations had been met.

"Is this your way of punishing me because I didn't accept your illogical conclusions about C. L. Chambers?" Nacona growled sourly.

July gasped in outrage. "Do you think I intend to withhold sexual privileges just to get you to agree with my theories? If you do, then you're a bigger fool than I am, Nacona Bleu!"

"And just what the sweet loving hell is *that* supposed to mean?" he demanded in a gruff voice.

"Oh, never mind." July wheeled toward the table where Killer was helping himself to the leftovers. "Go about your slinking, master sleuth. I have my own matters to attend to."

With a wordless scowl, Nacona whipped open the back door and slammed it shut behind him, provoking Killer to bark. Now what was the matter with her? Nacona wondered. He'd thought the two of them were getting along superbly, except that they didn't agree on investigative approaches. Then that temperamental hellion had decided to evict him from her bed, despite the splendor they had shared. What bee did she have in her bonnet now?

If she wants to be bullheaded, I'll let her, Nacona thought bitterly. July wasn't the only female in the county. Cheyenne boasted thirty-five saloons teeming with calico queens, and prostitutes were available in dozens of bordellos. He would find somebody else to accommodate him, just to prove to her that she was not leading *him* around on a leash.

Nacona broke stride and cursed at the thought that penetrated his sulky mind. He had left the people of Cheyenne with the impression that he was hopelessly devoted to his wife. He had to maintain that impression.

Or did he? There were such things as lovers' spats. If he didn't know better he would swear he and July had just had one, even if she didn't exactly love him and he didn't exactly love her. No doubt, she was trying to make some profound point. Too bad he didn't know what the hell it was. But what man ever really knew where he stood when it came to a woman? Nacona had once heard it said that any man who claimed to understand the workings of the feminine mind was either a fool or a complete idiot. Nacona chose to be referred to as neither.

Drawing himself up, he stormed toward the barn to saddle a mount. He could outwait that sassy spitfire, just see if he couldn't! One day she'd come to *him*, requesting to join him in *his* bed. And if she didn't . . .

Nacona growled in irritation. That green-eyed nymph had become a habit it was difficult to unlearn. He had grown accustomed to their companionable silences, their lively debates, the mindless pleasures of passion. Though he had assumed July enjoyed those things as much as he did, her present attitude indicated she had only catered to him because of the terms of their bargain. Now the honeymoon was over and they were back to pistols at twenty paces. How could he puzzle out who was responsible for the local thievery while he was so preoccupied with that infuriating vixen? She was making him crazy.

C. L. Chambers behind the robbing and rustling? Nacona rolled his eyes skyward. What kind of warped logic was that? No wonder he couldn't understand the woman. That was the most ridiculous conjecture he had ever heard, almost as ridiculous, in fact, as letting himself believe that he and the feisty blonde could ever be compatible for more than two days at a time.

Chapter 17

Leaving Killer to guard the house, July ambled past the corrals to locate a mount. She could hear the murmur of voices in the bunkhouse and was relieved that no one was around to question her departure. The comment Nacona had voiced earlier kept drumming against her mind. Since it was only a mile to town, July intended to snoop around while he was doing his nocturnal prowling on the perimeters of the Golden Spur.

Even though Nacona was certain she was barking up the wrong tree, July planned to test her theories. The instant she arrived in town she spied Jordon Milner, one of the small-time ranchers she had met at the club. After the incident in Denver in which she had very nearly become a victim of abuse, July decided not to press her luck. Milner would make as good an escort as the next man. She could wheedle information out of him while she strolled the streets, searching for evidence to support her theories.

"What are you doing back in town all alone?" Jordon queried incredulously. "I didn't think that doting husband of yours would let you out of his sight for more than five minutes."

July sent him a look of frustration, and since she was mad at Nacona already, she didn't have to call upon her theatrical abilities. "We had a verbal sparring match," she explained as Jordon fell into step beside her. "Nacona is much too possessive at times. I need space in which to breathe." That's a laugh, she thought. The real Nacona Bleu was anything but possessive. He didn't care what she did or with whom.

"Your husband won't call me out for escorting you down the street, will he?" Jordon asked. "Considering his reputation and all—"

"No need to worry." July waved away his concerns. "His irritation is with me and only me."

The lanky rancher relaxed as he ambled beside her, giving her the grand tour of Cheyenne. He pointed out Shingle and Locke's Saloon and Frenchy's, where more than just rotgut and snake head whiskey was served. The saloons ranged from one-room shanties with dirt floors to long, clapboard buildings with painted and wallpapered interiors, ornately carved mahogany bars, lively piano music, and oil paintings that depicted ladies in various states of undress. Jordon assured July that fine liquors, the latest mixed drinks were available, even anchovies and Russian caviar could be found on some menus. He also seemed especially pleased to announce that Wild Bill Hickok had once wrecked the premises of Greer Brothers Gold Room when a Mississippi cardsharp had tried to cheat him.

July was only half-listening while Jordon spoke. She was busy surveying the activities on the street and peering

268

through the opened doors of the gaming halls and saloons. She wanted to familiarize herself with the faces of the men who frequented Cheyenne's infamous watering holes. Her gaze narrowed when she saw Hub Butler pass beneath a street light, heading toward a questionable-looking establishment at the end of the block. Several cowhands had just exited that building—men July had seen milling in front of the Cheyenne Club earlier in the day.

"Just what is that building over there?" she asked curiously.

Jordon chuckled. "That's no place for a lady like you. I can tell you that."

"A dance hall?" she prodded as they strolled down the shadowed boardwalk.

"No," Jordon replied, biting back a grin. "There is some dancing going on, but it isn't the main activity at Cheyenne Rose's Pleasure Parlor."

"A bordello?" Her pensive gaze narrowed on the three-story building.

"The most popular one in town," Jordon confirmed.

"And do you frequent that parlor?" she dared to ask.

Jordon looked amused by the brash question, and a tad bit uncomfortable.

"I'm sorry. That is none of my business."

"Rose's girls are . . . um . . . er . . . expensive," he explained as delicately as he knew how. "They maintain high standards for their clients." Jordon tugged at the collar of his shirt to relieve the mounting pressure. "They cater to . . . I shouldn't be discussing such things with a lady like you."

July patted his arm and flashed him a spellbinding

smile. "I didn't mean to make you feel uncomfortable, Jordon. But I am sorry to report that I am as curious as a cat. I noticed Hub Butler going inside the Parlor and well . . . I was under the impression that he and Angel Chambers . . ." She purposely let the comment dangle like bait on a hook, hoping Jordon would bite. Sure enough, he did.

"So you noticed, did you?" Jordon chortled before stepping forward to shield July from a stumbling drunk. "Hub and Angel have been . . . er . . . well, I think you already know that. You are very astute."

"Too much so perhaps." July's lips twitched as she glanced at Jordon. "I'm afraid I got the same impression about you, and a few of the other ranchers I met this afternoon. Angel is a very stunning woman, I must agree."

Jordon threw back his head and laughed heartily. "Are you always this straightforward, July?"

She tossed him an impishly charming grin. "I'm afraid so. And being new in town, I don't want to cast glances in the wrong directions."

Jordon beamed at the insinuation. "A glance in my direction would be quickly accepted. And for the record, my involvement with Angel is shallow. I think she keeps company with me on occasion just to make Hoyt Simpson and Hub Butler jealous. In her eyes, we small ranchers aren't quite good enough for her expensive tastes. When she married money, she became accustomed to it in a hurry. Angel spends most of her time fraternizing with the ranchers who can afford her while C.L. is busy making money and poring over his ledgers. Why, I even heard that C.L. had background investigations done on everyone who has a loan with him, just to see if he could dig up any dirt."

July tucked that tidbit of information in her mind and then proceeded with her subtle investigation. "If Hub and Hoyt are Angel's most frequent companions, why was Hub strolling into the Pleasure Parlor?" July questioned.

Jordon grinned rakishly. "Men have varied tastes, my dear lady, as do some women."

He seemed to speculate as to whether July might be one of those women. As Nacona had insisted, she took advantage of her escort's growing interest. Curling her hand around Jordan's arm, she gestured toward the nearest restaurant.

"Would you consider joining me in a cup of tea, kind sir?"

Jordon returned her engaging smile. "Nothing would delight me more . . . at least for the moment," he added with a suggestive tilt of his brows.

All things considered, July thought she was having a very productive evening. Jordon Milner had turned out to be a walking encyclopedia of useful knowledge, and by the time they had sipped two cups of tea, July had begun to put the names and faces of ranchers and cowhands together. She also came up with the names of several cattle detectives who were working for various ranchers in the area. Jordon made no bones about the fact that ranchers had hired more than guns to protect their livestock from rustlers and from neighboring ranchers who might be tempted to change a few brands for profit.

The most puzzling piece of information July acquired as they hopped from one topic of conversation to the other concerned the bank and train robberies. Jordon mentioned that several banks had been robbed during storms. The thunder and lightning had kept most folks off the streets and had concealed the explosions necessary to gain entrance to the bank safes. July certainly didn't venture out during storms unless absolutely necessary. She stayed safely tucked away from lightning. But such timing for the crimes was ingenious. The thefts went virtually unnoticed until the following morning, and by then tracks that might have led a posse to the culprits had been washed away. Even some of the train holdups had occurred during storms which had made it impossible for guards to see or hear the approach of riders until the thieves were upon them. July sensed that she was dealing with a cunning mastermind rather than a hapless band of desperadoes.

Was C. L. Chambers that clever? He probably had a good mind. After all, he was in charge of the bank. Playing the model citizen, he could be making a fortune by having a band of thieves rob banks and make off with railroad payrolls and rustle cattle that could be shipped off and sold at forty dollars a head to meat-packing plants in Chicago. If the rustling and the robberies were connected, the scheme was exceptionally clever.

When Jordon escorted July back to the street, she stopped short at seeing Angel Chambers sashaying down the boardwalk on Hoyt Simpson's arm. Angel regarded July with a devilish smile and then glanced at Jordon.

July could almost see the cogs in Angel's mind turning as she ambled past them. That woman was trouble, she decided. But she couldn't pass up the kind of gossip Nacona had suggested she use to her advantage. No doubt, word would spread that she was available for extramarital adventures.

The shaft of light that splintered from the bank window indicated C.L. was working late—on some fiendish plot to rob another train or bank, July surmised. While Angel was cavorting about town with one of her lovers, C. L. was scheming to get even in his own way.

"I'm sorry," Jordon apologized as he guided July toward her steed. "Knowing Angel, I am sure you will be the subject of much gossip."

July shrugged nonchalantly. "My disagreement with my husband is a private matter. Just because a woman is married doesn't mean she cannot enjoy various types of friendships. Angel obviously shares the same philosophy."

Jordon peered up at the bewitching blonde who had settled herself upon her horse. "You have a very liberal outlook on marriage, it seems."

July elevated one delicate brow to a challenging angle. "Don't most men, Jordon? What's good for the gander is good for the goose, I should think."

That said, July reined her steed toward the Golden Spur and trotted away. When she passed Cheyenne Rose's Pleasure Parlor, Hub Butler stepped outside. He stopped dead in his tracks and glanced around, expecting to see Nacona somewhere in the near distance. When he didn't, a rakish smile curved his lips.

"Riding alone at night, July?" he questioned, his voice a seductive purr.

"Yes, as a matter of fact, I am." She sent him a sultry smile. "Would you care to accompany me home?"

Hub flashed her an accommodating grin. "I would be delighted. I was just headed in that direction myself."

July waited a moment for Hub to retrieve his mount, and together they cantered down the path that led to the Golden Spur and on to the Cabestro Ranch.

"You surprise me," Hub remarked a few minutes later.

"Do I? In what way?" July forced herself to toss Hub a seductive smile.

"Your husband seems hopelessly devoted to you, and I can see why. But I had not expected to find you out and about at night." He cast her a speculative glance.

"Nor did I expect to see you sauntering out of Cheyenne Rose's Pleasure Parlor," she parried with a teasing grin. "Perhaps we have misjudged each other, Mr. Butler."

"Hub," he corrected. "And perhaps we have."

"We shall make good neighbors, I think," July said in a provocative voice.

"Better than most," he countered in a suggestive tone.

July decided then and there that Hub Butler, like Hoyt Simpson and Jordon Milner, was indeed a man of varied tastes. His seductive glances and tone of voice indicated that he wouldn't be opposed to keeping a handful of women at his disposal. It seemed Angel was only one of the females who appeased his male appetites. July had unveiled all sorts of interesting facts during this day and night, but one thread of discovery soured her. Men, it seemed, were governed by physical desire.

Loyal husbands and suitors seemed in danger of extinction, like the herds of buffalo. If she had thought that Nacona would care for her in the ways that truly mattered, she was the world's biggest imbecile. He was exactly like the rest of his gender.

The touch of Hub's hand on her arm brought July from her musings. The feel of cool lips playing on hers shocked her beyond words. With tremendous effort, she forced herself not to pull away, but the comparisons she was making during this unexpected kiss rattled her. If not for this charade Nacona had designed, July would have doubled up her fist and knocked Hub out of his saddle. Blast it, why did she feel she was betraying Nacona when he didn't care what she did in pursuit of information, even bedding other men.

"You taste as good as you look," Hub murmured as he resettled himself on his perch. "A pity your husband isn't man enough to satisfy a woman like you."

July struggled to maintain control of her temper. She yearned to tell this arrogant rascal what she thought of his kisses, to assure him that Nacona was more of a man than he could ever dream of being. Unsure of what to say without inviting another amorous assault, July said nothing at all. Hub, Hoyt, and Jordon obviously were men who moved very quickly in their pursuits of women. July only hoped she could remain one step ahead of them.

"By all means come to the Cabestro Ranch and let me show you around sometime soon," Hub invited as he closed the distance July had placed between them.

"I will," she assured him, easing her steed away. "I volunteered to help Nacona take the livestock census. It gives me an excuse to go where I please." She mustered a provocative smile. "Is tomorrow too soon?"

Hub grinned like a starved shark. "Not soon enough, sweetheart. I'll be counting the minutes. . . ."

So would July, and with trepidation. Her shoulders slumped in relief when she veered through the arched gateway that led to the Golden Spur ranchhouse. She had an impulsive urge to dash up the steps—straight into Nacona's arms, whether he wanted her there or not. At the moment, sharing his lust would be enough. July didn't like the taste of Hub's kisses on her lips or the memory of Jordon's arm gliding familiarly around her waist as he escorted her toward her steed. Both men had become more familiar with her than she preferred. Damn this charade. It went against the grain!

A ferocious bark made it impossible for July to make a discreet entrance into the house. Before she could grab the knob, the door whipped open. Nacona loomed over her, looking like the very devil, puffing on his cigar until he had surrounded himself in a cloud. His eyes glittered so dangerously that July automatically retreated a step.

"Where the hell have you been?" he boomed out.

Before July could respond, steely fingers clamped around her forearm, jerking her inside. She had always considered this awesome giant faintly dangerous. But the thunderous scowl that now puckered his features would terrify the most courageous of souls.

"You're hurting my arm!" she bleated when her hand began to tingle from lack of circulation.

"I'd like to break it," he snarled. "Now answer me, damn you!"

When he yanked her toward him, July shrieked. That was all it took to upset Killer. With a snarl of his own, the great beast bounded forward, displaying his sharp teeth.

Nacona could see them all when the great dog reared up to place giant paws on his shoulders.

"Good God!" Nacona nearly strangled on his cigar when Killer's snout was stuck in his face and the dog growled.

"If you let go of my arm, I'll order Killer to get down," July bargained.

At the moment she wasn't sure who looked the fiercer—Nacona or Killer. When the viselike grip on her arm slackened, she stared at Killer, face-to-face. He was that tall when he stood up on his haunches.

"Killer, go back to bed," she ordered firmly.

Eventually, the large mongrel dropped onto all fours, cast one last warning glance at Nacona, and returned to his braided rug. After circling thrice, Killer plopped down to rest his head on oversize paws.

"I'm moving that mutt outside, first thing in the morning," Nacona muttered.

"Oh really? You and whose army?" With a saucy toss of her head, July swanned across the parlor to enter her boudoir.

Nacona counted to ten twice and then cursed. What the blazes was the matter with him? He never lost his temper. He had iron-clad control. But when he had returned to find July gone, he had lost it.

July was so annoyed by Nacona's irrational behavior that she forgot all about modesty and just yanked off her dress and wormed into her nightgown while he loomed at her door. With a flair for the dramatic, she flounced onto her bed and snuffed out the lantern, ignoring her unwanted visitor.

For several moments, Nacona stood at the entrance to

her room, puffing on his cheroot, staring at the shadowed form in bed. He had been worried about July. Knowing what an impulsive, unpredictable imp she was, he'd suspected she had trotted off to do her own nocturnal prowling. For an hour, he had paced and stewed, wondering if she had managed to embroil herself in trouble. She certainly wouldn't have to go far to find it, considering the state of affairs locally.

Nacona wasn't accustomed to fretting over anyone else. He was unfamiliar with worry and concern. And July wasn't helping his black mood by defying him.

Scowling to himself, he pushed away from the door jamb and stumbled over the furniture in the darkened parlor. Favoring an aching shin, he groped his way toward his own room. That impossible woman was going to be the death of him sooner or later, he thought disgustedly. She had his emotions riding up and down like a teeter-totter. She drove him mad with desire at one minute and made him mad with anger the next. Why did he let her do that?

The faint scratching at the front door brought July awake. She swung her legs over the edge of the bed and padded barefoot through the darkened parlor to find Killer sniffing at the door. When she let him outside, he trotted around the side of the house and growled. July stepped across the stoop to survey the moonlit lawn, and her gaze fastened on the silhouette of the man scurrying around the corner of the barn.

She presumed the cowhand had had the same intention as Killer, who had seen to his needs and then had trotted back to his rug. When July pivoted toward her room, she saw an ominous form poised in the doorway.

"Now what are you up to?" Nacona demanded grouchily.

"If you are not smart enough to figure out why Killer needed to go outside in the middle of the night, I'm not going to bother telling you." With that snide remark, July veered into her room, slammed the door, and tucked herself in bed.

Although she begged for uninterrupted sleep, it was slow in coming. She kept picturing Nacona towering over her, scowling and demanding to know what she was doing. Suddenly, he had become like her overprotective brothers, behaving as if he were responsible for her, aggravated that he had to shoulder the blame if she got herself in trouble. Honestly! If she thought he actually cared enough to be worried, she might have been flattered. Instead, she was insulted that he assumed she was going to bungle the investigation. Nacona had been upset because he considered her an inconvenience. He had said as much during their debate that afternoon.

Just forget him! July lectured herself sternly. She would be much happier if she remained emotionally unattached to that dark-eyed devil. He could conduct his investigation in his way and she would do likewise. Hopefully, one or the other of them would come to the correct conclusion and solve the case. That, after all, was her sole purpose for being in Wyoming. Tomorrow she would throw herself into her duties and attempt to arrange the scattered pieces of the puzzle that were floating, disjointed, in her mind.

* * *

When July awakened to the morning sun glaring through the uncurtained window, Nacona was already up and gone. Not that she cared one whit, mind you. It was too early in the day to face his sour mood. After "oohing" and "ahing" over Cookie's mouth-watering biscuits and green-grape jelly, July garbed herself in a riding habit and strolled down to the stable to saddle a horse. Ot Knott was one step behind her, insisting that he tend to the task for her.

"Mr. Bleu certainly got an early start this mornin'," Ot remarked as he tossed a saddle on the buckskin mare.

"My husband is an early riser," July replied for lack of much else to say.

"He must have needed more supplies from town since that was the direction he was headed. Are you joinin' him, ma'am?"

"No, Hub Butler invited me to tour his ranch operation."

Ot was quiet for a moment while he busied himself with the girth strap. "Ma'am, I know this ain't none of my business and all, but Hub Butler, Jordon Milner, and Hoyt Simpson have reputations as ladies' men in these parts. They don't seem to care who lays claim to the ladies who catch their eye. The mister might not take kindly to yer payin' such a house call without him."

The *mister* could take a flying leap in a briar patch, for all July cared. Tossing Ot a reassuring smile, she settled herself on her mount. "I can take care of myself, Ot, but I do thank you for your concern."

When July trotted down the path, she found Killer trailing her. No amount of coaxing, no terse commands, would send the mongrel back to the house. If July hadn't

280

known better, she would have sworn Nacona had persuaded the oversize mutt to keep an eye on her while he did whatever he was about in town. A devil cavorting with an angel, no doubt.

Before July could dismount at the spacious country house, Hub stepped onto the veranda to flash her a roguish smile. His pleasant expression evaporated when Killer growled uncordially at him.

"Don't tell me Bob Foster's mutt has adopted you," he grumbled. "That vicious dog should be done away with, to put everybody else out of out of their misery."

"I find Killer to be a good companion," July contradicted. "He and I get on splendidly."

Warily, Hub stepped off the porch to fetch a steed. While July followed him to the immaculate stables, Killer paused to growl at one of the cowboys who had made the mistake of wandering out of the bunkhouse. But to July's relief, Killer voiced no protest when several other wranglers moseyed outside to pay their respects and await an introduction. It seemed Killer was particular about whom he liked, just as Ot Knott had said. Some men invited Killer's warning growls while others did not.

Once Hub had saddled a strapping black stallion that had as much interest in her buckskin mare as his rider did in July, they cantered across the pasture to take count of the livestock.

"You have a grand ranch," July complimented, surveying the blacksmith's barn, the hen houses, and the various and sundry whitewashed buildings that surrounded the residence. "The Cabestro Ranch appears very self-sufficient."

"I have visions of setting up an empire that spreads as

far as the eye can see," Hub assured her. "This ranch has been quite successful, despite the rustling. Some of the other ranchers have been hit hard by cattle losses, and the bank holdups have drained their savings. In the case of the former owner of the Golden Spur, his losses proved fatal."

Although July posed several questions, she was sorry to admit that her interview with Hub was proving less than enlightening. She had learned very little that she didn't already know about the other ranchers, and Hub avoided commenting when she casually mentioned C. L. Chambers and his wife. However, July did manage to escape from a close encounter with Hub when they paused by the stream to water their horses. When he took a step toward her, Killer leaped in front of her like a shield, and July made a mental note to take Killer with her each time she ventured within ten feet of any of the smooth-talking ranchers. Hub and Jordon had already been closer to her than she preferred, but in the future Killer would provide the necessary protection. July might even sic Killer on Nacona if he . . .

July forced the spiteful thought aside and concentrated on the investigation. She was not going to become side-tracked by her illogical attraction to Nacona Bleu. She had come to Wyoming to launch her career and prove to her overprotective brothers that she could be an asset to the family's detective agency. That was her purpose and she was not going to allow herself to forget it.

The Mackenzie brothers sailed out of the hotel in Dodge City and marched toward the marshal's office like a three-man army on parade. The expressions on their faces did their handsome features no justice. They were not a happy lot. After tracking July's telegram to this hell-raising cowtown, they had boarded the earliest train from Kansas City. Their good humor had not returned and it didn't look as though it would until they located their sister and dragged her back home where she belonged.

According to the proprietor at the hotel, their vagabond sister had been in town for two weeks before flitting off again. The proprietor had been hesitant to offer any details. He had sent them to the marshal's office for explanation. Why the famed Bat Masterson should have to answer their questions, the MacKenzies didn't know, but they were anxious to find out.

Deputizing himself as the spokesman of the group, Gresham burst into the office and thrust out a hand. "Mr. Masterson, I am Gresham Mackenzie, and these are my brothers. We have come all the way from Kansas City to locate our missing sister. We were told you could shed some light on this perplexing matter."

Bat peered at the somber threesome and then glanced at twenty-nine-year old Wyatt Earp who had just ambled in with a cup of coffee in hand. The Mackenzie brothers glanced at the cup in Wyatt's hand, assuming the worst, and then looked down their noses at him. Bat knew Wyatt never drank anything stronger than coffee, but these stoic detectives probably wouldn't believe that. They held Western lawmen in low esteem.

When Bat's younger brother Jim, who had arrived the previous week to lend a helping hand, followed in Wyatt's wake, he was treated to the same snobbish glances Wyatt had received.

After another round of stiff how-do-you-dos, Gresham stared grimly at the law officials in charge of this rowdy town. "Our sister has been missing for a month and we are anxious to find her," he declared. "We were told you might know where she is."

Bat studied the citified detectives, noting the striking family resemblance between July and her brothers. He wasn't at all sure he wanted to convey the information the fashionably garbed detectives wanted. He didn't cotton to their looking down from lofty heights and implying he didn't meet their expectations for Western peace officers.

"Well?" Calvin demanded impatiently. "Do you know where July is or don't you?"

"The last I heard she was on her way to Cheyenne," Bat informed them.

"Cheyenne?" Ethan croaked. "Why the devil would she go from here to there? This town is bad enough. Cheyenne is probably worse."

Bat shifted uncomfortably beneath the probing stares. "I suppose she and her husband are enjoying their honeymoon there."

"Her *what?*" Gresham yowled.

"Husband," Bat repeated. "She married Nacona Bleu and they——"

"Bleu?" Calvin howled in disbelief. "I heard he'd been shot down outside Waco, Texas, while on assignment."

"Nacona is married?" Wyatt Earp questioned in astonishment. He had only returned from the gold fields of Deadwood the previous evening, and no one had bothered to tell him the famed pistolero had taken a wife.

"I think you had better start at the beginning, Mr.

Masterson," Gresham insisted. "I'd like to know what the hell's going on!"

"It's a rather involved story," Bat hedged.

"We'll make time to listen," Ethan assured him.

Bat organized his thoughts and began. "Well, you see, July and Nacona had a tussle of sorts and . . . um . . . she pressed charges against him for assault. Then—"

"That gunslinger assaulted her?" Calvin roared, unable to contain his Scotch-Irish temper another second.

"I never did know all the details myself," Bat admitted. "But July filed charges, so I had to put Nacona in jail. After several days, your sister returned to make some sort of arrangement with Nacona. When I asked him how they had resolved their problem and why she decided to drop the charges, Nacona said he had to marry her to pacify her."

"Had to?" Gresham erupted like a geyser. "*Had* to?"

"It was the night my brother was killed," Bat murmured ruefully. "I had too much on my mind to quiz Nacona. He stayed to help me with the funeral arrangements and then he and July rode north. He didn't say when they would be back."

The shocking news left the MacKenzies completely miffed. They knew their sister better than anyone alive—or at least they thought they did. But they didn't know Nacona Bleu, except by a reputation that did nothing to endear him to them. Bleu did not sound like the kind of man July would marry under any circumstances. She was sophisticated, intelligent, and refined. From what the MacKenzies knew about Nacona Bleu he was none of those things. In fact, he represented everything the MacKenzies detested.

"If you like, I'll wire Sheriff Pinkston in Cheyenne to confirm Nacona and July's arrival," Bat volunteered.

"That won't be necessary," Gresham muttered. "We want to see our sister for ourselves and hear *her* explanation."

When the MacKenzies wheeled around and stalked out in single file, Wyatt eased a hip onto the edge of the desk and stared thoughtfully after them. "What do you think of those snobbish detectives?"

Bat plunked back into his chair and heaved an audible sigh. "I think Nacona is going to have a lot of explaining to do when those three men get hold of him."

Wyatt's blue eyes focused on Bat. "I'm certainly not taking their side, but the incident leading up to that whirlwind marriage does sound a mite suspicious. If the young lady in question is as stuffy as her brothers, I can't imagine why Nacona would dally with her."

The faintest hint of a smile pursed Bat's lips. "You didn't have the pleasure of making the aforementioned lady's acquaintance, Wyatt. I assure you, you would have known exactly what Nacona and every other man saw in her if you'd gotten a good look at July MacKenzie."

"That pretty, huh?" Jim Masterson questioned with a rakish grin.

Bat nodded affirmatively. "They don't come any prettier, or better designed, than that little firecracker."

"All the same, I'm afraid Nacona's in-laws are going to give him trouble," Wyatt prophesied.

Bat heartily agreed. The MacKenzies had not taken the news of their sister's marriage well.

Chapter 18

Making his customary visit to the Sheriff Pinkston's office to check the wanted posters, Nacona found no leads as promising as the one in Denver. He was anxious to conclude this assignment and head back to Colorado to continue his crusade. Absently, he moseyed past the saloons that lined the streets, gathering bits and pieces of information as he went. His seemingly casual conversations with the patrons and off-duty cowhands had earned him several interesting facts. One was the unspoken rivalry between the big-time ranchers and small farmers who pretended to be companionable while they milled around the Cheyenne Club. As Nacona had learned, most of the ranchers had problems with fences, livestock, and water rights. But he also had heard that several cowhands, always seemed to have funds in their pockets to purchase whatever they desired. Considering the average wrangler's salary of thirty-five dollars a month, that seemed suspicious to Nacona.

Mulling over the possibility that an intricate ring of thieves was operating in the area, Nacona ambled toward the Cheyenne Club late in the afternoon. A curious frown furrowed his brow when he glanced back toward Cheyenne Rose's Pleasure Parlor to see Jordon Milner and Hoyt Simpson ambling inside, followed by several dusty cowhands. My, that uppity brothel seemed to be doing a thriving business day and night. Part of the clientele that filed in and out of the place was not what he had expected. Nacona recalled hearing about cowhands who could afford luxuries out of reach of the average wrangler. It was a shame he had played the devoted husband. He would like to take a look around the Parlor. Well, he'd just find an excuse to get in there without drawing suspicion. He'd figure out something.

The instant Nacona sauntered into the Cheyenne Club, he decided Angel Chambers was a permanent fixture. She was lounging at a table at which Derrek Paine, John Gilman, and Hub Butler sipped whiskey and tried their luck at poker. Nacona knew something was brewing when Angel excused herself and flashed him a devilish smile.

His dark, perceptive eyes wandered over Angel's seductive gown as she sauntered toward him. Nacona mentally offered his compliments to Angel's seamstress. Gold satin material fit her voluptuous figure so well it might have been painted on her ivory skin, while a plunging neckline revealed the hilly terrain of her bosoms to alluring advantage and tucks at the waist suggested a man's hands could easily encircle her there. There had been a time—and not too long ago—when Nacona would have taken full advantage of this provocative brunette. But these days there was a feisty blonde on his mind.

Irritably, he cast his preoccupation with July aside and

returned Angel's smile. "You look stunning, as always, Angel," he complimented as she sidled up beside him, ensuring that her ample bosom brushed against his arm.

"Do I, love?" she purred throatily. "I'm glad you noticed. I was afraid you were too bewitched by that little wife of yours."

How could he not notice this vixen? She made every man focus on her. Nacona allowed himself to be steered toward a vacant table. He could tell something was on Angel's mind by the way she kept flinging him speculative glances.

"I saw your wife last night," Angel said conversationally, or so it would have seemed.

"Did you?" Nacona braced himself, afraid he wasn't going to like what he was about to hear. With extreme effort, he glanced at Angel with a well-disciplined stare that revealed none of his thoughts.

"Yes." Angel's forefinger circled the rim of her glass, and her sultry gaze drifted over the broad expanse of Nacona's chest. "She was gadding about town on Jordon Milner's arm." She gauged Nacona's reaction, dismayed that his expression never wavered. "It seems to me that you are far more devoted to your wife than she is to you. A pity." She sighed dramatically. "You shouldn't deprive yourself when she does not."

It was most fortunate that Nacona had learned to mask both utter boredom and murderous fury behind a carefully blank stare. The news had hit him like a rock slide. He felt bruised inside, but mustering his composure, he glanced away from Angel's taunting smile to monitor the activity in the room. The detective in him wanted to believe July had been seeking information. The man in him was seething at the thought of her hanging on the blond rancher's arm.

"Sometimes it seems a man and woman don't share an equal amount of affection for each other," he managed to say without spitting out the words in disgust. "July is young and accustomed to the eager attentions of many men. When a man from my station in life marries a woman like her, he has to be prepared to compromise and sacrifice for what he wants to keep."

"Well, your vivacious young wife seems to be making no sacrifices in this marriage," Angel declared. "I heard tell she took the grand tour of the Cabestro Ranch with Hub this morning."

Nacona silently damned her and that wife of his.

Angel reached across the table to trail her fingers over the taut muscles of Nacona's forearm. "If you decide you don't want to make all those sacrifices, love, you know where to find me. . . ."

Although Angel chitchatted about this and that, Nacona's thoughts were elsewhere. He knew perfectly well that many bachelors would leap at the chance to court the gorgeous July, yet he had ordered her to make herself available. Now he was suffering, wondering just how many privileges July was doling out in her pursuit of knowledge, especially since he had *demanded* that she do whatever it took to dig up facts.

Since Angel offered no pertinent information for his investigation, Nacona unfolded himself from his chair and ambled over to converse with the other ranchers congregated around the billiard table. He wasn't sure whether Angel's comments had influenced him or whether he simply harbored a natural dislike for these ranchers. The men kept smiling, as if they harbored some secret they refused to share. No doubt they thought they had hoodwinked him while flirting with July.

"What's this I hear about you moonlighting as an agent for the Census Bureau," Hoyt Simpson questioned as he strolled into the club after his brief but undoubtedly intimate visit to the Pleasure Parlor.

Nacona shrugged a broad shoulder. "I hoped the job would help pay for the new ranch," he offered in explanation. "All I have to do is calculate the number of livestock in the area and report it to the government for their surveys. They're trying to determine if the cattle, sheep, and hog production can meet consumers' demands. You don't mind complying with the request, I hope."

Hoyt grumbled sourly. "Personally, I don't like anybody snooping into my business. I'd rather the government send someone to investigate the rustling and robberies. I've lost one hundred head of cattle in three months. I could have gotten forty to fifty dollars a head for them at market. The loss could become staggering if this keeps up. My investors might decide to back out. If the Census Bureau wants to take surveys, it ought to take count of the livestock that've been *stolen* from the ranchers."

"I'll make a note of that," Nacona assured Hoyt. "Maybe the information will convince law officials to do something about the problem."

"When you showed up in town, I thought maybe you had come to investigate," Hoyt commented before sipping his brandy. "Then I saw your lovely wife and figured that was a wild speculation." His look suggested he was doing some more wild speculating—about July.

Nacona strangled the glass in his hand rather than Hoyt's neck and nodded affirmatively. "My days of investigation are over. I have a wife and a ranch of my own to protect, so if it comes to using my gun again to stop thieving, I intend to use it to protect my own interests."

Hoyt leaned close to convey a confidential remark. "Then maybe you wouldn't mind joining the Wyoming Vigilante Committee. We're trying to band together to put a stop to this rustling and that includes hanging offenders on the spot."

"You can count me in," Nacona volunteered. "Just because I'm no longer in the business of hiring out my gun hand doesn't mean I won't fight to protect what belongs to me."

That said, Nacona strode off to check into several matters that demanded his attention. He conferred with C. L. Chambers to determine when the next Union Pacific payroll was due to arrive and to acquire details on the last bank robbery. Then he ambled to the depot to check the train schedules. Although July had convinced herself that C.L. was involved in a master scheme to bleed all his wife's former, present, and future lovers dry, Nacona was skeptical. He wasn't at all certain that the rustling was linked to the bank and railroad robberies, either. July was laboring under the theory that jealous revenge was the motive for the thefts and robberies, but Nacona clung to the belief that greed was the root of all evil in Wyoming. He hoped he was right because that sassy female would never let him hear the end of it if he was not.

* * *

While Nacona was making his rounds, searching for clues, July was on a mission of her own. She traveled from one ranch to another with Killer following at her heels. She had seen very little of Nacona the past few days. It seemed he would return home when she was leaving, and he no longer demanded to know where she was going. For the most part he ignored her, and not to be outdone, July ignored him in return. Their private war was fought in silence, but the glares they tossed back and forth were hot enough to melt rock. As far as July was concerned, the less said the better. She was trying hard to concentrate on her investigation and to forget her attraction to her temporary husband. Still, all too often she found her thoughts straying to that midnight-haired rake. . . .

Killer's low growl jolted July from her musings. She glanced up to see one of the cowhands at Hoyt Simpson's ranch shying away when Killer bared his teeth and snarled a second time.

"You really should do something about that mutt," Hoyt insisted as he stared at the oversize beast. "He's a nuisance."

"Killer has deputized himself as my body guard," July said, favoring Hoyt with a charming smile. "And I have developed a certain fondness for him."

"I hope you aren't planning on bringing Killer to town for the celebration," Hoyt grumbled. "There are plenty of us who'd like the pleasure of dancing with you. With that beast underfoot, we'll be deprived of that anticipated privilege."

"I'll see that Killer doesn't make a scene," she assured Hoyt. "I do love to dance."

"Will you save a dance for me?" he questioned hopefully. "Or will your husband demand all your attention? He seems very devoted to you, although I have seen him in Angel's company a time or two the past few days."

July was certain Hoyt was baiting her. He, like Hub, Jordon, and John Gilman, with whom she had spent the previous afternoon counting livestock, seemed curious to know if she was as promiscuous as Angel Chambers. "My husband understands my need for freedom," she declared. "Nacona isn't the jealous type. I doubt he will mind if I have several dance partners."

Hoyt sent her a suggestive glance. "Then I will look forward to the dance on Saturday night."

July smiled and let him think his shallow charm was getting to her. "So will I, Hoyt."

After playing up to almost every rancher in the county the past week—and barely escaping what had almost become an amorous tête-à-tête with Hoyt that very afternoon—July wondered how beneficial her flirtations would prove to be. Thus far, she had no sound evidence that any of the ranchers were involved in rustling or robbery. All she had done was leave herself open to one sordid approach after another.

A disheartened sigh escaped her as she reined her steed toward the Golden Spur. She was beginning to doubt that she had the patience for a long, involved investigation. She and Nacona had been in Cheyenne for well over a week, but she had not one substantial lead. Nothing was going as she had anticipated.

The instant July breezed in the door, she screeched to a halt. Nacona was lounging in the rocking chair, puffing on his cheroot. His probing gaze wandered over her in silent inspection.

"And just who have you been gallivanting with this evening, my dear wife?" he asked without offering a civil greeting.

The silent war was over. Nacona was back to demanding to know who and where again.

"Hoyt Simpson, if you must know," July replied as she plopped down on the chair across from him.

"I suppose Hoyt offered all sorts of vital information to aid in our investigation." His tone suggested that he supposed nothing of the kind.

"No, actually I feel I wasted my time," July admitted, trying to ignore his black mood.

"And did our friend Hoyt come away feeling disappointed, too?" he asked with a ridiculing smirk.

July glared at him. "You're the one who insisted I employ my feminine charms to pry into the affairs of every man in the county."

Yes, he had, and he regretted doing so. It had begun to haunt him.

"No doubt, you've been utilizing the same tactic on Angel," July added on a bitter note.

"Would that I could," Nacona grunted between puffs on his cigar. "But I made the mistake of leaving the impression that I was hopelessly infatuated with my wife, who never stays home long enough to—"

"To do what?" she demanded tersely.

"Nothing." Nacona scowled, disgusted with himself for feeling so damned possessive. But every time he came within ten feet of Angel she made it a point to tell him who had last been seen in July's company. "I thought you might like to know I'm taking the train to Laramie to investigate the bank robbery that occurred last night."

"Last night?" July frowned pensively. "But there wasn't a storm to camouflage the holdup, was there?"

Nacona chuckled. "I hate to burst your theoretical bubble, my dear July, but not every robbery occurred during a storm. Our ring of thieves is careful not to become predictable. The bandits were greedy enough to steal the railroad payroll that had just been deposited in the Laramie bank."

"So what do you plan to do, sniff out their trail to determine where it leads, great scout?" she questioned caustically.

"It beats the hell out of flitting from one ranch to the other, trailing dead-end leads," he countered in the same sarcastic tone.

July tilted her chin. "I'll have you know I've made some interesting discoveries."

He snorted disdainfully. "I'll bet you have. For all your prowling and cavorting, you should have cracked the damned case by now."

July bolted to her feet to glower at him. "I don't know why you care what I've been doing or with whom, my *dear* husband." She made the endearment sound like a curse. "Rumor has it you've been seeing quite a lot of Angel, though you claim to be loyal and true blue. I'd like to see you explain *that!*"

Nacona sprung to his feet. "I'll be happy to explain what Angel and I have been doing as soon as you explain what you've gleaned from all the damned ranchers in the county!" he roared.

"How many women have you had, Nacona?" she tossed at him unexpectedly.

His response was a wordless scowl that did his handsome face no justice.

More than he cares to count, the philandering swine, July thought. "Well, maybe I've decided I want to be as experienced and worldly as you are, maybe I want to know my fair share of men. For the sake of this investigation, of course. Still, Wyoming is the state of equality. A woman has the right to equal pay, equal *position*—"

Nacona looked positively murderous as he broke in on her tirade. "Who did you sleep with, July?" he growled.

"That is none of your business," she snapped, stubbornly belligerent. Let him think whatever he liked. She didn't care.

But the instant Nacona snatched her to him, she realized she *did* care. Too much in fact. The feel of his arms encircling her sent her heart racing in triple time. It seemed months since she had been close to this ruggedly handsome giant, since she had inhaled the masculine scent of him, felt the warmth of his muscular body. July's preoccupation with the investigation had not been very effective in countering this ill-fated attraction. The plain and simple truth was, she longed for Nacona's touch. She remembered the magic they had created, and her betraying body yearned for more of it.

July peered into stormy black eyes, the truth hitting her like a ton of rocks. She had tried to ignore her feelings for Nacona, but they seemed to have sneaked up and engulfed her while she was busy denying them. Lord have mercy, she *was* in love with this man! She had this week spent time in the company of a dozen men, unwillingly making comparisons to this sensual giant. The others had all fallen short of the mark.

A muddled frown creased Nacona's brow when he noticed July's startled expression. She was staring at him as if he had sprouted horns. "What's the matter with you?" he demanded.

The question jostled her back to her senses, and she wormed free, presenting her back to him. "Nothing," she declared. "Just go away and leave me alone."

Nacona grabbed her arm and spun her around. His penetrating gaze burrowed into her. "I asked you a question, minx. Now answer it!"

She wished she had let Killer back in the house. He protested when Nacona clutched her to him or raised his voice. "I thought you had a train to catch."

"I have time for you to tell me what's the matter with you," he guaranteed. "Now what the hell's wrong?"

"I'm frustrated," July replied, struggling to concoct a believable way to conceal the truth. "I want to solve this case, but it is taking forever. The information I've gathered is drifting in my mind, refusing to be linked together."

Nacona stared at her for a long silent moment. He doubted this elusive sprite was being honest with him. He had become practiced at reading people's faces over the years. July might have spoken the truth, but there was still something she wasn't telling him. And stubborn as she was, it would require a crowbar to pry it out.

Damn it to hell, why did this female exasperate him so? Knowing she had been with half the men in the county, and probably had their fingerprints all over her, cut him to the quick. It shouldn't have. He and July had no hold on each other. That was the agreement. For the past week he'd felt they were drifting farther apart. Had she truly found a man to replace him? That was possibile since she had her pick of the crop. Nacona wanted to trust the whispers of his heart, to believe July would remain faithful to him because of their marriage vows, even if they had been a means to an end. But he was accustomed to dealing with females who spent their lives making a lot of men happy, not a woman who had devoted the past few weeks to making one man miserable. Quite honestly, Nacona wasn't sure he could trust this sassy beauty, and he knew for certain he couldn't trust the lusty ranchers who had designs on her.

He was beginning to understand the full meaning of jealousy for the first time in his life. The thought of another man touching this bewitching nymph tormented him. July was his wife, temporarily or no. His pride had taken a beating, thanks to Angel's grating remarks and observations, though he knew her own marriage was a fiasco.

With a scowl, Nacona jerked July to him. "If you won't tell me what's on that complicated mind of yours, at least tell me good-bye, good and proper. You'll have all the freedom you want for the next few days. The price is a kiss."

He didn't wait for her to initiate the kiss, for fear the contrary hellion would reject his request. Instead his mouth came down on hers in fierce, impatient possession. It was as if all the emotion that churned inside him exploded the instant he lost himself to the honeyed taste of her, the tantalizing scent of her perfume, the delicious feel of her supple body. This was what had been missing from his life the past week, he realized with a tormented groan. He only felt whole and alive when July was in his arms. He had been craving her like a starving man hungers for a feast. He couldn't seem to get close enough to her. It was maddening to be so lost in a woman.

July couldn't muster the will to resist, not even for a second. Her body eagerly responded, wanting him in the wildest ways. Her arms glided over his powerful shoulders to clutch him closer. And suddenly the tension between them burst into a flame fanned by unappeased passion. Instantly and totally aroused by this rake's masterful touch, July craved things she had never wanted in her brief relationships with other men—mutual affection and love and sharing a life.

It was demoralizing to know that Nacona was only killing time with her during lulls in this frustrating investigation. But even that didn't cure her desire for this raven-haired giant. He was going to break her heart. Her traitorous body settled for Nacona's passion. Even if that was all he could offer, she wanted him. She wanted to forget the touch of every man who had tried to court her this past week. Only Nacona could set her pulse to pounding.

A muffled groan rattled in Nacona's throat as rising passion engulfed him. Desperate to appease the hunger that had been gnawing away at him, he felt hot and cold and shaky. His body was making fierce demands on him, and yet, even in that hazy darkness that accompanied urgent desire, he couldn't bring himself to do something as rough and reckless as ripping away the garments that separated them. Not with this particular woman. Even though she frustrated him more often than not, July was a sophisticated lady. She wasn't some hapless female who made her living satisfying men. She deserved to be loved well. Pleasing her had somehow become as important to him as pleasing himself.

Entangled in that thought, Nacona hooked his arm beneath July's knees and lifted her off the floor. His hungry eyes dropped to her enchanting face, only to become mesmerized by rippling emerald pools surrounded by long, sooty lashes. Another shudder of intense longing wracked him as he strode toward her bedroom.

So fixed was he on her eyes, he caught his foot on the rocking chair. With a startled yelp, he stumbled forward and then struck an end table as he reared back to maintain his balance. But gravity had a fierce hold on him. With a crash and a thud, he hit the floor, doing his level best to break July's fall without squashing her.

The commotion set Killer to barking his head off, and once July caught her breath, having had it forced out of her by Nacona's weight, she burst into giggles. Ordinarily, there was nothing clumsy about this agile giant. He was poetry in motion. But with his mind on more arousing activities, he'd managed to trip himself up. It was ever so nice to know Nacona was human. Until now, July hadn't been too sure of that. He always seemed in perfect control until his male desires got the better of him, and it was gratifying to know that she was the reason for his distraction. Though loving her was not within the realm of his capabilities, for now it was enough that he wanted her.

The scowl that creased Nacona's brow disappeared when he levered up on an elbow to bask in the warmth of July's elfin smile. She had not voiced one complaint about landing on the rug that lay before the empty hearth, and he was relieved that he hadn't set the logs to blazing when he'd returned home to find July gone. Otherwise, her mane of blond hair might have been set afire when he accidentally tripped and fell with her clutched possessively in his arms.

"You do have a most unique way of sweeping a woman off her feet," July tittered as she reached up to limn the sensuous curve of his lips.

Nacona didn't take time to question why July hadn't scorned him for his obvious intentions. He had expected her volatile temper to burst out as it had a few minutes earlier. This gorgeous female was a marvel to him. He just never seemed able to predict her moods or reactions. But he was glad she didn't rant and rave at him for dumping her in an unladylike heap on the rug. There was precious little time left before he had to catch the train to Laramie, and he had no inclination to spend it fencing with words.

His head moved toward July's as if drawn by some magnetic force, and his frustration evaporated. The fall had knocked the impatience clean out of him. Suddenly he was drifting on a languid wave, hypnotized by the feel of the luscious body lying beside his. His hands scaled the silky curve of her thigh, pushing ruffled petticoats aside to greet soft flesh. His lips trailed across her cheek to monitor the rapid pulsations in her throat. His embarrassing bout with the rocking chair and end table were instantly forgotten as his body responded to July's arching to meet his seeking hands and lips. She, too, seemed entranced by the ungovernable spark of passion that vibrated through them and between them.

Nacona was overcome by the compelling need to brand a memory of him on this lovely nymph's mind.

Knowing he would be gone for at least two days and she would be gadding all over creation with every man in the county, he wanted it to be *his* face she saw in the swaying shadows, *his* voice that whispered to her in the wind. It was becoming increasingly important that he mattered to her, that he was the only man who could ignite her ardor and satisfy her desires.

As Nacona's reverent caresses and kisses flooded over July, her body begged for his touch. She fed on the warm drafts of breath that whispered over her quaking flesh, sending shock waves rippling through her every nerve and muscle. Her mind dallied in the cloudy corridors of desire while Nacona skillfully brought to life each sensitive part, leaving her to burn with a fever he could cure.

July floated on a cloud of pleasure. Though Nacona could be rough, domineering, and forceful, when he set his hands upon her, he became a gentled giant. It was as if he were worshipping her, cherishing her. His expertise marked him as a skilled and practiced lover, of course, but for the moment July allowed herself to believe in magic.

His moist lips hovered over her skin, making incredible feelings unfold, like the velvety petals of a rose, inside her. His fingertips probed, satisfying her aching needs, exciting and teasing her. A soft moan broke from her throat when he paused to remove her gown. Those tormenting moments when she was deprived of his seductive touch caused the maddening cravings to increase tenfold. She lay there, watching him undress her, watching him undress himself. His whipcord muscles, his bronzed face, were increasing her craving for him.

Ah, love was such a bewildering emotion, July thought as she reached up trace the corded tendons and taut

303

muscles of his arms. In the beginning she could barely imagine being married to this man, much less allowing him to touch her in such wildly intimate ways. But something about this raven-haired rogue drew her to him, like a moth to the proverbial flame, even though she knew she'd singe her wings before they went their separate ways. Falling in love knew no rhyme or reason and . . .

When his sleek, masculine body half covered hers, guiding her thighs apart, July forgot how to think, how to breathe. She merely reveled in the feel of his hair-roughened flesh. The velvet warmth of him became a white-hot flame inside her, and his powerful body engulfed her, absorbing her energy and strength. Scalding kisses . . . hungry nips at her shoulder . . . hands upon her. He moved with the growing impatience of mindless passion.

July feared she had left claw marks on his back when she'd clutched at him. Even when they were as close as two people can get, nothing seemed to satisfy the riveting need that pulsated through her. His name was on her lips in a breathless plea as he drove into her and she answered each hard, penetrating thrust.

And suddenly the dark universe exploded into a kaleidoscope of blinding colors. Intense heat burned its way up from the core of July's being to flood through her every nerve and muscle. Then she felt the helpless surge of Nacona's muscular body, and gloried in the rapturous sensations that spilled through her, cooling the flames that had very nearly burned her alive.

A wobbly groan rattled in Nacona's chest, and he forced himself to loose his fierce grasp on July. He feared he had crushed her, but when the maddening need to possess her overwhelmed him, he always became the prisoner of his own savage needs. No matter how tender he tried to be, he always wound up with passion getting the better of him. He had thought time would cure his insatiable craving, that he would tire of this firebrand. But the opposite was true. Each time he made love to July was like a stepping stone to yet another mystifying realm of pleasure.

How was he going to appease this kind of maddening desire that fed upon itself, demanding more and more? What kind of hold did this sorceress have on him anyway? He couldn't put her out of his mind. She was always there—like a skipping shadow, tormenting him, satisfying him beyond his wildest dreams, and then tormenting him again. She kept his emotions swinging back and forth like a pendulum. Hell, he couldn't think straight or even maintain his balance when he got within five feet of her.

"Nacona, I . . ." July swallowed her foolish confession before it leaped off her tongue and embarrassed her.

"You what?" he whispered before dropping an impulsive kiss on her lush pink lips.

July shook her head, afraid to trust herself to speak without blurting out the words Nacona didn't want to hear. He wanted no ties, and she had known that from the beginning. She hadn't wanted any either, until her foolish heart had begun to rule her head.

A frustrated sigh tumbled from Nacona's lips when he felt that invisible wall go up between them again. July glanced away, as if the furniture had suddenly demanded her attention. "You'll what, minx?" he grumbled in question. "You'll miss me while I'm gone?"

The taunting remark broke her silence in one second flat. Even though she was a fool for caring, she'd die before she let this cocky rapscallion know he had stolen her heart. "Miss you?" She smirked to salvage her stinging pride. "I'd miss a festering boil more."

Nacona muttered under his breath and rolled away. He seemed to have a knack for irritating this proud beauty. He never did say the right thing at the right moment. "I gotta go. Stay out of trouble, July."

She clutched at her discarded clothes. "*You're* the trouble," she mumbled half-aloud. And he was. He had given her serious heart trouble.

"Me?" Nacona snorted as he thrust a bare leg into his breeches. "I didn't ask for this assignment." He shoved his feet into his boots and snatched up his shirt. "And damn it, don't try to sidetrack me, woman. You watch your step while I'm gone. This town is full of potential disasters. I don't want to come back to find you got in the middle of one."

"I didn't really think you cared," she scoffed as she wormed into her gown.

"I—" Nacona very nearly bit off his tongue in an effort to halt the reckless confession that stampeded to his lips. If he told this spitfire he was worried about her, it would be a mistake. Sure as the devil, she would never let him live it down. "I'll be back Wednesday. Thursday at the latest," he threw over his shoulder on the way to the door. Without a backward glance, he scooped up his satchel from the sofa and disappeared into the night.

July expelled the breath she had been holding. How could something so wild and sweet turn sour so quickly? One moment she was gliding over rainbows in the magic circle of Nacona's arms. The next instant she was cursing herself for caring about him. She was going to have to channel her energy into solving this case as quickly as possible so she could go home. Her dreams of launching a career and building a name for herself had caused her to run headlong into catastrophe. She had made a crucial error when she'd bargained with that devil. Nothing had worked according to plan, and now she had fallen in love with a reckless tumbleweed of a man who was so independent and self-reliant that he needed no one to make his life complete.

Life was certainly full of unexpected twists, turns, and surprises, she thought glumly. Not all of them were pleasant, though, as July was about to find out. . . .

Chapter 19

Gresham MacKenzie expelled an exasperated sigh and squirmed uncomfortably in the third-class passenger car fitted with rows of narrow wooden benches as hard as rocks. The MacKenzie brothers had not been blessed with the good fortune of acquiring first-class accommodations during their rail ride to Colorado. The passenger car, which had been coupled to freight cars, was constantly being shunted aside, so they had faced several delays already. The meals at the roundhouses, which turned out to be no more than crude wooden shacks on the plains, were barely fit for human consumption. And the information the MacKenzies had received in Dodge had set as well with them as the indigestible food they'd been forced to choke down.

"I think we need to decide on a plan of action," Gresham declared.

"I'm all for ganging up on that gunslinger and shooting him down," Ethan muttered acrimoniously. "No man abuses our sister and gets away with it!"

"I agree with Ethan," Calvin put in. "I want Nacona Bleu tried, convicted, and punished—after we blast him full of holes."

Gresham was equally vindictive. Like his brothers, he took exception to his sister being legally bound to a social outcast. However, being an attorney who adhered to the law, he was aware of other complications that might arise from this predicament.

"I think we have other issues to consider besides our need for revenge," Gresham said.

"Don't start spouting the law at me, Gresh," Ethan grumbled. "Bleu obviously holds himself above it. His reputation has gone to his head. He thinks he can do whatever he wishes to whomever he wishes because he's quick on the draw and he's a friend of men like Masterson and Earp."

"You seem to have overlooked the fact that he and July are married," Gresham pointed out.

"Not for long, they won't be!" Calvin growled spitefully.

"July cannot testify against her husband." Gresham crossed his arms over his chest and stared at some distant point at the front of the crudely furnished passenger car. "If you recall, Masterson said Bleu had to marry July. Distasteful though the idea is, not to mention its complications, it poses an unsettling problem that we have to consider. What if she is carrying his—"

"Good God, don't say it. Don't even think it!" Ethan shuddered. "The very idea of having a niece or nephew fathered by that bullying gunslinger sickens me!"

"The law maintains that Bleu has the right to see their child, if there truly is one on the way, and I cannot fathom

310

why July would marry such a scoundrel if there weren't extenuating circumstances. What other possible reason could there be for her actions?" Gresham questioned reasonably.

"I think we should just call Bleu out, shoot him down, and be done with it," Ethan decreed. "July will thank us. She can't possibly approve of this marriage. It was most likely performed to conceal her shame and humiliation . . ." When the train wobbled to a halt, Ethan scowled crankily. "Damnation, what now?"

The locomotive hissed and sputtered and paused at a remote outpost on the edge of nowhere to take on water.

Calvin scowled in irritation. "At this rate, it will take us over a week to reach Cheyenne."

"Then we will have a week to decide how to handle Nacona Bleu and save July from a miserable fate," Gresham announced.

"I still vote to shoot him and be done with it!" Ethan repeated vehemently. "Destiny may have frowned on July, but she deserves better than this!"

"You know perfectly well we are too civilized to resort to the disgusting tactics the barbaric gunslingers and the disreputable marshals in cowtowns employ to solve problems," Gresham chided his younger brothers. "But one way or another, we are going to dissolve this ridiculous marriage and take July back where she belongs."

The MacKenzie brothers agreed on that point. They just hadn't determined how to remove Nacona from their sister's life without breaking any of the laws they were sworn to uphold.

* * *

July heaved a weary sigh and plopped down on the rocking chair. Claiming to be Nacona's assistant for the Census Bureau survey, she had visited nearly every ranch in the area, noting the numbers of cattle and of the missing livestock. She had seen no brands that looked as if they had been tampered with. Whoever had taken possession of the stolen cattle had been careful not to add them to a ranch herd. The calves were either being held on some remote range or they had already been sold and shipped to slaughterhouses.

She glanced over at the huge mutt lying on the braided rug beside the door. A puzzled frown clouded her brow as she peered pensively at Killer. During each visit to the surrounding ranches, one or two cowhands always set him to snarling and growling. And each time July ventured to town, Killer barked at some of the wranglers who milled around Cheyenne Rose's elaborate bordello. That truly baffled July. It seemed Killer was trying to tell her something, but she didn't have the foggiest notion what it was.

A warning growl jolted her from her thoughts. The oversize mongrel was on his feet in a single bound, pawing at the door. July watched an envelope slide across the floor. Killer latched onto it immediately. July heard a rider racing away, but when she scurried to the window, she couldn't identify the man who thundered off into the darkness.

Although Killer was reluctant to relinquish the envelope, she finally got him to give up the mysterious missive. Her narrowed gaze swept over the parchment, which had been addressed to Nacona. According to the note, C. L. Chambers requested a private conference at Nacona's

312

earliest convenience. Since Nacona wasn't around, July intended to meet C.L., even if the man didn't consider her capable of handling the investigation.

Quick as a wink, she scuttled to the stable to fetch a mount. With the oversize mongrel loping along beside her, July headed toward town. As usual, the lantern was blazing in C.L.'s office window long after dark. It was little wonder, though, that C.L. made the bank his life, considering the kind of woman he had married.

Without arousing unnecessary curiosity, July tethered her horse a block away from the bank and darted into an alley. She had every intention of making a discreet entrance into C.L.'s office. When she rapped on the back door, however, she was met with silence. She turned the latch and the door creaked open. But C.L. wasn't lounging in his chair. He was sprawled face up on the floor!

A gasp erupted from July as she peered at the peaked face devoid of expression. She forced herself to inch toward the motionless form. Grimacing at the unpleasant sight, she hunkered down on the floor beside the banker. A pearl-handled dagger lay beside him. She picked it up to examine it. Lord, had she expected the murderer's initials to be engraved on the handle? But the most unsettling part of all was that the dagger was similar to the one Nacona kept strapped to his right hip!

Her attention shifted to a crumpled envelope that lay beneath the desk. Curious, she contorted her body so she might grasp it. Killer's quiet growl caused her to glance toward the partially opened door, and July cringed when Sheriff Pinkston appeared from the shadows.

"What the hell . . . ?" Pinkston croaked, aghast.

July knew perfectly well that having the murder

weapon in her hand while she was positioned over the dead body did not bode well for her. Of course, holding the dagger was only circumstantial evidence at best; still . . . She was in the kind of trouble Nacona had warned her away from. In fact, if she had been prosecuting herself in a court of law, she would have considered this an open and shut case.

"Missus Bleu, I'm afraid you're going to have to come with me," Sheriff Pinkston said grimly. "And I hope you can explain why I found you hovering over C.L. Chambers while I was checking the doors to all the businesses after dark."

"I assure you, Sheriff, this is not what it seems," July replied, her voice nowhere near as steady and convincing as she had hoped.

Another figure appeared from the shadowy alleyway. Then a piercing scream nearly shattered July's eardrums and caused Killer to howl like a coyote. Angela Chambers cannoned into the room, shrieking at the top of her lungs and blubbering over her husband as if the moon rose and set upon him.

"You killed him! You little tramp!" Angela wailed.

July glared at the hypocritical woman. "I did no such thing. Your husband was lying on the floor when I walked in here."

Already infuriated by her predicament, July was angered further by Angel's theatrical display. To her knowledge, this was the first time Angel had shown her departed husband the slightest bit of affection. She spent most of her time throwing herself at other men.

"You came in through the back door?" Angela glowered accusingly at July. July glowered back. "If you had

had respectable intentions you would have entered by the front door. And what are you doing here at this late hour?"

"Why were *you* coming through the back door at this late hour?" July fired back at her.

"Because I heard the sheriff's voice in the alley," Angela explained. "If I known you had—"

"That's enough," Pinkston snapped. "I'll handle this investigation, if you don't mind."

Resigned to a long night of being forced to answer questions rather than asking them, July dropped the dagger and rose to her feet. She did have the presence of mind to tuck the crumpled envelope in her pocket before the sheriff or Angela noticed it. While Angela breezed out the door to inform the whole town that July had murdered Clarence Lee, the sheriff clutched her arm to lead her away.

Killer's growling protest prompted Pinkston to release his grasp on July immediately. "If you don't call off that mutt, I'll have to shoot him for obstructing justice," he warned.

July reassured the growling beast, but Killer made certain he remained between her and Pinkston, who followed a cautious distance behind them. By the time July reached the street, a crowd had congregated and murmurs rippled through it like waves on an ocean. Disheartened, July trudged toward the jail. She didn't have the foggiest notion how she was going to explain herself. If she mentioned the letter sent to Nacona, that might invite questions she hesitated to answer without first conferring with him. And she was not about to plead self-defense to a murder she hadn't committed. She was a victim of

315

circumstance and Angel—witch that she was—was trying to turn public sentiment against her. July wouldn't have been the least bit surprised to discover that Angel had disposed of her husband for control of Chambers's fortune.

Trail-weary, Nacona arrived on horseback. The safe at the Laramie bank had been opened with explosives, as had the one at C.L.'s bank in Cheyenne during a thunderstorm. But this time there had been no booming thunder to conceal the explosion, only the whistle of the train that had rolled into the depot. The holdup had taken place in the cover of darkness, and witnesses had been unable to describe the thieves' physical appearance, though the bandits had been reported to be wearing long linen dusters and masks.

Nacona had followed the robbers tracks east until the band had scattered in several directions. They had converged north of Cheyenne, only to split again. To say Nacona was frustrated by this investigation was an understatement. To compound his frustration, he hadn't been able to get that blond-haired hellion off his mind. He'd spent every spare minute wondering what she was doing and who she was with.

"Mr. Bleu!" Ot Knot's voice shattered the silence.

Nacona drew the mount he had purchased in Laramie to a halt when the wiry little foreman came charging out of the bunkhouse to intercept him.

"Lord, ya shoulda bin here," Ot shouted in frustration. "While ya was gone the most awful thing happened. I can scarcely believe it myself, and the other men have bin walkin' 'round in a daze all the livelong day. I didn't know what to do, 'cept wait 'til ya got back from wherever ya went. Ya shoulda told me where to reach ya."

A feeling of dread weighted Nacona down as he swung from the saddle. His first thought was that something terrible had happened to July. He should have known better than to leave that green-eyed terror to her own devices. The woman attracted trouble. She delighted in seeing if she could wade out of calamity as easily as she leaped into it. And if she had gotten herself killed . . . Nacona scowled at the unnerving thought.

"What happened?" His anxious gaze darted toward the darkened ranchhouse. "Where's my wife?"

"That's what I've bin tryin' to tell ya," Ot gushed. "She ain't here, and she ain't bin here since last night. I tried to rescue her, but they—"

Nacona yanked the smaller man up by his shirtfront and shook him soundly, trying to bring him to his senses. "Slow down, Ot." Nacona scowled into his face. "Now tell me where July is."

"Jail," Ot bleated. "They locked her up last night, and they won't let her out. An' Killer won't let nobody go near her. He just sits in front of her cell and snarls. They have to send her meals in through the barred windows. That crazed mutt tried to chew off Sheriff Pinkston's leg twice and—"

"What the devil is July doing in jail?" Nacona growled.

"They say she killed C. L. Chambers, but I know yer wife would do no such thing. Somebody made a bad mistake."

Somebody had made a mistake all right. And it well might be that daring little wife of his. Cursing, Nacona swung back into the saddle and thundered off to town. He had left her alone for three short days and she had wound up in jail for murder! And why had she killed C. L. Chambers? Had she discovered that C.L. was behind the holdups and the rustling, then confronted him with the evidence? Chambers might have attacked her. If he had, couldn't she have simply walloped him over the head?

Nacona was still stewing when he reached the sheriff's office. The instant he zoomed through the door, Pinkston was on his feet, sighing in relief.

"I thought you'd never show up," the sheriff muttered. "Where have you been?"

"I was in Laramie, tending to some business." Nacona stared at the closed door that led to the row of cells. "Why the hell did you lock up my wife?" His glistening black eyes riveted on the sheriff. "You ought to know she's no murderess," he felt compelled to say in July's defense.

"Well, Angela Chambers and her lawyer seem to think she is," Pinkston countered. "Angela has been spouting off about lynching and immediate justice and I don't know what all! And when I walked into C.L.'s office, your wife was bent over his body, clutching the dagger that killed him. She looked pretty damned guilty to me, too."

"I'd like to see my wife," Nacona demanded gruffly.

"So would Angela's lawyer, and so would I," Pinkston snorted. "That dadblamed dog won't let anybody near her. I couldn't even lure Killer away with food. He nearly took off my leg when I tried to go in there."

Heaving a frustrated sigh, Nacona strode across the office and eased open the door to the cells. Sure enough, there sat Killer, looking as immovable as the Rock of Gibraltar. Behind the iron bars was a very subdued, visibly distressed, and badly rumpled July MacKenzie Bleu. This untoward development had taken the wind out of her sails, that was obvious. Now she knew how exasperated Nacona had been while in the Dodge City jail. He had half a mind to keep her locked up so she wouldn't embroil herself in even more trouble.

July peered up at the towering giant who looked as tired and haggard as she was. From all indications, Nacona had been tracking outlaws night and day. Much as she relished the sight of him, July had been dreading this moment.

"I suppose you are surprised to find me here," she began lamely, pushing herself off the cot to confront his condescending glare.

"Surprised? No. I've learned not to be surprised at anything you do. Annoyed? Yes, most definitely." He lit his cheroot and puffed upon it. "Now suppose you tell me why you killed one of the men who hired us. Don't you think that was a mite drastic, July, just to ensure we don't have to pay back half the fee—in the event that we fail to solve this case."

July glared at Nacona. Leave it to him to ridicule her. "Oh, for heaven's sake, you don't really think I killed C. L. Chambers," she snapped.

"According to the sheriff, you entered C.L.'s office through the back door, late at night. Pinkston caught you holding the murder weapon." Nacona expelled a disdainful snort. "Damn it, July, don't you ever stay home?"

She stamped her foot. "I had a perfectly logical reason for going to the bank at that late hour," she declared self-righteously. "Someone delivered a message, asking you to meet C.L. as quickly as possible. Since you were in

Laramie, I went in your stead. The sheriff was making his rounds to secure the businesses for the night, and he saw me. Then Angel came along. She started wailing like a banshee, claiming that I had murdered her dear husband—which, of course, I didn't. I just happened to be at the wrong place at the wrong time. If you ask me, Angel killed C.L. and framed me."

Nacona leaned negligently against the wall, mulling over what July had told him and puffing on his cheroot. "And if you ask me, you're recklessly leaping over intervening steps in the reasoning process," he said calmly.

July peered into the bronzed face that sported three day's growth of whiskers, and then she frowned, bemused. "What do you mean?"

"First of all, you cannot say for certain that the messenger was sent by C. L. Chambers. Has anyone come forward to confess they delivered a message to the Golden Spur?"

July gave her tangled blond head a negative shake.

"I thought not," Nacona remarked blandly. "C.L. was probably already dead when the message arrived. And, if you recall, the message was addressed to *me*. Perhaps *I* was to be framed for murder rather than *you*."

July plunked herself down on the smelly cot and rolled her eyes ceilingward. "And why do you think Angela wanted to frame *you*? In my estimation, she sees you as a prospective lover." She glanced at Nacona as if he had already become one. The thought disgusted her. "I would have thought Angel saw a chance to get me out of the way so she could get to you."

"Perhaps it was as Angel claimed. Maybe she had nothing to do with the murder and just happened along,"

Nacona speculated. "She may have only seized the opportunity to retaliate against you—her rival. After all, you have turned the heads of her lovers since you arrived in town. And—" a mocking smile twitched his lips—"this perplexing twist blows holes in your theory that C.L. was the ringleader."

"Not necessarily," July pointed out. "Perhaps one of C.L.'s henchmen got tired of taking orders and decided to take control of the operation."

Nacona scowled. July was clinging fiercely to her ridiculous notion. She was so stubborn she couldn't bring herself to admit she was wrong.

July glanced discreetly toward the door before fishing the rumpled envelope from her pocket. She thrust it through the bars for Nacona's inspection. "I found this under C.L.'s desk," she said quietly. "There was no letter inside it, but I think it bears consideration. Jordon Milner told me that C.L. was checking the backgrounds of some of the ranchers in the area. I thought perhaps C.L. had dug up some incriminating information about one of Angel's lovers. Maybe she or that lover—thought it necessary to dispose of C.L. before he spread it all over town."

Nacona noted the address and frowned.

"I was going to send off a telegram to request that a second copy of the letter be returned to us as evidence for the case," July explained. "But unfortunately, I wound up in this foul-smelling jail with nothing to do and all day to do it."

Nacona tucked the envelope in his pocket and smiled down at the bedraggled beauty. "I'll see what I can do about springing you. After all, a wife's place is in the home, not the jail."

July rolled her eyes at this attempt at humor, refusing to be amused. "Just get me out of here. Please!"

In two strides, Nacona was beside her, staring at her through the bars. Recalling Dodge City, where July had sought to bargain with him when he was in the calaboose, he reckoned it was time to employ the same tactic on her.

"And if I do manage to set you free, I expect compensation for my trouble," he insisted with a devilish grin.

July couldn't resist the ornery twinkle in those ebony eyes, or the rakish smile that turned up his sensuous mouth. "If you get me out of here, your wish is my command, my dear husband," she purred suggestively.

Two dark brows jackknifed at the implication, and Nacona peered curiously at July. What? No loud protest? No sassy retort? My, my, a stint in jail had certainly changed this hellion's tune. "*Any* wish?" he prodded. "You'll grant me *any* whim if I set you free?"

July reached between the bars to rearrange the tousled raven hair that drooped over his forehead. Having Nacona back came as a tremendous relief. At first seeing him again, her heart had leaped with excitement. Having overheard Angel ranting and raving about a lynching, she had decided it was best to reap every pleasure, just in case she did wind up swinging from a rope. After all, Wyoming had come to be known as the equality state. Women were equal enough to be hanged, right alongside men.

"For my freedom, I'll grant you any whim," she assured him.

Nacona stood there for a half minute, studying the indecipherable expression on July's weary face. God, what was it about this green-eyed witch that stirred him so? At her slightest touch, he was on a slow burn. And he had missed her while he'd been gone. Though he wanted to get this blond-haired vixen out of his system, he always wound up wanting her.

"I'll see what I can do about your predicament." Nacona's voice was heavy from the effect of her caressing touch.

"Take Killer with you," July requested. "I intend to see that the stench is removed from this cell while you're gone. This jail is revolting. I'm not planning to be here much longer, but my successors deserve better than this."

Nacona glanced down at the mongrel and voiced the command to follow. Killer didn't budge from his spot.

"Go on," July demanded. "With your sensitive nose, you can't stand much more of this offensive smell, either, Killer."

Reluctantly, the beast trailed behind Nacona, but not without casting one last glance in July's direction.

Sheriff Pinkston backed behind his desk when Nacona ambled into the room with Killer one step behind him.

"My wife requests that her cell be cleaned," Nacona announced. "And I want her out of there as quickly as possible."

"I can't just turn her loose. Angela Chambers and her lawyer will be over here, protesting to high heaven!"

Nacona braced his hands on the edge of the desk to stare Pinkston squarely in the eye. "Come now, Sheriff. You don't really believe July is responsible for the murder, do you? One look at my dainty, sophisticated wife should be proof enough that she is hardly the type to go around killing people for no apparent reason. Why, she almost never stabs bankers, and if she did she wouldn't hang around to get caught." His tone was mocking.

"Well, she *was* at the scene of the crime—for no other apparent reason." Pinkston had been casting wary glances at Killer.

"She had a perfectly legitimate reason," Nacona confided. "But she refused to tell you until I returned. The fact is, a mysterious message was delivered to our home that fateful night, requesting that I meet with C.L."

Pinkston blinked. "Why was he summoning you at that hour?"

Nacona's broad shoulders lifted in a shrug. "I wish I knew the answer to that question. But whatever happened, I was the one C.L. wanted to see. July only went on my behalf. It seems to me that whoever killed Chambers was trying to frame me, and July wound up in the wrong place."

Pinkston combed his handlebar mustache with his fingertips while he mulled over Nacona's remark. He had to admit there was a certain degree of logic to the explanation.

"C.L. may not have sent that message at all," Nacona reasoned. "The murderer might have delivered the note after disposing of him. And whoever the killer is, he or she is running around loose while my wife suffers for it. I would like permission to investigate this case. After all, I was a detective before I put down roots in Wyoming," he added, twisting the truth to suit his purpose. He was still a detective, and one of his clients had just turned up dead. That wasn't good for business!

"You have my permission," Pinkston granted. "But you'll have to talk to Angel about dropping the charges since she filed them and she's been carrying on about a quick trial and a hanging. If it was up to me, I'd release your wife. But I don't need Angela and her lawyer threatening to have me ousted from office if I go easy on July. They'll claim it was because she's female and pretty to boot."

"I'll have a talk with Angela," Nacona volunteered. "And while Killer is with me, round up somebody to clean those cells. They're disgusting."

That said, Nacona wheeled around and stalked off. Had he known what lay ahead of him, he might not have bothered to leave.

Chapter 20

A provocative smile pursed Angel's lips when she opened the door of her elegantly furnished home to see Nacona standing on the porch. "Do come in, love." She stepped into the light, revealing the black negligee that exposed her feminine assets to advantage.

Nacona assessed the sultry brunette and scowled to himself. Angel was wearing black all right, but it wasn't the kind of mourning garb that befitted a grieving widow. If Nacona didn't know better, he would swear this seductive sorceress was expecting a late-evening guest. Who? Nacona didn't have the faintest idea. The lady, if one could call her that, had a stable of studs at her beck and call. Nacona hadn't cared much for C. L. Chambers, but he did sympathize with the departed man for making the mistake of marrying this vamp. Angel was a curse, not a blessing that enriched a man's life.

Now she smoothed the provocative gown over her curves, calling even more attention to them, and with a noticeable swing to her well-shaped hips, she sashayed across the room to pour herself a drink.

As far as Nacona knew, this woman was rarely without a drink in hand.

"I suppose you have come to plead for your wife," Angel guessed. With a flair for the theatrical, she slipped onto a chair, allowing the hem of her gossamer gown to reveal a generous amount of bare leg.

Nacona eased the door shut, forcing the oversize mongrel to wait on the stoop. "I want July out of jail. Despite the incriminating circumstances, she has committed no crime."

Raspy laughter bubbled in Angel's throat. "You truly are blinded by your wife's beauty, aren't you, love?" Her gaze slid over Nacona's striking physique, assessing him as thoroughly as if she'd reached out to map his masculine contours with her hands. "And so devoted, too." Her smile became more mischievous as she studied him over the rim of her glass. "Just how devoted, I wonder? Are you willing to do anything to see those charges dropped, Nacona?"

This witch was definitely without scruples. Her smile and the downward path of her gaze indicated what she wanted in exchange for July's freedom. Angel employed all sorts of blackmail, Nacona imagined. She was accustomed to getting what she wanted by utilizing her beauty and her sexual appeal. Nacona couldn't help but wonder if this seductive creature had manipulated one of her lovers into disposing of her husband. But the mysterious message July had received puzzled him. Someone had tried to frame him, but he didn't know what role this sultry vixen had played in her husband's death. Or what he was going to have to do to free July.

Gracefully, Angel rose to her feet and sashayed toward

Nacona. Her arms glided over his broad shoulders to toy with the jet black hair at the nape of his neck. "I think you would be a most satisfying lover," she murmured as her shapely body brushed suggestively against his. "So good in fact, that I might find it in my heart to dismiss those charges against your wife. But I cannot imagine that she is woman enough to please a virile man like you." Her hand drifted down to measure the wide expanse of his chest. "You need an experienced lover who knows how to make a man glad he's a man . . ."

Nacona was startled by the repulsive shiver that trickled down his spine. This temptress, for all her outward beauty, was wicked to the bone. That made him realize how open and giving July was, once he'd broken through her defenses. July was passion awaiting release, and she responded to him with instinct and emotion. Angel, however, preyed on men's needs for physical satisfaction. She obviously delighted in lusty affairs—the more of them the better. But there was little sincerity or sensitivity about her. She always seemed to have an ulterior motive.

"Well, my handsome stag, just how much are you willing to give to rescue your wife?" Her fingertips dipped between the buttons of his shirt to caress his chest.

Nacona's temper snapped. He wanted this sorceress a respectable distance away from him. Now! Until the previous month, he had never really considered himself a man of discriminating tastes. But after he had married July his perspectives had changed. He hadn't realized just how much until Angel threw herself at him. The very idea of sleeping with this vixen repulsed him. Evidently July had ruined his bad reputation and had given him the kind of respectability he'd never thought he would want.

"Stop it, Angel." He abruptly set her away from him. "I didn't come here to bed you." He glared disdainfully at the sultry tramp C.L. had foolishly married. "You should at least have the decency to wait a week after your husband's death before you start propositioning everything in breeches."

Angel staggered back as if he'd struck her. "You stupid bastard," she spat out. "I can have any man I want! You're a fool if you think I'll drop the charges against that bitch you wed, and if you don't know that she's been sleeping around while you remain true to her, you're an even bigger fool."

Nacona snatched the crumpled envelope from his pocket and waved it in front of her flushed face. "I'm not as big a fool as you would like to believe," he countered, watching the startled expression that came to her face before she could mask it. "Unless I miss my guess, and I doubt I have, your husband discovered something about one of your lovers and tried to run him out of town by threatening to expose him. Did you plot your husband's murder, or were you merely an accomplice to the crime, Angel?"

His scornful gaze flicked over her barely clad figure in blatant disapproval. "How convenient that you inherited C.L.'s stock in the bank and all his worldly possessions. I think July might be right in thinking you were the one with a motive to kill him. Had C.L. grown tired of being the laughingstock of Cheyenne? Did he threaten to divorce you if you continued your dalliances?"

In a burst of fury, Angel snatched up her glass and hurled it at Nacona. She missed him, and the glass shattered. "You bastard! You'll pay dearly for this, I swear you will. I'll see to it that the bank forecloses on your mortgage. After July is hung, you'll be run out of town on a rail!"

"So the pot is calling the kettle black." Nacona smirked insultingly. "My wife is everything you could never be. And, believe me, she knows how to make a man thankful he's a man. You can't find satisfaction in one bed, much less a dozen of them. I pity the fool who thinks you're a prize worth taking."

Another furious screech exploded from Angel. Then, outraged, she scooped up the decanter of brandy and hurled it. Nacona artfully dodged the oncoming missile, and liquor splattered over the brocade wallpaper. Cursing like a trooper, Angel picked up the delicately carved end table and heaved it across the room. It cartwheeled across the floor and clattered against the wall.

"Get out!" she hissed at him.

"Gladly." Nacona obliged, slamming the door behind him with such force that the window panes rattled.

Killer growled when Nacona stormed onto the porch, but the dog's attention seemed to be focused elsewhere. When Killer bounded toward the railing, Nacona quickly called him back and stalked down the steps.

Damn it, he had handled the situation poorly. But the instant that witch had touched him, he had lost his composure. Angel's insulting remarks about July had set him off, too. Criticizing July was a privilege that Nacona reserved for himself. It had become second nature to him to defend her, verbally as well as physically. The nauseating bargain Angel had proposed had infuriated him, even if he had been guilty of employing a similar technique in his dealings with July. Now he regretted having done so.

Scowling, Nacona swung into the saddle and trotted down the street. He took time to rouse the telegraph operator and request that a message be sent to the address on the crumpled envelope. July was right. The letter had played a significant part in C.L.'s death. Nacona had noticed the shock on Angel's face when he'd thrust the envelope at her. Once he and July knew what was in the letter they would have a valuable clue.

By the time Nacona returned to the sheriff's office, things had progressed from bad to worse. Lo and behold, there stood Angel Chambers, a cloak barely concealing her figure, hysterical tears spilling from her. There was a welt on her cheek, a rip in her gown, and Nacona had the sickening feeling that he had been framed for the second time.

July had feigned an assault to get him stashed behind bars, and now Angel seemed to be up to the same trick. Nacona was certain that it would work as well for Angel in Cheyenne as it had worked for July in Dodge.

"I want this brutal savage arrested!" Angel blubbered.

The way she was pouring out the tears, Nacona wondered if this vamp had spigots in her head.

"This man barged into my home and threatened me, struck me!" she wailed as she indicated the red welt on her cheek. "He wanted me to drop the charge of murder against his wife. When I refused he abused me!" Another round of howls gushed from her lips. "Put him away, Sheriff, or my lawyer will have your job!"

At this point, Pinkston was on the verge of telling Angel's lawyer that he was welcome to this thankless job.

Muttering to himself, Pinkston gestured toward the door that led to the cells. "Well, Mr. Bleu, it seems your method of persuasion has granted you the right to visit your wife . . . indefinitely."

"I didn't lay a hand on this woman," Nacona protested. "In fact, she propositioned—"

"That's a lie!" Angel railed as she spun to face the sheriff. "He's trying to save his miserable neck by putting the blame on me. I have marks on me to prove how vicious this scoundrel can be. Now lock him up before he returns to punish me for speaking out against him and his murdering wife!"

It was no use. Nacona knew he was doomed. Angel and her lawyer had already been hounding Pinkston. The sheriff was forced to do his duty, if only to shut Angel up. She was making such a racket that Killer was barking his head off outside the door. It did indeed look as if Nacona's attempt to free July had worked in reverse. Now the two of them were facing charges for crimes they didn't commit.

July had heard the carryings-on in the outer office, but it had been difficult to determine exactly what was happening. She presumed Angel was putting up a fuss about her being released from jail. Expelling a long-suffering sigh, July bounded to her feet the instant the portal creaked open. But when the sheriff unlocked her cell and gave Nacona a nudge inside, she frowned, bewildered.

"What's going on?" July demanded to know when Pinkston slammed the barred door shut.

"Your husband assaulted Angela when she refused to

drop the charges against you," Pinkston explained. "Now she has brought charges against him."

July stared incredulously at the scowling giant. "The idea was to get me *out* of here. Not *join* me! Blast it, why didn't you—?"

Nacona clamped a hand over her mouth and stared grimly at the sheriff. "Those were trumped-up charges. I refused Angel's lurid proposition, so I insulted the *un*grieving widow. She threw a glass of whiskey, the whole damned bottle, and an end table at me. Then she vowed to get even with me for turning her down. I left and . . ."

His voice trailed off when a fleeting thought skipped across his mind. Nacona had been too perturbed at the time to recall Killer's behavior on the stoop. But now the incident began to make sense.

"Killer was waiting for me on the porch, growling and craning his neck around the side of the house, as if he'd heard something." Nacona peered straight into Pinkston's dubious frown. "I think someone was eavesdropping at the window out there. Probably the same man Angel was expecting when I showed up. Considering the way she was dressed, she had to be anticipating someone's arrival, and it certainly wasn't mine because I'd just returned to town."

Thick eyebrows, like woolly caterpillars, drew together on Pinkston's forehead. "Are you sure about that? Am I supposed to rely on your word and the growl of a crazed dog?"

Nacona loosed July to clamp his hands around the bars. "I swear to God I didn't touch that scheming female. She wanted me to . . ." He glanced back at July and then refocused on Pinkston before continuing in a quiet voice. "For an hour of pleasure she promised to drop the charges against my wife. When I refused, she threw her tantrum."

There was nothing wrong with July's hearing. She deciphered the hushed words and gasped in outrage. "That witch! Didn't she even have the decency to let her husband rest in peace for a day or two before she resumed her sordid affairs? She's disgusting!"

To further convince Pinkston, who wavered in indecision, Nacona slipped an arm around July's waist and drew her to him. He stared deeply into her face. "I love my wife," he declared without taking his eyes off the vivacious blonde. "As much as I wanted July out of jail, I refused to stoop so low as to accommodate that pathetic woman. July has become my life." To add credence to his declaration, Nacona placed a passionate kiss on her lips and drew her possessively to him. While he nuzzled his chin against the top of her head, he glanced back at Pinkston. "Believe me, Sheriff, I have all I want. I've been dodging Angel's suggestive innuendos since I arrived in town."

Pinkston couldn't help but be touched by the loving display. July was peering up at Nacona as if he were the moon and Nacona stared at her as if she were the stars. The sheriff had heard the rumors that Nacona was hopelessly devoted to this saucy beauty who was not quite as stuck on him. But the look on July's face indicated the feelings were mutual, no matter what the bachelors in town wanted to believe. Mismatched though this couple appeared to be, Pinkston could almost feel heat radiating from their cell.

Heaving a sigh, he pivoted toward the door. "I'll go talk

to Angela after she has a chance to simmer down. But if I pressure her, it could cost me my job. Then that lawyer of hers will buy off my replacement, who will undoubtedly see that you two are locked away permanently."

"Take your deputy with you," Nacona advised. "Angel may accuse you of molestation, too. Then the three of us will be mildewing in jail."

Pinkston half turned and managed a grin. "Good idea. I should have volunteered to accompany you. Maybe none of this would have happened."

When the sheriff closed the door behind him, Nacona stared down into July's beguiling face. There was no need for him to go on holding her now that his performance was over, but he couldn't make himself let go. It seemed months since he had captured this bewitching goddess in an embrace. After his fiasco with Angel, he felt the need to replace the sense of revulsion with warm, heady pleasure.

"Welcome home," July teased as her arms entwined around his neck, bringing his head to hers. "I think it well advised to continue this charade, just in case Pinkston comes back, don't you?"

"Mmm . . . most definitely," he agreed in a husky tone. "We want to make absolutely certain Pinkston is convinced of our sincerity and devotion."

July stared into those glistening obsidian eyes, and a wave of pleasure rolled over her. She didn't have to play a charade for Pinkston's benefit. Loving Nacona had become as natural and instinctive as breathing.

"Did you truly reject Angel? Why?" she questioned as her lips feathered over his sensuous mouth.

"Because of this . . ." His mouth took urgent possession

of hers, and his aroused body fitted itself against her shapely curves. "And this . . ." His hands glided over her hips, drawing her ever closer, allowing her to feel his hungry desire for her. "She wasn't you." Nacona pressed a kiss to the sensitive point beneath her ear. "And even though Angel insists you haven't remained faithful to me, I keep coming back to the fire to see just how hot it can burn."

"That witch!" July gasped in outrage. "I flirted with those other men because you told me to. But you should see how adept I am at dodging an octopus's arms. That Jezebel never moved away from a man's groping touch in her life."

The confession July had blurted out in a fit of temper pleased Nacona beyond words. During their stormy affair, he'd kept wondering if July had fallen into another man's arms, just to spite him. It was a relief to know she hadn't. She didn't love him, he knew. But at least she cared enough not to humiliate him while they played out their charade for the sake of the investigation.

The need to slake his thirst for kisses was more intoxicating than brandy. Nacona gave way to temptation, craving one and then another. It was in mid-kiss that Pinkston barged back inside, carrying the dinner tray the deputy had brought from the restaurant. If the sheriff hadn't been convinced before, he certainly was now. No matter what anybody said or thought, the Bleus had something that caused sparks to fly. With a wife who possessed July's beauty, spunk, and charm, Nacona had no need for Angel Chambers.

A yelp erupted from Pinkston's lips when something big and powerful and hairy slammed against the back of his knees, knocking him into the bars and very nearly upending the tray. Killer was back in full force, and he had no intention of remaining separated from his new mistress and master.

"Oh, hell," Pinkston muttered as he dug into his pocket to retrieve the keys. "I may as well go talk to Angela now. Between the two of you steaming up the cell and that mutt snarling and growling all over the place, I'll never have a moment's peace. With any luck, I'll catch Angel with the 'visitor' Killer spotted in the bushes."

Pinkston didn't even bother to lock the barred door after he shoved the tray at Nacona. "Enjoy your supper while my deputy and I talk to Angela. And don't you dare leave. You don't need to add a jail break to your alleged crimes. I'll be back as soon as I can."

With that, the sheriff took a wide berth around Killer and hurried out to summon his deputy. In less than a minute, he was on his way to speak with Angel, and July and Nacona were left to enjoy their meal.

By the time July and Nacona finished eating, Pinkston and his deputy returned. The instant Nacona noticed the sheriff's bleak expression and his lack of color, he knew something was amiss.

"Now what's happened?" Nacona questioned as he walked out of the open cell to confront the visibly shaken sheriff.

"Bad news," Pinkston croaked. "The worst."

"Don't tell me Angel accused you of attacking her," July muttered, following on Nacona's heels.

"She didn't accuse me of anything." Pinkston gulped. "She couldn't. She was . . . dead."

As the words crackled in the silence, July swayed against the bars.

"What?" Nacona stared goggle-eyed at the pale-faced sheriff.

Pinkston nodded in grim confirmation. "She was lying abed in that skimpy negligee of hers—face up, staring sightlessly at the ceiling." He shivered. "At first I thought she was in a drunken stupor or something. The lady was known to drink a bit. But when I shook her, she didn't move. . . ."

Nacona was out the door and gone. July was right behind him, with Killer bringing up the rear. The threesome darted down the street toward the Chambers' spacious home. Nacona found the parlor just as he'd left it two hours earlier. Brandy stained the wallpaper and shards of glass were embedded in the carpet. The upended end table was still in the corner.

July surveyed the ransacked room, certain the incident had occurred just as Nacona described it. Angel wouldn't have wasted a drop of good liquor unless her temper had exploded. She was a drinker.

Bracing herself, July strode into the elaborately decorated boudoir to see Angel lying motionless in bed. Nacona was standing at the foot of it. His gaze bounced back and forth from the dead widow, to the furniture, and then to the open window. Hesitantly, July approached the bed to peer into Angel's waxen features. Her astute gaze lingered on the smudges of makeup on Angel's cheeks, and a curious frown knitted her brow.

She picked up the pillow beside Angel and turned it over in her hands.

"What the devil are you doing?" Nacona quizzed.

"Searching for clues. Angel obviously wasn't strangled or there would be marks on her throat. No doubt, the murderer would like us to believe she drank herself to death." July indicated the empty flask and the empty glass beside it. Grimacing, she eased the other pillow from beneath Angel's head and turned it in her hand. *"Voilà.* Just as I suspected."

Frowning, Nacona eased up beside her to see smudges of makeup on the underside of the pillow. "She was smothered," he said. "Our murderer was far more clever in disposing of Angel than in getting rid of C.L."

July nodded in agreement. "The letter must have prompted the killer to dispose of C.L.—and quickly. I'm beginning to agree with your theory that the mysterious message I received was an afterthought. C.L. was probably already dead when it arrived at the Golden Spur. Our killer was looking for someone to frame—to protect himself. Since we are the newest residents in town, we were probably prime targets."

A muffled groan escaped Nacona's lips. "It was my fault Angel wound up dead. After she propositioned me, I accused her of being an accomplice to her husband's murder. I waved that damned envelope under her nose, and she looked shocked by its existence. She must have confronted her husband's killer with the information."

"Or perhaps she tried to blackmail the murderer with her knowledge," July speculated as she reached down to examine Angel's hands. "And it looks as if she tried to

340

fight back while she was being smothered." She held up the dark hairs entangled in Angel's fingers.

"Brown," Nacona muttered. "Only half the males in Cheyenne have brown hair. It could have been anybody."

"But one male has a few hairs missing," July added.

"That knowledge is useless," Nacona grumbled. "We're right back where we started—no clues, no probable suspects, only a hypothetical motive."

July frowned thoughtfully. "We do have one."

"Oh, really? Who might that be?"

July met his curious stare. "Whoever inherits control of Chambers bank."

"In which case the demise of Angel and C.L. may have nothing whatsoever to do with your initial investigation. We may have just acquired another case," Nacona muttered.

"What did you find out in Laramie?" July questioned as Nacona shepherded her out of the room.

"Only that there were a few similarities between the latest robbery and the one at C.L.'s bank. I followed a set of tracks east, but they diverged, converged, and then went in all directions again."

"If whoever killed Angel and C.L. is linked with the robberies, he's shrewd and clever, I'll give him that."

"Not as clever as you are, I'll wager," Nacona commented. "Nice work, July. I'm ashamed to say I doubted your skills as a detective. But you know what you're doing. I didn't check the pillows. I thought Angel drank herself into eternity. That was just what our murderer wanted me to think."

The compliment pleased July, and she rose on tiptoe to place a fleeting kiss on his lips.

Nacona frowned curiously. "What was that for?"

"For giving me the chance to prove myself—to you, at least—even if the rest of the world won't believe a woman has enough intelligence to seek out and analyze evidence."

His arm curled around her trim waist, drawing her possessively against him. "You're damned good, July," he admitted. "But I want a promise from you. Don't ever go off alone to investigate a lead without first consulting me. We are dealing with someone capable of murder. I don't want you to become a victim."

"But what if you're gone again and—?"

Nacona pressed his forefinger to her lips to silence her. "No ifs, ands, or buts, July," he told her firmly. "This is a dangerous business. I don't want you to end up like Angel. I already have her death on my conscience. Having yours would be infinitely worse."

"And just why is that?" she prodded, wishing just once he would take her into his confidence and tell her exactly how he felt about her. Then perhaps she would know whether she was wasting precious emotions on this man who had stolen her heart. If he could just bring himself to like her, that would certainly go a long way toward compensating for this one-sided love she was harboring.

When Nacona peered down into her lovely, inquisitive face, his heart was jolted. He knew if he didn't get hold of himself, he was liable to blurt out some reckless confession. He cared more for this rambunctious imp than he should. Thoughts of her preoccupied him, but a crusade awaited him when this investigation was completed. Two years ago, he had made himself a promise, and he never made promises he didn't keep. Despite his growing attachment to July, he could not—would not—forsake his search for his brother's killer.

"Nacona?" July halted in the street, waiting, hoping for even the slightest declaration of affection. She wanted him to love her as he had claimed to in the sheriff's office. "You didn't answer my question."

His breath came out in a frustrated rush. "Jeezus, July. Do you think I have no heart at all? We've been together through thick and thicker. We're partners—man and wife—at least temporarily. Even that oversize mutt has become attached to you. Don't you think it possible for me to get attached to you, too?"

Getting Nacona to confess to love, or something like it, was worse than dragging a mule where he didn't want to go. "Killer likes me because I feed him and let him out in the middle of the night. I suppose this attachment you feel for me is simply because of sex," she burst out, her pride wounded.

Nacona wheeled around and stalked off. "We are not having this discussion or the argument that always follows when I try to talk to you. We're going home to get a decent night's sleep. Sleep, July, not sex—which you seem to believe is all I ever think about. Anyway we don't have sex," he clarified. "We make love. If you were more experienced you'd know the difference."

When he swung into the saddle and extended a hand to assist her up behind him, July simply stood there staring up at his ruggedly handsome face. He owned her soul, that was a fact. She loved him. He offered her his hand, but she wanted his heart—not temporarily but forever.

"Are you coming or not?" he questioned irritably.

"Not," she replied. "I don't want to be around when the termites bore into your wooden heart!"

"Now what the hell did I say wrong?" he asked with an exasperated scowl.

"What have you ever said right!" July inhaled deeply to bring her runaway temper under control and shooed Nacona on his way. "The sheriff left my mare in the livery stable. I'll fetch her and make my own way home."

Nacona studied the curvaceous beauty for a long moment before he nodded in compliance and reined toward the Golden Spur. He had the feeling that July needed to be alone, especially after her stint in jail. It was better to part company for a few minutes, he assured himself. He, too, needed time to get himself in hand and to ponder the new developments in this case.

If July had been riding with him, her ripe feminine body meshed against his, he probably wouldn't have been able to manage a sane thought. She distracted him too easily. Lord a-mighty, if he didn't watch himself he *was* going to fall in love with that adorable nymph. He had never been in love, and he didn't want to be now. The prospect, the complications, scared him. He cherished his freedom, thrived on it, needed it. He'd been born under a wandering star, and he was too old to change his ways. Besides he had to bring Shandin's killer to justice, no matter how long it took. If he was smart, he wouldn't be sidetracked by his attraction to that emerald-eyed minx. They were as mismatched as two people could be, and nothing could change that.

Chapter 21

The MacKenzie brothers were in the worst of all possible moods. Their train connections from Dodge City to Pueblo, Colorado, had been marked by one frustrating delay after another.

"We should have purchased mounts and traveled by horseback to Cheyenne," Calvin grumbled sourly. "We would have been there by now. By the time we do arrive in Wyoming, there'll be no telling where that unscrupulous gunslinger will have taken July."

"I have the assurance of the engineer that repairs on the locomotive will be finished in a few hours," Gresham informed his disgruntled brothers. "We should be on our way to Denver this afternoon."

Ethan pulled his plug hat from his sandy blond head and sighed wearily. His green eyes settled on the looming mountains to the west. He might have enjoyed the magnificent scenery, if he hadn't been so concerned about his sister. Ethan simply could not imagine how July had gotten mixed up with a man of Nacona Bleu's reputation. She had been pursued and courted by the wealthiest, most upstanding gentlemen in Kansas City. No doubt, she was sickened and heart-broken at having virtually become a slave to a domineering tyrant. Only MacKenzie pride had kept her from begging for her brothers' assistance, or Bleu had kept such close tabs on her that she'd had no chance to make contact with her family. And if the truth be known, Nacona Bleu was probably the one who had sent those misleading telegrams.

"I still can't figure out what July was doing in Dodge City in the first place," Gresham mused aloud, staring unseeingly at distant peaks of mountains.

"That doesn't really matter now," Calvin commented. "Thanks to this Bleu character she has been there and gone."

"And Bleu is going to be here and gone when I get my hands on him," Ethan muttered spitefully. "He's going to rue the day he laid his filthy hands on July."

Ethan had voiced the brothers' sentiment. Three pair of eyes—of various shades of green—focused on the rugged terrain to the northwest. But none of the MacKenzies could see the grandeur of snow-capped peaks. They were simply staring into the distance, fearing the worst and thinking vindictive thoughts about their new brother-in-law.

The two mysterious murders in Cheyenne put a damper on the festivities scheduled to celebrate the town's tenth year of existence. Nevertheless, the townsfolk and residents of the surrounding areas turned out in droves to enjoy the rodeo in which wranglers from various ranches displayed their skills at bronc riding, roping, and steer wrestling. A traveling group of dramatists was also on hand for the celebration, as were the musicians who played for the street dance. Horses that had been groomed and trained, lined the street in preparation for a series of races.

July had lost track of Nacona more than two hours before the dance began, but the faithful Killer had never let her out of his sight. She accepted every invitation to dance. However, she noted each partner against whom Killer voiced his disapproval with a growl or a snarl. Again, as she had on several other occasions, she found herself wondering what the dog was trying to tell her. Killer even snapped at Hoyt Simpson when Simpson tried to kick him out of the way, and he growled at Hub Butler and Jordon Milner when they tried to hold her a little closer than necessary while swaying to one of the slow-tempoed tunes.

Although July would have preferred to be in Nacona's brawny arms, staring into those onyx eyes that could steal her breath away, she did enjoy the lively celebration. Until she saw Nacona ambling out of Cheyenne Rose's Pleasure Parlor. The thought of what he had been doing in such a place cut her to the bone. Even though he had insisted he'd wanted nothing to do with Angel's propositions, he wasn't beneath bedding the harlots who worked for Cheyenne Rose, the renowned madam.

July scolded herself for feeling betrayed. She had no hold on Nacona except for their bargain. Because she had fallen in love with him, nothing had changed. She was the one who had assured Nacona that he was free to do as he pleased during this marriage arrangement. Still, it hurt to know he felt no particular loyalty to her, despite what he'd told Sheriff Pinkston.

"It seems your husband has a wandering eye after all," Hub Butler remarked when he noticed where July's gaze had strayed.

She gently pushed Hub back into his own space, trying very hard to control her temper. It was harder than she'd expected. "And it seems you have remarkable resilience," she countered. "As I heard it told, you and Angel were intimate friends. You seem to be taking her passing in stride, considering how close the two of you were reported to be."

Hub's face clouded over, but he quickly masked his irritation. "Life goes on, July. I have learned not to look back or dwell on the past. But you, my lovely lady, should consider your future. As I suggested once before, I will always be around when you realize your supposedly de-voted husband is enjoying far more freedom than he would have you believe." His arms tightened around her, bringing her body into close contact with his. "I want you, July. I have since the moment I saw you."

July gulped hard and forced herself not to pull away. Hub was pressing her, just as Hoyt Simpson had a few minutes earlier. Hoyt had even stolen a few kisses, forcing July to clamp down on her temper to keep from lambast-ing him for taking privileges with her. It was difficult not to express her irritation at both ranchers, but she could not afford to make enemies if she wanted to glean infor-mation from every available source. Someone around here had caused the Chambers' demise, and someone led a band that was stealing gold from the banks and railroads. To determine *who* July must keep all lines of communication open.

She seriously doubted Hub Butler was responsible for disposing of C.L. or Angel. He and his ranch were prospering. He had no need to dispose of C.L. in order to get his hands on Angel's fortune, not when he had amassed one of his own. The same held true for Hoyt Simpson. Both men had sound financial backing, and they had often been seen in Angel's company. If Angel's favorite lovers weren't responsible, who the devil had killed her and her husband? As of yet, July had not ascertained who would inherit a controlling interest in the bank, but that might prove to be an important clue.

"We could easily lose ourselves in this crowd," Hub whispered against July's neck. "Or you could meet me at my ranch. Most of my men are in town enjoying the celebration. We could have the Cabestro all to ourselves. . . ."

After a moment, July nodded agreeably. "I would like to see the Cabestro at night," she murmured in her most provocative voice.

Hub's face beamed like a lantern blazing on a long wick.

Although he was full of anticipation, July was silently plotting the latter part of the evening. If she was lucky, she could quiz Hub about Angel and her stable of lovers. There had to be some jealous man provoked enough to kill. Perhaps Hub could offer the clue for which she searched, but if he thought he would get what he wanted from her, he was sorely mistaken. He had nothing she wanted except answers to a perplexing mystery that had evolved from thievery to murder.

"Just what is Cheyenne Rose like?" July questioned, switching the topic of conversation before Hub gave way to another urge to slobber on her neck, or to some other disgustingly hungry display. "I would at least like to know what Nacona finds so fascinating about the Parlor."

A wry smile pursed Hub's lips. "You and Rose have never met? A pity that. You are alike in many ways—saucy, spirited, and very desirable."

July had the feeling Hub was saying this to create a strain between her and Nacona. If July went to Hub, determined to spite her husband, the wealthy rancher would ultimately get what he wanted from her. Hub obviously knew Cheyenne Rose quite well. July had seen him going in and out of the Parlor on three occasions. He dallied with Angel and then turned his attention elsewhere while Hoyt Simpson—and only God knew who else—gallivanted about town with her.

"But as for myself," Hub went on to say as he swirled July around the dance area. "I find you far more desirable than any woman I've met in a long while. It grieves me to covet my new neighbor's lovely wife. Yet, I envy what he has and I have not." After giving her hand an affectionate squeeze, Hub stepped away to allow Hoyt Simpson to take another turn in her arms. "Until later, my dear July. I am anticipating a most memorable night. . . ."

While July was spinning in Hoyt's arms, trying to keep him a respectable distance away, her thoughts were growing more bitter by the second. As Nacona made his way across the street, women seemed to materialize out of nowhere to latch onto him. It didn't upset her that she was in another set of arms because she knew she had no interest in any other man. But she was sad to report that she could not say the same for Nacona. He hadn't come near her since the night he'd kissed her in the jail cell for Pinkston's benefit. Was that normal behavior for a man who honestly cared about his wife? July didn't think so.

Several moments later, Nacona cut into the long waiting line to take his turn at dancing with his wife. "You seem to be the center of attraction around here," he observed.

The sluggish tone of his voice assured July that he had been doing hand-to-glass combat with either a whiskey bottle or the spiked punch. Maybe both.

"I'm sure you've been enjoying yourself without me," Nacona added on a sour note.

"Every bit as much as you seem to be enjoying yourself without me," July flung at him. "Is the inside of Cheyenne Rose's Pleasure Parlor as gaudy as the outside? And how, my dear devoted husband, did you find Rose?"

The hiss in July's voice caused Nacona to cock a dark brow. "Am I being accused of wrongdoing?"

"When one associates with wrongdoers, one is subject to accusation," July rapped out.

"And you have convicted me." He smiled devilishly. "Really, sweetheart, if you keep pretending to be jealous, you'll have me thinking you really care."

She did and that was what was killing her, bit by agonizing bit.

His sinewy arms fastened around her, forcing her traitorous body to respond to the feel of his muscular contours. "Do you care, July?" he queried as his lips grazed her forehead. "Or is it that your catlike curiosity and intractable pride have a fierce hold on you? You don't really want me, but the woman in you doesn't want anyone else to have me—is that how it is?"

Nacona couldn't say what had possessed him to pose this probing question. Maybe it was the sight of Hub Butler and Hoyt Simpson squeezing the stuffing out of her. Or perhaps it was the whimsical thought that July had become possessive enough to care what he was doing and with whom. And it didn't help that he'd had a tad too much whiskey this evening at the celebration. That made him too reckless and a little too straightforward.

For the past two days, Nacona had been testing himself, refusing to go near this blond-haired temptress. He had needed to know just how great a hold she had on him. And sure enough, it was almost as bad as he'd thought. He wanted this high-spirited sprite, even when he didn't want to want her.

Nacona had not known fear or anguish since, as a young man, he'd faced his first skirmish in eastern Kansas during the war. Then he had been inexperienced and ill prepared. But with the passage of years he had become hard, tough, and cynical. He had seen and done all there was to do in this world. He had become a seasoned fighter hardened by blows he had had to endure. Yet, nothing had prepared him for the emotional beating he was taking from July MacKenzie. Nacona again reminded himself of his vow to avenge Shandin's death, and it bothered him that he *did* have to remind himself because this green-eyed siren kept distracting him.

Becoming emotionally involved with a woman like July would demand a man's constant attention, and Nacona didn't feel that he was in position to give it, not with a private crusade awaiting him. July needed continuous supervision—because she was so daring and independent and because she thought she could take care of herself in every situation. Why, even the most reckless angels wouldn't walk where this woman trod! Even her brothers hadn't been able to keep track of her, and they were detectives.

If Nacona had any gumption at all he would simply come right out and tell that he wanted her back in his bed, sharing her uninhibited passion for as long as it would last. But he wasn't comfortable with the direct approach, not in this situation. He felt vulnerable, and he didn't like that one whit. In his profession, vulnerability bred disaster. It could get a man killed. In this case it could wound his pride and his heart, even though July didn't seem to think he had one. And yet, he wanted to re-create their splendrous moments even if he and July didn't have a future together. His predicament was frustrating.

Nacona's ridiculous question about her not wanting him but also not wanting another woman have him set off July's temper. She would have slapped him silly for taunting her if she'd thought she could get away with it. But Nacona was overpowering, especially when he'd been drinking.

Annoyed with herself for being so sensitive to everything he said, July pried herself loose and headed toward her next dancing partner. She refused to dignify Nacona's goading questions with responses that admitted to a commitment he wouldn't return.

If Nacona wanted to dally with Rose or somebody else in the Pleasure Parlor then let him! July was going to get over her frustrating fascination with him, but she hoped he found out that she intended to meet Hub Butler at his ranch. It would serve him right. If Nacona refused to be honest in his feelings then she could be just as bullheaded as he. Stubbornness, after all, was a MacKenzie trait. Nacona could do what he wanted. She was tired of caring because it wasn't doing her one bit of good.

When Nacona saw July practically throw herself at her waiting dance partner, he decided the battle of wits he kept trying to play with her hadn't worked out well. She was too hot tempered. She would not admit to wanting him, even under penalty of death. If he really wanted to know if she would accept him in her bed, then he was going to have to come right out and tell her that he had missed having her in his. That approach, however, might invite outrage and ridicule, and Nacona wasn't that desperate yet. He'd be damned if he let that woman know what kind of hold she had on him. She would laugh herself into a coma.

Rankled at that thought, Nacona aimed himself toward the punch bowl to help himself to another drink. . . .

Something very peculiar occurred while July was being shuffled around by the men who requested a dance with her. She suddenly realized that Killer hadn't growled or snarled at anyone in the past half-hour. Those the mongrel found offensive seemed to have vanished from sight.

Now that set July to thinking. And although she solved dilemmas far better in solitude, staring meditatively into the distance, rather than twirling through a crowd to the beat of music, one single thought persisted—Killer growling for what she considered no particular reason except an unexplainable dislike of certain men. And she recalled those times when Killer had demanded to be let out during the night and she had spied a fleeting silhouette venturing away from the bunkhouse. She also recalled her visits to the various ranchers, when Killer had snarled at one or two of the cowhands, and the times when she had passed Cheyenne Rose's Parlor, only to have the huge mutt voice an objection to several of the men who milled around the establishment. She also recollected what Nacona had said about Killer growling at the shadows the evening Angel had been murdered. There was something uncanny about the dog's reactions to certain men in the community. It was almost as if . . . July missed a step, causing Jordon Milner to stomp on her foot.

"I'm sorry," Jordon said contritely.

July managed a smile and stepped back. "It was my fault. My mind seems to be elsewhere tonight. I keep wondering if we will be able to keep our loan now that Angel and C.L. have been killed. Do you happen to know who now has control of the bank?"

"Hoyt Simpson, of course," Jordon replied as if that were common knowledge. "His Eastern investors have been stockpiling their money in Cheyenne, and Hoyt has made enough with the ranch to buy stock."

Where else was Hoyt acquiring money? July asked herself. "Please excuse me, Jordon, I need to sort something out. Until I do, I'm afraid I won't be good company."

He winked down into her lovely face. "I always find you interesting company, July. I'd prefer to enjoy your company in privacy. I only wish . . ." His voice trailed off when a foreboding shadow fell over him.

"What were you wishing?" Nacona smiled pleasantly enough, but there was a dangerous gleam in his eyes. He knew exactly what Jordon—and half the male population of Cheyenne—was thinking when it came to this curvaceous beauty.

"You've been drinking again," July said reproachfully.

"Thank you for calling my attention to the fact." Nacona snorted.

"Excuse us, Jordon." July clutched Nacona's arm and steered him away from the dance area that had been roped off in the street. "What the devil are you trying to do, start a brawl?" she demanded.

"I am only protecting what belongs to me," Nacona argued.

That was the wrong thing for him to say. July puffed up like an inflated bagpipe. "I do not need your protection," she assured him huffily.

She had just stumbled onto an intriguing possibility when along came this black-eyed giant who'd been drinking and carousing when he should have been paying attention to business. How the devil was she to explain her theory when Nacona couldn't digest more than a five-word sentence without his brain malfunctioning?

"I need you sober," July muttered sourly.

His arm went around her waist as he unsteadily wove his way down the street. "And I need to ask you something," he mumbled. "It's been on my mind a good long while. But it took several drinks before I finally got up enough nerve to spit it out."

Despite July's irritation, she couldn't suppress an amused smile. She had never seen Nacona drunk. Ordinarily, he was very much in control, but tonight his movements were sluggish and he was so much at ease that he was comical. However, he could have selected a better night to get himself soused. Something was brewing. She could feel it in her bones. Her keen intuition was hard at work, trying to link the scattered pieces of this mystifying puzzle.

"What I want to know is—" Nacona was cut off by a yelp and a growl and the eruption of fisticuffs in the dance area.

He suddenly grabbed July and presented her with the kind of kiss a soldier might bestow on his ladylove before charging off to battle. Abruptly releasing her, he stumbled off, shouldering his way into the middle of the brawl. July rolled her eyes in disbelief. It was obvious that several of the men had sampled the spiked punch too many times during the course of the afternoon and the evening. Now they were spoiling for a fight—Nacona included. He had been forced to play the reformed gunslinger far too long, and was definitely not the kind of man who stood aside when trouble erupted. In fact, he seemed to enjoy a challenge.

Resigning herself to the fact that she would have to pursue her theory by herself, July wheeled toward her mount and summoned Killer to her side. It seemed more than a coincidence that a fight had broken out just after dark, preoccupying almost everyone. It was too convenient. July rather imagined the brawl had been instigated by a person or persons who had something to gain from it.

Her gaze darted toward the bank. It might be a target for robbery, but July doubted that. No, tonight was a prime time for rustlers to strike. Most of the ranchers and

357

wranglers were on hand for the celebration, leaving only a skeleton crew on the ranges. She didn't have time to drag Nacona out of the scuffle and present her theory to him. Besides, she had Killer for protection. He was worth two good men.

Although July had promised Hub that she would meet him at his ranch, she had no intention of fending him off when other activities might be brewing. Unfortunately, she wasn't sure where to begin her search. She supposed the Golden Spur was as likely a place as any to start. There was a wrangler there Killer disliked. Perhaps that man would lead her in the right direction. . . .

July suddenly recalled something Nacona had said the night they'd arrived at the Golden Spur. It had sparked a wild conjecture she had immediately discarded. But now that she thought about it, and linked the idea to Killer's reaction to various cowboys, it was beginning to make perfect sense. Nacona had scouted the area, trying to determine how familiar the rustlers had to be with the grazing meadows in order to cut cattle from herds and move them to isolated locations without being spotted.

"That *is* it!" July declared to the world at large. There was a very logical reason why the rustlers had been so successful and elusive. And thanks to Killer, it had finally occurred to July. The setup was so clever that she had to compliment the ringleader who devised it.

Veering north to the least populated area, July trotted down the moonlit trail, pausing occasionally to listen for sounds that might alert her to nocturnal activity—rustling in particular. When she reached the crest of a rolling hill, she spied a golden glow in the distance. A triumphant smile pursed her lips as she headed toward the not-so-mysterious light. If her predictions proved correct that glow was radiating from a campfire over which rustlers were heating their branding irons to mark stolen cattle.

Some brands were easily changed. Others were difficult to alter. Since it wasn't easy to brand a squirming calf, it wasn't unusual to see a smear here and there. Natural occurrence gave rustlers the edge in changing the brands. And no doubt, this group of rustlers had become quite proficient at their technique since they had yet to be caught.

Killer's quiet growl told July what she needed to know. This fiercely protective mongrel had been with his previous master the night cattle had been stolen from the Golden Spur. According to Ot Knott, Killer had been in the midst of the thieves, trying to protect Bob Foster. The dog had picked up their scents. That was why he growled at particular cowhands from time to time. He had been trying to communicate with July in the only way he knew. And his silence during the last hour of the dance indicated that the cowhands involved in the rustling had sneaked away. Why, the dog was a far better detective than she would ever be! He was also an eye witness, but she had failed to give Killer credit until the pieces of this perplexing puzzle came together.

July dismounted and tethered her horse to one of the trees that lined the creek. She needed to get a good look at a few faces. Perhaps no one would accept Killer's growl as evidence, but a positive identification would be admissible.

To her dismay, the rustlers took no chances whatsoever. Though they considered themselves alone and undetected, they still wore masks and long linen dusters to conceal their identities. That forced her to get even closer to hear voices. She hoped someone would momentarily remove his mask.

Then it happened. Killer couldn't keep his mouth shut when he was near the thieves. His growl caused one of the men to stare warily into the darkness.

"What was that?" one of the rustlers asked.

"What was *what?*" somebody else responded.

"I didn't hear nothin'," another voice declared.

"Everybody's in town. Nobody's gonna—"

July clamped her hand over Killer's mouth when he growled a second time.

"Damn it, I know I heard something," the first bandit insisted.

Frantic, July glanced around her. She refused to sneak away just yet, not when she was so close to an important discovery. She and Killer would have to mingle with the cattle herded into a makeshift pen constructed of scraggly trees and rope. The bawling of the calves would drown out Killer's growls. Hurriedly, July tied her skirts into a knot on her hip to prevent stumbling and tripping in case she found it necessary to dash off. She didn't relish the idea of crawling around in a corral, not amid stamping hooves, and sharp horns, but investigation often demanded sacrifices.

The knock-down-drag-out fight that erupted was just what Nacona needed to relieve his frustration. He had taken to drinking in the hope of curbing his continuous craving for July—which he had valiantly controlled for the past few days. But the liquor hadn't helped. In fact, it had almost made matters worse when he'd declared that he had something to ask her. Thank the Lord the fight had broken out before he'd made an ass of himself. All that drinking and thinking had led him to the exasperating conclusion that he was farther gone than he'd realized—and a mite more desperate. Nacona wanted July back in his bed, and he had been about to beg to have her.

That would have been disastrous. July would have been outraged at his besotted request. And when he sobered up, he would have regretted his recklessness. Fortunately, the fisticuffs had distracted him, and he had charged off to throw a few punches and have several beefy fists pound some sense into him.

Now, fifteen minutes later, Nacona had wandered off to locate July, who, of course, was not where he'd left her. A quick search of the premises showed that her buckskin mare was gone and so was she. Scowling at his own stupidity and July's impatience, Nacona swung into the saddle and thundered off. Three-quarters of a mile later he spotted a lone rider and an oversize dog silhouetted in the moonlight as they topped a hill. But when he got to the hill, he could no longer see the rider who should have been headed toward the Golden Spur. Nacona dismounted and lit a cigar, using its faint glow to inspect the tracks. Sure as hell, hoofprints and paw prints had veered off to only God knew where; Nacona damned sure didn't.

"Where the blazes could she be going at this time of night?" he asked the darkness.

Then, in a single bound, he was in the saddle again. He trotted off in the direction July had taken. A furious growl erupted from his lips when he spied a suspicious glow in the distance. He didn't have to be a genius to determine what was going on. What he couldn't figure out was how July had known where and when to search for rustlers.

Sometimes Nacona had the unsettling feeling that she was a better detective than he was. Of course, he'd cut out his tongue before he admitted any such thing. If he did July would gloat.

She should have revealed her speculations to him. Hadn't he demanded that she never traipse off alone again after she'd ended up in jail as a murder suspect? But she didn't listen. She just romped off as if she were invincible. If she got herself killed he was never going to forgive her for doing it. And if she didn't, he was seriously going to consider shooting her.

Chapter 22

July grimaced uncomfortably when a sharp horn rammed her in the hip. Just as she had hoped, the milling herd made enough noise with intruders in its midst to drown out Killer's snarls, and the rustlers went about their business of disguising brands. The smell of burned hide and beef on the hoof permeated the air. Twice July had to pinch her nose and hold her breath to prevent sneezing, and her elegant gown had suffered irreparable damage. But that, she reminded herself, was just another hazard of this investigation.

"How many more do we have to brand?" a rustler asked.

A quick count of the cattle that lay on their sides, legs tied with rope, left seven head to be tended. July groaned to herself. As efficient as these rustlers were, they would be finished in ten minutes and would move the herd from the makeshift corral. Just what, she wondered, was she going to do? She had yet to recognize a single voice. She had to get closer to the campfire. That was all there was to it.

Determined, she waddled between stamping hooves to

obtain a better view of the illegal operations. That turned out to be a mistake. Killer let out a full-fledged bark that even the bawling of the calves couldn't conceal. And suddenly everything seemed to be happening at once. Rustlers scattered. Killer pounced. The herd circled and knocked July flat. When she heard the curses and growls of angry men swarming about the corral like hornets, she made a frantic attempt to escape.

A pained yelp erupted from her when a hand reached over the rope corral to grab her by the hair. It turned into a shriek when she was dragged into a pair of unyielding arms. Fighting for all she was worth, July clawed at her captor's mask and bit savagely at the arms that imprisoned her.

"It's that Bleu woman!" the man bellowed at his companions. "Somebody give me a hand. She's ripping me to pieces!"

Reinforcements arrived within seconds, much to July's chagrin. But she didn't cease kicking, biting, and clawing for a moment.

"Get a rope!" one of the rustlers ordered.

That was when gunshots barked in the night and the thunder of hooves heralded the approach of a rider.

"Damn," somebody bellowed.

Then a few men cursed vehemently. The instant July felt her captors' attention shift to the charging rider who was firing from both hips, she rammed an elbow into the closest set of ribs and was released so abruptly she hit the ground with a thud. The rustlers fumbled beneath their linen dusters for weapons, but by that time Killer was having a field day chewing on legs and ankles.

A gasp of fear, not for herself, but for Nacona broke from July's throat. He seemed to be inviting gunfire as he raced toward the camp.

"Son of a bitch, it's Nacona Bleu," somebody croaked. "Let's get out of here!"

With Killer snapping at their heels, the rustlers darted toward their horses. Two of them, however, were braver than their cohorts. They rushed to the campfire to take up glowing branding irons. July winced in apprehension when one of the rustlers made a stabbing gesture at Nacona's leg with the searing-hot metal. His mount reared when the hot iron collided with its hip, and a shrill whinny pierced the night air as the horse leaped sideways and stumbled.

July marveled at Nacona's ability to bound from the terrified horse without being crushed as it fell. He hit the ground and bounced back to his feet to face the whirling irons. He had no time to reload or to retrieve his dagger from his boot, not while he was dodging the hot irons. Agility was all that protected him from being fried alive.

With pantherlike grace, Nacona leaped backward to avoid a scorching iron. In one lithe move, he snatched up the iron that remained over the fire. Metal clanked as he deflected oncoming blows, and July held her breath until she became lightheaded. Suddenly it was as if three swordsmen were matching their skills with flaming sabers. They lunged and retreated, and sparks danced in the air when the hot irons collided.

An agonized screech crackled through the air when Nacona's branding iron connected with fabric and flesh. The wounded rustler hurled his weapon at Nacona, and

365

then charged off. He didn't get far, however. A snarling Killer had returned from chasing the other rustlers, and he lit into the injured man.

Meanwhile, July had scurried over to retrieve the discarded branding iron. When Killer downed the outlaw, who was howling in agony, she shoved the glowing iron in the man's masked face, daring him to move and find himself branded for life.

"Killer, sit down," July ordered firmly.

With a snarl, the huge mongrel retreated a few inches from his victim and sat like a sentinel, in case the desperado had any inclination to attempt another escape.

"If he moves, go for his throat," July ordered the snarling dog. Of course, Killer didn't understand her, but her words gave the bandit food for thought while he stared up at sharp fangs.

July threw a quick glance over her shoulder to monitor the ongoing battle between Nacona and his opponent. Now that the odds were even, Nacona was making short shrift of the desperado. A howl soon burst from the outlaw as searing iron struck his thigh. When he reflexively stiffened at the burning, Nacona kicked the branding iron from his hand, sending it to the ground. Before the bandit could recover and take flight, Nacona flung his own iron aside and his hammerlike fists cracked against bone beneath the outlaw's mask.

Having seen Nacona in action in Denver, the night she'd come dangerously close to being molested, July knew the outlaw's fate. When Nacona was good and mad, he could pulverize a man in a matter of seconds. Sure enough, his opponent soon lay battered, bruised, and defeated. The outlaw had no strength or wit left to counter the bone-jarring blows he'd received.

With a snarl, Nacona yanked his dazed opponent to his feet and held him upright. He jerked off the mask to glare into the man's bruised features in the glow of the campfire.

His head swiveled in July's direction. "Do you recognize him?"

She squinted, trying to place the puffy face. "I've seen him at one of the ranches, but I'm not sure which." She reached down to remove the mask from the man she and Killer were holding hostage. "I don't know this one, either, not by name at least."

"Fetch some rope," Nacona demanded. "Somebody around here will recognize them."

July stared down at their captive who still lay sprawled in the dirt, nursing his various wounds. "Killer, you can go ahead and dispose of this scoundrel if he tries to—"

"I ain't goin' nowhere," the rustler hissed. "Just keep that damned dog away from me!"

Assured that she wouldn't have to chase the desperado down again, July raced over to fetch some ropes draped over the pommel of the saddle. Hurriedly, she bound the outlaw and then repeated the process on the man Nacona held prisoner. When both men were secured to their horses, Nacona wheeled on July, his scowl so vicious she impulsively shrank back two paces.

"You little fool!" Nacona hissed. "You could have gotten yourself killed. Don't you ever listen to me? I distinctly remember telling you never to rush off alone. Why didn't you wait for me?"

July tilted her chin to a militant angle. How dare he scold her as if she were a disobedient child. She had located the rustlers and he was chewing her up one side and down the other instead of praising her for a job well done.

"You were so eager to bash in a few faces and drink yourself blind that I couldn't reveal my suspicions to you," she said tersely. "There wasn't time to retrieve you and explain. This is all your fault."

"My fault?" Nacona let out his breath in an exasperated rush. "Jeezus, July, you're driving me crazy!"

Nacona hated being scared half to death by this daring hellion. When he'd seen trouble break out near the campfire, he had willed his steed to fly down the hill so he might rescue this horror in yellow satin—that was the color her gown had been until she'd slithered around in a corral full of calves. Terrifying visions had flashed through his mind as he'd raced toward the campfire, pistols blazing. Nacona had been afraid one of the rustlers would end July's life right then.

Forcing those unnerving sensations aside, Nacona clutched July by the arm and led her toward the horse she had tethered by the creek.

"I demand an apology," she insisted, setting her feet, only to be uprooted and dragged along.

"For what?" Nacona grumbled. "For saving your life? I swear, woman, sometimes I don't think you have the sense God gave a mule. Have you any idea what would have happened if I hadn't come looking for you, if I didn't know how to track fools who veer off the main road and risk getting themselves killed? How the hell did you know where to come anyway?"

"I simply sought out the most sparsely populated area and spotted the campfire," she explained as Nacona scooped her up and deposited her none too gently in the saddle. When he swung up behind her, she scooted forward to give him room. "Killer was actually the one who made me realize how this operation was organized and carried out. And you were the one who put the idea in my head in the first place."

"Me?" Nacona frowned, bemused.

July nodded affirmatively as Nacona reined his steed toward the waiting prisoners. "You scouted the area to determine how difficult it was for rustlers to learn the terrain and to know when and where to strike. That set me to thinking."

"Your thinking is damned dangerous, if you ask me," he muttered.

The hair-raising incident had had a sobering effect on Nacona. His head had long since ceased spinning and his sight was no longer blurred.

July twisted in the saddle to glare him down. "Do you want to hear my theory or do you simply intend to ridicule me?"

"Do go on," Nacona encouraged in a mocking parody of courtesy. "Forgive me for interrupting."

Despite his sarcasm, July continued, "Each time I visited the surrounding ranches, all of which had been subjected to rustling, Killer growled at certain cowhands. He also snarled at the wranglers who mill around Cheyenne Rose's Pleasure Parlor. I haven't figured out why he did that yet, but I do know why Killer behaved the way he did at each ranch. He was on hand the night of his previous master's murder. He knows the bandits better than anybody."

369

"Good Lord, don't tell me you're planning on having Killer testify in a court of law?" Nacona croaked in disbelief. "Lady, they'd laugh you right out on your ear."

July glowered at him. "I thought you were going to listen instead of interjecting your customary bits of sarcasm."

"I'm sorry. I forgot," Nacona mumbled, his voice nowhere near apologetic.

"As I was saying, Killer snarled at certain cowhands at various ranches. That, compounded with your comment about the rustlers knowing the country, led me to an intriguing theory. Perhaps these outlaws had infiltrated each and every ranch to learn its procedures and to gather important information needed to go about rustling undetected. The wrangler who works a ranch leads the attack on it. Since thieves hired on at all the ranches, they always knew when and where to strike."

Nacona slumped in the saddle and shook his head in astonishment. The theory sounded logical, the plan ingenious. "That's why ranchers usually don't even know part of their herd has been spirited away until days later." A slight frown furrowed his brow. "But how do these thieves know when to strike the banks and trains? I don't see how they could possibly be involved in those robberies if they're working the ranches."

"I have my suspicions but no positive proof," July confessed. "If the robbers and rustlers are the same outfit, perhaps our prisoners can provide the details."

Nacona stared at the two men they'd taken. He doubted either would be willing to talk without forceful persuasion. The phrase "thicker than thieves" generally held true. Nacona had tried to force confessions out of

370

several prisoners over the years. They didn't usually give in without strong-arm tactics.

In one fluid motion, he swung to the ground to inspect the cattle which had yet to be rebranded. Part of the livestock had come from the Cabestro Ranch which was operated by Hub Butler. Others carried Jordon Milner's and John Gilman's brands. No doubt the ranchers would be grateful to have their calves back. July had saved them from another round of losses. Nacona wondered what form the ranchers' gratitude would take. That thought spoiled what was left of his good disposition.

"I still think we should take the prisoners to the Golden Spur," Nacona advised when they reached the fork in the road.

"I see no reason why we should be responsible for them with a perfectly good jail at our disposal—one that has just been sanitized and cleaned," July argued as she reined toward town.

"I can think of a half-dozen good reasons why we should accept the responsibility."

"We are not above the law. The sheriff and his deputy are being paid to guard prisoners. Besides," she added, leaning close to make a confidential point, "we don't want anyone to know that we are professionally involved in this case."

"You went above the law to capture these crooks," Nacona pointed out. "So that makes us involved."

"I did nothing of the kind. I was only making a citizen's arrest after spotting trouble," July insisted.

At that point Nacona threw up his hands and

conceded. It did no good whatsoever to argue with this law-spouting female. July knew the rules forward and backward. But if Nacona had been in charge, he would have bypassed the local law enforcement. He had always believed there were times when a man had to take the law into his own hands. This blond-haired sprite believed in playing by the rules unless they didn't work to her advantage, in which case she either *bent* them or simply *ignored* them.

Why Nacona gave into her, he wasn't sure. Probably because she had located the desperadoes, even if he had saved her from disaster. And that still bothered him. July needed around-the-clock supervision. Nacona simply couldn't trust her not to court catastrophe when the spirit moved her. She seemed to thrive on adventure and excitement. How had he gotten mixed up with her anyway? She reminded him so much of himself at times, and that scared him.

When they reached town, the celebration had ended and the streets were deserted. Distant rumbles of thunder and streaks of lightning provided the only sounds and bright lights in Cheyenne. Since activity was at a low, it took only a few minutes to incarcerate the prisoners and explain the incident to Sheriff Pinkston.

He stared at the rumpled July and then shook his head in amazement. "Young lady, I would dearly like to know how you always manage to wind up in the midst of such dangerous goings-on."

"That's simple enough to explain." Nacona smirked. "My wife is attracted to trouble. She's worse than a bloodhound." His remarks earned him a condescending glare.

"In this case, Sheriff, it was Killer who led me to the

rustlers. I simply followed his instincts." It wasn't exactly the truth, but was close enough to pacify Pinkston.

Stroking his handlebar mustache, Pinkston paced the confines of his office. "Do you honestly believe this dog can identify the other desperadoes?"

"Without a doubt," July said with great conviction. "He already has, but because Nacona and I are new in town, we can't attach names to faces. And unfortunately the rustlers are cautious enough to wear dusters and masks, making them difficult to identify. Unless our prisoners decide to divulge the names of their cohorts and their ringleader, we'll be forced to bring them in after we've caught them red-handed."

"Bob Foster tried to do just that, and you know where it got him," Pinkston reminded July with a meaningful glance.

"I want you to make damned certain these scalawags are still here when I get back in the morning," Nacona demanded. "I intend to interrogate them."

"That's my job," Pinkston insisted. "You retired from investigation, remember?"

"Cattle have been stolen from my newly acquired ranch," Nacona countered. "That makes it my investigation, too."

A typical sheriff, Nacona thought, refusing to let anyone steal his thunder. Pride was so often more important than seeing justice served. Nacona was on the verge of informing Pinkston that this was indeed his case and that he had been hired to resolve certain problems in Wyoming, but Pinkston could have been on the take for all he knew. It had happened before. Sheriff Plummer had been the ringleader of a Montana outlaw gang that had plundered the gold fields a decade earlier. His badge had been nothing but a cover for his criminal activities. Nacona wasn't quite ready to trust Pinkston or his deputy, who could have been bought and paid for by the ringleader of the Wyoming thieves.

"I will be back bright and early in the morning to find out what you've learned from those men," Nacona promised with a stern glance.

"My advice to you," Pinkston confided after July sailed out of the office, "is, keep a careful watch on that rambunctious wife of yours. She has barely escaped disaster twice. I don't want to wager on her luck in escaping a third time."

Nacona regarded Pinkston suspiciously. "Is that supposed to be some sort of a threat, Sheriff?"

"Stop looking at me as if *I* were on trial here." Pinkston's tone was indignant.

Nacona stuffed a cigar in his mouth and leaned over to light it from the lantern on the desk. "I was a detective for a long time. I've learned to take no one for granted. Greed seems to have a way of corrupting the best of men— sheriffs, marshals, and deputies included. I've seen several good lawmen turn bad."

"I do not appreciate your insinuation," Pinkston huffed, "I'll have you know I rode herd over this town when train crews settled in for the winter to drink, stab, and shoot each other before romping off to advance the rails over Sherman Summit and on to Laramie. I came here to clean up this town, not ruin it. And I was doing a fair job of that until this cussed gang of outlaws started wreaking havoc in this place."

"So you think this ring of thieves is responsible for *all* the criminal activity in the area?" Nacona questioned. "Just how did you arrive at that conclusion?"

Pinkston scowled. "There you go again. You're pouncing on everything I say as if I were guilty of something—which I most certainly am not! For your information, Mr. Former Detective, both the robbers and rustlers seem too well organized to be different groups of desperadoes."

Nacona puffed on his cheroot, trying to decide whether he trusted Pinkston. Although the sheriff had done nothing to invite suspicion, he had done nothing to quell it, either. To Nacona's way of thinking, Pinkston was a mite too susceptible to public opinion—especially with Angel and her lawyer. Pinkston hesitated in taking action. He should have had posses combing the countryside, searching for clues. No doubt, that was why some ranchers were organizing the Wyoming Vigilante Committee. Local law enforcement wasn't strong enough to handle the disturbances in the area.

Mulling over a dozen suspicious thoughts, Nacona strode outside to find himself distracted by July, who was casting apprehensive glances at the storm clouds that had blotted out the moon. During the course of the long, eventful evening, Nacona had swung back and forth between a desire to shake the stuffing out of this vivacious nymph and a need to clutch her protectively to him. He had been jealous of every man who had held her in his arms under the pretense of dancing, and he'd been scared senseless when the rustlers had captured her.

This wife of his kept his emotions churning. And to complicate matters, this blasted investigation had him stymied. Even if July's theory held true, there was a world of difference between speculation and proof. What was he going to have to do to crack this damned case?

It was with a pounding head and an aching body that Nacona fell into bed that night, listening to the crashes of thunder that heralded the approach of the storm. He would have liked nothing better than to cuddle up beside July, if only to sleep beside her. But he wasn't sure he could trust himself with her these days. With every unsettling incident, he found himself growing more emotionally involved with her. Even now he found himself wondering if she was huddled beneath her quilt, reliving the tragedy that had left her afraid of storms. Did she need him now, as she had needed him that day on the plains of Kansas when inclement weather had caught them with little protection?

Damn it! He could not allow himself to be so aware of her needs—or to fall in love with that wild sprite. Love built walls around a man. It confined him, restricted him, made him vulnerable. And he couldn't forget his vow to Shandin. He had promised revenge while Shandin lay in his arms, breathing his last breath. That tormenting memory was too much a part of him to fade. Nacona owed Shandin. They were brothers. It could have been Nacona who had been killed that night. And in a way, a part of him *had* died.

"Nacona?"

The whispering voice jostled him from his troubled thoughts. His eyes swept open to take in July lit by a flash of lightning that speared through the window. She looked so delicate and fragile standing here, silhouetted by shadows and flares of silvery light. The impulse to reach for her was overwhelming, but Nacona exerted his willpower and stifled the maddening urge.

"I'm very grateful that you showed up when you did tonight," she murmured as she eased down beside him. "Would you mind very much if I shared your bed? The incident rattled me more than I first thought, and the storm isn't helping matters. I can't seem to get to sleep."

This independent female, out to show the world that she could stand on her own two feet, had swallowed her colossal pride and come to him for comfort? Nacona was surprised. July had always held up so well under pressure that he never thought she needed him at all, not for moral support or protection. It was only the threat of the storm that had lured her to him, he reminded himself. But for some unaccountable reason, he had wanted July to need him, to depend on him, since those first days when they had matched wits and challenged each other in Dodge.

Nacona had known an unexplainable sense of satisfaction when July had nestled up against him during that first thunderstorm. And now she had stolen quietly into his room and he couldn't resist her hushed request. But then, he'd never been able to resist her. That was the problem.

Flipping back the corner of the quilt, Nacona extended a silent invitation. July snuggled up against him like a trusting child and the strings of his heart felt a quick but forceful tug.

"Better?" he murmured as he brushed a light kiss across her brow.

"Much better," she said with an audible sigh.

What was there about those brawny arms that pacified

her despite all she had recently endured and the terrifying storm. Lying beside this muscular giant, she swore nothing could harm her. His strength somehow made her invincible. Why couldn't he feel the same overpowering emotions that always brought her back to him, despite her pride and her fear of having her heart broken?

July had lain awake, reliving the unsettling incidents that preyed on her emotions, hoping Nacona would come to her room. When he hadn't, she had swallowed her pride and gone to him, expecting him to take advantage of her weakness. But he merely held her, even when he could have anything he wanted. She couldn't refuse him—even when she knew it was only lust that drew him to her. But perhaps he didn't even crave her physically anymore.

The sound of an unidentified object being dragged across the floor brought Nacona and July straight up in bed. A deep skirl of laughter rose from Nacona's chest when he spied the oversize mongrel padding into the room, the corner of his braided rug clamped in his teeth. Killer dropped the rug at the foot of the bed, turned his customary three circles, and plopped down to expel an enormous sigh.

"The evening's event and the storm must have rattled Killer, too." Nacona chuckled as he drew July back beside him, oddly content just to have her with him. "He probably thought he was about to lose you when the pistols started barking. Now he's afraid to let you out of his sight."

"It's nice to know someone around here cares what becomes of me," July said, half-teasing, half-serious.

Nacona suddenly became very still. July could barely hear him breathing.

"I care." His deep baritone voice sent tingles skittering down her spine.

Although Nacona cursed himself for voicing his feelings, the words were out. It seemed he'd been on the verge of saying something to that effect the whole livelong night.

"And I care about you, too, Nacona Bleu," July whispered as she nestled deeper into his arms.

Admitting she cared was all she dared do with a man who didn't really need or want her love. Her friendship and physical affection? Yes. But love? July doubted it. She had come to understand Nacona's limitations. She wanted much more, even if she settled for what a man like Nacona could give. Knowing he cared in his own way was the balm that soothed the hurt of loving in vain. She knew her heart was dangerously close to being broken for the first, and last, time. She would never love again. Having fallen in love with a man like Nacona Bleu, she simply couldn't settle for second best.

"July?" His husky voice echoed in the darkness.

"Yes?" She waited with bated breath, hoping. . . .

Damn! He still had his pride! "G'night. . . ."

July smiled ruefully and closed her eyes. "Good night, Nacona."

And it was a good night, all things considered. Nacona slept more peacefully than he had in weeks. Even the pattering of the rain didn't rouse him from slumber. The contented feeling he derived from simply having July's soft, feminine presence beside him deluded him into thinking all was right with the world. Killer must have been lulled into that same sense of false security since he had dragged his pallet as close to July as he could get it.

This lively, adorable beauty seemed to attract males, even those out of her species. But she was hell on the ones from it, Nacona included. A man could gaze upon her, admire her, and fantasize about her, but he just couldn't resist her, no matter how hard he tried. Nacona was willing to admit he wasn't trying very hard at the moment. She drew him to her against his will. There was no getting around it. And every day with this strong-willed firebrand was an intriguing adventure.

Chapter 23

July concentrated on the newspaper article that had captured her attention. Engrossed in it, she absently sipped her coffee and nibbled on the fluffy biscuit Aud Ball—or Cookie as he liked to be called—had prepared for breakfast. She eased back on the sofa in the parlor to digest the featherlight biscuit and the information.

According to the report, Dull Knife, Little Wolf, and three hundred and fifty-three Northern Cheyenne had managed to elude the soldiers from various Western forts and had reached their destination in Montana. The reporter stated that the Indians had surrendered at a nearby Army post and had been allowed to remain on the Tongue River.

July was thankful the Cheyenne had been permitted to return to their native land. Maybe there was some justice in this world after all. . . .

When the front door of the ranchhouse slammed shut and the entire structure shuddered, she very nearly spilled her coffee. Wary green eyes lifted to see sunbeams spotlighting Nacona as he stalked into the parlor, looking angry. Although she and he had slept peacefully in each other's arms the previous night, he had returned from town to glare at her as if she had committed some unpardonable sin.

"I knew I shouldn't have listened to you," Nacona exploded. "I knew we should have kept those prisoners at the Golden Spur instead of in that damned jail!"

July slumped back on the couch and expelled an unladylike curse. "What happened?"

The query set Nacona to pacing back and forth across the room like a restless tiger. "Just before daybreak, a gang of outlaws hooked a rope to the barred window and pulled it clean out of the wall. According to Pinkston, who claimed he had fallen asleep in his chair, the prisoners escaped."

Nacona lurched around to glare at July as if the incident were all her fault. "Now we're right back where we started. If I had handled the situation *my* way, we would at least have had the chance to interrogate those men."

"If the rustlers broke their cohorts out of jail, what makes you think they wouldn't have swarmed down on the Golden Spur to release them?" July questioned.

"Because they wouldn't have known exactly where to look," Nacona blared in frustration. "We were too predictable and that—"

Killer's growl cut Nacona off in midsentence the instant before a knock sounded. In agitated strides, Nacona went to the door. Hoyt Simpson, Jordon Milner, and Hub Butler winced when they confronted him, for he was evidently having a devil of a time controlling his temper.

The night had been pure and simple torment for Nacona. He had awakened to find July's head resting on his shoulder, her mane of blond hair trailing over his arm. Her bent knee had been draped over his thigh, and her arm had been flung over his chest. It had felt so natural to have her beside him, so right and yet so . . . exasperating. He was getting *too* comfortable with her. This was not like his affairs with other women.

For God's sake, all he had done was sleep beside her. Now did that sound like the old Nacona Bleu? Hardly! *He* had never gone to bed with a woman and simply slept beside her. The fact that he now actually enjoyed merely holding July angered him. He feared he was becoming soft. He was uncomfortable with the unfamiliar emotions bombarding him. The tighter July's hold on him, the harder he struggled to free himself from the velvet chains that bound him.

"What the hell do you want?" Nacona demanded uncordially of their visitors.

July bolted to her feet and scurried over. "You'll have to forgive my husband."

To Hoyt, Hub, and Jordon, no one looked less in need of forgiveness.

"The harrowing events of last night have put him in a black mood," July explained. "He was very displeased with me for venturing off and spotting the rustlers' camp."

Her soothing voice put the ranchers at ease—partially. Nacona looming behind July, still looking dark as a thunder cloud, was difficult to ignore.

"Do come in, gentleman," she graciously requested, stepping aside and purposely blocking Nacona out of the way.

Hub Butler elected himself spokesman for the group. He stepped forward, taking July's hand and gallantly bowing over it. "We have come to offer our appreciation. Thanks to you, dear lady, and to your husband, part of our missing livestock has been recovered. Hoyt, Jordon, and I rode down to that makeshift pen to fetch our missing calves after we heard the news in town." His brown eyes ran over July's arresting figure. It was clear that he liked what he saw. "But I must agree with your husband. You walked into a dangerous situation last night. Do not forget that the former owner of this ranch lost his life trying to protect his stock. We would be beside ourselves if something happened to you."

Nacona had managed to regain control of his temper, though watching Hub make eyes at July had made it difficult. He couldn't force himself to like any of these three who constantly fawned over his wife. Not one of them made the slightest attempt to disguise his desire for her.

"We were disappointed to hear the prisoners escaped," Jordon commented. "That was as close as we've ever come to having a lead on the rustling."

"After having some of their cohorts caught, I wouldn't be surprised if those confounded rustlers become more cautious," Hub speculated.

"I think we need to put the vigilante committee into operation immediately," Hoyt suggested. "Pinkston doesn't seem to have much luck locating those scoundrels."

"And July should not be on the patrol," Hub advised, peering directly at her. "She is better suited for other activities than tracking outlaws."

July shifted uncomfortably beneath Hub's meaningful

stare. She knew perfectly well that he was referring to the rendezvous she had forgone in her pursuit of rustlers. "I will try to restrain my curious nature," she promised.

She then glanced suspiciously at Hoyt. She hadn't expected him to congratulate her for her part in the previous night's fiasco. In fact, she'd rather thought Hoyt would be disgruntled by her interference. But was he trying to throw her off the track in the hope of quelling her suspicions? He could be relying upon duplicity to disguise his true feelings. The rustlers' leader would be shrewd and cunning. July wasn't fooled by the supposedly charming smile directed at her. Though Hoyt had an innocent air about him, she knew damned good and well that none of his cattle had been stolen the previous night because she had rubbed noses with the livestock. She also knew that Hoyt was now in charge of Chambers Bank and she suspected he was involved with the ring of thieves.

After the ranchers took themselves off, Nacona rounded on July. "That remark Hub Butler made to you, what was it supposed to mean?"

July pivoted away, but his penetrating glare burned a hole in her back. "What remark?" she asked innocently.

Nacona grabbed her arm and spun her about. Seeing that angelic expression on her face, he decided he wasn't buying her innocent routine. "You know what remark. The one about your being better suited to other activities. What the hell's going on?"

"Butler invited me to his ranch last night, if you must know," July blurted out. "That's where I was headed when it occurred to me that the festivities were a perfect cover for rustling activities."

Lean fingers clamped down on her arms, drawing her to his hard, unyielding contours. "I want you to stay away from him and the other two," Nacona growled.

"Hub was one of Angel's lovers," she reminded him, tilting her chin defiantly. "I might have been able to learn something about—"

"You would have learned nothing pertinent to this investigation, I'll wager." Nacona snorted. "What Hub and Jordon and Hoyt want from you isn't going to help us locate the culprit. I don't like the way those men keep looking at you."

"And I don't like knowing that you've been gallivanting about Cheyenne Rose's Pleasure Parlor," July retorted.

"That was business," Nacona muttered.

"Business?" July hooted in contradiction. "I cannot imagine what business you have with Rose, other than the customary one of a man at a brothel. Business indeed!"

"I happen to think Rose's Parlor might be some kind of headquarters for the illegal activities," Nacona informed her. "You said Killer growled at the wranglers who milled around the place. They could be meeting there to convey information."

July believed Nacona's assumption was correct. Come to think of it, not only could information be passed from an outlaw at one ranch to a confederate who worked at another, even schedules for cash deliveries to banks and railroads could be channeled through Rose's.

"July, I want you to pack up and leave," Nacona demanded suddenly. "Go back where you belong and let me wrap up this assignment."

"Leave? Even if it wasn't for this investigation, I

couldn't leave," July protested. "I love you, you fool, don't you realize that?"

The confession, too long contained, had just popped out. Now July blinked in disbelief and silently cursed herself for making such a blunder. She had made herself and Nacona terribly uncomfortable. He wouldn't really welcome her confession. She had had Nacona put in jail, had forced him to help her to further her career, and had deterred him from his private crusade. She knew he resented her intrusion on his life, knew that he begrudged the time this investigation took. There simply was no room for love in his life. She had driven another wedge between them. When he had decided to send her packing, she had burst out with something he didn't want to hear.

For a moment Nacona simply stood there, gaping at the enchanting face that had haunted him for a month. Before he could find his tongue to respond to her comment, July wormed out of his grasp, intending to make her escape. But his hand snaked out to snare her before she had taken two steps.

"Why, July?" It was all he could manage to say. He'd been totally unprepared for her confession. What had he ever done to deserve this blond-haired nymph's love? Nothing. He had teased her relentlessly to keep his own chaotic emotions from getting the better of him, he had scolded her when she'd scared him half to death with her daring shenanigans, and he had jumped down her throat as if it were her fault the prisoners escaped. Finally, he had manipulated her to get what he wanted. He deserved nothing but her contempt.

"I'm going to my room," July insisted, humiliated.

"You aren't going anywhere until you tell me why you think you love me," Nacona assured her crossly. "You can't just blurt that out and then go on your merry way."

"What the blazes is this—your version of the Spanish Inquisition?" July launched herself out of his arms and streaked toward her bedroom.

Embarrassment reddened in her cheeks. She had never said those three words to any other man, and Nacona's reaction left her feeling awkward and unsure. Blast it, why did she have to explain why she loved him? Was that customary procedure or something?

As she fled across her room to position herself in the farthest corner, Nacona propped himself against the door jamb and studied her. "Have you ever been in love before, July?" he asked.

"No." She backed herself up against the wall when he charged toward her, leaving her nowhere to retreat.

He was bearing down on her, causing the world to shrink to the space he occupied, prompting her heart to pound like a tom-tom.

"Neither have I," Nacona admitted as he reached out to sketch the delicate lines of her flushed face. "So how do people know when they're truly in love?"

"I just feel different, that's all," July murmured, her voice trembling in response to his caress.

"Like when you are coming down with a disease?" he teased with a husky chuckle.

"Confound it, I don't know!" July blustered, feeling even more mortified with each passing second. "It's just different somehow—the way you make me feel. I like being with you, looking at you, having you watch over me, even when I keep insisting I can take care of myself.

I find strength in knowing you're there. I like . . ." She stared over his head, unable to meet his unblinking gaze. "Well, when we . . ." Her face turned all colors as she fumbled to explain the pleasures of his masterful touch. "I just know I love you, and if you didn't have the insensitivity of a rock you wouldn't be harassing me about it. You would simply say something diplomatic and let me down gently or tell me you love me, even a little. Since you don't, please leave so I can die of humiliation."

"No, July, I'm not leaving," he assured her softly.

An enormous sigh escaped his lips as he enveloped her in his arms. Nacona couldn't begin to explain the pleasure and satisfaction her words brought him. It would have taken a far better man than he to reject the love of a woman like July, even if she was better than he deserved. Nacona didn't feel like a seasoned fighter or an expert shootist at the moment. He felt like a jellyfish, a limp creature drowning in a sea of emotion. He stared down into those emerald eyes surrounded by thick lashes and knew he'd lost his last skirmish in this battle of mind and body.

Love had never been a word Nacona used. What little affection he remembered sharing had been the brotherly kind, with Shandin. As for his affection for women, well, love hadn't been a part of it. What he felt for July was totally different from satisfying his body but not his heart, his emotions. Sex had always been simple, not personal. An appeasement of a basic need. Nothing more. But this *passion* was tempered with caring and a sense of peace and fulfillment, and feelings Nacona had never realized existed until July had come into his life.

"I can't leave because . . . I think I love you, too," he

heard himself say. Though it nearly killed him to admit it, at last he had encountered something as strong as his need to avenge his brother's killing. It made him more vulnerable than he'd ever been.

Nacona swore the sun had just burst in to illuminate the room when July smiled up at him. He had been reluctant to put words to his feelings for fear of the commitment that entailed, yet now a tremendous weight had been lifted from his heart.

"You do?" Had her ears deceived her? She had wanted to hear those words so badly that she feared she dreamed them. Pleasure radiated from her face, her body, and her heart—most of all her heart.

His hands glided over her hips, exploring the luscious curves and swells that fitted so perfectly against him. "I do," he confirmed as his lips grazed her forehead. "I didn't want to. I've fought it all the way. But I've never felt like this in my life. Nothing has hit me so hard or endured so long. Being with you is like riding a runaway stallion. I keep holding on, even when I know I should leap to safety. You make me feel out of control. When you're in trouble, I sweat blood. When you're in another man's arms, I become jealous. And when you're in *my* arms the blaze inside me burns like wildfire."

July swelled with pleasure. This midnight-haired mountain of a man loved her.

Confession sometimes being good for the soul, Nacona now knew an inner peace. He still harbored a need to avenge Shandin, but he couldn't let July walk away without knowing how he felt about her. She wasn't the only one who had fallen prey to an ill-fated love.

"We are hopelessly mismatched, and I cannot ignore

my obligation to my brother," Nacona murmured as he enveloped her in his arms. "But all those sermons I delivered to myself about not getting involved were a waste. I was involved with you the minute you burst into my hotel room and into my life. I just refused to admit it for fear of becoming too vulnerable. You claimed there would be no strings attached to this marriage of ours, but I could feel them being spun around me like an intricate spider web."

July framed his ruggedly handsome face in her hands and pressed an adoring kiss to his lips. "I don't want my love for you to be a prison," she whispered. "Never that. I know how you feel about your brother, and I don't blame you. I took you away from your mission, but I understand that you must continue your search. I'm not asking for forever." Her expressive eyes held his captive. "I'm only asking that you love me . . . until you have to go away. And if you should want to come back . . ."

A muffled groan rumbled in his chest as he clutched July to him, devouring her, an impatient need exploding inside him. He didn't ever want to let her go—that was the hell of it. Nacona was torn between his affection for this feisty beauty and his obligation to his brother—to justice itself. But he wasn't going to frustrate himself with thoughts of tomorrow, or the day after, when July was in his arms, offering a special gift that he still wasn't sure he deserved.

Clients had needed him to resolve problems because he was quick on the draw and effective with his fists. But no one had ever needed him to stay around when an assignment was completed. Quite the opposite. He was like a freak in a circus each time a foray ended. People stared at him and gossiped behind his back, but they never tried to understand or accept him. This mere wisp of a woman had somehow come to know him better than he knew himself. She understood his long-harbored craving for vengeance, and she was offering unconditional love, not insisting on a commitment he couldn't keep.

Nacona closed his mind to all except the feel of July's voluptuous body molding itself to his. He wanted to love this bewitching goddess, to treasure the gift she had offered him and him alone.

"July," he rasped as his hands and lips drifted over her silky flesh. "I do love you, more than you'll ever know. You're in my blood—like an affliction I can't cure. I no longer even want to try. I look at other women and find myself comparing them to you. I close my eyes, and your delicious memory colors every thought. I know you're the last woman I should want as badly as I do, yet you're the only one my heart desires. I know I can't give you everything a lady like you deserves, but that doesn't stop me from craving you." He drew just far enough away to peer into those luminous green eyes. "Just love me and make the world go away," he whispered hoarsely. "I don't want to think or analyze. I only want to hold you until this fire in me burns itself out. . . ."

A breathless gasp tripped from her lips when sparks leaped from his body to hers and then back again. His gentle touch soothed away her lingering tension and spread a floodtide of pleasure over her sensitive flesh. She lived for his touch, for the feel of his sensuous lips whispering over her skin. She surrendered to him, returned each scintillating kiss, each arousing caress. Even if this was the kind of love that couldn't last, she relished the wondrous sensations that bombarded her. When she was in Nacona's muscular arms, all her senses came to life and nothing seemed as important as expressing her heartfelt affection, sharing the intense pleasure that burgeoned inside her.

July wasn't sure how and when they came to be on her bed. But they were, clutching at each other with urgent hunger. The world careened crazily about her when Nacona's open mouth sought hers once again. Her body quivered in helpless response as his brazen caresses tracked a path of living fire across her flesh. Sweet maddening torment engulfed her, leaving her to wonder if she could survive such wild, hungry pleasure yet not caring whether she did.

Like a magician, Nacona wove a spell around her, and she arched helplessly toward his seeking hands and greedy lips. He made her beg for more kisses and caresses, he dragged her to the very edge and left her quavering with the want of him. Shock waves rippled through her, arousing her until she cried out his name in a breathless plea for delivery from torment.

"Not yet, my love," Nacona murmured as his kisses glided over the trim indentation of her waist. "I have just begun to show you how much I love you. I want to unveil sensations you've never experienced . . . until now. . . .

Heat radiated through her as his lips traversed her skin, pausing to whisper over the peaks of her breasts and suckle at their dusky crests until her body curled upward in helpless response. His fingertips glided over her nipples as his moist breath skimmed her belly, spreading fires that left her moaning in tortuous pleasure.

Nacona lifted his raven head to stare at her supple

body, seeing passion flicker in her eyes, noting the rapid rise and fall of her chest. He smiled down at her, satisfied to have her helpless in his arms.

"Are you through killing me by inches yet? Come here, please, Nacona!"

July reached for him, but he grasped her hand and drew it over her flat stomach, letting her feel the gliding sweep of his caresses on her flesh. Another rakish grin pursed his lips as he nudged her knees apart to position himself between her legs. "You have only begun to die, July," he promised huskily.

He dipped his head and sensuous lips grazed her inner thigh, causing her to quiver. When his tongue flicked out and his fingertips glided lower, she trembled at the intimacy of his seduction. He felt the moist heat of the passion that he had called forth from her, tasting her, caressing her with his lips and fingertips; and he sensed the convulsive shudder that rippled through her very core. Hypnotized by the wild, ardent responses he was drawing from her, he vowed to evoke even more. He burned in the silken fire of her desire, absorbing the scent of her, the uninhibited sensations he wrested from her. And only when her passions rose again did he bring his lips back to hers, while his fingertips remained buried deep within the fire he had kindled, stoking the blaze.

The scent of her was on his lips as his mouth slanted over hers. His tongue invaded her mouth's sweet recesses imitating the intimacies of moments before, the silvery heat of her response scorched him, her uncontrollable shiver pierced the depths of own soul.

"I've never loved anyone in the secret ways I'm loving you," he whispered to her. "The taste of your luscious body is a taste of ecstasy. I want to savor and devour you in every conceivable way, to expand the limits of passion until you and I have experienced every sensation."

When his lips retraced their deliciously tortuous journey down her body, July waited, knowing he would send her over the edge and into oblivion again, certain she couldn't survive another barrage of such incredible sensations. And die she did, swirling through such exquisite rapture that time turned backward. Past moments' of pleasure became indistinguishable from those in the present. Her body shuddered under his hands and lips, and in hot, aching need Nacona glided upon her. Masculine strength, sheathed in the velvety length of him, penetrated the core of her, filling the fathomless ache wrought by his patient seduction. Only with the pulsating heat of his desire deep inside her did she discover the quintessence of life.

July thought she had died moments before, but this . . . this was the wild, sweet death Nacona could make her beg for. When his body moved rhythmically upon hers, it was as if she couldn't die fast enough to experience the explosive launch into life beyond physical boundaries. And then she was soaring, gliding, trembling with a need both fierce and demanding.

At last July found the cure for the fever that burned with the heat of a thousand suns. the rapid thud of her heart beat in unison with his, his masculine body was absorbing her. She was no longer an entity but a mystical part of a force so overpowering it consumed her.

Nacona gloried in the heady feelings that overcame him while he and this bewitching nymph were sailing past the stars. Riveting sensations converged upon him as he soared like an eagle in flight, uplifted by a draft of wind that sent him spiraling into infinity. When he had finally admitted to this love that he'd feared would confine him, he discovered boundless freedom. He had cautiously withheld a bit of his heart, but even that could not resist rapture that crested over him like a tidal wave.

Nacona no longer *thought* he loved this spirited beauty; he *felt* it in the deepest corners of his soul. It warmed his heart and vibrated through every fiber of his being. No wonder he had been so terrified by the thought of July perishing at the hands of the rustlers. This green-eyed nymph was a living, breathing part of him. No wonder jealousy ate him alive when other men stared at her, speculating as to what it would be like to make love to her. He was fiercely possessive of the magic between them. July belonged to him and he belonged to her. Like two pieces of a puzzle, they made no sense until they were one, sharing and satisfying the needs they aroused in each other. No matter where his frustrating search for Shandin's assassin took him, Nacona knew that he would never get over loving this woman. She had given his life new meaning. She *needed* him. She *loved* him. And he loved her—so completely that passion bound them in a fiery union.

An uncontrollable tremor shook him, sending him plummeting from the dizzying heights of rapture to the deepest abyss of ecstasy. He clutched July to him as a numbing splendor engulfed him. No words could express his feelings. Loving July had suddenly become as natural to Nacona as the batting of an eyelash.

He found himself wondering if he hadn't loved her

from the very first moment he'd seen her standing in the hotel lobby, staring up at him with those spellbinding emerald eyes alive with intelligence, curiosity, and spirit. He had simply refused to admit the truth. But in the end, he hadn't been able to resist the lures of this captivating imp. Not even in the beginning, he silently admitted.

As for July, she was bubbly as a glass of champagne. The ecstasy of their lovemaking, compounded by knowing she was loved, made her dizzy with pleasure. Playfully, she propped herself on his chest to peer down into glittering ebony eyes. She didn't want to fret over how miserable she was going to be when he set off to search for his brother's murderer. She wasn't going to deprive herself of a moment they could share.

"Do you know, I've always found you incredibly attractive," July confessed as she sketched intricate designs on his hair-matted chest. "In fact, when I burst in to find you lounging in your bath, I was thinking the most sordid thoughts."

Black eyebrows jackknifed, and a rakish grin quirked his lips. "Were you now?" He was basking in the free and easy companionship between them. They had no more secrets, and it delighted him to hear July's private thoughts. "I had suspected that *revealing* incident prompted you to have me arrested."

July trailed her forefinger over his full lips and then traced the smile lines that bracketed his mouth and eyes. "I had you arrested to railroad you into helping me." Her eyes twinkled with impish amusement. "I bargained to marry you, just in case you proved to be more than I could handle, which you most certainly did. A lady has to salvage her dignity, you know. How could I have lived with myself if I gave in to you after I'd discovered I couldn't keep my hands off you?"

Nacona burst out laughing. This feisty elf had had as much difficulty denying the attraction as he had. Too bad they'd both been so proud and cautious and stubborn. They had wasted too many nights trying to appear emotionally detached. They had fooled each other, but not their own hearts.

Still chuckling, Nacona draped an arm over her hips and twisted so that her pliant body was beneath his. Now he was gazing down at her, and at a waterfall of silky blond hair cascading over the pillow. "July MacKenzie Bleu, you amaze me. You're as much the rogue as I am. Couldn't keep your hands off me, could you?"

"At least you're the only man I've ever felt that way about," she countered. "You, of course, couldn't keep your hands off dozens of others." The thought spoiled her lighthearted mood.

Nacona tensed. They had landed on shaky ground. July had the curiosity of a cat, and he had the uneasy feeling she was going to pry into his past. Sure enough, he could see the questions in her eyes, even before she put them to tongue.

"Just how many other woman *have* been in your arms, Nacona?" she wanted to know.

A teasing grin pursed his lips. "Well, there was the brunette in Waco, the redhead in Denver, a voluptuous blonde in Omaha, and . . . argh!"

July jabbed him in the ribs. "Philanderer!"

"If you didn't want me to answer that damned-fool

question, you shouldn't have asked it." His teasing laughter dwindled as he bent to kiss away her exaggerated pout. "But the truth is, my curious one, I didn't know what love was until I found you. I was a man with a man's appetites, but passion was never so sweet until I found you. You've made a difference, July, and that's the truth."

When his lips drifted over hers in a worshipping kiss, she forgot her irritation. Suddenly his past didn't matter. She had won his wild heart, at least for a time. And she wasn't going to waste one precious moment stewing about the women long gone from his arms. She would ensure that her initials were carved on his heart and would pray that love would bring him back to her, no matter how far away his personal crusade took him.

That was the last thought to filter through her mind before Naconas practiced hands again wove a spell. July gave herself up to it, expressing her love in touch and movement.

It turned out to be a long, wondrous afternoon, one July swore she would never forget. Their walls of restraint and caution had come tumbling down, and passion now raged like a storm—not the kind July feared, rather the kind that showered them with ineffable pleasure.

Love, couldn't get better than this, she decided much later. But just in case it could . . . With that amorous thought in mind, she blazed a path of adventurous caresses and kisses over Nacona's flesh, igniting a fire in him. And lo and behold, their loving seemed to feed upon itself, growing stronger, more electrifying with each reverent caress and savored kiss. July had never known anything so wild and sweet and satisfying. Each time they made love they seemed to improve upon perfection. She now regretted being so stubborn and cautious. More days and nights could have been spent in the circle of Nacona's arms, exploring the boundless dimensions of paradise.

Chapter 24

Cavalierly, Nacona tugged July into his arms and planted a sizzling kiss on her lips. Their afternoon of splendrous lovemaking left him feeling giddy and carefree, but it was time to get back down to earth . . . just as soon as he helped himself to a few more kisses to tide him over for the rest of the day.

"Where are you off to?" July murmured when Nacona reluctantly set her away from him and pivoted toward the door.

A wry smile quirked his lips as he glanced back into those spellbinding green eyes that no longer tried to disguise the love she felt for him. "I thought I'd better do a little investigating," he informed her, his tone husky with the aftereffects of pleasure. "We were working on a case . . . until I got sidetracked by a siren who cast a potent spell on me."

July returned his mischievous smile. "I didn't hear you complain two hours ago, Mr. Bleu."

"I wasn't even on the planet two hours ago, Missus Bleu." He chuckled rakishly, then ambled toward the door. "I'm taking Killer with me so I can round up every cowhand he growls at."

Reluctantly, July forced attention back to their investigation. "So you have decided my theory might be correct?" she teased.

"I have," Nacona admitted as he reached for the latch. "And this time, I'm bringing the prisoners here, not to jail, so I can interrogate them in my own way."

July didn't ask what methods Nacona planned to employ to glean information. She had a feeling the long arm of the law was about to end in a fist that would pound out answers.

"And while I'm gone, I want you to start packing," he said, his expression now somber. "I was serious, July. I want you to go back to Kansas City before pandemonium breaks loose here."

Her chin tilted to that stubborn angle he had come to recognize. "I'm not leaving. This is my case as much as it is yours. In fact, I'm the one who accepted it—"

"On the strength of my name and reputation," he reminded her with a stern glance. "I don't want you hurt."

July was touched by his concern, she truly was. But she had never run away from trouble or a challenge, and she wasn't about to do it now. She was a doer, not a watcher. "I'm not leaving, and that's all there is to it."

Nacona pivoted to stare into her determined face, then he expelled a sigh. "If you loved me, you'd go so I wouldn't have to worry about you."

"I do love you," she countered. "And if you loved me, you wouldn't ask me to leave when I want to be with you, no matter what."

"Those rustlers may think you can identify them," he pointed out. "They might try to dispose of you. I don't want to take that chance."

"Then I'll just have to exercise caution, won't I?" July sauntered over to slip her arms around his neck and plant a very persuasive kiss on his lips.

Nacona groaned in defeat. He had never been able to say no to this vivacious minx. He'd probably regret letting her stay, but he couldn't make her go.

"All right," he begrudgingly conceded. "But don't go racing off like a one-woman posse again." He stared at her long and hard. "I mean it, July. Sooner or later hell is going to break loose, and I don't want you caught in the crossfire."

When Nacona stamped off, having lost another battle with July, her laughter brought him to a screeching halt. He lurched around to see her smiling impishly at him. She held his boots and holsters in her hands.

"Won't you be needing these, Mr. Detective?" She clucked her tongue and grinned again. "And *you* were worried about *me?*"

Muttering, Nacona reversed direction and tromped across the porch. "It's your fault I can't think straight," he accused. "How's a man supposed to concentrate on his purpose while you're distracting him?" He gathered in his boots and holster in one hand, July in the other, drawing her delectable body against his. "Stay out of trouble, woman."

When he'd soundly kissed her for the last time, July performed a saucy salute. "Yes, sir. I'll be on my best behavior while you're gone."

With a dubious glance, Nacona stuffed his feet into his

boots. He strapped on his holsters on his way to the barn. When he called to Killer, the dog was hesitant to go with him. Killer's gaze went back and forth between July and Nacona, until she made a stabbing gesture with her arm, urging him to his feet. Under July's command, the huge mongrel trotted after Nacona.

Dreamily, she leaned against the supporting beam of the porch and smiled to herself, remembering the wondrous hours she and Nacona had spent together. They had finally come to confess what was in their hearts. The foolish, adorable man! How could he think that she would leave him, loving him the way she did?

Shaking off these thoughts, July ambled back to her room. She had the feeling that Nacona's actions were going to break this investigation wide open. Word would spread like wildfire when he began gathering up suspects with Killer's assistance. Despite Nacona's insistence that she remain behind, July wanted to be in an advantageous position when the shock waves of Nacona's actions began to ripple through town. July intended to be at the place Nacona had mentioned that morning—Cheyenne Rose's Pleasure Parlor. There she might overhear conversations that would provide evidence against the mastermind of the outlaw gang.

Hurriedly, she dug out the breeches and shirt Nacona had purchased for her before they'd made their overland trek from Dodge City to Oakley. With her hair tucked beneath her hat, a knife in her boot and a pistol in her pocket, July ventured outside. She grimaced when Ot Knott caught her inching toward the barn.

The foreman eyed her warily and then drew himself up in front of her. "Missus Bleu, I don't have the foggiest notion where ya think yer goin' or what's goin' on 'round here. But Mr. Bleu gave me specific instructions to keep my eyes on ya. He told me not to let ya outa my sight."

July muttered to herself. She should have known Nacona would put a guard on her. He knew her much better than she wished.

"You have no need to fret, Ot," July assured him breezily before continuing on her way. "And if Mr. Bleu returns before I do, which I doubt he will, simply tell him that I'm gathering roses."

"Roses?" Ot's thin brow puckered over his pale blue eyes.

"Roses," she repeated, biting back a sly smile.

"But . . ."

That was all Ot was allowed to say before July disappeared into the barn to retrieve the steed Ot had saddled for himself. Just as Ot veered around the corner, July came trotting out, atop his horse. With a wave and a smile she thundered away, leaving Ot mumbling to himself.

"Why don't nobody ever tell me what the blazes is goin' on 'round here?" he asked the world at large. Heaving an exasperated sigh, he yanked his hat off his head and slapped it against his hip.

"What's-a-matter?" Aud Ball questioned as he ambled out of the kitchen that sat between the ranchhouse and bunkhouse, carrying a supper tray.

"Yer wastin' yer time totin' that food to the Bleus," Ot grumbled in frustration. "They ain't here. Mr. Bleu said he was goin' to take Killer for a walk and Missus Bleu went to gather roses."

Aud halted in his tracks and frowned, puzzled. "At this time of the evenin'? There ain't any roses for miles around, and nobody takes Killer for walks, least not that I ever heard of. Killer goes where he pleases and nobody ever tries to stop him."

Ot raked his hands through his wiry hair and shrugged. "All I know is what they said, though it didn't make no sense to me neither."

Grumbling to himself, Ot stalked off to saddle another horse while Aud wheeled back to the kitchen with tray in hand. Walking the dog and gathering roses? Aud thought that sounded odd. Likable though the Bleus were, they had some mighty peculiar habits. They were always traipsing off somewhere or other. Those two people just never could seem to stay put!

By the time July reached the outskirts of Cheyenne, darkness had settled over the countryside. As usual, Rose's Parlor was a hub of activity. The establishment was situated close to the meeting place of Wyoming's legislators, who were known to retire to the parlor to break a few of the laws they'd voted on.

After tethering her horse, July moved inconspicuously along the boardwalk and ducked into the alley. Using caution, as Nacona had advised—though he would have skinned her alive if he'd known where she was—she tip-toed past the windows to observe the goings-on. Since she had never been inside the bordello she found herself gaping at its gaudy wallpaper and lavish furnishings. A hand-carved liquor cabinet stood in one corner of the north parlor and platters of fruit rested on tables beside which shiny gold spittoons were positioned.

The thirty-year-old Cheyenne Rose was certainly

doing a thriving business! July had managed to learn that the madam's girls worked on commission and split their fees with the house. The harlots charged five dollars for a few minutes of lusty pleasure and up to thirty dollars for an entire night. Judging from the number of men who lounged in the elaborately decorated room in which a piano player was pounding out tinkling melodies, Rose was having another prosperous evening.

A wave of disgust washed over July as she watched Hoyt Simpson whispering—she could well imagine *what*—in a doxie's ear. She wasn't the least bit surprised to see him at Rose's. In another corner of the parlor that graced the lower level of this den of sin, John Gilman was slobbering over a flamboyantly attired seductress for hire. At that point July almost felt sorry for the departed Angel, who had been seen in the company of these men as well as many others. Men seemed to have very little loyalty to any particular female. It made July wonder just how faithful Nacona would be when the newness of his affection for her wore off. When he went on his way to search for his brother's assassin, would he find passion in other willing arms? She forced herself not to think about that just now. She had come to snoop. If she became distracted by unsettling thoughts, she could wind up in trouble.

Composing herself, she crept past a second parlor that teemed with besotted patrons and more prostitutes, to survey the dining room where several wranglers were taking a meal with three more ladies of the evening. July began to recognize several faces as she went about her nocturnal prowling. The men in the dining room were cowhands Killer had growled at each time he passed them. Nacona was probably right on the mark in thinking the Pleasure Parlor was the headquarters of more than one kind of sinister activity.

Determined to locate the madam of the house, July eased open the back door and stepped into a hall that led toward the kitchen and a narrow staircase. The three-story brick house, with its two parlors, ballroom, kitchen, and dining area, appeared to have at least twelve to fifteen bedrooms in the upper stories—for the convenience of male patrons. And somewhere in this gaudy monstrosity of brick there had to be an office Cheyenne Rose utilized when she wasn't tripping the light fantastic with one of her special clients.

Glancing about, July tiptoed up the steps to survey the second story of the palatial bordello. When she peered into open bedrooms, she couldn't believe what she saw. Most of them were decorated in red velvet. Mirrors lined their walls and even their ceilings. The thought of Nacona ambling through this sordid establishment had July muttering disrespectful epithets. The things that man had seen here and elsewhere, yet he claimed to remember no woman but her. Ha! She was going to have a few choice words to say to that rake when she got home.

The murmur of hushed voices jerked July from her resentful musings. She darted into the elaborately decorated bedroom at the end of the hall—and decided she must have happened into Cheyenne Rose's private quarters. The boudoir was far more spacious and luxurious than the others. No expense had been spared in furnishing it. Costly trinkets and hand-painted dressing screens were everywhere. A marble-topped table sat in one corner, two velvet upholstered chairs graced the corner adjacent to the bed, and a crystal chandelier dangled from the ceiling. The bed, with its lace and satin canopy, looked like something Cleopatra would have delighted in utilizing. Cheyenne Rose had created an aura of wealth in this lurid den.

July edged toward the closed door that adjoined the boudoir, certain she had located the madam's office. A slight frown knitted her brow as she listened to the conversation, between a man and woman, going on behind the door. She didn't recognize the woman's sultry voice, but there was something familiar about the male's. Sinking down on her knees, July peeked through the keyhole and then gasped at seeing Hub Butler lounging at Rose's desk—as if *he* owned the place. Her astounded gaze shifted to a voluptuous, auburn-haired woman adorned in gold silk, jewels, and scads of dainty lace.

"I want you to tell the men we are shutting down our operation for a while," Hub was saying. "I've decided we need to keep a low profile until I can figure out what to do about Nacona Bleu."

July blinked like an owl adjusting to bright sunlight. Hub Butler? But he couldn't possibly be involved with this ring of thieves. She had seen the Cabestro brand on cattle the rustlers were branding, and Butler had come by to thank her for rescuing some of his calves. She'd thought Hoyt Simpson a more likely suspect. Something was very wrong here. . . .

Rose leaned across the desk to brush her fingertips over Hub's hand. "Why don't we take a vacation," she purred at him. "When we come back . . ."

Hub withdrew his hand and grumbled under his breath. "Leaving won't resolve the problem. Bleu is the problem. I tried to set him up as C.L.'s murderer, but that inquisitive wife of his came in his stead. The other ranchers have never posed any problems, but Bleu's reputation as a detective and gunslinger is a threat. I'm beginning to think someone hired him to investigate the robberies and rustling. If it wasn't for the fact that he's married and has bought the Golden Spur, I'd swear to it."

July digested the information she had overheard and then swallowed hard. Hub had set Nacona up for a murder charge, so he must have been the one who'd disposed of Chambers. But why? July frowned ponderously. She had assumed the envelope she had confiscated from under C.L.'s desk was connected with the assassination. But was it? And what about Angel? She was reported to be one of Hub's conquests, or vice versa. Nacona had thought he'd precipitated Angel's death by questioning her about the envelope. But perhaps she had known Hub had murdered C.L. and had tried to blackmail him. Hub could have . . .

Her thoughts trailed off as she concentrated on the man she viewed through the keyhole, seeing Hub Butler from an entirely different angle.

Hub propped his arms against the edge of the desk and stared into Rose's painted face. "You're going to have to help me get rid of Nacona Bleu."

"I rather like the looks of the man." Rose tittered as she struck a provocative pose.

The comment did not set well with Hub. In fact, it put him in a rage. To July's utter disbelief, he growled and backhanded Rose, sending her head snapping against the back of her chair.

"God damn it, I told you the man's a threat to our operation," he snarled.

Rose's whimpers didn't seem to faze Hub one iota, and July quickly recalled the welt on Angel's face the night she had been suffocated with her own pillow. She was now certain that she was staring at a murderer who only played the part of an even-tempered rancher. Beneath those expensive clothes and pretentious manners lurked the soul of a demon. July could see the diabolical sparkle in Hub's eyes when he glowered at Rose, who was inspecting her stinging cheek with her fingertips.

"Now you listen to me." Hub sneered maliciously. "I want you to lure Nacona to your room. Send him a message—say anything to get him here. I'll have one of my men on hand to do the killing, but you'll have to set the stage and see that your girls corroborate your story. I want that bastard out of the way. Do you understand me?"

July watched Rose gather her feet beneath her and rise. If her rigid back was any indication of the suppressed anger that churned inside her, July was sure the madam was as furious with Hub as he was with her. But Rose was wise enough not to cross him in his present mood.

"I'll make the arrangements," she promised.

"Good." Hub relaxed in his chair. "Once we—"

"Hey, kid! What the hell are you doin' in Rose's room?"

Sickening dread came over July when the drunken cowboy poked his head into the boudoir to see her kneeling in front of the keyhole. She knew Hub and Rose had heard the big galoot. His voice carried like a bugle!

Left with no option, she bounded to her feet, lowering her head, and, like a billy goat, barreled out of the room. A pained groan erupted from the man's chest when July's forward momentum sent him slamming against the wall. She was wearing men's clothes, so she wasn't fretting over being recognized—unless she got caught, which she had no intention of doing. She shot down the hall like a bullet, only to hear Hub's furious snarl echoing behind her. Her heart hammering, July took the steps three at a time in her haste to escape. She had just pivoted onto the bottom step in order to dart toward the back door when a body collided with her, knocking her flat. Frantically, July gouged and jabbed at her captor, but to no avail. Squashed flat, she winced apprehensively as the barrel of a pistol stabbed her in the back.

"What the hell were you doing upstairs, kid?" Hub Butler growled as he shifted his weight to turn the small captive over onto "his" back. A muddled frown plowed his brows when he recognized July's shadowed features beneath the brim of her oversize hat. Outrage exploded in him as he jerked the hat off, sending her blond tresses spilling onto the floor. "You sneaky little bitch!"

"You murd—"

July had no time to voice the accusation. Hub clamped a hand over her mouth and rammed his pistol into her belly. Hurriedly, he bounded to his feet and yanked her up with a back-wrenching jolt. Before she could bite his hand, he stuffed his handkerchief in her mouth and dragged her up the steps. July considered battling her way to freedom, but the loaded Colt .45 discouraged her from defying this infuriated murderer.

She really hadn't cared to see the inside of Rose's office, but that was where she wound up, meeting the buxom madam of the bordello face-to-face.

Rose's jaw gaped in amazement when she stared at the

female garbed in men's clothes. "Isn't that Nacona's wife? Good God, did she overhear us?"

Hub nodded grimly and gestured toward the waterfall of red velvet drapes. "Fetch those cords to tie her up," he demanded impatiently. "It looks as if I'm going to have to take a vacation after all. You can see to it that word spreads I went to meet with my investors to discuss the ranch."

"I want to go with you," Rose insisted as she handed him the improvised ropes.

"No." He refused gruffly. "It might look suspicious if you and I and this little witch all disappeared at the same time."

July was dismayed to learn that Hub Butler was very good at knot-tying. By the time he finished, she and her chair had become inseparable. He was also very thorough in searching for and finding the pistol she had stuffed in her pocket. He did not, however, think to check for the dagger in her boot, not that she could reach it.

"I want you to keep an eye on this sly piece while I gather my belongings and check the train schedule," Hub told Rose. "Don't let anyone know she's here."

"What about Butch?" Rose glanced at the cowboy who had slammed his head against the wall and passed out after July had knocked his legs out from under him.

"When he wakes up, tell him some lad was sneaking around up here to further his education," Hub suggested. "Butch probably won't even sober up for days, if he runs true to form."

Before Hub sailed out the door, Rose clutched his arm imploringly. "Hub, please take me with you."

He shook himself loose from her grasp and left the

room. When Rose expelled several unladylike curses, July peered at her puckered face and saw that it boasted a welt very similar to the one Angel had sustained. Unless July missed her guess, Hub was the man Killer had seen outside Angel's home the night she was murdered. The mongrel had always greeted Hub with a growl. It was a shame Killer couldn't talk. He could have resolved this case in one whale of a hurry.

"You have just signed your own death certificate . . . July, isn't it?" Rose taunted as she gave her captive the once-over, twice. "It seems you know far too much for your own good." A gloating smile pursed her lips as she pirouetted to sashay to her room. "I had the feeling Hub had become infatuated with you. He certainly mentioned you often enough these past few weeks." Rose leaned against the door latch and half-turned to glance in July's direction. "But he is mine, and he always will be. Even that Chambers woman couldn't sink her claws into him and hold him. Hub needs me. He always comes back to me."

July wasn't sure who Rose was trying to convince, her captive or herself. As far as she could tell Hub Butler had no capacity in that rock he called a heart for love. Why this woman was attached to the man was beyond comprehension. Hub had struck her, yet she wanted to run away with him. And she still aided him in his illegal activities by passing information to the men he had planted at various ranches. July knew if a man struck her she would never go near him again. Rough-edged and domineering as Nacona could be at times, he had never come close to striking her.

Nacona . . . Misery clouded July's mind. She wondered

414

if she would ever again gaze into his ebony eyes or feel his sensuous lips melting upon hers. Blast it, hadn't Nacona warned her to stay out of trouble? Now it didn't look as if she'd live long enough to divulge the information she had overheard. Hub Butler had evil designs on her, that was for certain. She was a threat to him, just as C.L. and Angel Chambers must have been. She might not even live long enough to discover why Hub had decided to dispose of the banker and his promiscuous wife.

Determinedly, she blinked back tears. She wasn't dead yet, she reminded herself fiercely. Sooner or later Hub would have to untie her from this chair and drag her off to dispose of her. And when he did, she would use the knife in her boot to defend herself. But this time Nacona wouldn't be coming to her rescue. Even if he did manage to pry the information out of the bandits he rounded up, it would be too late, No, this time July was on her own. If she escaped it would have to be by her own skill and wit. She told herself she should have listened to her brothers and Nacona when they suggested she pursue a safer profession. This time her stubborn daring could prove to be fatal!

The Mackenzie brothers were in the worst of all possible moods by the time they finally stepped off the train in Cheyenne. The journey, which should have taken only a few days at the most, had evolved into a full week of travel. Their frustration had festered with each delay, and they were now eager to take out their fury on Nacona Bleu, the unscrupulous gunslinger who had abused, raped, and then coerced their little sister into marriage.

The MacKenzie males, like three musketeers, paced down the street toward the sheriff's office. There they found a lawman asleep beneath a newspaper, snoring up a storm. Disgusted with the entire week and with this careless excuse for a marshal, Gresham plucked up the paper and slammed it down on the desk.

Pinkston jerked back in his chair and his feet flew off his desk. The chair reared up on its hind legs and crashed to the floor, leaving him sprawled in a most undignified position.

"The local marshal, symbol of law and order, I presume," Calvin smirked disdainfully.

"County sheriff," Pinkston corrected as he climbed to his knees and then to his feet. Sleepy-eyed, he surveyed the three men in dusty but elegant waistcoats and matching breeches. Their strong family resemblance was recognizable at a glance. And they reminded Pinkston of someone else. He was just too damned groggy to figure out who that was.

"We are looking for Nacona Bleu," Ethan declared without bothering with introductions. "Where is he?"

That was it, Pinkston decided. These three men bore a striking likeness to July Bleu—similar color of the eyes, similar shade of blond hair. The only difference was that July had eyes like polished emeralds and her brothers' eyes were a paler shade of . . .

"My brother asked you a question," Gresham pronounced each word clearly and distinctly, even though his voice rumbled with irritation. "Where is Nacona Bleu?"

"Are you relatives of his?" Pinkston queried as he smoothed his handlebar mustache into place.

Calvin flashed the sheriff a look one might expect to

receive after asking to share the same bath water or eating utensil. "We're his brothers-in-law," Calvin responded, very nearly gagging on the words.

"I thought you reminded me of Missus Bleu," Pinkston said with a confirming nod. "I got to know her while she was locked in jail."

"Jail!" the MacKenzies croaked like a trio of bullfrogs.

Pinkston stepped back a pace when three pair of narrowed green eyes riveted on him. "Well, it was a mistake, of course. Missus Bleu didn't kill anybody. I knew that for sure after I had her *and* her husband locked up and—"

"Murder?" Gresham howled. His incredulous gaze drilled into the sheriff. "Who was killed?"

"The banker and his wife," Pinkston hurriedly explained.

Gresham glanced bleakly at Calvin, who stared dismally at Ethan. Then all three MacKenzies glared at Pinkston.

"Just tell us where we can find Nacona Bleu," Calvin demanded through clenched teeth.

"I suppose he's on the ranch he bought from the banker before Chambers was killed," Pinkston speculated. "The Golden Spur sits a mile north of town."

Like soldiers on parade, the MacKenzies performed a perfectly executed about-face and filed out of the office. With swift strides they propelled themselves toward the livery stable to purchase horses for their journey.

"What do you make of this, Gresh?" Ethan questioned.

"I'm beginning to think that gunslinger has decided it's more profitable to be on the wrong side of law and order."

"Then he has forced July into being an accomplice to murder," Calvin predicted. "Utilizing his strong-arm tactics, Bleu has probably decided to take over the whole damned town."

"He won't live long enough for that to happen," Ethan seethed. "If I have anything to do with it, he'll be dead by dawn!"

"Calm down," Gresham snapped, struggling to control his own frustration. "First we'll listen to what July has to say. She won't be afraid to speak out against Bleu with us here to protect her."

"Fine. We'll listen to her and *then* we'll take care of Bleu," Calvin announced. "There's nothing worse than a hired shootist turned bad. Such a man thinks he is above the law. But Nacona Bleu is going to become an example to everyone who has ever considered turning to crime."

In murderous frames of mind, the MacKenzies galloped past Cheyenne Rose's Pleasure Parlor, unaware they had been a mere hundred yards away from their sister and that she was in a far more dangerous predicament than they imagined.

Things were heating up in Wyoming, but it wasn't because of the fire in Aud Ball's stove. He had given up serving dinner to the Bleus on this day.

Chapter 25

Ot Knott glanced up when he spied the owner of the Golden Spur returning from walking the dog. A muddled frown puckered Ot's brow when he realized Nacona had a string of men behind him, all of them bound. One of these men worked at the Golden Spur.

"Now what the devil is goin' on?" Ot demanded as he strode toward Nacona. His befuddled gaze dropped to the huge mutt who was growling.

Nacona didn't bother answering the question. He swung to the ground to voice a command, "Fetch all the men who are in the bunkhouse. I have an assignment for them."

Still frowning, Ot scurried off to do as he was told. With a rough jerk, Nacona dragged each and every rider out of the saddle and then double-checked the rope that bound them to one another like a string of ponies. When he had his prisoners all in a row, Nacona glanced at the cowhands Ot had gathered.

"These men are suspected of rustling and robbery," he announced. "It has already been proved that Pinkston and his jail can't hold them. Although I have led all of you to believe I had retired from being a detective, the truth is my wife and I were both sent here to investigate certain crimes."

The moment July's name was mentioned a ripple of murmurs undulated through the cluster of men, just as Nacona had expected it would. After all, he had reacted the same way when he'd discovered the little spitfire had made criminal investigation her profession.

"I am telling you this in the strictest confidence. And if anyone in Cheyenne learns of it, I will find out who passed the word I wanted to go no farther than the boundaries of this ranch, and the guilty party will answer to me." The accompanying stare he leveled at each individual dared the wranglers to abuse his trust.

"I anticipate trouble," Nacona continued in a grim tone. "As of yet, these renegades have refused to name their ringleader, who may very well be gathering a strike force to free them. I intend to deputize all of you to ensure that doesn't happen."

The wranglers scattered to collect their weapons and ammunition, while Nacona herded his prisoners into the storehouse situated beside the bunkhouse. By the time he had secured the desperadoes, some of whom were nursing wounds sustained during escape attempts, the wranglers had regrouped.

Nacona glanced at Aud Ball who looked far more comfortable with a skillet in his hands than a rifle. "Go tell July to come outside. She might be able to identify some of the men she saw in the rustlers' camp."

"I don't reckon I kin do that, Mr. Bleu," Aud replied in his customary slow drawl.

Nacona frowned, wondering if Aud thought he shouldn't leave the prisoners he was guarding. "We can do without you for a few minutes."

"I'm sure you kin, Mr. Bleu," Aud acknowledged. "I ain't much of a hand with a gun nohow. But Missus Bleu can't come outside if she ain't inside."

"Then where the hell is she?" Nacona growled impatiently.

Ot stepped forward to meet Nacona's annoyed stare. "Missus Bleu said she was gonna go gather some roses while you was walkin' the dog."

"Roses?" Nacona blinked in astonishment.

"Roses," Ot confirmed. "That's what the missus said. There ain't all that many roses 'round these parts, but—"

"Damn it to hell, I told you not to let her out of your sight!" Nacona blared, losing his grasp on his temper.

"Well, she took off on my horse afore I could stop her," Ot protested. "I don't mean to be makin' excuses, but that wife of yers is like a cyclone when she blows off to wherever she's decided to go."

"Roses?" Nacona repeated ponderously.

Rose's! When the message finally soaked in, Nacona let out a string of curses. July wouldn't dare snoop around that brothel, he told himself. But he knew she would. Spewing out several more oaths, he leaped into the saddle in a single bound.

"Don't let anyone near those prisoners—not even the sheriff himself." He fired out the order as he wheeled his steed around to thunder toward the golden archway that glowed in the moonlight.

He hadn't even reached the gate when three stony-faced men blocked his path.

"We're looking for Nacona Bleu," Gresham MacKenzie announced.

"Well, you've found him, but I haven't time to—"

Nacona was the one who was interrupted for a change when Calvin MacKenzie came uncoiled like a striking snake. His doubled fist shot out of nowhere to connect with Nacona's jaw. The unexpected, well-aimed blow sent Nacona sliding sideways in the saddle. Before he could right himself, Ethan Mackenzie took a turn at pelting him with a punch to the left eye. Then all three men were taking cracks at him. They might have leveled several more brain-scrambling blows if Killer hadn't attacked the horses upon which they sat.

By now Nacona was wondering if *three* vicious masterminds had been discreetly operating the gang of thieves from a safe distance. As of yet, he hadn't got a good look at the shadowed faces of these ruthless strangers. He didn't realize his brothers-in-law had come all the way from Kansas City to pound him into the ground for molesting their poor little sister and dragging her into a deplorable marriage, as well as for various and sundry other crimes they thought he'd committed.

Had it not been for Killer, Nacona knew he would have been overpowered, dragged from the saddle, and beaten to a pulp. When he'd reached for his pistols, they were no longer in his holsters. When he'd tried to answer the blows, arms had shot out to block him. Only when the oversize dog caused the horses to circle, did Nacona have the opportunity to throw a few retaliatory punches. But all three men then leaped at him, forcing him to the ground. Killer came to his rescue once again and his attackers reluctantly backed off just enough to appease the snarling mongrel. Nacona found himself at gunpoint—gunpoints to be exact—while he licked his bloodied lips.

The silence vibrated with hostility. "Where's our sister, you miserable son of a bitch?" Ethan snarled.

Killer had nothing on Ethan. Both man and beast were frothing at the mouth.

"Your sister?" Nacona parroted out of the least swollen side of his mouth.

"And don't pretend you don't know who or where she is." Calvin sent him a lethal glare. "We know you molested her in Dodge and forced her to marry you after you'd raped her. Now where is July!"

Nacona blinked—with one eye. The other was swollen shut. "You're the MacKenzie brothers?" he chirped.

"That's right, Mr. Bleu." Gresham, who prided himself in honoring the law, wanted to yank this bastard up and pistol-whip him. But Killer's deep growl prevented Gresham from enjoying his revenge. It appalled him to realize he had already broken the law by committing assault and battery. This unfortunate incident with July had turned him wrong side out. He had thought physical violence and brutality beneath him . . . until now.

"We also know you connived to have July put in jail, for a murder *you* obviously committed. You probably thought no one in Wyoming would convict a female. Did you grease a few palms and voice a few threats to beat a murder rap?" Calvin snarled.

With a scowl, Nacona heaved himself off the ground and dusted himself off. "And you call yourselves detectives?" he snorted in disdain. "I never heard such a ridiculously erroneous theory in all my life."

When Ethan tried to launch himself at Nacona,

Gresham felt obliged to grab his youngest brother by the nape of his waistcoat and jerk him back. "Steady, Ethan. That mutt will chew you up and spit you out." Stormy green eyes drilled into Nacona. "Explain that remark, Mr. Bleu."

"I don't have the time to explain a damned thing," Nacona muttered. "That sister you are so fond of protecting could be up to her pretty little neck in trouble at this very moment. You can either help me find her or get the hell out of my way. I don't particularly care which!"

That said, Nacona scooped up his pistols, bolted onto his steed, and shot off like a lightning bolt. Quick as a wink, the MacKenzies mounted up to follow in his wake.

Cursing all MacKenzies—July in particular—Nacona licked puffy lips and squinted his good eye at the distant lights of Cheyenne. When he got his hands on that idiotic wife of his he was going to let her have it. He had specifically told her to remain at the ranch until he returned. But did she ever listen? *Never*, damn her gorgeous hide. What went on at that bordello was not for her to see. And what the sweet loving hell did she expect to find out there anyway? Was she trying to identify the rustlers she'd seen the previous night? Or did she think she could acquire information about the Parlor being the headquarters of criminals. He should never have revealed his suspicions to her. If the rustlers Nacona had been unable to locate had spotted her, she could wind up dead—or worse!

The thought of any man laying a hand on July caused Nacona to burst into another round of curses. He had the sickening feeling in the pit of his belly that July was in dire straits. Why else wouldn't she have returned home by now?

* * *

July tensed apprehensively when Hub Butler whizzed back into the room, carrying a huge wool sack. She didn't have to be a genius to know who was about to be placed in it. Perhaps Hub planned to heave her into the river, never to be seen or heard from again.

"Rose, fetch me that concoction you give some of your rowdy clients to put them to sleep," Hub demanded when the madam appeared in the doorway.

With a nod of compliance, Rose reversed direction to mix the brew of gin, whiskey, and laudanum that left hell-raising customers in a stupor. When she returned with it in a glass, Hub grabbed July by the hair of her head, forcefully tilting her chin up. Quickly, he removed her gag and poured the potion down her throat. When July spit it back in his face, Hub cursed foully and yanked harder on her hair. Despite July's determination to keep her mouth closed, the fierce tug on her hair caused her lips to part in a soundless shriek. Hub rammed the glass at her mouth and then held the lower portion of her face with his hand, forcing her to swallow. Although July did manage to let out a small screech, he repeated the process until she had consumed the entire sleeping potion.

She felt the effects immediately. Various parts of her body were already numb from being tied up so tightly, and the potion made that condition worse. Furthermore she was becoming more dizzy and sluggish by the second. The office in which she sat seemed to turn a fuzzy shade of gray as she battled to keep her wits about her, but she was fading into oblivion. The two faces above her kept splitting and then merging before vanishing completely. . . .

Satisfied that July would pose no problem when he untied her, Hub worked the drapery cords loose. He caught July in one arm before she tumbled from the chair.

"Help me get her into this sack," Hub commanded. "I don't have much time before the train pulls out."

"When are you coming back?" Rose wanted to know.

Hub didn't respond. He merely slid the sack over July's limp body until she was completely covered.

"You aren't planning to come back at all, are you?" Rose speculated. "I'm coming with you."

Still Hub said nothing. He was intent on stuffing linen and blankets around July to disguise her form. Hurriedly, he hoisted July over his shoulder and strode toward the door, anxious to load her in the wagon with the stolen money and his belongings. He glanced back to see that Rose had returned from her boudoir with a satchel in each hand.

"You aren't coming with me," he growled in a tone that brooked no argument.

But Rose was determined. With chin held high, she approached him, only to be backhanded across the cheek when she got within arm's reach. With a startled squawk, she stumbled backward over the chair in which July had been tied.

"You stupid whore," Hub jeered. "Do you really think I'd let you chase after me?" Her raked her with a scornful look. "You're just like Angel. She tried to hold me down, and you know what happened to her. The Parlor is now yours to control. That's all you'll get from me."

"I don't want this house," Rose wailed as she massaged her stinging jaw. "I only wanted you!"

"But I don't want you," Hub told her cruelly.

"You need me!" Tears ran down her flushed cheeks, sending streaks of makeup running to the corners of her quivering mouth.

With a furious snarl, Hub backhanded Rose again when she bounded to her feet to chase after him. Her head snapped backward when the punishing blow launched her across the office. A dull groan ripped from her bloodied lips when her head struck the corner of the desk, and she wilted into a motionless heap.

Scowling over the waste of valuable time, Hub surged out of the room and down the back steps. Hastily, he tossed July into the back of the wagon beside his trunks and satchels. Without sparing Rose another thought, he bounded onto the seat and snapped the reins over the horses, in haste to reach the depot on time for the train.

A sly smile pursed his lips as he glanced back at the satchels that held the cash his men had stolen from banks and trains and ranchers. He had made a killing in Wyoming the past few years—enough to live out the rest of his life in the lap of luxury. He hadn't intended to leave for another year, but Nacona Bleu's appearance and the incidents of the past few weeks had prompted him to change his plans. After he satisfied his yen for this curvaceous blonde and disposed of her, he would be on his way to California.

Hub explained to the railroad agent that he would be away for a few weeks, meeting with his investors. Then he personally saw to the loading of his belongings in the freight car. He stashed his trunks and the lumpy bundle alongside sacks of flour, barrels of molasses, and crates of shovels, nails, and hammers being shipped west.

As calmly as you please, he then presented his ticket to the conductor and settled himself in a first-class seat. A triumphant smile quirked his lips as he glanced around the crowded car. He had outsmarted the legendary Nacona Bleu who prided himself in being such a successful shootist and detective. Well, this was one case Bleu would never crack, and Hub would enjoy ultimate satisfaction when he took his pleasure with Bleu's lovely but daring wife. It was a pity he couldn't inform Bleu that he was the last man to touch July before she met her demise. That would really put him in a fury. But at least he would have the pleasure of knowing he had hoodwinked the gunslinger!

Hub treated himself to a self-satisfied chuckle when the train whistle announced their departure from Cheyenne. The passenger car wobbled as the locomotive rumbled westward, and he leaned leisurely back in his tufted seat to catch a nap before making his way to the freight car to check on July. She would be unconscious for several hours. And when the drugging potion wore off, he would sample the feminine charms of the woman who had caught his eye but had eluded him. Tonight he would find long-awaited pleasure before he launched her into eternity. . . .

With Killer hot on his heels and the MacKenzie "musketeers" only a few paces behind him, Nacona jerked his steed to a halt in front of Cheyenne Rose's Pleasure Parlor. Wearing a snarl and muttering a curse, Nacona powered his way through the men congregated around the front door. With fiendish haste, he darted into each room on the ground floor, searching for his missing wife. His efforts, however, turned up nothing but a bunch of drunken men with paid paramours.

After taking the steps two at a time, Nacona sped down the hall toward Rose's office. He stopped short when he spied Rose sprawled beside the desk. His abrupt halt caused the MacKenzies to back-end him, making him stumble into the office before he was prepared to enter it. Uprighting himself, Nacona stalked across the room to prop Rose up. He shook her three times before her head rolled from side to side and a pained moan tripped from her blood-caked lips.

"Where's my wife?" Nacona demanded as he stared at the satchels strewn around the room. He didn't like what he saw—or the implication of packed bags. The welts on Rose's face reminded him of another female who had been struck before she wound up dead.

Ever so slowly, Rose's lashes fluttered up to see the chiseled face peering at her. There had been a time not so long ago when Rose had cheated, lied, and stolen for the man she loved. But Hub's heartless words and hasty departure had made her bitter. She didn't care if this towering mass of masculinity beat the tar out of Butler. She now despised him for treating her so ruthlessly.

"Where's July?" Nacona demanded a second time. "And who did this to you?"

Rose licked her lips and struggled to formulate her thoughts. Her head was pounding like a sledgehammer, and her mouth was as dry as the Mohave Desert.

"Hub Butler," she croaked at long last.

A muddled frown clouded Nacona's brow. "Where is he?"

Rose inhaled a steadying breath and slowly expelled it. "He took the train. But I don't know his destination."

"What about July?" Nacona queried apprehensively. When Rose glanced away, Nacona emitted a scowl. "Damn you, woman, tell me what's happened to my wife!"

"She was sneaking around the house, and Hub caught her," Rose admitted shakily. "After he drugged her, he put her in a wool sack and took her with him to the train depot."

Cursing up one side and down the other, Nacona levered Rose up against the desk and bolted to his feet. It was becoming alarmingly clear that Hub Butler was responsible for the rustling and robberies in the area. Even though Nacona had never warmed to the rancher, he had assumed his animosity had been due to jealousy. Obviously July had uncovered some incriminating facts that put her life in jeopardy. Hub had abducted her to silence her— permanently.

"Who is this Hub Butler character?" Gresham questioned as he followed Nacona into the hall. "Why would he take July?"

"He is undoubtedly the one who's been in command of the thieves who've terrorized Wyoming," Nacona hurriedly threw over his shoulder. "And that daring sister of yours knows too damned much."

The comment put bleak frowns on the MacKenzie brothers' faces. Their frustration with Nacona Bleu was momentarily forgotten because of their concern for July.

Her position sounded grim, so they all matched Nacona stride for stride.

Suffering, Nacona swung into the saddle and charged down the street to the railroad depot. Before he could dismount to check the departure of the train, the telegraph agent ambled outside to flag him down.

"I just received this message. I was on my way to deliver it to you," the agent announced.

He reached up to hand the note to Nacona. Eyes blazing, Nacona read the message and then exploded in a volcanic growl. The telegram was a response to the wire he'd sent off a week earlier, requesting a copy of the information C.L. Chambers had received before his death.

A shiver of dread slithered down Nacona's spine as he reread the information C.L. had requested about Hub Butler. The man Nacona knew as Butler did not fit the age or physical traits. According to this response, Hub Butler was a round, plump individual of forty-seven years of age. He had organized a syndicated ranch through Eastern banks with foreign investors participating, and he had gone west in '76 to hire cowhands to establish a ranch with funds he had received. The man who managed the Cabestro Ranch must have assumed the identity of the real Hub Butler. Nacona had the sickening feeling he knew what had become of the Missouri-born man who had never reached Wyoming and had never turned up to contest the new owner's rights to the land.

A terrifying thought followed that realization. The nondescript characteristics of the man who had long tormented Nacona suddenly came to mind. That individual had been in need of a new identity and a new life after his

431

exodus from Indian Territory. Charley Brazil. Nacona could only speculate that Brazil had chanced to meet the Wyoming-bound Butler and had taken advantage of a golden opportunity. The telegram stated Butler had been an orphan who'd elbowed his way through life to make something of himself. He had left no family behind in Missouri when he'd ventured West.

Opportunity had been staring Brazil in the face. Brazil had acquired valuable information from Butler, had disposed of the man, and had assumed his identity. That was why it had been impossible to track Brazil down. The man had disappeared from sight. He had shaved off his woolly mustache and beard, had clipped his scraggly mane of hair, and had turned up in the far reaches of Wyoming with the funds to start life all over again.

Nacona hoped he was wrong, but he feared he was not. The crimes in Wyoming hinted at a mastermind at work, the likes of Charley Brazil in his clandestine dealings in Indian Territory, two years earlier. The scoundrel had always been cautious, cunning, and discreet. He had been impossible to pin down, to second-guess. He was as analytical and deadly as they came. Nacona well remembered that he and Shandin had had the feeling they were chasing a disembodied spirit while they searched high and low for the outlaw who had been difficult to identify even then.

And who better than Charley Brazil to lure old cronies from his corrupt days in the territory into Wyoming? He could have planted his former cohorts at the various ranches to spy and thieve for him. The man's criminal mind bordered on genius. Now the bastard had left Cheyenne, burning bridges behind him, taking the one person who probably knew too much about his criminal activities to go on living.

"Mr. Bleu?" Gresham frowned in concern when Nacona turned as white as a suntanned man could get. "What was in that telegram?"

The deep insistent voice brought Nacona out of his gloomy trance and spurred him into action. He bounded off to interrogate the ticket agent and check the train's scheduled stops. He feared he wouldn't have a chance in hell to catching up with the train if it wasn't stopping to take on freight, water, and passengers.

Horrible images of July being abused and murdered kept leaping into his mind. Hub Butler—Charley Brazil or whoever he really was—would certainly be planning her demise. If he had confined her to a sack, that suggested she was traveling in the freight car. At his convenience, Brazil could slide open the door and shove his unwanted baggage from the speeding train. July would be dead and gone and none of the railroad agents along the way would be the wiser. In the darkness, the watchmen would never hear or see anything over the racket of the train rumbling down the tracks.

A lump constricted Nacona's throat, and he struggled to inhale. July had frightened the living daylights out of him a time or two in the past, but those incidents couldn't compare to this. Nacona was sweating bullets, and going through hell. The only good and decent and cherished part of his life was about to be destroyed by a murderer and thief who had already proved he would kill each time he was threatened. Nacona was terrified. The train that carried July to her death had a head start on him. He knew the direction in which it was traveling and where it would stop. He wondered if that would do July much good by the time he caught up with her.

Lord, he hadn't needed a second reason for wanting Charley Brazil to roast in the fires of Hades! Knowing he would have to leave July sooner or later to continue his search, he had tried to imagine his life without her, but had found that would be like living without the sun, moon, and stars—without air to breathe. If he lost July, he lost everything worth wanting or keeping.

Grappling with that unbearable thought, Nacona bounded into the saddle and urged his steed to its swiftest pace. With a cloud of doom hovering around him, he followed the steel rails that seemed to stretch out forever. . . .

Chapter 26

July let out a groggy moan, reflexively tried to stretch, and realized her ankles and wrists were tightly bound. Jolted awake, she found herself staring at the inside of the wool sack in which she'd been stuffed. Panic seized her when she felt the train on which she had been stashed begin to roll away from the roundhouse where it had stopped. If she had awakened a few minutes earlier she might have been able to cut herself loose and escape.

July contorted her body so that she could reach inside her boot and retrieve the dagger. Once she'd grasped the weapon she stabbed at the sack and slit it open enough to worm free. Levering herself upright, she then cut away the improvised ropes and massaged her arms and legs until they began to function properly. Although she smelled like a sheep and the oily substance of the wool clung to her skin and clothes, she inhaled a breath of air to clear her senses.

Her discerning gaze circled the darkness. Unable to see a blessed thing besides a few splinters of moonbeams that slanted through the wooden car, she fumbled her way over the unidentified sacks and crates that blocked her path. She managed to push the sliding door open just enough to shed some light and fresh air on the inside of the freight car. Pensively, she studied the crates and sacks, hoping to locate something that would serve as a weapon.

Apprehensively, July glanced outside, watching trees whiz by at an alarming pace. Although she didn't relish the idea of waiting around for Hub Butler to arrive upon the scene to dispose of her, she wasn't anxious to leap from the train at full speed, either.

Think, July, she ordered herself. She had to decide on a plan of action and get to it. Perhaps if she climbed atop the train and made her way to the engine she would be safe until the train stopped. Then she could escape while Hub was unaware of her whereabouts. She didn't want to have to chase that murdering scoundrel to the ends of the earth to see him get his comeuppance, but better that than winding up dead.

There was a hitch in July's plan, however. Maneuvering around the partially open sliding door in order to reach the steps that ascended to the top of the car was no small feat, especially while the train was rumbling full speed down the tracks. In fact, from where July stood, craning her neck around the door, the task looked damned near impossible.

Before she had the opportunity to devise a safer mode of escape, she heard a scraping noise on the top of the freight car. Fear chipped at her composure when she realized Hub Butler was about to make his entrance, via the trap door atop the car. Quickly, she eased the sliding door shut and picked her way around the freight to hide. She had one advantage, she reasoned, and she intended to make the most of it. Hub didn't know she had gotten free, and he didn't know where to locate her among the sacks and crates. With the element of surprise on her side, and with any luck at all, she could club him over the head with a makeshift weapon, stack the crates up like a ladder, and climb atop the train.

With her heart pounding, July scrunched down between the sacks of flour and the crates of shovels, her gaze lifting as moonlight filtered through the trap door. A shadowed form loomed in the light and then dropped to the floor of the car with a soft thud. July assumed Hub had landed on a sack of flour since puffs of white rose around him. He sputtered, coughed, and cursed as he stumbled over the sacks, half-blinded by the flour. But he was now easier to see in the moonlight since he was as white as a proverbial ghost.

While he fumbled his way toward the corner where he had left July, she used her dagger to quietly pry open one of the crates which contained shovels. She kept one eye trained on the floured wraith and the other on the crate, hoping no sound would betray her. When the nails creaked as they were pried up, she halted her efforts until Hub's stumbling camouflaged the sound. When he reached the far corner and found the empty wool sack, a furious growl exploded from his lips. July made use of the noise to wedge another nail loose.

"I know you're in here." Hub jerked his pistol from beneath his jacket to point it in every direction. "You won't escape me."

July disagreed. She gave herself a sporting chance. Slim but sporting.

When the ghoulish vision inched along the wall, July

slipped her hand inside the crate to grasp the handle of a shovel. Ever so gently, she eased the spade toward her, but it scraped against the shovels beside it. She cursed inwardly when Hub wheeled toward the sound and fired, flattening herself on the floor. Curse the man! He wasn't going to give her half a chance.

"I've dealt with far more clever individuals," Hub assured her as he eased toward the sound. "That wily husband of yours, for one. He didn't . . ." His voice trailed off and taunting laughter rumbled in his chest as he zigzagged around the crates, careful not to expose himself as a target.

July frowned at his words. Nacona didn't *what?* she wondered. Recognize him perhaps? July's heart catapulted into her throat as understanding dawned on her. Was Hub implying that he had fooled Nacona? July swallowed hard. Was this man actually Charley Brazil without beard and mustache, living under an assumed name?

Icy dread ran up July's spine. She had the unnerving feeling she knew why Hub—or Charley Brazil—had tried to frame Nacona for C. L. Chamber's murder. Hub had known Nacona by sight, but Nacona had had only a vague description of him. Could it be that the elusive outlaw truly had been in Wyoming all this time? July had said he might be here to get Nacona to agree to take this case. Well, this could be Charley Brazil living under an assumed name. No wonder Nacona swore the man had dropped off the face of the earth. Suddenly, July froze. If her assumptions were correct, she was in more trouble than she'd first thought.

"You may as well show yourself, July," Hub insisted as

he dashed behind another crate for protection. "If you do, I'll go easy on you. In fact, we might even strike a bargain."

How stupid did this desperado think she was? July inched the shovel closer. Although she was competent with the dagger, thanks to her brothers' instruction, she didn't dare use it except as a last resort. If she missed her target, she would have nothing but the shovel when it came time to square off against his loaded Colt .45. July didn't like the odds. They weren't in her favor.

"You know I've wanted you since the moment I saw you." Hub slid past one crate to position himself behind another. "Angel and Rose meant nothing to me. They were only available and convenient. But you're more than enough woman. Together we can make a new start and live a life of luxury."

July would rather be dead than allow this murdering viper to touch her. The very thought made her nauseous.

"What do you say, July? Do we have a deal?"

She said nothing. She simply leaned back to slit open the flour sack behind her. If Hub pounced, July intended to blind him and wallop him upside the head before he filled her full of lead.

Hub scowled at the infuriating silence. "Very well then, you leave me little choice." He aimed toward the sound he'd heard earlier and fired.

July ducked away as sparks and bullets ricocheted off the shovels beside her. That was close! Twelve inches to the left and she would have been a goner! If only she could hold out until Hub crept within spade-length. But her nerves were on edge, and her hands were shaking. She knew she was dealing with a deadly assassin. The nefarious Hub Butler was rotten to the core. He had proved himself a killer.

"Enough of this," Hub sneered maliciously, his patience depleted. "Come out where I can see you, or I'll fill this freight car full of—"

July leaped forward, certain she'd have no other chance before Hub began firing wildly. As the knights of old charged into battle with lances poised, she attacked, shovel in one hand, a fistful of flour in the other. The instant Hub cocked his pistol, July hurled flour in his eyes and swung the spade toward his Colt. The bullet zinged off the steel head of the shovel, and July whipped her improvised weapon back to make a second strike.

This time the spade connected with Hub's head. A furious roar escaped his lips when he staggered sideways. But to July's dismay, the blow didn't knock him unconscious. It only infuriated him. When he bounded up to attack, she swung wildly and stepped back, stumbling over the open sack of flour. Another puffy cloud fogged the car, and July cursed her own clumsiness. Now she was as easy to see as Hub was.

The instant she saw him make a dive toward her, she scooped up two handfuls of flour and flung them in his face. Before he landed atop her, she rolled to the floor and twisted to retrieve her shovel. As luck would have it, Hub found it first. With a snarl, he swung the makeshift weapon, but July was not only curious as a cat, she was as agile as one, too. She hurtled toward the nearest crate, seeking protection. The spade shattered the wood and answered July's hasty prayer for deliverance. A crate of lanterns might not be considered weapons by anyone else, but to July they were as good as grenades. With both hands, she hurled the missiles at Hub, giving him no time to gather his legs beneath him and strike her with the spade. Glass shattered everywhere, leaving Hub to curse a blue streak.

With a mutinous sneer, he defied the oncoming projectiles by deflecting them with his spade. July let out a shriek when he raised the shovel over his head like an ax and swung down with such force that he could have severed her neck from her shoulders. But fear had put her on her feet, and she was up and gone before the hatchetlike blow shattered what was left of the wooden crate. In frantic desperation, Hub swung the shovel up like a spear and heaved it at the white apparition that darted toward another corner of the freight car.

A howl of pain erupted from July's lips when the spade stabbed her shoulder. Before she could recover, Hub sprang at her, forcing her down onto the sacks of grain.

"Now, little witch, you'll pay for defying me!" he vowed as he straddled her hips.

But taking this feisty wildcat was too great a temptation. Hub had ached to steal Nacona's Bleu's wife right out from under his nose. Well, this was his chance, before he permanently silenced this cunning vixen. Roughly, he grabbed the front of July's shirt, but his satisfaction departed when he felt a knife at his back. July had retrieved her dagger from her boot. As Hub arched back to rip the fabric of her shirt, the blade grazed his side before he knocked the weapon aside, sending it cartwheeling over the sacks of feed and out of sight.

Desperation overwhelmed July in that horrifying moment when he groped at her. She doubled her fists and swung at him with both. The simultaneous blows earned her a backhand across the cheek—Hub's favorite method of retaliating against females, other than outright murder.

Suddenly, his need to appease his lust was overshadowed by fury. This she-cat was almost more than he could handle. She was the most competent female he had ever met, and he thought better of risking his life for the sake of male desire. If he didn't dispose of this tigress and quickly, she might get the best of him. She'd come too damned close already.

Hub grabbed July by the hair and jerked her up, forcing her to stand. Although July fought with every ounce of strength she possessed, he dragged her toward the sliding door. She kicked and screamed, but Hub's fierce grasp on her hair made it difficult for her to attack him and impossible to squirm away.

Horrified, July watched him push open the door of the swift-moving car. When he tried to shove her out, July set her feet and anchored herself to the edge of the door. Even her toes curled like cat's claws in an attempt to dig in. The timbered embankment below her looked like instant death as she clung to the edge of the door. She saw the silvery reflection of moonlight on water not far off and spied a trestle. If she could hold out for another few seconds she could plunge into the river instead of the trees, giving herself a better chance of survival.

July prayed as she clutched at the wooden door and dug in her nails. Hub braced himself behind her. He was as determined to force her into the trees below as she was not to fall. She pushed backward when he shoved her forward, but the instant she could see water beneath her, she unclamped her fists from the door and wheeled about

442

to sink her nails into Hub. She might wind up dead, but, by God, she was taking this murderer with her. At least Nacona would have some consolation in knowing she had disposed of the ringleader of the thieves, even if he didn't realize that this was his brother's killer.

A yelp of disbelief burst from Hub's lips when July caught him off guard. Without her resistance, his forward momentum launched both of them off the speeding train and into a vast nothingness. Worse, July had twisted in midair leaving him on the bottom and her on the top as they plunged into the river. Water shot upward as they sank beneath the surface.

July had taken a deep breath before their dive took them into the inky depths. Now, curling her legs beneath her, she pressed her feet against Hub's shoulders, employing him as a springboard to propel herself upward while he floundered beneath her. Since the fall hadn't killed her, July burst to the surface and paddled toward shore. She wasn't about to risk having Hub drown her.

Although she didn't consider herself a strong swimmer, she was adequate. Fortunately for her, Hub was not. It took him longer to reach the shore, giving her a head start. July thrashed through the reeds and scrabbled up the steep incline toward the cover of the timber. Braving a glance over her shoulder, she saw Hub clambering ashore, gasping for breath. Now was her chance to put some distance between them and save herself from another harrowing experience like the one in the freight car. With fierce determination, she ran as fast as her legs would carry her. She knew beyond a shadow of a doubt that this murdering scoundrel was as intent on catching her as she was on escaping.

* * *

Nacona reined his steed to a halt at one of the round-houses situated between Cheyenne and Laramie. Since he had checked the schedule, he knew the train had stopped once again to take on passengers and water and supplies. Each time it was delayed, he gained on it. Every precious minute brought him closer to July, and he refused to let himself consider what might happen to her while he frantically raced along the tracks, closing the distance between them.

Nacona's gelding was lathered with sweat and breathing heavily, and had begun to stumble from sheer exhaustion. He had pushed the steed to its limit, just as he had pushed himself in his attempt to rescue July from certain death. His desperate gaze circled the depot and landed on a string of saddled horses. He dismounted from his steed and leaped into the nearest saddle.

"That's outright theft!" Gresham MacKenzie exclaimed as he reined to a stop. "Horse thievery is punishable by hanging."

Nacona's blazing black eyes drilled into the man who was two years his senior and who spouted law at the most ridiculous moments. "Your problem, MacKenzie, is that you don't know how to bend the rules or simply ignore them the way your sister does."

"I broke them when I took a few punches at you," Gresham reminded him huffily.

"Then break another one and confiscate a fresh horse," Nacona ordered as he wheeled his new steed around. "You can live by the law, but that won't do July a helluva lot of good right now. She may have little time left!"

The words whipped past Gresham as Nacona galloped off. Gresham thought about what he had said and glanced back at his brothers.

"Steal yourself a horse," he commanded as he reined close enough to hop onto a fresh mount.

Calvin and Ethan followed suit. Killer lagged behind, his tongue hanging out. But when the rescue brigade trotted off once again, Killer quickened his pace.

Bullets spattered in the dirt behind them when the men who owned the horses realized that persons unknown had made off with their mounts. But neither Nacona nor the MacKenzies glanced back to monitor the activities of the men outside the railroad roundhouse. They were intent on pursuit. Nacona had voiced the gloomy truth. July was in the clutches of a known murderer!

Hub braced himself against a tree and sucked in huge gulps of air. Damn that tigress. She had more stamina and endurance than he'd thought such a dainty female could possess. He considered trying to catch up with his luggage and the satchel of stolen money that was headed to California without him. But with July running around loose, he would be doomed. He had to dispose of that wily minx. If he could overtake her . . .

His calculating gaze circled the surroundings. July would travel parallel to the tracks since she was in unfamiliar territory. Hub had traveled this area several times while planning train holdups. If he could follow a higher trail while July raced along by the tracks he could easily compensate for the distance between them. Mulling over that logical theory, Hub dashed up the slope, a sinister smile on his face. This time the element of surprise would be on *his* side. Before long July would be running straight toward him, and he would put an end to this bundle of trouble.

Panting for breath, July clutched at a tree for support. Her lungs felt as if they were about to burst. Apprehensively, she glanced behind her, but the shadowy image that had darted in and out of the moonlight had disappeared completely. She could only hope Hub had collapsed in exhaustion. But she wasn't counting on it, though she was near collapse herself. Racing up and down hills, zigzagging around trees, and forging through the underbrush had cost her considerable strength and energy. But she refused to allow herself to pause for more than a minute before bounding off again.

Concerned about the possibility of getting lost in unfamiliar terrain, July stuck to the steel rails. She knew there was a depot somewhere to the east since the train had stopped while she was regaining consciousness. But it was difficult to estimate how far the train had traveled while she was matching wits and shovels with Hub. Her only hope was to follow the tracks until she found someone who could protect her from this killer.

Inhaling deeply, July pushed away from the tree and trotted down the slope. She had just topped another rise when a shadow sprang out at her. A bloodcurdling scream exploded from her lips when she realized Hub had somehow managed to cut her off. Instinctively, she raised her knee, kicking him with deadly accuracy in the most vulnerable part of his anatomy. When he groaned and reflexively doubled over to protect himself from another punishing blow, July sailed off. Now only a few precious feet separated her from disaster.

As she dashed eastward, Nacona's black-diamond eyes came to mind and silently commanded her to push herself to the limit despite complaining muscles and burning lungs. She had to think about what awaited her in Cheyenne—about the man whose love had become the most important thing in her life. The thought of never seeing that midnight-haired giant again was agonizing.

A tormented moan gushed from July's lips when she caught her foot on a fallen log and skidded across the grass, banging her chin as she went. She seemed to be moving in slow motion as she dragged herself onto all fours to dart off again. She had just gained her feet when Hub pounced on her. His arms locked around her knees, flinging her forward to mutter curses into the grass. Although July bucked and swung about wildly, he grabbed her shoulders and forced her to turn her head to meet his diabolical sneer. As his curled fingers clamped around her neck, July screeched at the top of her lungs.

Spasms of pain crossed her face when Hub leered down at her and dug his fingers into her throat with deadly intent. In panic, she clutched at the hands fastening around her neck like a vise, cutting off precious air. But she was no match for the snarling brute who was slowly but surely choking the life out of her. Her grasp on his hands, and on reality, was ebbing away. The dark world around her faded into gray shadows as she gasped for one last breath of air. . . .

Chapter 27

July's terrified scream went right through Nacona, bringing with it stark fear. Desperate, he urged his steed through the underbrush, trying to locate the source of the sound. It was as if he were reliving that fateful day when his brother had been bushwhacked. Cold dread encased him as his mount thrashed through the maze of trees, guided by moonlight and pure instinct.

A second shriek—one that lacked the intensity of the first—sent a chill rippling through Nacona. For a moment it was as if his life-sustaining functions had ceased. His breath froze in his throat.

Another strangled groan pierced the night air and speared his tortured soul. Nacona mercilessly kicked his weary steed, refusing to let the animal break stride. He kept waiting for another sound to encourage him, to reassure him that July was still alive. But now there was nothing but the creak of leather and the huffing of his winded steed.

The instant Nacona spied the two silhouettes in the clearing, something inside him snapped. He had arrived in time to watch July collapse, unable to fend off her assailant, the man Nacona suspected of haunting him for the past two years. As he closed the distance between them he prayed that July would stir, would give him some indication that she was still alive. But she didn't move . . . because she couldn't. She, like C.L. and Angel and maybe even Shandin, had fallen victim to this murdering bastard.

In those tense few seconds, while his steed pounded out a death knell with its hooves, Nacona saw nothing but red, heard only the echo of July's cries in the silence.

Swearing colorfully, Hub released his death grip on July's neck and bounded to his feet. The gargantuan man racing toward him like a centaur through the timber struck a chord of panic in him. As a rumble shook the earth Hub stared up at murderous anger and black hair caught in the moonlight. He had prided himself on outsmarting the famed detective. But terror surged through his veins as Nacona, like a vengeful demon, blazed a path toward him. The need to turn and run overwhelmed Hub. He couldn't seem to move fast enough to escape the savagery of Nacona's attack.

A growl reminiscent of that of a pouncing lion resounded through the trees and hung in the damp night air. Nacona was fury incarnate. Seeing July lying motionless on the grass had sent him over the edge. He saw neither the trees nor the steel rails gleaming above him. He saw only the man who represented all that was cruel and destructive in this world.

Nacona displayed no mercy as he raced his winded steed toward Hub. Leather creaked and hooves pounded the ground. Nacona knew July's fate. Vengeance was all he had left, and that consumed him.

Without batting an eye, he galloped straight into Hub.

A howl of pain burst from Butler's lips as one thousand pounds of horseflesh slammed against him, forcing him onto the grass. Frantic, he rolled away from the deadly hooves and clawed his way back to his feet, despite a searing pain in his leg and back, but before he could burst into a run, Nacona leaped from the saddle and took him back to the ground.

Pent-up anger was behind each power-packed blow Nacona delivered. Fists drove into Hub's chin and cheeks, his eyes. In desperation, he shoved Nacona away and darted off like a frightened jackrabbit. He was halfway up the embankment, hoping to climb through the wooden trestles of the track that spanned the gully, when Nacona launched himself through the air.

Nacona knew he had lost July forever, but he refused to let her assassin escape. He had lost his brother and now his wife—the only woman who had ever mattered to him. Not July, too! his tortured mind screamed.

Curses burst from his lips as he pounded Hub into the ground. Flesh smacking flesh, Hub moaning and groaning but unable to deflect the blows. Each time he tried to throw an answering punch, an infuriated Nacona responded by sending blow after blow to Hub's jaw. Butler was no match for this looming giant. The bone-jarring blows were beating the life out of him. . . .

* * *

"Oh my God, no!" Gresham gasped when he spied July's lifeless body sprawled in the grass.

Killer had spotted her first, leading the MacKenzies to their motionless sister. The mutt whined and howled like a dying coyote before licking July's ashen cheek as if to urge her back to life. But she simply lay there with arms outstretched, her tangled blond hair spilling onto the ground like a pool of faded sunshine.

All three MacKenzies were off their horses in a single bound to gather around July. Gresham propped her head against his shoulder while Calvin pressed the heels of his hands against her abdomen, desperately trying to force her to breathe. But that did not revive her. Frantic, Gresham rolled her limp body over his lap so Calvin could press his hands against her back.

And while they tried to rescuscitate their sister, they heard the thud of body blows and the vicious snarls that erupted from Nacona's lips. Even when July finally began to breathe on her own accord, her brothers found their attention partially on the ominous giant throwing punches like a madman.

July's lashes fluttered up to see Nacona spotlighted in moonbeams. He and Hub were halfway up the slope that led to the tracks. The wooden trestle that spanned the ravine cast crisscrossed shadows on the rocky hillside. Although she had seen Nacona in action before, she was no less awed by the imposing figure of a man who lifted Hub up by the lapels of his coat to bury a meaty fist in his soft underbelly. Each time Hub's legs began to fold beneath him, Nacona jerked him upright with another blow that slammed belly against his backbone.

"Good Lord!" Ethan croaked, goggle-eyed.

The MacKenzies had pounced on Nacona at the arched gateway of the Golden Spur several hours earlier. They had caught this powerful hulk of a man unaware, and they had still wound up with puffy lips and swollen jaws. But when Nacona Bleu was prepared for battle, he could turn a man into mincemeat. Without a platoon of reinforcements, confronting this giant was suicidal.

"Bleu is going to beat the man to death," Calvin declared.

Once July was breathing normally, and Killer had wedged his way between the MacKenzie brothers to offer his affection, Gresham bounded to his feet. He rushed up the hill, Ethan and Calvin following. Before Nacona could throw another punch, Ethan grabbed his right arm and Calvin latched onto his left. Gresham stepped between Nacona and Hub, who slithered to the ground like a snake.

"Bleu! July is still alive!" Gresham blared. He honestly wondered if anything could shatter the icy glaze that frosted those black eyes. The man was in a murderous rage, numb to all except his need for vengeance. "Don't kill that bastard with your bare hands. The law demands that he be tried and sentenced in a court of justice."

Nacona shook himself from his trance when Gresham's words soaked into his tormented mind. His ruffled raven head swiveled to stare at July who had levered herself up against a tree, her arm draped over the huge mutt that nuzzled affectionately against her.

"July? You okay?" Nacona questioned, refusing to take Gresham's word for anything.

"Yes, but I must admit I've enjoyed better days," she bleated, her vocal cords half-collapsed. She laid her head back and drew in a refreshing breath. Ah, it was nice to breathe again. Hub had come within a hairbreadth of launching her into eternity.

When the taut muscles in Nacona's body relaxed a smidgen, Ethan and Calvin eased their restraining grasps. To their surprise, Nacona shook himself loose and shoved Gresham aside as if he were a hundred-pound weakling. To Nacona's way of thinking, Hub Butler deserved no trial. His list of crimes was extensive, and the long arm of the law was about to deliver the remainder of its punishment.

"Bleu, the law states—" Gresham bellowed and then snapped his mouth shut when Nacona wheeled around to glare bullets at him.

"Not this time, MacKenzie," Nacona growled in a voice that rumbled with barely controlled fury.

In pronounced strides, Nacona followed Hub to the tracks atop the hill. Hub's puffy eyes widened in fear when he saw the towering mass of fury stalking him. Stumbling, he scurried along the tracks and then halted when he heard a low, threatening snarl behind him. He glanced back at Nacona's dark, foreboding face, and then he peered at the trestle that bridged the boulder-covered gully below.

"This one's for July." Nacona drew back a fist and struck out, two hundred and ten pounds behind the blow.

Hub threw up his forearm to block the attack, but Nacona's surge sent him stumbling backward. He teetered precariously on a boulder, in desperation attempting to latch onto the trestle that was just beyond his reach. Then, with a terrified howl, he toppled over the edge to collide with the boulders that filled the deep ravine.

454

Without one ounce of regret, Nacona watched Hub's feless form tumble over rocks to finally land in a broken eap. Then came deafening silence. For a time, Nacona tared over the cliff, recalling all those tormenting weeks nd months of searching for a man he had been unable o recognize or locate. He was relatively certain Hub 3utler was Charley Brazil, the mustache and beard which aad once disguised his ordinary features now shaved. Charley had undoubtedly taken a new name and set aimself up in a new life, but he had reverted to his old vays of stealing and killing, even devising new ways to go about them. Shandin Bleu had been just one of many victims who had been cut down by the desperado who aad played the respectable citizen in Cheyenne.

While Nacona stood poised on the ledge, silhouetted by moonlight, July dragged her feet beneath her. Although he was curious to know what her brothers were doing in he middle of Wyoming, her attention was on the towering giant who loomed like a monument on the ridge above her. As if she were in a trance, she rose and headed oward Nacona. She longed to tell him of her suspicions about Hub, to share the grief he had harbored for two ong years, to help him put the past behind him at last.

"July, get hold of yourself," Ethan muttered when he saw his sister amble past him. "Now's your chance to escape that maniac."

"We'll have the marriage annulled," Gresham promised her. "It's only a matter of a few legal documents. I'll have them drawn up."

It was as if July heard not a word. And when Calvin reached out to detain her, she pried his fingers from her forearm without glancing at him, then eagerly ascended

455

the hill. She had come within inches of losing her life.
Each moment was now like a cherished bonus—a second
chance she wouldn't have had if Nacona hadn't arrived
when he did. Somehow he had found her before Hub
finished her off.

Her arms went up to caress his broad muscular back,
feeling his whipcord muscles flex and relax beneath her
tender touch. "I love you, Nacona Bleu," she whispered.
"I can't bring your brother back, nor can I take his place,
but I think perhaps you just found the man you hunted."
She moved in front of him to frame his face in her hands,
holding his unblinking gaze. "I will always be here when
you need me, just as you were at the moment I needed
you most."

July was suddenly engulfed in protective arms.
Nacona's entire body shook as he held her to him and
nuzzled her throat to kiss away the memory of Hub's
vicious attack. His hands coasted down her body in a
gentle massage that soothed her like a healing balm. For
a long, shuddering moment, Nacona clung to July before
lifting her clean off the ground to devour her with a kiss
that bespoke the riptide of emotion churning inside him.

"Well, if that isn't the most pathetic thing I've ever
seen," Ethan snorted disgustedly. "The man's a certifia-
ble lunatic, and July has become as deranged as he is.
After all he has done to her . . . now this." He expelled a
derisive snort. "She almost got killed because of him."

"It makes absolutely no sense," Gresham agreed, staring bewilderedly at his sister who had always made a habit
of keeping men at an arm's length. July had practically
invited this crazed man to take her in his arms. Why, any

456

second now, Bleu would probably hurl *her* off the cliff to join his first victim!

"I think we should have them both committed," Calvin advised, watching his sister snuggle into Nacona's arms as if she belonged in them.

"Well, I, for one, do not intend to stand here all night," Gresham declared. He straightened his cuffs, squared his shoulders, and plowed up the hill to retrieve his dazed sister. "July, we are leaving this very minute. Say your last good-bye if you feel you must, and let's go!"

Nacona glanced over July's shoulder to see the Mac-Kenzie males approaching. "I can see why you abandoned those stuffy brothers of yours." His chin nuzzled her satiny cheek. "One is extremely hot tempered, the second is quick to react, and the third spouts rules and regulations like a talking law book."

July twisted to see her brothers marching toward her. "I wonder what they're doing here in the first place?" she mused aloud. "And how they found me?"

Nacona's arm glided around her waist to pull her against him as he dropped a quick kiss on her cheek. "They said they came to save you from me. They somehow got the idea that I had raped and abused you, and then forced you into wedlock. They also said something about me framing you for a murder I'd committed. For detectives, they certainly didn't get their story straight before they tried to drag me out of the saddle and beat me to a pulp."

July peered up to note that Nacona had a puffy jaw and the makings of a magnificent black eye. She had assumed Hub had landed the blows, but she should have known

457

better. Butler couldn't have matched Nacona's massive size and overpowering strength. No, it would take at least three men to compete with Nacona Bleu.

"July, we're going home. Now," Gresham declared with his customary tone of authority. He was the eldest MacKenzie, and for years he had been in charge of the younger ones.

July's chin tilted to a stubborn angle. "No," she said flat out.

Three pistols slid from their holsters. Nacona would have done likewise to counter the threat, but he had drawn July against his right hip, making it difficult to get his hand on his Colt. His other pistol had fallen by the wayside during the scuffle with Hub.

Quickly, Calvin snaked out a hand and pried July out of Nacona's grasp. "Gresh said we're leaving."

"And you, Mr. Bleu, can expect to see us in court when we press charges against you," Gresham said sharply.

"Oh, for heaven's sake," July grumbled. "If the three of you would just listen, I—"

"Quiet, July. We'll handle this," Ethan insisted as he steered her down the hill. "You're out from under that devil's spell now. You don't have to lie and defend him. He no longer poses a threat."

Although July resisted, her brothers forced her along and shepherded her toward their tethered horses.

"You have a lot of explaining to do," Gresham muttered to his sister. "I do not appreciate receiving telegrams that stated you were having a wonderful time at Aunt Betty's, especially when our dear aunt wrote to inquire when the four of us were coming for a visit."

So that was how they had discovered she wasn't where

she'd said she'd be. Aunt Betty had fouled up her well-laid plans.

"Or did Bleu order you to send those messages to us?" Calvin questioned.

"You cannot imagine how we felt when we arrived in Dodge City to learn that you had been attacked by that rapscallion who is a friend of Masterson and Earp," Ethan added. "Civilization has yet to catch up with that rowdy town."

"And we had the most exasperating train ride across the plains," Calvin put in. "So many delays and mechanical breakdowns."

July realized her brothers were hell-bent on giving her a blow-by-blow account of all that had occured on their way to her. When she tried to interrupt them to explain the error of their thinking as it pertained to Nacona, she was scolded harshly and her brothers assured her that the black-eyed devil had somehow bent her to his will. Finally, July gave up. She was totally exhausted after her arduous experiences. One terrifying ordeal had followed so quickly on the heels of another that her strength had been sapped.

She propped her head on Ethan's shoulder and clamped her arms around his waist while his steed trotted eastward. July didn't blame Nacona for keeping his distance. Her brothers refused to listen to reason, and he had had an exhausting night himself. If her suspicions proved correct, he had just clashed with his past, so he had a great many ghosts to lay to rest. If he truly wanted her in his life, after sorting out his emotions, he would come back to her. No one could stop Nacona, not even her brothers.

In the meantime, July would catch up on much-needed

rest. Her body ached all over. She leaned against her brother for support in the saddle and fell asleep from sheer fatigue.

Nacona did a great deal of soul-searching during his journey back to Cheyenne. He purposely didn't catch up with the MacKenzies. They had come a long way to ensure that their sister was safe and sound. Safe anyway, Nacona qualified. The MacKenzie men had made it obvious that they did not believe July of sound mind. What they thought of Nacona and of men in his profession was obvious. But Nacona wasn't fond of July's brothers, either. He had them pegged for snobbish muckamucks. Their holier-than-thou attitude didn't suit him.

July had told Nacona how overprotective her brothers were and she had not exaggerated one iota. Even to Nacona, it had been almost amusing to watch them fuss over her as if she were a helpless child. And the MacKenzie males had minds like mortar. Once they were set, it took a sledgehammer to make a crack in them. Those stoic musketeers had decided Nacona wasn't good enough for their precious little sister; they believed the worst about him. Nacona didn't know how they had managed to get the facts mixed up, but they certainly had. He wouldn't ask those uppity detectives to investigate the simplest case. They leaped from one wild conjecture to another.

Nacona heaved a sigh and set such spiteful thoughts aside. Though he longed to have July with him, he did need this time alone to sort out his feelings. The shock of realizing that Hub Butler might very well have been

Charley Brazil had knocked him for a loop. He still had no positive proof, but his intuition told him he had found the man he'd hunted. When the past collided with the present, and July wound up in that bastard's clutches, Nacona's composure had cracked. Glimpses of his brother's last few moments had bombarded him, converging into the tormenting fear that he would be left holding July's lifeless body in his arms, just as he had held Shandin's, watching him slip away. When Nacona had seen July lying so still and lifeless, something inside him had shattered. He truly had become mad, so intent on revenge that rational thought had been impossible.

Now he had gotten his long-sought revenge and his brother could rest in peace. At least he *hoped* he had discovered Shandin's killer. He might never know for certain, and as time went by, he would probably begin to wonder if he had leaped to an erroneous conclusion. Damn, he had to know one way or another. He wanted satisfaction, but what he'd gotten was an inescapable feeling of loneliness and uncertainty. His investigations had always been carried out for one ultimate purpose—to locate Charley Brazil. Now Nacona had no motivation. And without that rambunctious beauty to preoccupy him, he had no direction.

As the shock of what had happened wore off, Nacona became angry at July. She had practically invited death by snooping around for more information. He should have nailed her feet to the floor when he'd left her at the ranch. Even then, he'd have worried about her while he was gone.

July was a daredevil. How she had eluded her captor, Nacona didn't know. Luckily, she was almost as good at getting herself out of trouble as she was at getting into it. But if he hadn't showed up when he did, she would be dead. How dare she put him through such torment! If he managed to convince those bullheaded MacKenzies that his intentions toward their sister were honorable, he would have to contend with this rambunctious female. He would have to read her the riot act. From now on, when he told that feisty nymph to stay out of trouble while he was gone she'd damned well better! She had already scared him enough. If she didn't slow her frantic pace, she would drive *him* to an early grave. And if she ever . . .

Nacona let out his breath in a rush and halted in front of the Cheyenne Hotel. He might as well sleep the rest of the night away. He wasn't in the mood to storm the ranch to confront the MacKenzies. When that time came, he planned to be armed to the teeth and spouting a few orders of his own. If those three thought they were taking the best thing that ever happened to him away, they had damned well better think again! July meant everything to him. After coming so close to losing her earlier in the evening, he was not about to have her whisked out of his life, no matter how many laws and threats the MacKenzies spouted at him.

Chapter 28

It was with quiet precaution that July eased open her bedroom window and clutched her skirts around her prior to climbing outside. Silvery beams and darting shadows skipped across the ground as fluffy clouds paraded past the moon. A nap had relieved her exhaustion, and now she was as restless as a caged cat. Although her fiercely protective brothers demanded that she recuperate from her near-fatal ordeal, there were still several questions she wanted answered, and that must be done immediately.

July had trained herself to marshal the facts while pursuing an investigation. Nacona had once told her that a good detective never relied on assumptions. Since she had been unable to get a complete confession from Hub Butler—or Charley Brazil—she intended to interrogate the one person who seemed to know the man better than most—Cheyenne Rose. She refused to wait until Rose had gotten wind of Hub's demise, fearing the madam of the Pleasure Parlor would then disappear into thin air. She owed Nacona something in return for all the trouble she had caused him. If she could confirm her suspicions through Rose, she could take a tremendous load off his mind.

With the silence of a stalking cat, July tiptoed across the lawn to reach the stables. She had learned from the cowhands that Nacona had posted sentinels to keep watch on the outlaws he had collected. Nonetheless she hoped to sneak inside and retrieve a horse without having to explain herself. No such luck. Ot Knott arrived in the barn a few seconds after she did.

"Now Missus Bleu, I know it ain't my place to tell ya what to do—"

"Then don't," July advised, casting him a warning glance. It didn't faze Ot. She wondered if perhaps the darkness caused her practiced stare to be ineffective. Whatever the case, Ot seemed bent on spouting his opinions come high water, hell, or both.

"Mr. Bleu was powerfully put out when he came back to find ya gone. I don't know what the blazes is goin' on 'round here 'cause nobody seems to have the time to tell me nothin'." He heaved a frustrated sigh as he watched July lead her steed from the stall and wrestle with the saddle. "If Mr. Bleu was here—"

"Which he isn't," July pointed out. She then realized she had become as bad about interrupting as Nacona was.

"He wouldn't like ya traipsin' off in the middle of the night. He had a conniption fit when ya raced off in the middle of the day, ya know. And wherever ya think yer goin', I don't think ya oughta go!" Ot loudly protested. It was a waste of breath.

"This can't wait." July reached beneath the mare to

fasten the girth. "I appreciate your concern, Ot, I truly do." She grabbed the bit and nudged it into the steed's mouth, waiting for the mare to roll it over her tongue before pulling the bridle into place. "I need some answers, and the person who can supply them might not be there in the morning. Perhaps is not even now."

"I wish ya wouldn't do this," Ot pleaded as July swung into the saddle, her skirts and petticoats settling over the mare like a blanket. "I'm liable to catch hell again from them brothers of yers, just like I did from Mr. Bleu."

July trotted her steed up to the wiry little man who blocked her path. "You have nothing to tell my brothers because you weren't here. We didn't have this conversation, Ot," she told him meaningfully.

"But—" Ot wasn't allowed to finish his objection. He had to leap sideways to prevent being sideswiped by the mare and her very determined rider.

With a curse, Ot snatched his hat from his head, slammed it to the ground, and stamped on it. "That woman is the worst daredevil I ever did see!" he muttered.

Still grumbling over his—and everybody else's—inability to control July, Ot stalked back to his post. The lovely, high-spirited hellion seemed to thrive on danger. When Ot had first met July and Nacona, he'd considered the delicate beauty a mismatch for the swarthy, powerful gunslinger. But the better Ot got to know them, the more he realized they were just alike. They were confrontational individuals who refused to let well enough alone. And all things considered, Ot wasn't so sure that even the ominous giant who had rounded up the rustlers could handle a woman with such a reckless spirit. As far as Ot

Knott was concerned, it was an understatement to say that Nacona Bleu had his hands full with that rambunctious wife of his.

All was quiet at Cheyenne Rose's Pleasure Parlor when July arrived. The first rays of sunlight were lightening the sky, bathing the world in molten gold and blue. Tethering her mare, July crept in the back door of the bordello and made her way up to Rose's room. She grumbled under her breath when she surveyed the boudoir to find it devoid of the madam's belongings. Unless she missed her guess, Rose had packed up and left town. Either she'd heard what had happened to Hub or she'd finally given up on him and skipped town with whatever cash she had on hand.

Reversing direction, July descended the steps. Retrieving her mount, she trotted toward the railroad depot, hoping to intercept Rose before the madam caught a train. When she heard a whistle, a curse burst from her lips. She had no time to dawdle if she intended to catch the train that chugged southward, a puff of black smoke rolling over it in a tunnel-like cloud. July might be on a wild-goose chase, but she couldn't even waste a moment to interrogate the ticket agent.

Although she could handle a horse as well as the next person, trick riding wasn't her specialty. It might have to be, she told herself resolutely as she raced after the train, peering at the platform of the caboose. Had she known she was going to have to make a daring leap from the saddle to the railing of that car, she would have dressed appropriately.

466

Nudging her mare into a swifter pace, July drew her legs beneath her and clutched the pommel of the saddle for support. Her heart thudded in her chest as she focused on the speeding train. Then, with a prayer on her lips, she sprang from her steed and reached for the railing, her full skirts billowing about her.

Her jaw clenched in determination, July threw one leg over the railing and inhaled deeply. That had been simple enough. Well, perhaps not, she qualified, but at least it had been feasible. She was still in one piece. And after her death-defying plunge from the freight car into the river the previous day, this had been mere child's play.

Casting this thought aside, July scaled the metal ladder to the top of the caboose. She peered into the windowed hatch atop the car to see two agents dozing in their bunks. Certain that she hadn't been noticed, she made her way along the top of the car as quietly and carefully as possible considering where she was. Finally she eased down at the end of the caboose to tie her hampering skirts into a knot on her hip, to make it easier to walk atop the train without toppling to her death.

She then leaped onto the freight car and crawled along its top. She repeated that procedure until she reached the back end of the second-class passenger car that carried travelers south to Denver and beyond. Jumping onto its roof, July climbed down the ladder onto the platform. She then untied and fluffed out her skirt. After rearranging her windblown coiffure as best she could, she opened the door as casually as you please to survey the passengers on the wooden benches. Crammed together like sardines, they were attempting to sleep during these early morning hours. July remembered that she and Nacona had had to endure similar accommodations during their trek from Oakley to Denver.

She ambled down the aisle, searching for Rose. But the woman was not among the dozing passengers. July refused to be discouraged yet. She hadn't investigated the other second-class car, the sleeper or the parlor car, or the first-class accommodations.

Bound and determined, July eased open the door to be met by a rush of wind. Clutching the supporting beam, she opened the portal that led to the adjoining car. When she failed to locate Rose in that one, she felt discouraged. The sleeper posed more problems. July was forced to peek between curtains to inspect the inhabitants of upper and lower berths. Still no Rose. Had she miscalculated the woman? Had Rose rented a wagon or carriage and left town? Or was she calmly sitting inside the depot, awaiting another train? Maybe Rose hadn't heard about Hub's fate and had caught an earlier train, hoping to meet him in California. July had leaped to a conclusion. If Nacona had been with her, he would have admonished her.

Feeling a mite depressed, July wandered through the elaborately decorated parlor car that provided entertainment for first-class passengers. An unattended piano sat in one corner, and unoccupied tuft chairs lined the lavish velvet walls. Frustrated, July plunked down on a chair to relax for a few minutes. She felt like scolding herself for bounding from one conjecture to another. If Rose was aboard she had to be in the first-class car or the dining car. But the odds were now slimmer.

* * *

"Ethan," Gresham grumbled from his sandwiched position in bed, wedged between Calvin and his youngest brother. "Go let that whining mutt outside. He's been pawing at the door for an hour. July must be sleeping so soundly she can't hear him."

When Gresham nudged him with an elbow, Ethan rolled sideways, and the floor came up and hit him with incredible speed. Groggily, he fumbled his way across the unfamiliar room, annoyed that furniture kept darting out to trip him up. After feeling his way through the parlor, Ethan opened the door. Killer didn't stir a step. He merely cocked his head to the side, laid back his ears, and peered at Ethan.

"Well? Do you want to go out or not?" Ethan grumbled impatiently. "I don't know why July keeps a big mongrel like you in the house anyway. . . . Now, don't go off and sulk, you ugly hound. Come back here!"

When Killer padded toward July's bedroom, Ethan felt his way along the wall to fetch the mutt before July was aroused. She needed rest after her ordeals. Anger seized him when he spied Killer perched on the incongruous form beneath the quilts. The damned dog was going to wake July.

Ethan dashed over to retrieve Killer, but his irritation was transformed into suspicion when the lump on the bed didn't stir beneath the weight of the dog. Ethan flipped back the quilt to see pillows lined up to look like a sleeping body.

"Gresh! Cal! Get in here pronto!" Ethan shouted, causing Killer to bark.

At his distressed calls, bare feet hit the floor. To Ethan,

who was now fully awake and in a full-fledged snit, the commotion in the other bedroom sounded reassuring. Within moments, his bleary-eyed brothers stood wedged shoulder-to-shoulder in the doorway.

"What's the problem?" Calvin demanded as he massaged his aching knee.

"The usual one," Ethan muttered as he scooped up the pillows that should have been his sister. "July isn't where she's supposed to be. The dog brought me in here to point out the fact."

"Where the hell could she have gone now?" Gresham mused.

"Probably back to that no-account gunslinger," Ethan deduced.

"Get dressed," Gresham demanded. "When we catch up with that ornery little sister of ours, we're carting her onto the train and heading back to Kansas City. It's obvious she won't be her old self until that pistolero is out from underfoot. And bring that mutt with you," he added in afterthought. "Killer seems to understand July and her warped thinking better than anybody else around here."

With extreme haste the brothers stabbed arms and legs into clothes and scurried outside to saddle their mounts. Ot Knott took July's advice and pretended their conversation hadn't occurred. He simply made himself scarce when the MacKenzies jogged to the stables to saddle up and thunder off.

Armed to the teeth and expecting to find July nestled in Nacona's bed at the hotel, the MacKenzies tramped down the hall. Killer had his nose to the floor, checking

470

scents. When he sank down in front of one door and glanced up, Gresham shoved the door open and surged inside, pistol in hand.

Nacona came awake with a start and automatically reached for his Colt which lay on the night stand. His hand halted in midair when he realized the three musketeers were looming in the doorway, their weapons trained on him. He glanced at them in disgust. What nuisances these citified detectives were.

"Where is she?" Gresham demanded sharply.

"Where's who?" Nacona daringly propped himself against the headboard, despite the loaded pistols that were taking his measure.

"You know perfectly well who," Calvin muttered. "Where is July?"

"She's *supposed* to be with you." Nacona snorted insolently.

"Well, she's not. She sneaked off, and we expected she'd come to you since you seem to have some hold on the poor girl!" Gresham grumbled resentfully.

Nacona was on his feet in nothing flat. He grabbed his breeches and stuffed himself into them while hurling daggerlike glares at the MacKenzies. "And you called *me* a maniac?" He scoffed derisively. "You come bursting in, pointing pistols at me." He snatched up a pair of socks and hurriedly tugged them on. "You hauled July to the ranch, supposedly to keep an eye on her." He jerked on a boot and scowled when his left foot wound up in his right boot. "Don't tell me, let me guess. July escaped the master sleuths from Kansas City while they were snoring away." His mocking gaze raked the MacKenzies one by one, leaving little doubt as to what he thought of them.

471

"It's a wonder you have any clients or that you've solved a single case. You can't even keep track of one female who's related to you."

Ethan scowled, affronted by the insults. "You know how July is. She defies orders just to prove she can." He glared at Nacona. "Now where did you stash her?"

"I didn't stash her anywhere," Nacona snapped as he thrust a sinewy arm into his shirtsleeve. "I haven't seen her since last night. Maybe she got fed up with the three of you bossing her around and lit out to find someplace where she could breathe."

Gresham puffed up like a bullfrog. "The last thing we need from the likes of you is snide criticism, Mr. Bleu. We have yet to determine all that you coerced our sister into doing. But I assure you, when we gather all the facts, you'll be throwing yourself on the mercy of the court and viewing the world from behind bars. Furthermore, this ridiculous marriage will be annulled as soon as I can file the document. You are nowhere near good enough for a woman of July's breeding and education."

Nacona came dangerously close to planting his fist on his brother-in-law's condescending face. If he hadn't been concerned about July's safety, he might have done just that. But as usual, time was an issue when she was missing. Only the Lord knew what madcap caper she had launched herself into. Nacona wished he could read July's mind. Unfortunately, he didn't have a clue as to what was motivating her now. Maybe she had decided to shed her overprotective brothers. Or maybe she, like he, had considered quizzing Rose for answers. She might even have tried to locate Nacona in Cheyenne and been overtaken

by one of the drunken rakehells who prowled the streets.
. . .

Wheeling about, Nacona glanced down at the shaggy
mongrel July had relied heavily upon during the investigation. If anyone could locate her, Killer could. The poor
dog spent most of his time making sure his adopted owner
didn't get out of his sight, and when she did, he was
restless as a confined tiger.

Squatting down on his haunches, Nacona peered into
Killer's big black eyes. "Where is she? Go find July." Of
course, Nacona didn't expect the mutt to know what the
hell he said, but desperation prompted him to voice the
question and the command.

Lo and behold, Killer bounded up and trotted down
the hall. Grabbing his holsters and pistols, Nacona followed in his wake, the Mackenzies close behind. Nose to
the ground, Killer zigged and zagged from one side of the
street to the other, circling, doubling back, and then
romping off.

"I think you're giving that mutt more credit than he
deserves," Calvin grumbled sourly.

"You're welcome to get up your own search party if
you wish," Nacona offered sarcastically. "As for me, I'm
sticking with Killer."

A quarter of an hour later, even Nacona was ready to
give up on the shaggy mongrel. Killer appeared confused.
But when the mutt wound up at the train depot and then
rushed down the tracks like a house afire, Nacona's faith
was restored. What July might be doing on a southbound
train, he didn't know. But who was he to attempt to
second-guess that wild-spirited female?

An uneasy feeling constricted the region around his heart when he spied the buckskin mare July had become partial to riding. The horse was grazing along the tracks, and July was nowhere in sight. Nacona wondered if that woman was worth all the trouble she dragged him into. She never had a care about his concern for her safety. She just raced off, leaving him to fret and stew. He was beginning to understand why the MacKenzies were so fiercely protective of their younger sister. She needed a full-time chaperone.

"Has she always been like this?" He heard himself ask as he grabbed the reins of the riderless steed.

"Only since she was old enough to walk and talk," Gresham said begrudgingly. "The first words out of July's mouth were 'I can do it myself' and off she went to do just that." The eldest MacKenzie studied Nacona with a critical eye. "I still haven't figured out what is going on between the two of you, but I assure you, Mr. Bleu, you have misjudged us."

That makes us even, Nacona thought.

"July has always been too daring for her own good. She's been prepared to take on the devil himself if he dares to cross her." Gresham shot Nacona a glance that implied the rough-edged gunslinger ought to know all about devils, being one himself. "And she's keenly intelligent, impulsive, and unpredictable."

"There was a time, after we'd lost our parents, when July decided to carry on Papa's desire to race his thoroughbreds," Ethan said, adding his two cents' worth. "She garbed herself like a man, entered a race without our permission, and walked off with the prize. Immediately after that we sent her to a girls' boarding school in St. Louis to teach her to become a proper, dignified lady."

"Unfortunately, no walls could hold her." Calvin took up where Ethan left off. "She ran away twice in the first six months. The school administrator finally decided she was too difficult to handle—and that she was setting a bad example for the other young ladies."

"That was when we brought her back home and allowed her to join our detective agency and enroll in law school," Gresham continued as they trotted along beside the tracks. "That, too, was a mistake. July was born with too much spirit to be restricted to the acceptable confines for women. We were aware of that, but we thought we could watch her, permit her to do things that challenged her mind."

"But the problem was, the duties you assigned July didn't satisfy her," Nacona said. "She has always been a free spirit, by your own admission. You taught her to defend herself, to use all sorts of weapons, but then you refused to let her utilize the skills she'd strived so hard to perfect. You left her standing in your shadows, as if she counted for nothing." He flashed all three of them an accusing glance that scolded them for refusing to consider July's feelings.

"You have known July all your lives, yet you don't really understand her," Nacona chided. "You refuse to let her be the woman she is, and you have restrained her as if she were a child. She wanted to gain your notice, win your respect, and prove her worth, but you wouldn't allow her to live up to her potential. You smothered her until she rebelled against the limitations you set for her because she was a woman. July has strived to be just like the three of you, but you still see her as an obligation and a responsibility. She hates that most of all."

"Now see here, Bleu—"

Although Ethan tried to interrupt, Nacona hadn't finished saying his piece. "July wanted to make a name and a place for herself as a criminal investigator. She came to me in Dodge, demanding that I assist her in the investigation she had taken on in Wyoming, using my name and reputation as backing."

The MacKenzies gaped at Nacona and then frowned warily. The story he told was in direct contrast to their assessment of the situation. They had assumed their daring sister had left herself open to the rough-edged shootist and lust had gotten the better of him. Still, they now listened to Nacona's explanation.

"I refused July, of course," Nacona insisted. "But I needn't bother telling you that she does not accept no for an answer. She rushed to Bat Masterson's office, claiming I had attacked her, and she saw to it that I was herded into jail. She kept me there until I agreed to help her."

Nacona squirmed uneasily in the saddle. He had arrived at the difficult portion of the explanation. He knew the MacKenzies would have trouble believing this since they were fond of their sister, no matter how cunning and mischievous she was. He formulated his thoughts and stared at Killer, who was trotting beside the track as if he knew where he was going. If the dog did, he was the only one, Nacona mused glumly. He certainly hadn't determined the whys and wheres of July's disappearance—yet.

"Then what happened?" Calvin asked impatiently when Nacona paused longer than he deemed necessary.

"After mildewing in jail for several days, I agreed to assist July on one condition." Nacona wisely chose to stare straight ahead. The MacKenzies already believed him to be a scoundrel, and his next remarks would confirm their opinion. He wasn't in the mood to deflect venomous glowers.

"And what condition might that have been, Mr. Bleu?" Gresham's suspicious frown indicated that he already had a pretty good idea what a man like Nacona wanted from an irresistible young beauty like July.

"Privileges," Nacona admitted, his voice a little on the unsteady side.

The hot-tempered Ethan exploded like a keg of blasting powder. "You rapscallion! If you bargained for the kind of stipulations I think you did, you are beneath contempt! I should have blown you to kingdom come when I had the—"

"Clam up, Ethan," Gresham demanded in an authoritative tone. "I may not like what I hear—and I seriously doubt I will—but I would like to get to the bottom of this revolting business once and for all."

Ethan snapped his mouth shut, but muffled curses still spewed from between his clenched teeth.

"My terms were to have July in my bed," Nacona forced himself to say. When the MacKenzies glared, he hurried on. "I knew she would be outraged by my counterproposition. That was why I offered it—so that *she* would be the one to refuse. As I said, July balks at being told no. So I figured she would be more amenable if *she* was the one to say no."

"And was she?" Calvin questioned, scrutinizing Nacona from beneath the brim of his hat.

"She returned a few days later with a counterproposal of marriage." Nacona waited for their green eyes to grow wide. Sure enough, they did.

"She proposed to you, just to get you to join in this investigation?" Ethan yowled. "How could she do a thing like that? You're hardly good marriage material."

Nacona willfully overlooked the insult. Just when he was about to accept the MacKenzies for what they were, one of them blurted out a remark that tempted him to ram his fist in their faces.

"July, as you surely must know, is willing to go to great lengths to get her way or solve a mystery. It's simply her nature. Since I was getting cabin fever in jail, I agreed to the marriage and off we went to Wyoming to find ourselves embroiled in a most complex case of murder, theft, and robbery."

"Which of course our dear sister thrust herself into with her customary panache," Gresham interjected on a sour note. "It seems my brothers and I owe you a partial apology. July was as much to blame for this shenanigan as you were."

Partial? Nacona snorted indignantly. "To my way of thinking you owe me a *full* apology. I tried to keep a tight rein on your sister, but she is unmanageable, as you know. While I was in Laramie, investigating a bank robbery, she took it upon herself to respond to a message I received from our client. In my absence she dashed off to town and wound up at the scene of a murder, for which she ended up being toted off to jail. I had to do some fancy talking to convince Sheriff Pinkston that she didn't kill the banker who hired us to investigate. Then the banker's promiscuous wife tried to seduce me. In exchange for my "cooperation" she said she'd get July released from the calaboose. It wasn't until the banker's wife wound up dead, while July and I were both locked in jail for crimes we didn't commit, that Pinkston realized he'd made a mistake. The man who abducted, and tried to kill, July had committed the murders because his victims threatened to expose him for what he truly was."

"Just exactly who was he?" Calvin inquired.

Nacona's face clouded over as he urged his steed into a faster clip. "I'm still not certain. But I think he was the man who ambushed my brother when we rode for Judge Parker in Indian Territory. There is a chance that outlaw assumed the identity of the rancher sent to Cheyenne to organize a syndicated cattle operation."

"Very shrewd," Gresham mused.

"Yes. Charley Brazil killed my brother two years ago, and I'd had no luck tracking him down. Even in the beginning we couldn't recognize Brazil on sight. He was clever and elusive. I never had a face to attach to the name, only sketchy descriptions that could have fit a thousand men."

"I'm sorry," Ethan sympathized, glancing at his own brothers and imagining the anguish Nacona had suffered.

"So was I." Nacona let out a sigh. "I thought Brazil had dropped off the face of the earth, but when I received the telegram from Missouri, describing the real Hub Butler, I suspected the bastard might be Charley Brazil. I may never know for certain whether I found my brother's killer."

Gresham straightened himself in the saddle and stared at the imposing figure beside him. "It seems my brothers and I have misjudged you to some extent, Mr. Bleu. But

I think you realize as well as we do that this outpost of civilization is no place for July. The very fact that she is remarkably daring makes it essential that she reside in a relatively safe city, away from the dangers she feels compelled to pursue. My brothers and I have selected a very suitable man for July to marry. Since this wedding of yours was arranged for convenience, I'm sure you will be willing to have it dissolved so you can pursue your life without July strapped to your coattails."

Now Gresham sounded exactly like the lawyer he was—silver-tongued and diplomatic. Nacona's dark eyes narrowed on him as he cleared his throat and continued.

"I think it best that we locate July and immediately return to Kansas City. We will see to it that her future husband provides well for her, offering her the luxuries to which she has grown accustomed. You will have no further need to feel responsible for her, Mr. Bleu."

"Hogwash!" Nacona blurted out, unable to contain his festering temper. "Any citified dandy you chose for her will be so henpecked that he molts semi-annually. And he'll never slow that firebrand down. Damn it, she's still my wife, and I'll decide what to do with her."

The horses sidestepped in response to Nacona's explosive tone, and Killer barked.

"Mr. Bleu, please be reasonable. We have your best interest at heart."

Gresham's patronizing attitude infuriated Nacona all the more. "And quit calling me Mr. Bleu," he fumed. "The name is Nacona, and I *am* being reasonable. You are an unrealistic snob!"

The MacKenzie brothers swelled with indignation as, with a snort, Nacona spurred his steed to a reckless pace.

He'd exchanged pleasantries with the MacKenzies for as long as he could stand. They were muleheaded, but he wasn't giving July up just because her highfalutin brothers thought he should. No matter how outrageous their bargain, Nacona had fallen in love with that cyclone of a female. He wasn't going to politely bow out and let her go off with a wave of good-bye. Hell yes, she was trouble personified. And she was well bred, but she loved him—or at least she had said she did. The way Nacona had it figured what was between him and July was their own business. And if her brothers didn't go back to Kansas City and leave him alone, he was going to pound them flat and mail them home.

Chomping on that gratifying thought, Nacona took off like the wind, wishing he knew where the hell he was going and where his wife was. He was ready to wrap up the loose ends of this investigation, sit July down—if he could find her—and discuss the future with her as if they were two normal adults. Of course, according to the testimony of her own brothers, she had never been normal. But predictable females had never appealed to Nacona. Maybe that was why he was so crazy about the gorgeous July. She herself was an adventure. She led a man on many a wild chase . . . like the one Nacona was on now. With her, he never knew quite what to expect, just that it would be something unique and special. Because, Nacona reminded himself with a faint smile, that was just the way July MacKenzie Bleu was.

Chapter 29

After catching her breath, July prepared herself for disappointment. She turned the latch and stepped into the first-class passenger car. And there sat Rose—or a woman who resembled Rose. Her face and head were covered by a hat and a dark veil, but judging by her reaction, it was no other.

Rose bounded to her feet as if she'd seen a ghost, then raced down the aisle in her haste to escape. July charged after the madam. When the train ground to a halt at a roundhouse, one of its scheduled stops, July was launched into the laps of two immaculately dressed gentlemen. She reared up and craned her neck over the seat to keep an eye on Rose, who had been flung against the door. While July scrambled to her feet to give chase, Rose hurled herself through door and onto the platform. Even before the train rolled to a complete shop, Rose bolted off it and hurried away in a fleeting cloud of taffeta and lace.

July was only yards behind when Rose clambered onto the seat of an abandoned wagon and popped the reins over a team of mules. Her practice in leaping and jumping certainly paid off. She didn't even hesitate to project herself through the air, and she landed spread-eagled in the back of the racing wagon. Her nails dug into feed sacks, and she clamped her knees around objects as if she were a rider on a bucking bronco. The wagon careened as Rose switched direction to head east. Dust billowed from beneath the wheels, and July nearly choked when a brown cloud settled over her.

While Rose did her damnedest to get her unwelcome passenger out of the wagon bed, July lunged forward and grabbed the back of her dress. A shocked squawk erupted from Rose when she was jerked backward and her feet flew up in her front of her. Her frilly petticoats, caught by the wind, flipped up in her face as she fell back off the seat into the wagon bed. The startled mules veered north and took off like cannonballs when given free reins.

Rose came up clawing and fighting, and July had to defend herself. No doubt, the madam saw her as a threat and was fighting for her life, when July only wanted answers to a few questions. The way Rose was behaving suggested she was guilty of quite a few crimes.

She tried to force July out of the wagon, scratched and bit her. July fought the desperate madam, breaking her hold when she tried to choke her, even taking a bite out of Rose's arm as they rolled across the feed sacks and slammed against the sideboards of the wagon. And all the while, the mule team plunged wildly over the countryside, causing the wagon to bounce wildly due to the rough terrain.

An outraged shriek burst from July's lips when Rose very nearly succeeded in ripping the hair off the crown of her head. That, compounded by the bouncing of the wagon, gave July a headache. She reared back an arm, as she had seen Nacona do, and shot forth a fist. Rose howled like a wounded hound. Incensed, she again thrust herself at July. The jarring of the runaway wagon flung them apart momentarily, but they were screeching and smacking each other within moments.

July gritted her teeth and pushed Rose away when the madam flopped on top of her. She was oblivious to the tree-lined creek ahead of them, unaware that they were on a collision course with disaster. Her concentration was focused on Rose who apparently was no novice at brawling. The madam was so good with her feet and fists, July had her hands full, so she didn't see the mound of earth in the mules' path until she and Rose were very nearly catapulted from the wagon bed. They hit the sacks with thuds, and the battle started all over again. . . .

The color waned from Nacona's cheeks when he heard female screeches and the rumble of a wagon on the far side of the tree-lined creek.

"What now?" he asked himself as he veered from the tracks to search out the source of the sound.

Fearing the worst, he forced his laboring steed through the brush. When his mount hesitated, he gouged him in the flanks, forcing him to leap the creek and lunge up a steep incline, snorting and panting as he went. Nacona's eyes popped when he topped the hill to see a runaway wagon heading toward him. Skirts billowed in the breeze as infuriated screeches erupted from the wagon bed.

Nacona knew right away who was in that wagon headed toward catastrophe. Where there was trouble, there was July MacKenzie Bleu. Damn her daring hide!

His heart slammed into his ribs as he charged toward the approaching wagon. If he didn't halt the runaway mules the wagon would plummet into the ravine, launching its passengers into orbit.

Maybe he should leave this wild-hearted woman to her stuffy, aristocratic brothers, Nacona thought as he raced toward the wagon. She could get in and out of trouble faster than a speeding bullet. She was destined to cause him heart failure if she didn't slow her insane pace.

Nacona reached the wagon, and raced along beside it. Expelling a growl, he sprang from his horse onto the wagon seat. A curse burst from his lips when he reached for the reins to find them gone. They were flapping against the mules, spurring them to an even swifter pace. Left with no other option, Nacona bounded onto the back of a mule and sprawled out to retrieve the reins. His entire body tensed when he glanced up and then wished he hadn't. They were dangerously close to the ridge that dropped off into the creek. Frantic, he jerked back on the reins and steered the team to the left. Not a moment too soon. The wagon skidded sideways on the cliff and the wheels on the left side of the vehicle dropped off the ledge and whirred in midair. July and Rose were hurtled through the air as feed sacks split and grain tumbled down the slope. Two startled squawks erupted the instant before the two women landed slapbang in the mud.

Breathing heavily, July propped herself upon all fours and wiped slime from her eyes with the clean spot on her left sleeve. Her gaze swung up to the ledge to see a pair f muddy boots and then powerful thighs and hips. The massive chest was unmistakable. July now peered into a ugged face and snapping black eyes.

Nacona stood with feet askance, his swarthy arms rossed on his heaving chest. The look he gave July was ne of smoldering fury.

"July! For God's sake!" Gresham hooted as he side-tepped down the embankment.

"You almost got yourself killed again!" Calvin blared, kidding down the slope behind his older brother.

"You did that yesterday too!" Ethan muttered grouch-y, bringing up the rear. "Don't you ever take a day off?"

"Trying to set a record for death-defying shenanigans, re you, Missus Bleu?" Nacona's brooding scowl dis-olved into the faintest hint of a grin.

When she extended her arm, silently requesting that he ssist her to her feet, he stared at her muddy hand as if she vere offering him a four-day-old fish.

"You got yourself into this gooey mess. I reckon you an get yourself out of it," he declared unsympathetically.

Ethan gasped at Nacona's refusal to lend July assist-nce. Flashing Nacona a scathing glare, he stretched out o offer July his hand. Nacona quickly lifted his foot and ave the off-balance MacKenzie a shove in the seat of his oreeches. Ethan flapped his arms like a duck preparing for light, but gravity had a hold on him. With a yelp, he fell *ersplat* in the mud beside Rose who could barely move fter being sucked into the goo.

"You devil!" Calvin snapped furiously. "That only goes o show you aren't fit to have July for a wife, or Ethan for our brother-in-law."

Nacona was getting sick and tired of hearing what these

muleheaded MacKenzies thought of him. He had enjoyed sending Ethan sprawling. He felt twice as good when Calvin leaned over to offer assistance and wound up nose-diving into the mud beside his brother—with the help of Nacona's well-aimed kick to the seat of his pants.

One mocking brow elevated, challenging Gresham to take his turn at hoisting July from the sloppy grime. "Go ahead, *Mr.* MacKenzie," Nacona invited. "By all means, pull your baby sister up if you think she deserves a helping hand after tearing off without giving anybody any notice."

Gresham looked at his sister and his brothers and then stared long and hard at the ornery giant. His first reaction had been outrage. But after giving the incident a moment's consideration, he began to see Nacona's point. For years, the MacKenzie men had been rushing off to rescue their mischievous sister from her most recent escapade. She had strained against their protectiveness and against all types of authority. Of course, a properly bred gentlemen in Kansas City would think July helpless and defenseless in this situation. She was anything but. July had insisted on making her own way, and maybe it was time her brothers stood back and let her do just that. Only one man around here seemed to have enough sense to treat July as an equal rather than a responsibility.

Maybe, just maybe—though it killed Gresham to admit it—he had been wrong about this hard-bitten, rough-edged shootist. Only Nacona Bleu had given July the opportunity to prove herself in criminal investigation. She had obviously scared the living hell out of Nacona a time or two, but he had restrained himself and had allowed July her chance at success. Perhaps this brawny giant was exactly what she needed after all. She certainly hadn't been satisfied with any of the prospective beaus who had courted her in Kansas City over the past five years. And she did seem fond of this man, though only God knew why. Gresham begrudgingly admired this iron-willed gunslinger, but he didn't like him.

"Well?" Nacona prompted when Gresham simply stood there, analyzing the situation.

"As you said, Nacona," Gresham replied, forcing himself to employ the man's given name, "she got what she deserved."

"Thanks for nothing," July muttered as she heaved herself out of the mud and floundered up the slippery slope. She fell twice, but she finally reached the ledge to confront Nacona and her oldest brother.

"If you don't mind my asking, what in the hell were you doing in that wagon?" Nacona demanded. Though he longed to pull July into his arms and hug her, he refrained. That would probably set Calvin and Ethan off again. They still thought he was poison.

July half turned to stare down at Rose who was squirming about to no avail. The madam's heavy skirts held her fast. "I only wanted to ask Rose a few questions," she explained.

"It looked as though you were trying to beat answers out of her." Nacona smirked.

"She attacked me," July declared self-righteously. "I leaped off my horse and onto the moving train to locate Rose, but—"

"You did *what?*" Gresham croaked in astonishment.

July didn't bother to repeat herself. "—Rose bounded off the train at the depot and scrambled into the wagon to escape me. I had to hurl myself onto the wagon to catch her a second time."

"Hurl yourself . . . ?" Ethan gasped as he trudged up the embankment.

"That's when the battle broke out," July continued. "Last night Hub made a remark that piqued my curiosity about his past. Rose knew about his activities, so I thought she might be able to clear up a few things." Her gaze dropped to the muddy madam. "I had hoped to get her off with a lighter sentence if she agreed to tell me everything she knows about Hub Butler. But Rose never gave me a chance to explain. She kept trying to choke me and claw out my eyes and rip out my hair."

Nacona reached up to trace the red scratch above July's brow. "It looks as if she almost succeeded."

July moved cautiously down the hill to confront the mud-soaked harlot who had managed to pry both arms loose from the slime and sit up. "My oldest brother and I are lawyers," she informed Rose. "And we are prepared to help you if you will answer my questions. Despite what you thought, I don't want vengeance, only answers."

Rose peered up at July's smudged face and finally nodded in compliance. "I have no loyalty left for Hub Butler. What is it you want to know about him?"

"Who he really was would be a start," July prompted.

Although Rose had once fancied herself in love with the no-good scoundrel, her infatuation had died a quick death due to his cruel treatment the previous day. She saw no sense in defending a murderer when she had her own future to consider. Hub hadn't been faithful to her anyway; she had been nothing but a pawn to him.

"I don't know his real name," Rose admitted, causing

Nacona's shoulders to slump. "But once, when he was well into his cups, he confessed to me that he wasn't who he appeared to be." She struggled to her feet and steadied herself in the slime. "He said he had hightailed it out of Indian Territory after he'd killed a federal marshal and that he'd had another one hot on his heels. He'd met up with a braggart on a train in Kansas. The man flashed his money and boasted of how he'd convinced English investors to back a ranch in Wyoming. How Hub disposed of the *real* Hub Butler, he didn't say. But I do know he sent for some of his old friends in the Territory so they could help him with rustling and robbing."

Rose scooped up her grimy skirts and sidestepped up the slope. "Hub planted men at every ranch, even his own. When cattle were rustled, he never was suspected since the Cabestro was victimized too. He had the stolen cattle branded and driven to Ogallala, Nebraska, to be sold to cattle buyers from Chicago. His foreign investors covered his losses, and he made profit on the stolen cattle. A few months ago he started getting greedy, and he played up to Angel Chambers for information about train and bank payrolls. He used the bordello to discreetly meet his men and pass information, and he paid me to run the place and keep my mouth shut."

Her eyes took on a distant stare, and she was silent for a moment. "Fool that I was, I thought his feelings for me were real. But he used me, just like he used Angel and everybody else. C.L. didn't like his wife cavorting about town with everything in breeches, and he did some checking on Angel's favorite paramours. From what Hub told me, C.L. confronted him with a letter that denied Hub was who he said he was. Chambers didn't have a clue that

Hub was involved with the thefts, but he did try to black
mail him into keeping away from Angel."

"I guess Hub was afraid of complications, so he dis
posed of C.L.," Rose added as she used a tree to pul
herself onto the ledge. "I don't know why he tried to
frame Nacona, except maybe his wandering eye had
fallen on July."

Nacona knew perfectly well why Hub wanted him ou
of the way, even if Rose didn't. Hub wanted the last laugh
on the marshal who had spent two years tracking him
down. Hub Butler was Charley Brazil, Nacona decided
All the pieces of the puzzle fit perfectly. Robbing and
thieving was Charley's trademark. At long last Nacona
had achieved his goal. Now he could put the past to rest
for he had found Shandin's killer.

"I don't know how Angel found out about the letter,"
Rose went on to say.

Nacona did. It was his fault that Angel had met with an
untimely death.

"But she tried to blackmail Hub into marrying her with
the information she had obtained. Hub had always been
her favorite, but he got rid of her when she started pressing him. I had nothing to do with it," Rose insisted. "I
found out about it later."

A pensive frown furrowed Nacona's brow as his gaze
bounced from Rose to July. This intelligent imp had been
incredibly adept at reasoning out the incidents involved in
the case, though she had gotten sidetracked by Angel's
infidelity. Neither he nor the MacKenzie brothers had
realized just what a beneficial role July could play in
investigation, even if her crusading instincts were a mite
overactive.

492

"Well, now that that's settled and out of the way, I'd like to go home," July declared.

"I can't wait to do that myself." Calvin surged up the embankment to shepherd his sister toward her horse.

July set her feet and refused to stir. Her emerald eyes lifted to Nacona. She wondered if, now that he could wash his hands of her and go on his way, he would. He'd made no lasting commitment to her, and he was a wanderer. After the wild chases she'd led him on, he might very well want to see the marriage she had engineered dissolved. His declaration that he wanted to resolve his brother's killing might have been an excuse to take his leave when he'd felt the need to roam. July wondered if he cared enough to stay with her?

"Well?" she asked the towering giant.

"Well what?" Nacona responded.

"Come on, July," Ethan urged. "We have a detective agency to run in Kansas City. We've been gone too long as it is. When you come back, we'll let you handle a few cases on your own."

When Calvin and Ethan tried to propel her toward the horses, July wormed free. It was a simple feat, considering she was as muddy and slippery as an eel. She turned back to Nacona, hoping he would give her a sign that he wanted to give their marriage a chance.

A wry smile quirked his lips as he studied the muddy bundle of irrepressible spirit. His smile grew wider when he deciphered the expression in her wide green eyes, the question that MacKenzie pride refused to let her pose in front of her brothers. Nacona cocked his head and lifted one dark brow.

"It's your move, Missus Bleu," he drawled with affec-

493

tionate amusement. "What are you going to do? Go with these mothering hens you call your brothers or stay with the man who loves you, though I don't know why he should since you persist in dashing off into danger without giving a thought to how much it scares him every time you do."

Voicing his affection in front of the MacKenzie brothers was well worth the radiant smile Nacona received from July. Her face lit up so she could have guided a stranded traveler through a raging Wyoming blizzard. Laughter gurgled in her throat as she rushed toward Nacona, her arms outstretched. He didn't mind getting muddy when she leaped up to wrap her arms around his neck and her legs around his hips. However, he hadn't anticipated her overzealous reaction or her amorous display in front of her disapproving brothers. Her momentum threw him off balance.

As Nacona stepped back to steady himself, he slipped on the spilled grain that had tumbled down the slope. Since he was top heavy, with July in his arms, he stumbled down the embankment and landed with a splash.

Three blond heads appeared atop the ridge to survey the damage. Ethan sighed in dismay. The very idea that July would settle for this ornery scamp when the world was teeming with eligible, dignified gentlemen seemed mad.

Calvin scowled at his sister's choice in men, but Gresham merely smiled to himself. Minute by minute, he was beginning to realize that Nacona was an exceptionally good sport. He had taken on a responsibility that all three MacKenzie brothers had been unable to handle. Though Gresham loved his sister dearly, he was the first

494

to admit that she was incredibly rambunctious and independent. Nacona had accepted the challenge . . . and the
consequences.

"I'll make the arrangements with the circuit judge in
Rose's behalf," Gresham volunteered. "And my brothers
can herd your prisoners to jail to await trial." He grinned
into Nacona's mud-splattered face. "You, Nacona Bleu,
already have your hands full. I wish you luck. I assure you,
you're going to need it."

Chapter 30

When the congregation retreated from the edge of the cliff, Nacona focused his attention on July who was sprawled half-off, half-on him. Determinedly, he set her beside him and tipped her face to his annoyed gaze, accidentally smearing more mud on her chin than was already there.

"I have heard it said that the Lord looks after little children and fools. You're twenty-one so just what do you think that makes you?" He didn't give her the chance to answer; he rushed on in a condescending tone. "I didn't say this in front of your brothers, but damn it, your shenanigans are driving me up the wall. I do not intend to spend the rest of my life, wondering where the devil you are and what sort of calamity you're courting. Sometimes love requires that you tell me where you're going and why. So does common courtesy. I respect your independent nature, but I want you alive, not lying in a pine box, a victim of your insatiable curiosity."

At one moment this dark-eyed rascal was telling the world he loved her, and the next minute he was jumping down her throat. His curt tone riled July, and she found herself spouting out the thoughts that had hounded her while she'd been snooping around the Pleasure Parlor.

"And I do not appreciate knowing you were gallivanting in a brothel with scoundrels and painted harlots," she shot back.

Nacona's brows jackknifed. He wondered why she had veered onto that topic while he was reading *her* the riot act.

"When I think of the disgusting sights I viewed in that deplorable place, knowing you had undoubtedly participated in such activities more times than I care to count, I cursed you. I refuse to be married to a man who frequents dens of iniquity while I remain loyal to him."

Nacona chuckled at her explosive tone, her possessiveness, and at the idea that he would seek out another woman when he'd found the very best. Impulsively, he dropped a kiss onto the clean spot on her lips. "July MacKenzie Bleu, you really are something," he murmured. "Mud and all . . ."

The unexpected compliment, coming from a man like Nacona—a man who had seen and done everything, and was difficult to impress—put a smile on her face. "Do you really think so?"

"Mmm . . . I most certainly do," he assured her as he struggled to his knees and hoisted July up beside him. "After we find a spot where the channel is wide and deep, we can shuck these soggy clothes and bathe, and then I intend to prove to you just how much I do appreciate you."

His suggestive look and the caressing huskiness of his

voice said it all. July blinked mud-caked eyelashes and peered inquisitively up at him. "In the water?"

A roguish grin pursed his lips as he ushered her downstream, the devoted Killer following at their heels. "Have you ever made love in the river before, Missus Bleu?" he questioned.

As if he doesn't know, July thought to herself. This brawny, sensual giant was all the experience she had had, all she ever wanted. "No, Mr. Bleu, I can't say that I have. Have you?"

When he scooped her up and held her close, she felt and heard the vibrations of his bright ringing laughter. "You're my very first time," he said with perfect assurance.

"At least I'm your first time at something," July countered, her tone a tad resentful.

Nacona set her on her feet and peeled away the grimy gown that concealed her luscious curves. "You're my first time in love, July," he murmured in a voice as soft as black velvet. "You're my best time of all. . . . The *very* best time of all . . ."

When his lips slanted over hers, July drowned in the sweetness of a kiss more potent than wine and twice as addictive. Her body responded as it always had to the hard, muscular contours familiarly meshing with her body. Her heart thumped, as if it were a wild bird caged inside her ribs, and shock waves of pleasure rippled through her as his tongue thrust into her mouth, promising the intimacies to come.

July nimbly worked the buttons of his chambray shirt and pushed it away from his powerful shoulders until his flesh was against her trembling skin. Her senses absorbed the sight and feel of him, and hot flames danced down her spine as his masterful caresses sought every sensitive point on her flesh and brought it to life.

. Breathing heavily, and noticeably disturbed by the arousing effect this gorgeous sprite had on him, Nacona took her hand in his and led her into the channel. His dark, smoldering eyes never left her for a moment. One look, one touch had always lit a slow burning fire in the core of his being. July had made him want things he'd never considered before—a real home, a family, and love to last a lifetime. But at this moment he wanted only the wild, fiery splendor that consumed him when his blond-haired siren was in his arms.

With a tormented groan, he brought his mouth down on hers—demanding, savoring, devouring. He was making up for all the terrifying moments when he'd feared he would never see July again. She had flirted with disaster time after time. He'd been afraid he'd lose the one person who had become precious to him.

Even the cool water that swirled around Nacona didn't ease the fire of his longing as he clutched July to him. He swore the creek was carrying him away from the lingering fears and concerns of the past few days. Shaky and ravenous, he yearned for the rapture he'd always found in July's silken arms. Each time they made love it seemed like the first time, and yet it was always the same—spontaneous, explosive, shocking to his senses. This one woman with eyes like emeralds and hair the color of tropical seashores breathed new life into him with each honeyed kiss. With each adventurous touch, she made the sun burn brighter, the moon glow more silvery. She filled his world to overflowing, yet he could never seem to get enough of her. It was as if he fed on the passion that surged from his body to hers, as if he lived and breathed through her, *because* of her.

A soft moan tripped from July's lips as his seeking hands swirled around the throbbing peaks of her breasts and his greedy lips followed to suckle at each dusky crest. He had turned her in his arms so that she was suspended in the water, bobbing on rippling waves of ineffable pleasure. His erotic caresses and kisses teased and excited until July arched helplessly toward him. His roaming hands drifted over her abdomen to trail across the sensitive flesh of her thighs. A gasp broke from her when his fingertips delved to arouse and torment her in maddening degrees.

July felt she was floating toward a raging waterfall, about to be engulfed in a whirlpool of passion. Her heart hammered, her body ached with wanting this midnight-haired rake who had introduced her to the world of passion. He knew how to drive her wild with desire, how to leave her begging for what he alone could give her.

July's breath caught when Nacona pulled her to him, wrapping her legs around his lean hips, guiding her throbbing body to his to ease the maddening craving he had instilled in her. She surged eagerly toward him, meeting each hard, demanding thrust. Sensation after wondrous sensation avalanched upon her as their bodies moved in rhythm, setting the cadence of a love that was meant to last. The crescendo of passion built and intensified until she swore she could hear the melody pulsating in her ears, in her body, in her very soul.

July dug her nails into Nacona's back and held onto him for dear life as tidal waves of ecstasy swamped and buffeted her. Needs as ancient and instinctive as time itself flooded and ebbed and then swelled completely out of proportion.

The world vanished into oblivion as a compulsive tremor rocked her and set her heart to stampeding. Her bewildered cry echoed in the air, and Nacona caught the sweet satisfying sound in his kiss, groaning as raging passion seized his taut body. Her intense pleasure had always ignited his ardor. Now unbridled desire riveted him as July quivered in his arms, setting off a reaction that left him shuddering and clutching at her as if he never meant to let her go, *couldn't* let her go.

Sweet merciful heavens! Nacona thought shakily. Was it possible for a man to go all through life craving a woman as obsessively as he craved this lovely siren? Had any other man ever felt this way about the woman who caught his attention, who inspired his love? Surely not! And how could he survive such exhausting bouts of this all-consuming passion? Surely they would get to an aging man? Twenty years from now, this wild kind of hunger would surely kill him. As it was, he'd very nearly suffered heart seizure when in the throes of passion. Would this wildfire ever burn itself out, or at least dim enough for him to control it?

Nacona stared into the enchanting face that permeated his fantasies. The second he met passion-drugged green eyes and stared at kiss-swollen lips, he knew that nothing was ever going to bank the white-hot fires that sizzled within him. Loving July was paradise, and having her return his love was heaven on earth.

July watched the emotions that sparkled in his fathomless eyes that shone ebony black in the afternoon light. "Thinking troubled thoughts, Nacona?" she questioned, her voice thick with the aftereffects of indescribable passion.

"Very troubled thoughts," he admitted as he nuzzled against her satiny shoulder.

July withdrew as far as his encircling arms would allow to study his ruggedly handsome features. A frown ruffled her brow at wondering how he could be thinking of trouble when she was drifting in exquisite pleasure.

"The trouble is I can't get used to loving you," Nacona whispered before dropping another impulsive kiss on her heart-shaped lips.

July misunderstood his meaning. Her confused frown settled deeper into her elegant features. "But I thought you told my brothers that you wanted me to—"

His forefinger grazed her lips, shushing her, and he gave his damp head a contradicting shake. "I keep thinking I'll grow accustomed to the fires you ignite in me, that I'll be able to control this hot, sweet desire the way I can control all the other facets of my life. I'm in the prime of life now, but in twenty years . . ."

July's playful laughter filled the small space between them when she realized what he was trying to say. But Nacona didn't find his thoughts the least bit amusing.

"You're eleven years younger than I am," he reminded her seriously. "What if, in the years to come, I can't . . ." He stopped, trying to formulate a delicate way to say it. "What if I can't . . ." No good. There was no tactful way to express himself. "What if I can't perform in bed," he finally blurted out in exasperation. "You'll still be young and energetic, and I'll be a doddering old fool like C. L. Chambers, clinging to a woman who attracts men like flies."

July flashed him an annoyed glance. "Really, Nacona. I do not appreciate being compared to Angela."

"Well, maybe she wouldn't have turned out the way she did if her husband had been able to keep her content," Nacona countered.

July wormed free and waded ashore. "I can't believe we're having this conversation!" She reached down to grab her soiled gown and gave it a good scrubbing before glaring at the bare-chested giant who stood waist-deep in water. "Do you think it's only passion that holds me to you?" She sniffed, highly offended. "Do you think my affection is so shallow I wouldn't remain loyal to you, even if you never made love to me again?"

"Well, would you?" he wanted to know.

With a muffled growl, July scooped up his garments and hurled them at him. "Stop acting like a man," she muttered. "I swear, men seem to judge their usefulness and their contributions in life by sexual prowess. If I am to labor under your ridiculous theory, then I suppose when I grow round with child and waddle like a duck, and I cannot please *you* as well in bed, you will search elsewhere for physical affection."

"I would do no such thing!" Nacona protested indignantly.

"And what about those weeks that follow?" July persisted as she draped her clean gown over a limb to dry. "What will you do then, my lusty dragon? Wait for me to recuperate, attend me in my weakness, and share the responsibility of raising our child, our children? Or will you grow impatient for passion and find someone to replace me, simply for the sake of sexual satisfaction?"

Nacona scowled in irritation and stamped ashore to toss his garments over a nearby tree branch. "Just what the hell kind of man do you think I am, woman?"

A magnificently sculptured creature who knows no master and no equal, July mused as her appreciative gaze flooded over every masculine inch of him. An elfin smile quirked her lips as her eyes measured his inflated chest and frowning face. Quite honestly, she could not imagine the time when age would restrict this powerfully built giant, though she supposed it would come and he would not be as impulsive and urgent in passion as he was now.

A fleeting thought skittered across her mind, and her smile grew wider as she reached up to draw Nacona down beside her in the shallows of the creek.

"Come here, my love," she implored silkily. "I will show you what kind of man you are, the kind of man you will be when the two of us grow old together."

Her gentle hands flooded over him, mapping whipcord muscles and sleek flesh. Nacona melted like butter left on a hot stove as her tender kisses and caresses swept over him in the most languid and tantalizing manner imaginable. There were no traces of urgency, no heated demands; there was only a warm, unhurried expression of love in its sweetest, purest form. Her touch was embroidered with sunshine and made his skin glow. His mind wandered down a new, previously unexplored corridor of desire.

In the past, their need for each other had swept him up like a churning flood, draining his strength and energy. But this new brand of passion that July had invented to make her point was something else. It seemed to create energy when there was none. This was . . .

A quiet moan escaped Nacona's lips when her magical touch gently but gradually took him to a higher plateau of pleasure, bringing to him a strange and yet remarkably satisfying kind of hunger that consumed him in an entirely different way. His body was not taut. It was relaxed and pliant beneath her coasting hands and petal-soft lips. She caressed him ever so tenderly with that delicious body of hers. And suddenly, he was learning something he'd never known about passion—and he'd thought he knew it all! She stroked him until he swore he'd sink into the shallows and drown. And then, as if the smoldering passion she'd aroused in him had sneaked up to catch him unaware, he wanted her just as he always had, but in a different way. If that made any sense. It did, and this mischievous imp knew it. He could see satisfaction on her face as she settled upon him, teasing him, guiding him to her to satisfy the hunger she had slowly but surely aroused in him.

"And this, my love, is how it will be when you're a century old and I'm a spry eighty-nine," she whispered as she moved upon him, setting the sweet cadence of passion. "I'll love you just as well *then* as I love you *now* . . . because love always finds a way to express itself and because being with you is all that matters to me."

Her softly uttered promise and the feel of her ripe body gliding upon his sent shudders of ecstasy spilling through him. Nacona shifted to bring her beneath him, to appease the maddening needs that had mushroomed inside him. The thought of growing old and being unable to satisfy such a vivacious sprite no longer concerned him. They

506

would always be discovering new ways to pleasure each other, creating the kind of magic that was ever-changing, like the colorful designs of a kaleidoscope. He would delight in exploring new ways to express passion and to satisfy the emerald-eyed siren whose love he had won. . . .

That was the last sane thought to filter through Nacona's mind before sublime desire overtook him and sent him rocketing toward the sun. He was scaling pastel rainbows and bounding over puffy white clouds. In the distance, he swore he heard harps playing a melody created only for the two of them.

Later, in the glorious aftermath of passion, Nacona cradled July against him and sighed in pure satisfaction. He glanced over to see her blond hair rippling in the shallows, and he grinned roguishly. "Now, about all these children we're going to have," he purred provocatively. "Don't you think we ought to have some place to raise the lot of them?"

July pictured a tiny toddler with dark eyes and a crop of raven hair, and she smiled broadly. "I really don't suppose we can go gadding all over creation to chase criminals with a passel of babies trooping behind us," she agreed.

"There is a perfectly good ranch going to waste just outside Cheyenne," Nacona reminded her. "And there is another just to the north that needs a new manager."

"Mmm . . . yes," July said thoughtfully. "I suppose the two put together would be spacious enough to raise a large family."

"And the townsfolk have already been informed that I have retired from my previous profession," he added.

Nacona propped himself up on an elbow to peer down into July's captivating features. "I want my children to grow up in a stable home," he said suddenly. "I don't want them shuffled around the way Shandin and I were, managing without a father. I want them to bask in the warmth of my love for you, no matter what form it takes in years to come."

The sincerity in his tone touched her heart. July reflected on this reckless tumbleweed of a man she'd met in Dodge City, marveling at the changes he'd undergone, the changes she'd undergone during the past few months. She had been out to show the world that she was any man's equal—and to slay a few dragons. Nacona had allowed her to be his equal, even though her brothers wouldn't. She had experienced more than her fair share of adventure and danger, to be sure. Now she longed for something she'd never thought she'd want. This brawny giant had made all the difference. He had changed her perspective.

July looped her arms around his shoulders, drawing him down to her. "Considering all the children we plan to have to help us manage a sprawling ranch, don't you think we should concentrate on what it takes to make them?"

One thick brow elevated in surprise. "I thought we just had," Nacona chuckled.

Seductively, July stirred beneath him, marveling at the insatiable love she felt for this mountain of a man. "I'm not taking any chances," she murmured.

"Not taking chances?" Nacona snickered playfully. "Woman, that's all you've done the past few days, as I recall."

"That was different." Her trailing hands slid down his muscular back, to instigate something more stimulating than conversation.

Nacona was reminded of just how determined this blond-haired imp could be when she set her mind to something. And one truth rang clear as he surrendered to the delicious magic of her breath-stealing kiss and bone-melting caresses: July couldn't get herself into trouble while she was in his arms, sharing the wondrous pleasures of their love. Mm. . . . They were going to enjoy delightful years, progressing from one phase of life to another. Nacona had buried the ghosts of his past and had appeased the restless cravings that had once nagged him.

Love had swept into his life the day July Beth MacKenzie barged into his room to demand his undivided attention. And it had come to stay, which never ceased to amaze him. This rambunctious woman had given him new purpose.

"How is it, sweet witch, that you took a self-sufficient man and unveiled a need in him?" he questioned in wonder. "I feel as if I've found a part of myself that I'd never realized was missing. Without you, I was just a half a man. God, I love you!" he rasped as emotion surged through him.

July swore she would never tire of hearing the words he spoke with such fierce sincerity. Nor would she tire of returning his intense affection. When she had earned Nacona's love she had met the greatest challenge of her life, and she had unearthed a treasure.

Her hands framed his bronzed face as she met a dark gaze that spoke of immeasurable love. "Not long ago, I set out to prove my worth to the world," she whispered, her voice ragged with emotion. "But now I want only to prove it to you, Nacona. You're my everything. I intend to cherish this silken bond between us. . . ."

And that is exactly what she did.

PINNACLE BOOKS HAS
SOMETHING FOR EVERYONE—

MAGICIANS, EXPLORERS, WITCHES AND CATS

THE HANDYMAN   (377-3, $3.95/$4.95)
He is a magician who likes hands. He likes their comfortable shape and weight and size. He likes the portability of the hands once they are severed from the rest of the ponderous body. Detective Lanark must discover who The Handyman is before more handless bodies appear.

PASSAGE TO EDEN   (538-5, $4.95/$5.95)
Set in a world of prehistoric beauty, here is the epic story of a courageous seafarer whose wanderings lead him to the ends of the old world—and to the discovery of a new world in the rugged, untamed wilderness of northwestern America.

BLACK BODY   (505-9, $5.95/$6.95)
An extraordinary chronicle, this is the diary of a witch, a journal of the secrets of her race kept in return for not being burned for her "sin." It is the story of Alba, that rarest of creatures, a white witch: beautiful and able to walk in the human world undetected.

THE WHITE PUMA   (532-6, $4.95/NCR)
The white puma has recognized the men who deprived him of his family. Now, like other predators before him, he has become a man-hater. This story is a fitting tribute to this magnificent animal that stands for all living creatures that have become, through man's carelessness, close to disappearing forever from the face of the earth.